VOYAGERS II
The Alien Within

"Where the hell are we, anyway?" Stoner asked. "Hawaii?"

Richards nodded. "The big island, just outside of Hilo."

"This isn't a hospital, is it? It feels more like some big laboratory complex."

Again Richards bobbed his head up and down. "Right again. That's three in a row. Want to try for four?"

Stoner laughed softly. "I have no idea of how long I've been – suspended."

"Eighteen years."

"Eighteen? . . ." Stoner felt the psychiatrist's eyes probing him. Past the man's suddenly intense face, he could see the row of display screens flickering their readout curves.

The silence stretched. Finally Richards asked, "How do you feel about returning from the dead?"

"I thought they'd bring me back a lot sooner than this."

"The alien spacecraft was recovered almost twelve years ago. You've been kept in cryonic suspension until the biotechnicians figured out how to thaw you without killing you."

"And the spacecraft?"

Richard's eyes shifted away slightly. "It's in orbit around the Earth."

"The alien himself . . ."

"He was quite dead. There wasn't a thing anybody could do about that."

BEN BOVA

VOYAGERS II

The Alien Within

A Methuen Paperback

A Methuen Paperback

British Library Cataloguing in Publication Data

Bova, Ben
  Voyagers II: the alien within.
  I. Title
  813'.54 [F]   PS3552.084

  ISBN 0–413–14130–6

First published in Great Britain 1987
by Severn House Publishers Ltd
This edition published 1987
by Methuen London Ltd
11 New Fetter Lane, London EC4P 4EE

Printed and bound in Great Britain
by Richard Clay Ltd, Bungay, Suffolk

To Ruth and Herbert S. Stoltz

Zeus now addressed the immortals: "What a lamentable thing it is that men should blame the gods and regard *us* as the source of their troubles when it is their own wickedness that brings them sufferings worse than any which Destiny allots them."

HAWAII

Death, be not proud, though some
   have called thee
Mighty and dreadful, for thou art not so

CHAPTER I

Slowly, reluctantly, Keith Stoner awoke. The dream that had been swirling through his mind over and over again wafted away like drifting smoke, evaporated, until the last faint tendrils of it vanished and left him straining to remember.

Faintly, faintly the dream sang to him of another life, another world, of beauty that no human eye could see. But as he reached out with his mind to recapture the joy of it, the dream disappeared forever, leaving only a distant echo and the inward pain of unfulfilled yearning.

He opened his eyes.

A smooth gray expanse encompassed him. He was lying on his back. He could feel the weight of his body pressing down on a soft, flat surface. Instead of the deathly cold of space, he felt comfortably warm. Instead of the sealed pressure suit and helmet he had worn, he was naked beneath a smooth clean white sheet.

I'm back on Earth, he realized. I'm alive again.

He reached a hand upward. His outstretched fingertips touched the cool smooth curve of gray a scant few inches above his face. It felt like plastic, or perhaps highly polished metal. Something went *click*. He jerked his hand away. A series of high-pitched beeps chattered, like a dolphin scolding. The gray eggshell slid away, silently.

For long moments Stoner lay unmoving, his eyes focused on the white ceiling overhead. It looked like a normal ceiling of a normal room. It glowed faintly, bathing the room in pale light. Turning his head slightly, he saw that he was not lying on a bed, but on a shelflike extension built into a massive bulk of intricate equipment. A whole wall of gleaming metal and strange, almost menacing machinery, like the cockpit of a space shuttle combined with the jointed arms and grasping metal claws of robot manipulators. The machinery was humming faintly, and Stoner could see a bank of video display

3

screens clustered at the far end of it. He recognized the rhythmic trace of an EKG on one screen, patiently recording his heartbeat. The wriggling lines of the other screens meant nothing to him, but he was certain that they were monitoring his body and brain functions, also. Yet he felt no electrodes on his skin. There were no wires or probes attached to him, not even an intravenous tube.

It was a hospital room, but unlike any hospital room he had ever known. No hospital smell, no odor of disinfectants or human suffering. More electronics and machinery than an intensive care unit. Stoner felt almost like a specimen in a laboratory. Propping himself on his elbows, he saw that the other half of the room was quite normal. The ceiling was smooth and creamy white, the walls a cool pale yellow. Sunlight slanted through the half-closed blinds of a single window and threw warm stripes along the tiled floor. An ordinary upholstered armchair was positioned by the window, with a small table beside it. Two molded plastic chairs stood against the wall. The only other furniture in the room was a small writing desk, its surface completely bare, and a walnut-veneer bureau with a mirror atop it.

Stoner looked at himself in the mirror.

None the worse for wear, he thought. His hair was still jet black, and as thick as ever. His face had always been longer than he liked, the nose just a trifle hawkish, the chin square and firm. But there was something strange about his eyes. They were the same gray he remembered, the gray of a winter sea. But somehow they looked different; he could not pin down what it was, but his eyes had changed.

He sat up straight and let the covering sheet drop to his groin. No dizziness. His head felt clear and alert. His naked body was still lean and well muscled; in his earlier life he had driven himself mercilessly in the discipline of tae kwan do.

In my earlier life, he echoed to himself. How many years has it been?

He gripped the sheet, ready to pull it off his legs and get out of bed. But he stopped and looked up at the ceiling. The smooth white was translucent plastic. There were lights behind it. And video cameras, Stoner knew. They were watching him.

He shrugged. Take a good look, he thought.

Yanking the sheet away, he swung his long legs to the

floor and stood up. The machinery on the other side of the bed emitted one small, faint peep. Stoner flinched at it, startled, then relaxed into a grin. His legs felt a little rubbery, but he knew that was to be expected after so many years. How long has it been? he wondered again as, naked, he padded to the door that had to be the bathroom.

It was. But when he came out and surveyed his room again, he saw that there was no other door to it. Half stainless-steel laboratory, half cozy bedroom—but there were no closets, no connecting doors, no door anywhere that led out of the room.

CHAPTER 2

"I am *not* going into a board meeting until the experiment is decided, one way or the other."

Jo Camerata said it quietly, but with an edge of steel. The two men in her office glanced at each other uneasily.

The office was clearly hers. The textured walls blazed with slashing orange and yellow stripes against a deep maroon background, the dramatic colors of the Mediterranean. The carpet was thick and patterned in matching bold tones. If she wished, Jo could change the color scheme at the touch of a dial. This morning the fiery hues of her Neapolitan ancestry suited her mood perfectly.

Two whole walls of the office were taken up by floor-to-ceiling windows. The drapes were pulled back, showing the city of Hilo and, off in the distance, the smoldering dark bulk of Mauna Loa. Through the other window wall the Pacific glittered alluringly under a bright cloudless morning sky.

Although she was president of Vanguard Industries, Jo's office held none of the usual trappings of power. It was a modest-sized room, not imposing or huge, furnished with comfortable chairs and sofas and a small round table in the corner by the windows. No desk to form a barrier between her and her visitors. No banks of computer screens and

telephone terminals. No photographs of herself alongside the
great and powerful people of the hour. There was nothing in
the room to intimidate her employees, nothing except her
own dominant personality and unquenchable drive.

Jo sat in an ultramodern power couch of butter-soft leather
the color of light caramel. Designed to resemble an astronaut's acceleration chair, it held a complete communications
console and computer terminal in its armrests. Within its
innards, the chair contained equipment for massage, heat
therapy, and biofeedback sessions. It molded itself to the
shape of her body, it could swivel or tilt back to a full
reclining position at the touch of a fingertip.

But Jo was sitting up straight, her back ramrod stiff, her
dark eyes blazing.

The two men sitting side by side on the low cushioned sofa
both looked unhappy, but for completely different reasons.
Healy, chief scientist of Vanguard Industries, wore a loose,
short-sleeved white shirt over his shorts. Archie Madigan, the
corporation's top lawyer, one of Jo's former lovers and still a
trusted adviser, was in a more conservative shirt jacket of
navy blue and soft pink slacks: the business uniform of the
twenty-first-century executive male.

Jo was in uniform, too. For nearly twenty years she had
worked and schemed her way to the top of Vanguard Industries. She had brains and energy and a driving, consuming
ambition. And she never hesitated to use her femininity to
help climb the corporate ladder of power the way some men
use their skill at golf or their willingness to lick boots. She
was wearing a one-piece zipsuit with tight Velcro cuffs at the
ankles and wrists and a mesh midriff. Chocolate brown, it
clung lovingly to her tall, lush figure. The zipper that led
down the suit's front was opened just enough to suggest how
interesting it would be to slide it down the rest of the way.

Healy ran a hand through his thinning sandy hair. "It's
been a week now and he—"

"Six days," Jo snapped.

The biophysicist nodded. "Six days. Right. But he shows
no signs of awakening."

"We've postponed the board meeting twice now, Jo,"
said Madigan. He was a handsome rascal with a poet's
tongue, eyes that twinkled, and a grin that could look rueful

and inviting at the same time. This morning it was almost entirely rueful.

"I won't go before the board until we know," she insisted.

"Mrs. Nillson," Healy said softly, "you've got to face the possibility that he may *never* wake up."

Jo frowned at him, as much from being called by her husband's name as from his pessimism.

"He is physically recovered, isn't he?" she demanded.

"Yes. . . ."

"And the EEGs show normal brain activity."

With a shake of his head, Healy replied, "But that doesn't mean anything at all, Mrs. Nillson. We're dealing with a human being here, not just a bunch of graphs. All the tests show that he is alive, his body is functioning normally, his brain is active—but he remains in a coma and we don't know why!"

Jo saw that the scientist was getting himself upset. She made herself smile at him. "Back when I was a student at MIT, we used to say that hell for an engineer is when all the instruments check but nothing works."

Healy raised his hands, as if in supplication. "That's where we are. This is the first time anybody's ever brought a human being back from cryonic suspension—"

Madigan broke in, "The chairman of the board isn't going to sit in cryonic suspension. You can't dip your darling husband in liquid nitrogen and put him on hold."

Fixing him with a grim-faced stare, Jo said, "Archie, I'm getting tired—"

A chime sounded softly from the padded armrest of her couch. Jo cut off Madigan's reply with a quick movement of one hand as she touched a pad on the armrest's keyboard with the other.

"I told them not to disturb us unless he showed some change."

On the wall across the room, the glareless plastic cover over a Mary Cassatt painting of three women admiring a child turned opaque and then took on the three-dimensional form of Jo's secretary. The young woman was open-mouthed with excitement.

"He's awake!" she said breathlessly. "He just opened his eyes and got up and started walking around his room."

Jo could feel her own heart quicken. "Let me see," she demanded.

Instantly the secretary disappeared, and the three of them saw a view of Keith Stoner standing naked as a newborn by the window of his small room, staring intently out at the view.

"My God, he really is awake," Healy whispered, almost in awe.

"I didn't realize he was so big," said Madigan.

Jo shot him a glance.

"Tall, I mean."

She suppressed the urge to laugh. *He's alive and awake and just like he was all those years ago. I've done it! I've brought him back!*

She studied Keith Stoner intently, wordlessly, eyes picking out every detail of the face and body that she had known so intimately eighteen years ago.

Eighteen years, Jo thought. Suddenly her hands flew to her face. *Eighteen years! He hasn't aged a moment and I'm eighteen years older.*

CHAPTER 3

Stoner searched the drawers of the little bureau and found neat stacks of underwear, shirts, and slacks. No shoes, but several pairs of slipper socks.

Without even bothering to look at the size markings, he pulled on a pair of tan slacks and slipped an open-necked, short-sleeved buff-colored shirt over them. He did not bother with the socks. The floor felt comfortably warm.

Then he went to the window again and sat in the little armchair. The glass was all one piece; there was no way to open the window, and Stoner instinctively knew it would be too tough to shatter, even if he threw the chair at it.

Outside he saw lovely green landscaped grounds, dotted with gracefully swaying palm trees. In the distance, a highway busy with traffic, and beyond it a glistening white sand beach and a gentle surf rolling in from the blue ocean.

It did not look like Florida to him. California, possibly. Certainly not Kwajalein.

There were comparatively few automobiles on the highway, but those that Stoner saw looked only a little different from the cars he remembered. A bit lower and sleeker. They still ran on four wheels, from what he could see. He had not been asleep so long that totally new transportation systems had come into being. The trucks looked more changed, shaped more aerodynamically. And their cabs seemed longer, much more roomy than Stoner remembered them. He could not see any sooty fumes belching from them. Nor any diesel exhaust stacks. The trucks seemed to have their own lanes, separated from the automobile traffic by a raised divider.

It was quiet in his room. The highway sounds did not penetrate the window. The glistening bank of equipment that loomed around his shelf bed was barely humming. Stoner could hear himself breathing.

He leaned back in the chair and luxuriated in the pedestrian normality of it. Solid weight. The warmth of the sun shining through the window felt utterly wonderful on his face and bare arms. He watched the combers running up to the beach. The eternal sea, the heartbeat of the planet.

He closed his eyes. And for the briefest instant he saw a different scene, another world, alien yet familiar, vastly different from Earth and yet as intimately known as if he had been born there.

Stoner's eyes snapped open and focused on the enduring sea, unfailingly caressing the land; on the blue sky and stately white clouds adorning it. This is Earth, he told himself. The vision of an alien world faded and disappeared.

This is Earth, he repeated. I'm home. I'm safe now. Yet the memory of the flashback frightened him. He had never seen an alien landscape. He had never even set foot on Earth's own moon. But the vision in his mind had been as clear and solid as reality.

He shook his head and turned in the chair, away from the window. He saw that the curves of every monitoring screen had turned fiercely red and jagged. He took a deep breath and willed his heart to slow back to normal. The sensor traces smoothed and returned to their usual soft green color.

A portion of the solid wall between the bureau and the bank of electronic equipment glowed briefly and vanished, creating a normal-sized doorway. Through it stepped a smiling man. Behind him the wall re-formed itself, as solid as it had been originally.

"Good morning," said the man. "I'm Gene Richards."

Stoner got to his feet and stretched out his hand. "You must be a psychiatrist, aren't you?"

Richards's smile remained fixed, but his eyes narrowed a trifle. "A good guess. An excellent guess."

He was a small man, slight, almost frail. Thick curly reddish-brown hair and a neatly trimmed mustache. Thin face with small bright probing eyes and strong white teeth that seemed a size too large for his narrow jaw. He looked almost rodentlike. He wore a casual, brightly flowered shirt over denim shorts. His feet were shod in leather sandals.

Stoner dropped back into his chair while the psychiatrist pulled one of the plastic chairs from the wall and straddled it backward, next to him.

"Where the hell are we, anyway?" Stoner asked. "Hawaii?"

Richards nodded. "The big island, just outside of Hilo."

"This isn't a hospital, is it? It feels more like some big laboratory complex."

Again Richards bobbed his head up and down. "Right again. That's three in a row. Want to try for four?"

Stoner laughed softly. "I have no idea of how long I've been—suspended."

"Eighteen years."

"Eighteen? . . . ." Stoner felt the psychiatrist's eyes probing him. Past the man's suddenly intense face, he could see the row of display screens flickering their readout curves.

The silence stretched. Finally Richards asked, "How do you feel about returning from the dead?"

"I thought they'd bring me back a lot sooner than this."

"The alien spacecraft was recovered almost twelve years ago. You've been kept in cryonic suspension until the biotechnicians figured out how to thaw you without killing you."

"And the spacecraft?"

Richards's eyes shifted away slightly. "It's in orbit around the Earth."

"The alien himself . . ."

"He was quite dead. There wasn't a thing anybody could do about that."

Stoner leaned back in the chair and glanced out at the sea again.

"I'm the first man ever to be revived from cryonic suspension?" he asked.

"That's right. The scientists wanted to try some human guinea pigs, but the government wouldn't allow it."

"And the doorway you came in through, you learned that trick from the spacecraft."

Richards nodded again. "That . . . *trick*—it's revolutionizing everything."

"The ability to transform solid matter into pure energy and then back again," Stoner said.

"How would you . . ." Richards stopped himself. "Oh, sure. Of course. You're a physicist yourself, aren't you?"

"Sort of. I was an astrophysicist."

"So you know about things like that," the psychiatrist assured himself.

Stoner said nothing. He searched his mind for the knowledge he had just given words to. The alien's spacecraft had opened itself to him in the same way: a portion of the solid metal hull disappearing to form a hatchway. But he had never thought about the technique for doing it until the words had formed themselves in his mouth.

"How much do you remember?" Richards asked. "Can you recall how you got to the alien spacecraft?"

It was Stoner's turn to nod. "The last thing I remember is turning off the heater in my suit. It was damned cold. I must have blacked out then."

"You remember Kwajalein and the project to contact the spacecraft? The people you worked with?"

"Markov. Jo Camerata. McDermott and Tuttle and all the rest, sure. And Federenko, the cosmonaut."

Richards touched the corner of his mustache with the tip of a finger. "When you got to the alien's spacecraft, you deliberately decided to remain there, instead of returning to Earth." It was a statement of fact, not a question.

"That's right," said Stoner.

"Why?"

Stoner smiled at him. "You want to know why I chose death over life, is that it?"

Ben Bova

"That's it," Richards admitted.

"But I'm alive," Stoner said softly. "I didn't die."

"You had no way of knowing that. . . ."

"I had faith in the people I worked with. I knew they wouldn't leave me up there. They'd bring me back and revive me."

Richards looked totally unconvinced. But he forced a smile across his face. "We'll talk about that some more, later on."

"I'm sure we will."

"Is there anything I can do for you?" Richards asked. "Anything you want to know, anyone you want to see?"

Stoner thought a moment. "My kids—they must be grown adults by now."

The psychiatrist glanced up toward the ceiling, like a man trying to remember facts he had learned by rote. "Your son, Douglas, is an executive with a restaurant chain in the Los Angeles area. He's thirty-three, married, and has two children, both boys."

Thirty-three, Stoner thought. Christ, I've missed half his life.

"Your daughter, Eleanor," Richards went on, "will be thirty in a few weeks. She's married to a Peace Enforcer named Thompson; they make their home in Christchurch, New Zealand. They have two children, also. A girl and a boy."

"I'm a grandfather."

"Four times over." Richards smiled.

A grandfather, but a lousy father, Stoner told himself.

Richards's smile faded. Slowly, he said, "Your ex-wife died several years ago. A highway accident."

The pain surprised Stoner. He had expected to feel nothing. The open wound that their divorce had ripped out of his soul had been numbed long ago, covered with emotional scar tissue as thick as a spacecraft's heat shield. Or so Stoner had thought. Yet the news of Doris's death cut right through and stabbed deep into his flesh.

"Are you all right?" Richards asked.

Stoner turned away from his inquisitive face and looked through the window, out at the sun-sparkling sea.

"It's a lot to take in, all at once," he replied to the psychiatrist.

"Yes," Richards said. "We'll take it as slow as you like."

Stoner turned back toward him. The man was trying to keep his emotions to himself, but Stoner could see past his eyes, past the slightly quizzical smile that was supposed to be reassuring. I'm a laboratory specimen to him; an intriguing patient, the subject of a paper he'll deliver at an international conference of psychiatrists.

He looked deeper and realized that there was more to it. Richards truly wanted to help Stoner. The desire to be helpful was real, even if it was underlain by the desire to further his own career. And even deeper than that, buried so deeply that Richards himself barely knew of its existence, was the drive to learn, to know, to understand. Stoner smiled at the psychiatrist. He recognized that drive, that urgent passion. He himself had been a slave to it in his earlier life.

Richards misinterpreted his smile. "You feel better?"

"Yes," Stoner said. "I feel better."

The psychiatrist got to his feet. "I think that's enough information for you to digest for the time being."

"How long will I be here?"

Richards shrugged. "They'll want to run tests. . . ."

Stoner pulled himself up from his chair. He towered over the psychiatrist. "How long?"

"I really don't know."

"Days? Weeks? Months?"

Richards put on his brightest smile. "I truly can't say. Weeks, at least. Probably a couple of months." He started for the spot on the wall where the portal had opened.

Stoner asked, "Can I at least get out of this room and walk around the place?"

"Oh, sure," Richards said over his shoulder. "In a day or so."

"They're going to guard me pretty closely, aren't they?"

The wall glowed and the portal in it opened. "You're a very important person," Richards said. "The first man to be revived after cryonic suspension. You'll be famous."

Glancing around the bare room, Stoner asked, "Can you get me something to read? I've got eighteen years of news to catch up on."

The psychiatrist hesitated a moment. "Okay," he said. "I'll see that you get some reading material. But probably you ought to go slowly—there's a certain amount of cultural shock that you're going to have to deal with."

"Cultural shock?"

"The world's changed a lot in the past eighteen years."

"That's what I want to find out about."

"In due time. For the first few days, I think we ought to confine your reading to entertainment, rather than current events."

A sudden question popped into Stoner's mind. "Markov," he blurted. "Kirill Markov, the Russian linguist I worked with. How is he?"

Richards made a small shrug. "As far as I know, he's fine. Living in Moscow again. I believe he sent a message asking about you recently."

He stepped through and the wall became solid again. Stoner stood in the middle of the room, thinking that the first use of the alien's technology had been to make a jail cell for him.

CHAPTER 4

Jo Camerata did not sit at the head of the conference table. Vanguard Industries had long ago dispensed with such archaic hierarchical formalities. The president of the corporation sat at the middle of the table, flanked on either side by members of the board of directors, most of them male. A dozen muttered conversations buzzed around the table as Jo took her seat. Directly across from her sat the chairman of the board, Everett Nillson, her husband.

Nillson was a tall, rawboned Swede whose thinning blond hair and bushy eyebrows had been bleached nearly white by the Hawaiian sun. His eyes were such a pale blue that they seemed nearly colorless. His skin was so fair that strangers often assumed he was an albino. He was slow in speech and in movements, which led many an unwary adversary into believing Nillson's mind worked slowly, too. It did not.

He smiled across the polished mahogany table at his wife, his prized ornament, knowing that he had won her away from several of the other men seated in this plush, paneled boardroom. He had a long, bony, unhandsome face and a smile that looked more pained than pleasured. His hands were big, powerful, with lumpy, irregular knuckles and long, thick fingers. If it weren't for the perfectly fitted gray summer-weight suit and opulently decorated silk shirt he wore, he could easily have been mistaken for a farmer or a merchant seaman.

Jo smiled back at him, as much to discomfit some of the men seated around the table as to please her husband. She had dressed herself for this meeting in a demure starched white blouse with a high collar and a navy-blue knee-length skirt. Her only jewelry was a choker of black pearls, a diamond-studded pin shaped in Vanguard Industries' stylized V, and the plain platinum wedding band that Nillson had given her.

As chairman of the board, Nillson called the meeting to order. The room fell silent.

He let the silence hang for a long moment. All eyes were focused on him. Pungent smoke from several cigars and a half-dozen cigarettes wafted up to the ceiling vents. Nillson fixed his gaze on the computer screen set into the table top before him.

Finally, in his surprisingly deep, rich baritone he said, "The first item on our agenda this morning is a report on the cryonic project." He looked up at his wife. "Darling, if you will be so kind."

Jo said, "I have a videotaped presentation from Dr. Healy and several of his staff members. . . ."

"But he's actually awake and doing well?" asked one of the older board members, a heavyset, red-faced man who had received a heart transplant several years earlier.

"Yes," Jo said, not allowing herself to smile. "He is alive and as healthy as he was eighteen years ago. As far as the medical tests can ascertain, he has not suffered any detectable damage from being frozen."

She touched a button on the keypad in front of her with a manicured finger. The overhead lights dimmed slightly, and the wall to her left became a three-dimensional video screen. Everyone around the table turned to see.

Keith Stoner stood before them, life-sized and naked.

"This is when he first woke up," Jo told them.

One of the women board members whispered something. Jo could not catch the words, but the tone was carnal.

Stoner's image was quickly replaced by Healy's. The corporation's chief scientist began to explain, with charts and graphs, that Stoner's physical condition was so close to his condition as recorded eighteen years ago that the differences were undetectable. Then Richards, the psychiatrist, appeared and said that although Stoner's reactions appeared normal, he needed further study to "get deeper into the subject."

A male voice rumbled in the semidarkness, "The shrink's gay, is that it?"

"Maybe he's fallen in love with his patient," someone replied.

A few scattered laughs, most of them self-conscious.

The screen now showed Richards and Stoner strolling together along the grounds behind the building where Stoner was being kept. No walls or fences were in sight, only brightly flowering shrubs of hibiscus and oleander, which hid the lasers and electronic sensors of the security system. The area looked like a university quadrangle, bounded by multistory glass-and-chrome laboratory buildings. But no stranger or lab employee could get within a hundred yards of the carefully screened area where Richards and Stoner walked.

While the board members eavesdropped on their conversation, Jo sank back in her chair and studied Keith Stoner's handsome face. He had not changed at all. Or had he? His eyes seemed different, somehow. Nothing she could put her finger on, but different.

She had read every word of every transcript of every conversation Keith had taken part in. Not once had he asked about Jo Camerata. Not once had he spoken of the nights they had shared together, so long ago.

She turned slightly in her chair and saw her husband. He was not watching the screen. He was staring directly at her.

The videotape ended and the ceiling lights automatically came back up to full brightness as the screen turned opaque once more.

Jo tore her gaze away from Nillson's deathly pale eyes.

"Stoner appears perfectly willing to cooperate with us," she told the board. Then she added, "For the time being."

"What do you mean?"

"Sooner or later he's going to want to get out of our lab complex. He's going to want to see the world—after all, for him it's a new world. He's been asleep for eighteen years."

"He's much too important to let go," said the corporation's executive vice-president, a vigorous-looking man in his early forties, tanned and athletically trim.

"He's a vital asset," agreed the older woman sitting next to him.

"We've invested an enormous amount of money in this program," the corporation's treasurer added, waving his black cigar. "He can't just go wandering off where we can't keep him under study."

"What about the publicity aspects of this project?" Nillson asked, looking down the table to the new director of corporate public relations.

She was a stunningly beautiful Oriental, more than ten years younger than Jo. A face of hauntingly fragile delicacy, almost childlike except for the knowing eyes. A childlike body, too, slim and boyish, which Jo knew attracted her husband more than her own womanly figure. She was a protégée of Archie Madigan's. By rights she should not have been sitting in on a board meeting; but the chairman had invited her, and Jo knew better than to argue the point.

"The first man to be revived from cryonic suspension," she said, looking directly back at Nillson, "will be an instant global celebrity. Not only is he a former astronaut and scientist, and the man who went into space to meet the alien starship—he's the first man to be brought back from the dead. Properly handled, he can be worth billions in publicity, worldwide."

Jo nodded to show that she agreed with them all. "But I know the man. We worked together, before he . . ."

She hesitated just the barest fraction of an instant, her mind whispering silently, Before he went off into deep space and chose death rather than returning to me.

"Before he was frozen," she continued aloud. "Sooner or later he's going to want the freedom to come and go as he pleases."

"He's our property, dammit!" snapped the treasurer. "We spent the money to go out there and rescue him. He owes us his life."

"And there's the security question," the public relations director said, ignoring him and still looking straight at Nillson. "Competitors like Yamagata or Eurogenetics or even Avtech would *love* to get their hands on him. Until we're ready to reveal him to the world, we'd better be very careful with him."

Jo replied mildly, "But we don't own the man." Turning to the corporation's chief counsel, she asked, "Do we, Archie?"

Madigan smiled his poet's rueful smile. "Of course we can't be going against the provisions of the Fourteenth Amendment. But . . ." He let the word dangle before the board members.

"But what?" the executive vice-president demanded.

The lawyer made a slight shrug. "He's been frozen alive for eighteen years. He's been out of touch with civilization, out of contact with the world, for eighteen years. I think we could make a case that he's not fully competent to be responsible for himself. I think a friendly judge might allow us to maintain custody of him for a while."

The board members looked pleased at that.

"How long?" asked Nillson.

"Oh, a few months, I should think," Madigan replied. "Maybe a year."

"And how long will it be," Nillson asked slowly, "before the news media discover that he's awake?"

"There will be no announcement," Jo responded. "Not yet."

"Security has been airtight," Madigan added. "Only the staff scientists who work directly with him know that he's been revived. To the rest of the personnel he's just another volunteer subject for the pharmaceutical division."

Nillson shook his head. "This news is much too big to keep quiet for long."

The florid-faced heart transplant recipient nodded gravely. "The first man to be brought back from the dead. By God, the reporters will swarm all over him."

"And our competitors," the treasurer repeated.

"We'll move him to a more remote site as soon as the medical tests are finished," Jo said.

"That might be a very good idea," her husband agreed.

Jo touched the memo pad on her keyboard. The computer

would automatically highlight the previous ten lines of conversation when it printed up the transcript of this meeting.

The discussion moved on to other topics: Vanguard's pharmaceutical processing plant in orbit was conspicuously over budget; Avtech Corporation had hired away two of Vanguard's plant managers, one in Karachi and one in Rio: the corporation's interdivisional communications codes were being changed as a routine security precaution; terrorists from the World Liberation Movement had bombed the biotechnology factory in Sydney, nobody killed but half a million dollars' worth of damage to the organ-cloning production line; the European division's construction unit had run into unexpected snags in its contracts to build airports and civil improvements in Bulgaria ("Damned Commie bureaucrats want their bribes increased," groused one board member); angry crowds had staged a violent demonstration at the former corporate headquarters in Greenwich, insisting that Vanguard had developed a cure for cancer that it was keeping secret ("I only wish," Nillson murmured, drawing a big dollar sign on his scratch pad); the airline division was being sued in the World Court for its refusal to fly its scheduled routes into the countries involved in the Central African War.

In all, the corporation's profits for this quarter would be down some 8 to 10 percent, even though total sales volume from all its divisions appeared to be nearly 12 percent higher than the same quarter the previous year.

"Too much money being spent unproductively," Nillson said mildly.

The public relations director turned her most feminine smile on the board chairman. "And we don't really have any new products to show, to take the attention off the lower profits. Not unless we make a major effort on the frozen astronaut."

"It's too early for that," Jo snapped.

"Then the media's going to ask why our profits are down, and why R and D isn't producing."

Research and development was Jo's special area. She realized that the public relations director was openly challenging her.

Very sweetly, Jo said, "When you get old enough to be stricken by a terminal disease—like maybe cancer or a sudden stroke—you'll be willing to spend everything you have for the products of our *unproductive* R and D. Maybe you'll even want to have yourself frozen for a few years, until the medical people can work out a cure for whatever is killing you. Then the money we've spent on our cryonics and other R and D programs will seem like a good investment to you.''

The Oriental girl's lips pressed into a colorless line. But before she could answer Jo, Nillson said, ''R and D has been very important to this corporation's growth, we all know that. But we must keep a careful watch on expenses. No one in this organization has a blank check.''

Murmurs of assent spread around the table.

Jo smiled at her husband and realized that the woman was making a brazen play for him—and he seemed willing to see how well she could do. Looking around the table, Jo saw at least three people who would soon have a vital personal interest in being frozen until a terminal illness could be reversed. If it came to a real fight with the public relations director, Jo knew she would win.

But it won't come to that, she told herself. I'll have the little bitch out of here without anyone in this room knowing what happened to her. Or caring.

The meeting finally ended, and Jo started back toward her office. Nillson fell in beside her, and together they walked along the glass-walled corridor back to her executive suite.

They made a striking couple. She was dark fire, a long-legged beauty with the deep suntan, midnight-black hair, and stunning figure of a classic Mediterranean enchantress. He was pallid ice, taller than she, lean and spare, cold where she was fiery, wan where she was vibrant, a pale distant frosty Northern Lights compared to the blazing intensity of the tropical sun.

''You're not going back to your office?'' Jo asked as they strode in unison down the corridor.

''I want to ask you something.''

''Where we can't be overheard,'' she realized.

He dipped his chin slightly in acknowledgment. Offices can be bugged. Secretaries can be bribed. A busy corridor connecting the president's suite with the offices of the chairman of the board and the board's meeting room could be more private than any sanctum sanctorum.

''Did Healy tell you that he doesn't sleep?''

Jo looked up sharply at her husband. His face was perfectly controlled, no hint of any emotion whatsoever.

"What did you say?"

"He doesn't sleep," Nillson repeated. "Your man Stoner has not slept at all in the four days since he has been revived."

Jo said nothing. There was no need. Nillson knew full well that the scientist had not told her. Her thoughts swirled wildly. Keith doesn't sleep! Why? What's gone wrong? And why did that sonofabitch Healy tell my husband instead of me?

CHAPTER 5

Stoner and Dr. Richards strolled casually across the lawn outside his building. The late afternoon sun baked through Stoner's light open-weave shirt; he reveled in the warmth of it. The breeze from the sea was filled with the fragrance of tropical flowers. Since nine that morning Stoner had endured still another battery of physical examinations. Now he and the psychiatrist were out in the open air.

Like a prisoner taking his compulsory exercise, Stoner thought.

Richards was good, a smooth performer who seemed to be engaged in nothing more than relaxed conversation while he deftly probed his patient's innermost thoughts. Stoner smiled at him and nodded in the right places, keeping his end of the chatter going. But his eyes were focused on the space between two of the four-story lab buildings; he could see open ground stretching out to a high-wire fence. Beyond the fence was the highway and, beyond that, the beach and the ocean.

What would Richards do if I just sprinted off, ran between the buildings and jumped that fence and raced out to the highway? What would *I* do: flag down a passing car, or keep going into the surf and plunge in?

He thought about swimming in the ocean and remembered nights on Kwajalein when he and Jo had swum in the lagoon.

"Jo Camerata is here, isn't she?" he suddenly asked Richards.

The psychiatrist blinked in the slanting rays of the sun, his train of questioning derailed.

"Ms. Camerata? Yes, she's here."

"She must be pretty important," Stoner said.

"Would you like to meet her?"

"Of course."

Richards fingered his mustache. Stoner laughed and told him, "You're wondering why I never asked about her before this, aren't you?"

Trying to suppress a troubled frown, Richards said, "You have a way of telling me what I'm thinking."

Stoner lifted one hand in an apologetic gesture. "You wouldn't make a good poker player. I can read your face."

"It seems to me you can read my mind."

"No, nothing so . . ." The breath caught in Stoner's chest. He saw Richards's searching, inquisitive face, the dark eyes probing him. He saw the laboratory building behind the psychiatrist and the bright blue Hawaiian sky and the grass and graceful palms out by the beach.

But like a double exposure on a piece of film, Stoner also saw another scene, a completely different scene from a different world. A smooth, graceful tower, impossibly slim, incredibly tall, soared endlessly into a softly glowing sky of pale yellow. Stoner craned his neck painfully and still could not see the top of the tower. It rose heavenward against all the laws of gravity and sense, up and up until it was lost to his sight. He was standing at its base, atop a low, gently sloping hill. His feet were shod in metallic boots, and the ground was covered with brilliant orange blades of grass that seemed to shrink away from him and leave the ground where he was standing bare and sandy. He dropped to one knee, and as he did so, the individual blades of grass scurried out of his way, like frightened little creatures with wills of their own.

Stoner smiled at the strange orange blades, trying to see how they managed to move themselves. He put out a hand and saw that it was gloved in the same gleaming silvery metal as his boots. The motile grass backed away from his extended hand. He smiled. "I won't hurt you. Honestly, I won't. . . ."

The chanting made him look up. Far across the open orange field, a long procession was winding its way up the slope of the hill toward him. The grass was parting itself, making an open path for the people, a path that led straight to the spot where Stoner was standing. He could not make out the words they were singing, but the tone was mournful, sad. He saw they were carrying a body stretched out on a bier.

"That's me," Stoner realized. "It's my funeral procession."

He looked up again and saw Richards staring down at him. Stoner realized he was kneeling on the thick green grass of the laboratory lawn, the afternoon sun burning hotly behind the psychiatrist, framing his curly mop of hair with a halo of radiance.

Feeling almost foolish, Stoner got to his feet. A few of the employees walking some distance away were staring at them.

"Your funeral?" Richards asked. He was almost quivering with anticipation, like a hunting dog who had just scented its quarry.

His stomach fluttering, Stoner asked, "What did you say?"

"You said something about a funeral procession."

"Did I?" he stalled.

"What happened to you? What did you see?"

With a shake of his head, Stoner answered, "I don't know. I blanked out. . . ."

Richards's eyes were trying to pry the information out of him. "You went completely out of focus. You looked up at the sky, then you dropped down on your knees and muttered something about a funeral procession."

Stoner said nothing.

"You were hallucinating," the psychiatrist said.

"I've never done that before."

Abruptly, Richards turned back toward the building where Stoner's quarters were. "Come on, I want to see what the EEG looks like."

Stoner caught up with him in two long strides. "You've been recording me out here?"

Nodding, Richards said, "Every second. The equipment can monitor you anywhere in the complex—as far as the beach, maybe farther."

"You implanted sensors inside me?"

"Sprayed them on your skin. The technology's improved since you took your sleep. You can't feel them or wash them off, but they're there."

Instead of returning to Stoner's quarters, Richards hurried to a windowless room halfway down the antiseptic-white corridor. To Stoner it looked like a spaceflight control center: banks of monitoring display screens tended by a handful of young men and women in white lab smocks. The lighting in the room was dim, the people monitoring the screens looked like shadowy wraiths condemned to study the flickering green and orange glowing screens until they had atoned for the sins of their earlier lives.

Stoner remembered a similar room, on Kwajalein, where he and others had tensely watched radar screens that showed the approach of the alien spacecraft. That room had been cramped, hot, sweaty with fear and anticipation. This room was cool, spacious, relaxed, and so quiet that Stoner could hear the hum of electricity that fed the display screens.

No one bothered to turn around or look up as they came in. Richards went straight to the nearest unoccupied station and slid into the empty chair there. He touched the keyboard, and a convoluted set of ragged lines spread themselves across the screen.

For several moments he studied the display, touching the keyboard to bring up new data, then staring intently at the screen. Finally he gave a heavy sigh, punched a single button, and the screen went dark.

"What is it?" Stoner asked in a whisper as Richards got up from the chair. Whispering seemed the proper tone in this quiet, darkened chamber.

"What . . . Oh, nothing," the psychiatrist answered. "The EEG seems normal enough."

But even in the shadowy lighting Stoner could see that Richards was not telling the truth. His eyes avoided Stoner's.

"Nothing unusual?" he asked.

"I'm not a psychotech," Richards evaded. "Maybe somebody who's more expert than I will be able to see something in the EEG that I missed."

A single word pronounced itself in Stoner's mind, a word that seemed to flow from Richards's mind to his own.

Schizophrenia.

CHAPTER 6

Jo leaned back in her softly yielding leather chair and studied the faces of the two men. Healy looked distressed, like a freckle-faced little boy who had been caught doing something naughty. But Richards looked really troubled, a man with a frightening weight on his shoulders.

She had spent an hour in the office by herself, combing the walls, the ceiling, the furniture, the computer and phones, the windows and draperies, searching for bugs that might have been planted by an ambitious young rival such as the public relations director, or a suspicious board member, or an agent for a competing company, or by her husband. She remembered enough of her MIT training to feel that she could clean her own nest, but it bothered her that she had found nothing. Nothing at all.

Still, she had to have this showdown with Healy. It suddenly struck her that maybe her chief scientist was actually disloyal to her. Maybe he was the leak in her security.

She reset the office's colors to cool greens and blues, and selected just a hint of salt tang for the room scent. She lowered the air temperature several degrees: she was blazing hot enough. Then she waited, in a plain gray blouseless business suit adorned only by her corporate logo pin. The two of them arrived at her outer office exactly on time. Jo did not keep them waiting; she had her secretary usher them in immediately.

"I learned yesterday that Stoner has not slept since he's been revived," she said once the two men had taken chairs facing her.

Richards flicked a glance at Healy, who looked thoroughly miserable.

"I learned that information from the chairman of the board," Jo went on. "Why didn't I learn it from you?"

Healy replied, "We haven't put it into any of our reports yet. . . ."

"I know that," she snapped.

"We're still not sure of the significance of it," he said, squirming in his chair.

"A man doesn't sleep for five straight nights and you're not sure that it's significant?" Jo kept her voice low and icy calm.

"We . . . we're studying it," Healy said weakly.

"And how did the chairman of the board find out about it?"

Healy spread his hands. "I don't know! Somebody in the lab must have talked. . . ."

"Did you know that there was a disturbance at the outer fence last night?"

"A disturbance?"

"Security thinks somebody tried to break into the labs. World Liberation Movement terrorists, perhaps."

"How would they . . ."

She silenced him by raising one finger. "How many people are working with Stoner now?"

"Directly?" Healy's little-boy face pulled itself into a momentary frown of concentration. "There's Dr. Richards, here, and the medical team that's monitoring him . . . that makes seven—no, nine people."

"And indirectly?"

"There's the commissary crew, they prepare his meals and bring them to his room. And the data processing people, the electronics maintenance people, the—"

"Stop," Jo commanded. "I want the monitoring crew cut down to three people, one for each shift. Send me the files on the people who're working there now and I'll select the three I want. They will bring his meals to him when they start their shifts. All data processing will be done by our branch in Geneva, I'll clear a satellite channel for you. If there's any need for electronic repairs or maintenance, do it yourself."

"But I—"

"This is a burden on you, I understand," Jo said, her voice still steel-edged. "But security is absolutely imperative. The fewer people who are involved, the easier it will be to maintain security."

"But the whole board of directors knows about him!" Healy bleated.

"That can't be helped. They recognize his importance to the corporation, though. If they're smart, they'll stay quiet." She smiled, almost to herself. "At least long enough to grab as much Vanguard stock as they can without pushing the price sky high."

Healy looked unconvinced. Richards, on the other hand, was watching Jo intently.

She went on, "You've got to understand what we've got here. The man has been brought back from the dead. The technique for reviving him is worth billions—hundreds of billions. Do you have any idea how many people will want to have themselves frozen when they discover they have an inoperable cancer, or they're waiting for a replacement heart?"

"Yes, I know."

"If he's not sleeping, then there's something wrong, some- thing not normal. *We can't allow that information to leak outside these walls.*"

Healy nodded. Then, in a near whisper, he said, "But it was only the chairman of the board. He's entitled to know, isn't he? After all, he's the company's top man. And your own husband."

Jo stared at him for a long moment before replying. "If somebody's leaking information to him, out of channels, without your knowledge or mine, who else might they be talking to?"

"But I don't think—"

"I do! Now get back to your office and implement the procedures I just outlined. I want those personnel files on my screen within fifteen minutes."

Healy's face went white, as if Jo had slapped him. Dumbly he pushed himself out of his chair. Richards got to his feet beside him.

Jo let them get as far as her door before calling, "Dr. Richards, I almost forgot. I wanted to ask you a couple of questions about Stoner. Could you come back here a mo- ment, please?"

Richards turned back toward her. Healy hesitated, then opened the door and stepped out.

Jo indicated the chair nearest her own.

Sitting in it, Richards said, "If he wasn't your enemy before we came in here, he certainly is now."

Raising an eyebrow at him, Jo asked, "You think so? I'm not sure he has the guts."

The psychiatrist shrugged. "You emasculated him."

She laughed. "And you're assuming he had some balls when he came in here."

Richards smiled and ran a finger across his mustache.

"What do you make of Stoner's not sleeping?"

"I don't know. It doesn't seem to be affecting him physically. Of course, I never saw him before he was frozen, so it's a little difficult for me to say." His eyes shifted away from her.

Jo said, "What else?"

"I'm not sure what to make of it," the psychiatrist said. "He had a hallucinatory session yesterday. It was brief, but for a minute or so he was totally out of reality."

Jo felt her breath catch in her throat.

"It may be just the lack of sleep catching up with him. But there's a definite problem, and until we know what it is and what's causing it . . ."

"What does he *do* all night?"

"He reads. He sits around his room and reads everything that I give him. He's devoured half the books in my library—in less than a week."

"You're not giving him books about recent history or current affairs, are you?" Jo asked.

"No. I still think that he has to be introduced to the modern world gradually. But he's certainly catching up on the classics! He's like a student doing all his required reading for English lit. High school and college, all at once."

"What does he say about his not sleeping?"

Richards grimaced good-naturedly. "I asked him about it, and he said he'd been sleeping for eighteen years so he didn't feel the need for sleep now."

Jo nodded. "That sounds like him. He's good at covering himself."

"There's something more."

"What?"

"He's shown no interest in sex. Doesn't mention it at all. No nocturnal emissions. He doesn't even seem to pay any attention to the women who've been on the monitoring team.

And there are a couple of very pretty ones. No come-ons, no joking with them, no preening for them.''

Jo fell silent. As driven as Keith had been in his earlier life, he had still found time for sex. Not love, perhaps, but in bed he could unloose all the fiery passion that he had held in check through his tight-lipped, tension-filled days.

Richards asked, "You two were . . . close, weren't you?''

"We were lovers, for a short while." An image of herself as a star-struck student madly in love with the moody, brooding scientist-astronaut almost made Jo blush. What a fool, she scolded herself. What a fool!

"You were with him during the project to make contact with the alien spacecraft?''

"Yes, at Kwajalein. And I went with him to Tyuratam.''

"And he flew off to rendezvous with the spacecraft and didn't come back.''

"He *chose* not to come back," Jo said, her mind filling with the memory of it. "He chose to let himself freeze in the spacecraft with the dead alien's body instead of returning safely to Earth.''

Richards said nothing, and Jo finally realized that he was asking the questions, not she.

She smiled at him. "Your first name is Gene, isn't it?''

"Yes." He smiled back.

"You realize that we're going to have to move him from here. Too many prying eyes—and blabbing mouths.''

"I was wondering if you would come to that conclusion.''

"Will you go with him, Gene?''

"If you want me to.''

"I *need* you to," Jo said urgently. "Gene, I need your loyalty. I need a man I can trust.''

"You can trust me," he said.

She leaned forward and put her hand on his bare arm. "Can I, Gene? Not as employer and employee, but as friends? I need a friend. Desperately.''

"Your husband . . .''

"We don't see eye to eye on this. For the first time since I've known him, he's opposing me. Not openly. Not yet. But I don't think I can count on him, not on this project.''

Richards said nothing. Jo pulled her hand away.

He reached out to take it in his. "You have a reputation, you know.''

With a grin, she admitted, "I suppose I do."

"I don't want to get in trouble with the chairman of the board."

"I don't blame you."

"I'm still a married man."

"I've seen your file. You've been separated for six months now. Divorce proceedings started last week."

Richards gazed at her for a long, silent moment. Jo could see the mental calculations going on behind his bright brown eyes.

"Where will you take him?" he asked.

She shook her head. "I haven't decided yet. I have a house in Maine that's pretty secluded. Perhaps there." It was a deliberate ploy. If her people in Maine discovered a sudden new surveillance of the house in the next few days, she would know that Richards could not be trusted.

The psychiatrist let go of her hand. "I'll go with him, wherever it is," he said. "He's my patient, after all. And—I'd like to be your friend."

Jo smiled at him. "Thank you, Gene. You won't regret it."

"I'm going strictly on a professional basis, as Stoner's doctor. Any personal relationship between you and me . . . well, let's just allow nature to take its own course, shall we?"

"Go with the flow," Jo agreed, thinking silently, He's enough of a male to want to think that he'll pick the time and place. The male ego! How wonderfully predictable!

"And what happens to Healy?" Richards asked.

Jo looked into the psychiatrist's eyes, wondering, Is he asking out of loyalty or out of ambition? Is he trying to show me that he's loyal to Healy or that he wants the chief scientist's job?

"He'll stay here," she answered. "He's a competent administrator, even though I can't trust him with anything really sensitive."

"I see." Richards tugged at his mustache for a moment, then, "Can I ask you one more question? It's personal."

"Go ahead."

"Stoner has barely mentioned you, and he hasn't shown any burning desire to see you."

Jo felt ice chilling her blood. "I know that."

"Yes. But you haven't asked to see him, either. Why not?"

"I see the videotapes."

"But you haven't tried to meet him."

"Would you allow it?"

"I think he could handle it. It might even help to bring whatever he's suppressing up to the surface. But can *you* handle it?"

She finally saw the point he was driving toward. "You mean because we were lovers once, do I still have a feeling about him?"

Richards nodded.

"That was eighteen years ago," Jo said. "I was a kid, a student, and he was a very handsome, very glamorous, very important man."

"But you were in love with him then, weren't you?"

She hesitated, wondering what she should say. Then, "Frankly, I was using him to get ahead in what was then a highly male-dominated field. He wasn't very deeply attached to me, and I certainly wasn't madly in love with him."

It was a lie, and she thought she could see in Richards's eyes that he didn't believe her.

But he said, "I see."

They both let it go at that.

CHAPTER 7

The new Director of Corporate Public Relations for Vanguard Industries was An Linh Laguerre. To her, the frozen astronaut was more than a news story, more than a company project. It was a personal quest.

She had been born twenty-eight years earlier in a refugee camp in Thailand, a few miles from the border of Kampuchea, where Vietnamese troops and hard-eyed Communist administrators were turning the former Cambodia into an unwilling, starving colony of Vietnam. Millions had been killed in the years of fighting and massacres, and millions more had been driven from their homes, struggling desperately over shattered highways and tortuous jungle trails toward the relative safety of independent Thailand.

Relative safety. The camps were bursting with refugees, sick, wounded, dying. Their rickety, makeshift cabins and improvised tents overflowed with the tide of human misery. Rats fought human beings for scraps of food and often won. People died of simple infections, their bodies too malnourished to fight off the fevers that swept through the pitiful, ragged refugees.

In the torrid sun and paralyzing humidity of the jungle, amid the squalor and filth, the buzzing flies, the loud voices arguing over a cup of rice, the screams of a woman dying even as she gave birth—in such a camp was An Linh born. Her mother died of malnutrition and exhaustion before the sun set on her first day. A young French Red Cross worker, a harried, overworked volunteer, took that one baby out of the hundreds that she had seen orphaned at the camp, because the infant girl looked so pretty to her. Her husband, a surgeon who never volunteered for refugee work again after putting in three months at the camps, reluctantly allowed his wife to bring the baby home to Avignon with them. Eventually they adopted the girl, when it became clear that they could not have babies of their own. But he never allowed her to use his family name. He gave her an invented surname—Laguerre, the child of war.

An Linh's earliest memories were of Avignon, the medieval stone city with the bridge that had collapsed centuries ago and had never been rebuilt; it still went only halfway across the peaceful Rhone River. She spent many an afternoon at the crumbling edge of the old bridge, in the shadows of the chapel built upon it, straining her eyes to study the farther bank of the river. To her child's understanding, the other side of the river was her other life. Her Asian mother was there, she imagined.

She saw her French father as cold, aloof, unbending. As she grew older she realized that he treated her with formal propriety but never regarded her as his daughter. Slowly, An Linh began to understand that he had allowed her into his home because of his wife, An Linh's French mother. He loved the woman and could deny her nothing that was in his power to give. He simply did not have the power to love a child who was not his own.

But as distant as her adopted father was, her French mother was warm and close. To An Linh, she was the woman Monet painted, the mother who personified love and safety and happiness, the slim lady smiling tenderly in the afternoon sunshine of summer. She was Canadian by birth, a Quebecoise who had fled from the convent in which her parents had enrolled her and spent her life atoning for the guilt she felt at abandoning God. She had met the man she would marry, the proud, handsome son of a wealthy vintner, while she was at nursing school in Aix-en-Provence and he was an intern. They honeymooned in Paris while she talked him into volunteer work in Indochina.

To be a beautiful Oriental child growing up in Avignon was not without pain. When An Linh started school, the French children called her *Arabe* or *Africaine*. The Algerian and Moroccan children called her *Chinoise*.

She was ten years old when the American astronaut flew out to meet the approaching alien spacecraft and somehow stayed aboard it instead of returning home with his Russian cosmonaut pilot. An Linh watched the rocket's takeoff on television, but within a few days the story disappeared from view, just as the American himself drifted farther and farther away from Earth on the alien's retreating ship.

As An Linh grew into her teen years and began to menstruate, she suddenly saw her adopted father in a different way. He was a man, and she realized that now he was watching her as a man watches a woman. She was terrified, and all the more so because she could not bring herself to tell her French mother about this shocking secret.

She realized also that her mother was aging. While her father grew more handsome and distinguished with each year, her mother was visibly fading. Her golden-brown hair was turning dull, mousey. The sparkle in her eyes dimmed. She seemed tired, slow, withdrawn.

They sent her to the university at Aix, where An Linh studied journalism and quickly learned that sex was the greatest equalizer in the world. Among the students she was no longer the stranger, the outsider, the alien creature who did not belong. Even her nickname of *La Chinoise* became a term of admiration instead of mockery. She traded boyfriends with the other girls, eager to make them like her. She did well in her classes, so well that she could afford to avoid the male faculty members who pursued her.

By the end of her first year, as she rode the bus back toward Avignon, through the gentle hills dotted with nuclear power plants and neatly planted vineyards, she thought that she could at last face her adopted father as an adult, an equal, no longer afraid of the unspoken emotions that surged between them.

Her father was dead. He had been killed that very afternoon in an auto accident, senselessly, as he drove to meet her at the bus station. An Linh's mother collapsed. She had to take charge of the funeral arrangements herself, while her mother was taken to the same hospital where her father had worked.

There they found the cancer that was eating away at her body. And there they began the years of desperate therapies to save her life. Chemicals, radiation, lasers, heat, ice, diet— the doctors tried them all. To An Linh it seemed as though the woman she had known as a mother had been transformed into a haggard, passive, weak, and helpless experimental animal, melting away, visibly shrinking with each passing day. But deep within the woman's body, too deeply enmeshed with her vital organs for surgery or even X-ray laser beams to reach, cancerous tumors were growing. The body that could not conceive a baby created its own grotesque parody of life, cancer cells that multiplied endlessly. Like soldiers facing hopeless odds, the doctors slaughtered the enemy cells ruthlessly. But each tumor they killed gave rise to other tumors.

Her mother was dying. The chief internist of the hospital put it as gently as he could, but in the end he told An Linh that there was nothing more they could do except try to make the final days as painless as possible.

"But all the new medicines that have been discovered," she said, feeling a wild anger taking control of her. "The genetic techniques that have been developed . . ."

"Useless," said the physician. "We have tried everything."

Fighting down the fury that was making her heart pound so hard she could feel it in her chest, An Linh said, "Then freeze her."

The man's silver brows rose several millimeters.

"I want her frozen, like that astronaut was, years ago."

The chief internist's office was spacious and impeccably neat. He was not a man who tolerated slovenliness, not even sloppy thinking.

"But my dear child," he said softly, "that would be pointless. And quite expensive."

"I want her frozen as soon as she is pronounced clinically dead." An Linh had studied the possibilities for a school assignment. "I will sign the necessary releases."

"No one has ever been successfully revived after cryonic immersion. Neuromuscular function . . . the cytoplasm . . ." The physician was falling back on jargon in an unconscious effort to intimidate this willful, utterly beautiful but determined young lady.

"As long as she remains frozen there is always the hope that one day she can be revived and cured."

The internist shook his head sadly. "The cost . . ."

"I will pay," An Linh said flatly.

And she did. Her university days were finished. She applied the small legacy her adopted father had left to her mother's maintenance, then headed for Paris and took a job as a television news researcher. Within a year she had reached the bed of the company's chief executive and wangled an assignment to Indochina. She gained brief worldwide fame for her poignant, passionate story of her homecoming to that troubled part of the world and how it was finally taking the first timid, tentative steps toward peace and human kindness.

The Indochina story got her an offer from a Canadian news agency. An Linh accepted, partly because the pay was very good, partly because it got her away from the executive in Paris, mainly because it brought her closer to the United States, where the frozen astronaut was hidden away by the corporation that had rescued his body and returned it to Earth. After a year in Quebec, though, she longed for a warmer climate. And she had heard persistent rumors that the frozen astronaut was in a laboratory somewhere in the Hawaiian Islands.

She was too dedicated and too photogenic not to be noticed by the major news corporations. The offers started flooding in after only a few months of her being on-camera in Quebec. She stubbornly refused them all and set herself the task of getting to the frozen astronaut. It was not difficult for her to

gain a job in the public relations department of Vanguard
Industries' aircraft manufacturing division in California. The
woman heading the personnel department there said she was
overqualified, but the male division manager took one look at
her and, grinning, hired her on the spot.

Within six months she met Archie Madigan. She had been
able to fend off the division manager, but to get herself
promoted to corporate public relations, she went to bed with
the smiling, seemingly sensitive lawyer. Once she started
working in Hilo, she made certain that the chairman of the
board noticed her. Nillson made no sexual advances, but An
Linh rose rapidly to become director of corporate public
relations.

It was in her sparkling new office that she met Cliff Baker
of Worldnews, Inc. And he introduced her to Father Lemoyne.

Baker was the complete cynic, a journalist who believed in
no one and nothing except himself and his own talents. He
was nearly ten years older than An Linh, a ruggedly handsome Australian with golden-blond hair and a lean, muscular
body. He could have been a video deity, except for the
broken nose that marred his otherwise perfect face. His smile
was irresistible, his sky-blue eyes disarming. For the first
time, An Linh fell helplessly in love. It was not the first time
for Baker.

He casually mentioned the frozen astronaut to her, once
she told him about her mother waiting in a cylinder filled
with liquid nitrogen in Avignon. An Linh searched her office
data banks for every shred of data about the astronaut: his
past history, the details of how he flew aboard a Russian
Soyuz to rendezvous with the alien spacecraft, his decision to
remain aboard it with the dead alien, and finally the recapture
of the spacecraft. Vanguard Industries had spent a considerable fortune to reach the alien vehicle; it was the farthest
manned space mission in history. But once Vanguard's team
had brought the alien spacecraft back to an orbit around the
Earth, an impenetrable blackout descended. The file stopped
dead. Every attempt An Linh made to dig further was met by
the computer screen displaying RESTRICTED INFORMATION,
PER ORDER J. CAMERATA NILLSON, PRESIDENT, VANGUARD
INDUSTRIES.

An Linh soon realized that the marriage between Vanguard's president and the chairman of the board was a strange

one. She had a reputation for sleeping her way to the top and apparently did not care who knew about it. Nor did he, it seemed. Nillson's own reputation was the subject of whispers and strange rumors that hinted at odd tastes but offered no real facts. An Linh kept her own amorous liaisons as quiet as possible, maintaining a delicate balance between discreetness and desirability. She owed a debt to Archie Madigan, but he seemed content to leave her alone. Perhaps he was waiting for the debt to accrue interest, An Linh thought.

In a way, Jo Camerata Nillson became a role model for her, and she knew that sooner or later they would become deadly enemies, both seeking power through the same man: Everett Nillson.

Then came the board meeting, and the revelation that the astronaut had been successfully revived. An Linh's heart pounded inside her; she could see her mother being revived, recovering, returning to life.

That evening she told Baker. She knew she shouldn't, but she was bursting with the good news and she had to share it with someone.

"So he's alive," Baker said, his voice hollow with awe. "They've actually brought him back."

He was stretched out naked on the rumpled bed of his apartment, his body deeply tanned except for the narrow stretch that his briefs usually covered. An Linh lay beside him, still moist and warm from their lovemaking. A tropical downpour drummed at the bedroom's lone window.

"Cliff," she said, stroking his bare chest, "this is strictly between the two of us. Totally off the record. If you try to make a story out of it, I'll have to deny it."

Baker sat up abruptly, pulling his knees to his chin and locking his arms around them. He stared at his own image in the mirror above the bureau against the wall across from the bed.

"We'll release the story in a few months," An Linh went on, "and I'll make certain that you're—"

"Shh!" Baker hissed. "Genius at work."

She smiled up at his fiercely scowling face. Then, glancing at the digital clock on the dresser, she saw that she was running late for her dinner engagement. Leaving the Aussie to his own machinations, An Linh got up from the bed and walked lightly to the bathroom.

She was luxuriating in the steamy enveloping warmth of
the shower when she felt his hands on her.

"Soap my back, will you?" she murmured.

Baker complied, then slid his hands down her hips, her
thighs. She turned to face him, and he sank to his knees, his
hands reaching behind her now, grasping her slim buttocks,
his tongue searching between her legs. The hot water throbbed
against An Linh's shoulders and back. The steam swirled and
caressed them both. She dug her fingers into his golden hair
and tilted her head back, eyes closed against the delicious hot
shower. Her back arched, and she spasmed and gave out a
long, wrenching sigh.

With a knowing grin, Baker got to his feet and held her in
his arms for long silent moments. She twined her arms
around his neck and kissed him passionately, thankfully.

His grin widened. "My turn," he said.

An Linh smiled back at him. A small voice deep inside her
mind told her that he never gave without taking, but she
dismissed its warning and knelt before her handsome, smiling
lover.

CHAPTER 8

It was still raining by the time An Linh was dressed and
ready to leave for dinner. Standing in the apartment's living
room, she looked out through the windows at the rain drench-
ing the parking lot.

"Going to dinner?" Baker asked her.

She had not heard him approaching her. He had the knack
of moving noiselessly, like a shadow.

"I'm meeting Father Lemoyne, remember?"

He nodded. "Yeah, I know. How's he doing?"

"That's what I'm going to find out. He's just come back
from Boston, the medical people at Harvard."

"I've been thinking," Baker said, looking away from
An Linh toward his ghostly image reflected in the rain-

washed windows. "The priest might be the way for you to get me inside the Vanguard labs."

"I'll get you inside the labs, when the time comes. I'll make certain that—"

"Not 'when the time comes,' " Baker said. "I want to get in there now. As soon as possible."

"What do you mean?"

"You could arrange for me to do a story about Father Lemoyne, if he's really terminal."

An Linh felt the blood rising to her cheeks. "Cliff, you sound as if you *want* him to . . . to be terminal!"

He shrugged carelessly. "If he's not, that's wonderful. Of course. But if he *is*, then he could be a big help to us."

"That's awful!"

He clasped her wrist in his strong grip. "Now don't get sentimental on me, love. We're talking a big story here. You do want me to get the inside track on this frozen astronaut story, don't you?"

"Yes, but—"

"And once we get in among the scientists, we might even get a line on the cure for cancer they've developed."

"But they haven't!"

"Haven't they?" He smirked.

"Cliff, when you introduced me to Father Lemoyne, I didn't think it was for . . . for something like this."

"Now listen to me, love. There's a lot at stake here, and the least you can do is try to keep a professional attitude. After all, *we're* not making him sick, you know."

Pulling away from him, An Linh replied, "No, but you seem pretty damned quick to think of how we can use his illness for your own benefit."

"It's a big story, this frozen astronaut," Baker insisted. "It's important to the whole world, pet. They're going to sit on it, you know. They're going to keep it a secret for as long as we let them."

She shook her head. "No, they wouldn't."

"Wouldn't they?" Baker smiled at her like a grown man pitying a foolish child. "From what you told me about the board meeting, all they're interested in is keeping him under wraps."

"That's just for the time being."

"Really? I'll tell you what's going through their minds,

love. They're going to keep this all to themselves, like their cure for cancer. They want to have the secret of immortality for their own use. Not for you or me, pet. Not for the bleeding masses. For themselves and their friends. For the rich, who can pay millions. Not for us. Not for your mother.''

That was the magic word, and he knew it. An Linh listened numbly as Baker told her what he wanted her to do.

Minutes later she dashed out to the parking lot, wrapped in a monolayer raincoat and hood, so light and porous that it hardly hindered her hurried stride, yet totally impervious to the rain sweeping along the rows of parked automobiles. Her boots were similarly waterproof as she splashed through the puddles on the cement lot.

The apartment building had been built on a scenic hilltop overlooking the city. Even in the gray, driving rain, Hilo's soaring white towers and sprawling swirls of houses looked beautiful to An Linh. It was still a green city, despite the row of massive hotels that lined the beach like the wall of a fortress built to repel invaders from the sea. Flowers blossomed everywhere, and stately palm trees lined street after street.

But the city's charms were not uppermost in An Linh's mind. She ducked inside her car and slammed the door shut. Cliff wanted to use Father Lemoyne to get himself inside the labs and onto the inside track of the frozen astronaut story. He had introduced her to the priest months ago—was he thinking about this moment even back then? Was he thinking about it when he met me? she asked herself. Is Cliff using me, as well as the priest?

The answer was, Of course he is. But is that why he sought me out? Does he really love me, or am I merely a way to the story he's after?

But if he's right, she thought, if Vanguard really has developed a cure for cancer . . . and now they've revived the astronaut . . . Her thoughts spun. She saw her mother, alive again, young and vibrant and cured.

Cliff doesn't care about her, though. He doesn't care about Father Lemoyne, either. All he really wants are his big stories—the cure for cancer, and immortality through freezing. The biggest news stories of a lifetime.

An Linh shook her head as she tapped out the ignition code on the keyboard set into the console between the two bucket seats. I love Cliff, she told herself. That means I must trust

lim. He can go after the biggest news stories of the century,
hat's only natural. That's his profession. It doesn't mean that
ne's not in love with me. It doesn't. It can't!

The electric motor whined complainingly and then hummed
to life. Frowning at her inner thoughts, An Linh flicked on
the guidance computer, punched in the address of the restaurant downtown where she was to meet Father Lemoyne, then
studied the route that the computer marked in red on the
street map its screen displayed.

An Linh had to drive the car manually all the way, since
the computer's route avoided the electronically controlled
freeways with their usual crush of homewardbound traffic.
She parked as close as she could to the restaurant, then ran a
block and a half through the spattering rain.

Pushing open the door of the Japanese restaurant, An Linh
stepped into a haven of warmth and pungent, tantalizing
aromas. She slipped out of her raingear and accepted a plastic
token from the hat-check robot. A human maître d', a middle-
aged Japanese man who looked slim and ascetic enough to
have come recently from Japan, made a bow to An Linh
that was low enough to be polite but quick enough to be
obviously reluctant. He is from Japan, she thought. No
American-born would be so uptight about bowing to a woman.

"Father Lemoyne's table, please," she told him.

He blinked once, then understood. "Ah, the priest. Yess.
This way, prease."

He waved a kimono-clad waitress to him and left her to
guide An Linh to her table. The restaurant was long and
narrow, as if it had been built into a hallway separating two
buildings. Heads turned as she followed the waitress through
the closely packed tables. She still wore her board meeting
"business clothes," a simple long-sleeved Chinese red silk
blouse and light gray skirt, modestly adorned with accents of
costume jewelry. Yet she looked strikingly beautiful, her
short-cropped black hair like an ebony helmet framing the
ivory complexion of her high-cheeked face. Her body was
slight, almost boyish, her almond eyes wide, a tantalizing
conjugation of innocence and knowledge, of youth and
worldliness, that made her look somehow vulnerable, in need
of protection, utterly desirable. Men followed An Linh with
their eyes. Women stared openly.

Father Lemoyne was already seated at the very last table in

the place, his back solidly planted against the rear wall. Above him hung a cheap reproduction of a fine Japanese silk print showing beautiful ladies in blue-and-white kimonos against a background of snow-topped mountains.

Lemoyne looked like the ex-football player that he was. Ruddy face gone to jowls and creases, reddish hair fading to gray, big shoulders beginning to sag. He squeezed up from behind the table as An Linh approached. Even in his black clerical suit it was clear to see that his once powerful body had gone to fat.

"I'm sorry to be late," she said as the waitress held her chair for her.

"I only just arrived a moment ago myself," the priest said. A tumbler of whiskey sat before him.

For an instant they stood facing each other: the heavyset, florid priest in his collar and black suit; the Asian beauty who seemed as fragile as a porcelain flower across the table from him.

An Linh sat and ordered a *sake*. Lemoyne stared at his own drink, waiting.

"Welcome home," An Linh said. "I'm sorry it's such a rainy day."

"Better than the weather in Boston," answered the priest. "To think that I spent the first forty years of my life there."

"You got back this morning?"

He nodded, still eyeing the whiskey. "I've got a fine case of jet lag. They can fly your body to Hawaii in two hours, but your stomach's still in Boston."

She smiled at him. "You must have called me from the airport, then."

"I did. I was thinking about you while I was away."

"And the specialists . . . did they have good news for you?"

Lemoyne's face made a strange little half smile. "No, not really. To get at the tumor they'd have to cut away so much of my brain that I'd be a vegetable."

An Linh stared into his eyes. She saw no pain there, but no resignation, either. Lemoyne's eyes flamed with raw animal fear.

"I'm sorry," she whispered.

He grabbed for the whiskey and gulped at it. "Nothing to be done about it. God's will and all that."

"How long? . . ."

"I have a few months." He was trying to keep his voice from trembling and not succeeding. "Maybe as much as a year."

"They could be wrong, couldn't they?"

"Anything is possible if God wills it so. There could be what the medical people call a spontaneous remission. I could make a pilgrimage to Lourdes. The world might end tomorrow. . . ."

She reached out and touched his sleeve. Her hand looked frail as a child's next to his beefy clenched fist.

"It's painless," he said. "I'll just . . . lose my faculties as the tumor grows." Another gulp of whiskey. An Linh prayed silently that her own drink would come. She felt the need of something that could burn inside her, the need to join this dying man at least in the act of drinking.

"Imagine me in diapers," he joked feebly. "But it won't hurt. They assured me of that much. I won't feel any pain. Toward the end I won't even know what's happening to me."

Tears were blurring An Linh's vision as the waitress finally placed a ceramic bottle and tiny cup in front of her. "Another for you?" the waitress asked the priest cheerfully.

He nodded, then drained the last of his drink.

"There's nothing that the doctors can do?" An Linh asked, remembering the calm, grave face of the chief internist at her father's hospital in Avignon.

"It's God's will," Lemoyne said, just a hint of bitterness in his tone. "We all have to go to Him sooner or later. He just chose to make mine sooner."

"But . . ."

He patted her outstretched hand. His fingers were damp from clutching the glass.

"It's in God's hands," he said, trying to sound resigned. "There's not a thing we can do about it. Not a damned thing."

"But there is—"

"No, no. It's in God's hands. No more of it. It's too good to see you again, after all these weeks. I don't want to spoil it."

An Linh lapsed into silence.

"And how are things going with your new position?" he asked.

"Very well," she replied. "It's much easier to be the director of the department than one of the workers. All I have to do is give orders and let others do the work."

"That's great!" He actually laughed.

The waitress brought Lemoyne's second whiskey, and while she was at their table they both ordered sukiyaki. Another waitress, her kimono slightly stained and her hair a bit disheveled, cooked it at their table. An Linh enjoyed the pungent heat as the woman stirred in the vegetables and the sizzling slices of beef. After the waitress left them to their steaming bowls, An Linh and the priest ate in silence for several moments.

Then, "There is something that we can do about your . . . condition," she said.

He was struggling doggedly with his chopsticks. For a heartbeat or two An Linh thought he might not have heard her words, or that he was ignoring them. But he looked up at her finally, his blue eyes still wide with fear.

"And what would that be? A novena?"

It was meant to be a little joke, so she smiled at him. "We could have you frozen."

He frowned at the idea. "Like your mother?"

"Like my mother."

Waving the chopsticks almost angrily, Lemoyne said, "No, none of that for me. If I have to die, I'll die when my appointed time comes. I'll not have myself popped into some tin can filled with liquified air."

"The tumor in your brain," An Linh said gently, "will not always be inoperable. Someday medical science will learn how to kill the tumor cells without damaging your brain."

Maybe they already know, she added silently, unable to speak the suspicion aloud. Maybe they already have the cure but are keeping it to themselves.

Lemoyne was shaking his head slowly, unconsciously refusing to accept the possibility of hope.

"If they can keep an astronaut frozen for years and then bring him back . . ."

"They've brought him back?" he asked sharply.

An Linh hesitated. "I can't say it officially, but . . . yes, they have."

"They've brought him back to life? Really?"

She did not trust herself to repeat it. She merely gave the barest suggestion of a nod.

"There's been no news story about it; none that I've seen."

"There won't be," she said, thinking of Cliff. "Not for some time."

"But they've brought him back. Actually revived a man who'd been frozen for years and years."

She watched his face as the idea of it sank into his awareness. Lemoyne took another long pull on his whiskey, then attacked the sukiyaki with clumsy gusto. She said nothing more but returned to her dinner, too.

At length he looked up and asked, "Did you . . . miss me while I was away?"

"Of course I did."

"Did you go to anyone else?"

"No."

"Three months. You went without confession for three months?"

She made herself smile for him. "I haven't done anything I should confess."

"You're living with that Baker fella, aren't you?"

"Not living with him," she said. "I keep my own apartment."

"But you're sleeping with him."

"As often as I can."

"The Church still regards that as a sin, you realize."

"Do you?"

He closed his eyes. "An Linh, you are the one woman in the whole of my life who's ever made me feel a regret at having taken my vows. For me, you are a near occasion of sin."

"Your virtue is safe with me," she teased.

"I'm sure," he replied. "Too bad. Such a pity."

Inwardly, An Linh rejoiced. He was bantering with her, the pall of desperate fear that had hung over him had lifted, at least for a while. The idea of being frozen and then revived to be cured of his tumor had raised the cold hand of death from the priest's shoulder.

And from my mother's, An Linh told herself.

CHAPTER 9

Keith Stoner closed the book he had been reading, clicked off the tiny light clamped to its cover, and placed the book atop the stack next to his waterbed. He stretched out on the utterly comfortable, softly yielding surface, sending gentle waves across it. Stoner's room had changed. The waterbed took up a good deal of the floor space. The bed he had awakened in had been removed from the bank of sensors and monitoring instruments. Bookshelves lined the wall on either side of the waterbed, crammed with volumes of all sizes. Richards had offered Stoner an electronic reader, but Stoner preferred the paper-leafed books he was familiar with.

It had been the psychiatrist's idea to bring in a waterbed; he said he thought it might help to relax his patient. To Stoner, the waterbed was the nearest thing to the weightlessness of orbit that could be found on Earth. He wondered if the psychiatrist hadn't thought of the bed for that reason.

It was nearly midnight; pale moonlight slanted through the window and made a pool of silver on the tiled floor. The only other light in the room came from the ceaseless flickering curves wriggling across the display screens in the monitoring equipment that made up the room's farther wall.

Clasping his hands behind his head, Stoner stared intently at the screens. Slowly, slowly, he smoothed the ragged curves. Heartbeat, body temperature, breathing rate, even the EEG that recorded the electrical activity of his brain—he made them slow and smooth to the point where they were reporting that Keith Stoner had at last fallen asleep.

He smiled to himself. *I should have thought of this sooner. Richards is going to be pleased to see that I've finally had some sleep.*

The only thing that had surprised him about his sleeplessness was his lack of alarm over it. It seemed totally natural for him to stay awake constantly; the need for sleep struck him as archaic, primitive. Stoner knew this was not natural, but even though he felt he should be worried, or at least concerned, he found that he was perfectly calm. Even content. There were years' worth of books that he had always meant to read. Now he finally had the time to read them.

Hands still clasped behind his head, he looked up through the darkness at the ceiling, and the cameras behind the paneling, watching him. Darkness is no hindrance to them, he knew. They can see me as clearly as if it were daylight.

Maybe I can do something about that, too.

He got up from the bed and dressed quickly, silently, all the while concentrating on the display screens. They remained as calm as a sleeping infant's.

He went to the section of the wall where the portal was. After watching Richards and the younger assistants who brought his meals so many times, he knew that the doorway was activated by a heat sensor set into the wall. It would be turned off now, the portal closed for the night unless there was an emergency that overrode its computer command to remain closed.

Stoner made an emergency. The screens showing his heartbeat and blood pressure suddenly sprouted jagged, urgent peaks that turned blazing red. A chorus of electronic beeps wailed as Stoner stood patiently in the middle of the room, bathed in moonlight.

The portal glowed and opened, and a flustered young technician in a white lab coat rushed in, then skidded to a stop when he saw Stoner standing there.

"Wh . . . what the hell's goin' on?" the young man sputtered. He was tall and skinny, his hair a dark unruly mop, his coat open and flapping, pockets bulging. An intern, Stoner knew at once, stuck with the midnight-to-eight-A.M. shift.

"Looks like a glitch in the monitoring equipment," Stoner said calmly.

The youngster peered at the wildly fluctuating screens. "Jesus Christ! There's a crash wagon on its way."

With a grin, Stoner said, "You'd better tell them to relax and forget it."

"Yeah . . . yeah. . . ." The intern pulled a pencil-sized black cylinder from his shirt pocket and spoke into it. "Campbell, this is McKean. No sweat. He's okay. The goddamned electronics are screwed up.''

Stoner heard a tinny voice squawking angrily. The intern frowned as he said into the slim communicator, ''Well, then wake Healy up and tell him to check it out himself. I'm here with him and he's perfectly okay.''

Stoner smiled back at the youngster and slid an arm around his skinny shoulders. ''You got here damned fast.''

''That's what I get paid for.''

Together they stepped through the open portal, into the corridor outside.

''I'm going out for a swim,'' Stoner said. ''I'll be back in an hour or so.''

The intern blinked several times and knitted his brows, as if trying to remember something that kept slipping away from him.

''Why don't you just erase the videotapes and the monitoring records for the past half hour and the next hour or so,'' Stoner told him. ''They'll just be botched up anyway.''

''Yeah . . . I guess I should. . . .''

''Of course. That will be the best thing to do. No need to bother Dr. Healy.''

''Right.''

Stoner left him standing there in the corridor, looking befuddled, and walked swiftly to the nearest door that led outside.

It was a beautiful night, warm and scented with flowers. The tropical breeze sighed softly as Stoner strode alone across the lawn, through the gap between two lab buildings, and out to the fence that surrounded the Vanguard complex. He scaled the fence easily, crossed the highway—deserted except for a pair of huge tandem-trailer trucks barreling along almost silently—and sprinted out onto the beach.

The moon grinned down at him lopsidedly.

Stoner took off his slipper socks and rolled up the legs of his pants to the knee. He waded calf deep in the gentle surf, feeling the cool, delicious touch of the world ocean.

The eternal sea, he thought, bending down to scoop up a handful of salt water. It glowed slightly in his palm, reflecting the moonlight. Life began in the sea, Stoner said to himself. Did it begin that way on your world, too? Are there oceans on the planet of your birth?

He let the water drain from his hand as he turned his face up toward the heavens. There were few stars to see in the moon-bright sky. But several very bright ones hovered almost straight overhead. Space stations, Stoner realized. Looking back at the moon, he saw dots of light here and there on its mottled face. They've built bases on the moon. Big ones.

After a few minutes of stargazing he splashed back onto the sand and sank to his knees. The ocean stretched out before him, murmuring its eternal message, and beyond the horizon was the infinite span of the universe. Stoner knelt and waited, a worshiper, a supplicant, waiting for—for what?

He did not know.

Years ago he had seen the tropical sky of Kwajalein shimmering with the delicate hues of the Northern Lights. The alien's message, the announcement of its approach. But tonight the sky was exactly the way it should be: serene and lovely, everything so precisely in its ordained place that Isaac Newton could have predicted the location of each star and planet and moon.

How did I get that boy to let me roam free outside my room? he wondered. Hypnotism? Intimidation? Magic?

Clearly it had something to do with the alien. He was different now, Stoner knew. He could feel the difference within him. He had spent more than six years frozen in that spacecraft with the dead body of the alien. In that time, something—*something*—had gotten into him, seeped through his frozen flesh, enmeshed itself deeply inside his sleeping brain.

"I am Keith Stoner," he whispered to himself. "I am still the same man I was eighteen years ago."

But he knew that he was not *only* that same man. Not anymore.

For nearly an hour he waited, kneeling, on the beach. Nothing happened. The surf curled in ceaselessly. The warm wind caressing his cheek carried a delicate trace of the night-blooming cereus flowers from the shrubbery up near the highway. Behind him Stoner could hear the softly powerful thrumming of occasional trucks speeding along the road. But nothing more.

He got to his feet and walked slowly, reluctantly, back to the laboratory. I've spent most of my life locked into one sort of cell or another, he thought.

He clambered over the fence again and trotted back toward his room. He waved to the intern, sitting sleepily in front of his monitoring screens, arms hanging from his shoulders, eyes half-closed. The portal to his room was still open. He stepped in, and the doorway glowed and became solid wall again. Stoner wondered if the intern would actually erase the tapes as he had told him to.

He almost wished he wouldn't.

But in the morning they brought him breakfast as usual and Richards showed up almost at the instant Stoner finished his last sip of coffee.

"Good news," the psychiatrist told him as he drew up one of the little plastic chairs. "We're moving."

Seated at the chair by the window, his breakfast tray resting on a rolling cart in front of him, Stoner searched the psychiatrist's face. There was no sign that he knew about the night's little adventure.

"Moving? Where? When?"

Touching his mustache, Richards said, "Soon. A couple of days, I should think. I'm not sure where yet, but it'll probably be to the mainland."

"My son lives in Los Angeles, you said. I'd like to see him."

Richards nodded. "That can be arranged." But his eyes were saying, later. Much later.

"Have you told them I'm . . . alive?" Stoner asked.

"Your children? No, not yet."

"Don't you think they'd like to know?"

"I'm sure they would."

"So?"

Trying hard not to frown, Richards said, "Well . . . there are complications."

"What do you mean?"

"You don't sleep. And you hallucinated."

"Even if I'm crazy, my kids have a right to know that I'm alive again."

The psychiatrist lapsed into silence.

"Where is Jo?"

"Jo Camerata? She's right here."

"Yesterday you said she's pretty important to this operation."

"Very."

"I'd like to see her. Today."

"I'm not sure . . ."

Stoner leaned forward slightly, nudging the cart that held the remains of his breakfast. "I'd like you to call her. Now."

Richards looked puzzled for a moment, then lifted his left arm and touched his wrist communicator. "Mrs. Nillson, please."

Stoner felt a pang of surprise. "She's married."

The psychiatrist ignored his remark. He spoke to several underlings, then finally:

"Jo, he wants to see you. Today, if you have the time."

A long hesitation. Then Stoner heard Jo's voice reply, "Impossible today. Tomorrow. Lunch."

Jo touched the keypad that turned off the phone. He's finally gotten around to asking for me, she thought. I shouldn't have agreed to see him so easily.

She leaned back in her chair and touched the controls that gently warmed and massaged her. She needed to relax, to ease the tension that had suddenly made her neck as taut as steel cables.

The morning reports had troubled her. There had been some sort of glitch in the equipment monitoring Keith. The whole system had gone haywire for nearly two hours; everything had blanked out, as if somebody had erased all the tapes. The intern on duty was being interrogated by security, but not even the polygraph had turned up anything. Jo wondered briefly about the PR director; was she up to something? Then there had been a routine entry in the perimeter security log: something or someone had brushed the outer fence. Not once. Twice. Guards had searched the area and found nothing. Probably an animal, they concluded. There had been no sign of an unauthorized entry into any of the lab buildings themselves. An animal. A dog left to wandering by itself. Or a stupid nene bird with a hurt wing.

Or Keith Stoner.

The reports had troubled her. Someone had tested the security system from the outside two nights ago. Terrorists? Kids looking for drugs? A team sent to spirit Stoner away? The system had held; whoever it had been was scared away by the time the guards got to the fence. But then last night there had been another disturbance.

And now Keith suddenly wanted to see her.

He had gotten out last night. Jo was certain of it. How he did it, she had no idea. But she knew Keith, knew what he was capable of. If he wanted to get out, he would. No one she had ever met in her life could be so determined, so utterly single-minded.

But he had returned. And now he was demanding to see her.

Two things were clear to Jo. Keith had made a mockery of this facility's security. He would have to be moved to some-place much safer. And to keep him there, wherever she decided to put him, she would have to go with him. He would stay with her, she was sure of that. At least, for a while.

She got up from the chair and went to the bathroom adjoining her office. In the mirror over the marble sink, Jo examined herself pitilessly. Almost forty. Her face was leaner than it had been eighteen years earlier. The baby fat had been boiled away by the tough battles that had brought her to the top of Vanguard Industries. It would be a while before she needed a face lift, but there were lines at the corners of her eyes that not even cosmetics could completely hide.

She had gone to Vanguard Industries when the U.S. gov-ernment failed to move swiftly enough to recover the alien spacecraft. It was coasting away from Earth, out of the solar system altogether, with Keith Stoner frozen alive aboard it.

In those days, when she had loved Keith with the wild fury of youth, she had wanted to be an astronaut. Just as he was. She would become an astronaut and lead the mission to rescue him. He was alive, she knew he was alive. He had to be returned to Earth before the spacecraft bearing him and the dead alien swept so far away on its blind wandering that it could never be recovered.

She learned soon enough that a would-be astronaut had no power, and it would take power, a great deal of power, to move the people and machines necessary for the task of rescuing Keith.

Jo learned about power. How to get it, how to use it. The dream of leading the space mission faded as she devoted her blazing energies and ruthless drive to the task she had set for herself. Through the years, as she climbed over the bodies of friends and strangers, enemies and allies, lovers and rivals, her goal remained the same, but her reasons for pursuing it subtly changed.

She began to understand that power has its own rewards. Yes, returning Keith and the alien would be a staggering coup for Vanguard Industries. The alien spacecraft was a treasure house of technology. Who knew what secrets it would reveal to those who captured it? And if they could revive the frozen astronaut, bring him back to life, that alone would be worth untold billions.

She succeeded. The price of success was marrying Nillson and letting him parade her before former lovers and future possibilities as his possession.

But the rewards! Once they had brought the alien spacecraft back into a safe orbit around the Earth, Vanguard's scientists had dug into it like a swarm of ants stripping a carcass. In the first five years they found enough to change the world several times over, and to make Vanguard virtually an autonomous nation, such was the wealth and power uncovered.

And now, at last, they had brought the frozen human being back to life. Like Sleeping Beauty, they had revived the seemingly dead. Immortality was at hand. For that, the world would pay anything that Jo wanted.

But Keith Stoner had to be controlled now. At least for a while. Controlled and kept safe from harm. It wouldn't do for the world's first immortal man to disappear.

Or die.

CHAPTER 10

It was past eleven o'clock and Richards had not shown up yet. Stoner sat patiently in the chair by the window, reading *Don Quixote,* part of the lifetime's worth of literature that he had never gotten into before. He laughed at the antics of the emaciated old madman and his stout, earthy squire, Sancho. Like all the generations before him, Stoner saw something of

himself in the earnest lunacy of the Knight of the Sad
Countenance.

But within his mind, it was as though he were discovering
facets of the human race that he had never understood before.
It's all a sham, a voice within him whispered. Each human
being plays a role, presents a mask to the others around him,
and the others all hold up their own masks to hide their own
vulnerabilities.

No human is ever totally honest, Stoner realized. Not even
with himself. He put the book down on his lap and stared out
at the ocean. You knew that, he told himself. You've known
that almost all your life.

Yet there was a part of him that found the understanding
new and fresh and fascinating. A part of him that seemed to
be perceiving the human drama for the first time.

When the portal opened it made no sound, but the glow of
the wall's transmutation caught Stoner's eye. He turned to
see Richards stepping through.

The psychiatrist stared at the book in Stoner's lap. "You
just started reading that this morning," he said, his tone
almost accusing.

"Yes," answered Stoner, getting to his feet.

"You're damned near finished!"

Stoner glanced at the book, still in his hand. He turned and
put it down carefully on the windowsill next to the chair.
"My reading speed is increasing, I guess."

Richards bustled past him and picked up the book. "Seven
hundred and thirty-two pages! You've *read* it? Without
skimming?"

Stoner smiled. "Want to quiz me?"

"Should I?"

"Is it because psychiatry began among Middle European
Jews that you tend to answer a question with a question?"
Stoner asked.

Richards scowled.

"I'll tell you what I've learned from Cervantes," Stoner
volunteered. "And from the other authors I've been reading.
All of fiction is basically about one subject, and only one:
women choosing their mates."

"Women choosing . . . ?"

With a nod, Stoner said, "Yep. That's the common de-
nominator of all fiction."

"Not in *Don Quixote*," Richards objected.

"The don's adventures are just a frame to hold together a lot of little stories," Stoner said. "All of those little stories concern women deciding whom they're going to marry."

"But not all fiction! A lot of it's about men."

Stoner's grin widened. "Some of it seems to be about men and their adventures. But when you look closer, you see that what the men are really doing is trying to get certain women. And it's always the woman who decides. The men are constant, always striving to get the woman. The women are never constant; they're always trying to make up their minds about accepting this particular male or some other one."

"Hamlet?" snapped Richards.

"His mother chose Claudius, and that's what started all the trouble."

"Hemingway!"

Laughing, Stoner said, "I just finished *The Sun Also Rises* and *For Whom the Bell Tolls* last night. The women make all the decisions."

Richards stood there, frowning and tugging at his mustache.

"Try Jane Austen," Stoner suggested, "or *Gone With the Wind*."

The psychiatrist shook his head. Returning the book to the windowsill, he said, "I don't really have the time to discuss literature with you. Come on, you're going to lunch with Mrs. Nillson."

"I'm ready," said Stoner.

Richards led him through corridors he had not seen before, out to a parking lot and a sleek, silver, two-seated automobile.

"Alfa Mercedes," Richards muttered. "My sublimation machine." Stoner folded himself into the front seat as Richards slid behind the wheel and flicked his fingers over the keypad on the dash. The roof glowed briefly and disappeared. Stoner grinned. The same trick that turned a solid wall into an open doorway also turned the hard-topped car into a convertible.

"One of the fringe benefits of being relatively high up on the ladder of Vanguard Industries." Richards grinned back at him. "You get a lot of special features for your car, way ahead of the production models."

The engine purred softly, and the car eased out of the parking lot.

"Electric motor?" Stoner asked.

Richards nodded, swinging the car past the uniformed guards on either side of the parking lot's entrance and out onto the access road to the highway.

"Most vehicles are electrical now. One of the little gifts your dead friend gave us: fusion energy."

The car accelerated smoothly and quietly up onto the broad four-lane highway. Other cars whizzed past, as fast and quiet as a charging cheetah. Trucks rumbled along in their own lanes, passing all but the speediest of the autos.

"The trucks still use internal combustion engines," Richards explained. "Hydrogen fuel, though. No more kerosene."

"Nobody does fifty-five, do they," Stoner shouted over the rush of the wind that was tousling his hair.

Richards pecked out another combination on the dashboard keys, then took his hands off the wheel and leaned back in his chair.

"She's on automatic now. I won't have to pick up the steering again until we turn off the highway."

Stoner lifted his face to the glorious Hawaiian sun. He felt free and fine, the wind whistling by, the sunshine warm, the lovely beach racing past.

"There's no speed limit on the highways anymore," Richards told him. "No need to conserve fuel, so we adapted the European system. Besides, with magnetic bumpers and miniradar warning systems tied automatically to the computer that runs the engine, it's almost impossible to have a collision."

"There's no seat belt."

"Another gift from your friend," Richards shouted into the wind. "An energy shell absorbs any impact forces and keeps you safely in your seat.The car can be totaled, and you'll just get up and walk away from it. This'll go into the production cars next year, they tell me."

"Ought to please the insurance companies!"

Richards nodded happily.

Stoner eyed him for a moment. He could see through the psychiatrist's veneer of self-control. "How fast can this buggy really go?" he asked.

Richards smiled slightly, and his left hand unconsciously snaked toward the steering wheel. "Pretty damned fast."

"A hundred?"

"Miles or kilometers?"

"Miles."

"Easy." He reached into the compartment under the dashboard and pulled out a pair of skin-soft gloves. Stoner saw that they were worn nearly through at the palms and knuckles. Richards wormed them onto his hands, fastened the wrist clasps, then punched a single key on the dashboard. He gripped the wheel and leaned slightly forward. The car surged ahead with barely a murmur from the engine. Stoner felt the acceleration pushing him into the molded seat. But he missed the roar of power that he remembered.

The highway became a blur as Richards, hunching over the steering wheel, swung onto the leftmost lane and leaned on the accelerator. It was eerily quiet: only the rushing wind and the hum of the tires on the road surface. And the sudden, startling *whoosh* as they zipped past other cars. Fifteen minutes later Richards's silver convertible pulled into a parking area set off the highway, next to the beach.

The psychiatrist was grinning like a kid as he braked the car to a stop. "A hundred and seventy!" he exulted. "How'd you like that?"

"Fastest I've ever traveled on the ground," Stoner said.

Richards nodded happily. "I never had her up to that speed. Wow, she just glides along without a rattle, doesn't she?"

Pulling himself out of the bucket seat, Stoner admitted, "I never thought electric motors could produce such speed."

"Times have changed," Richards said, getting out of the car. "A lot of things have changed."

"I'm beginning to understand that."

They stood by the gleaming silver Alfa Mercedes in the bright noontime sun. Its warmth soaked into Stoner's shoulders and back; it felt good.

"Are we going to have a picnic?" Stoner asked.

Richards made an exaggerated shrug. "Search me. I was told to bring you here." Looking back at his car and grinning again, "We're a little early, of course."

Stoner nodded an acknowledgment and turned to look out at the ocean. It seemed to shimmer like a heat mirage. Concentrating every fiber of his attention on the waves rolling up to the beach, Stoner forced the shimmering to stop.

No hallucinations, he told himself. Not while he's watching
me. Then he heard the crunching of wheels on the parking
lot's macadam. Turning back again, he saw a long black
limousine gliding to a stop alongside Richards's sleek silver
sports car. The limo's windows were smoky dark; it was
impossible to see who was inside it.

He walked through the bright sunshine toward the limousine, Richards beside him. Its roof glittered in the sunlight.
Solar cells, he realized. They make enough electricity to run
the air conditioner and God knows what else, even when the
engine's off.

The chauffeur popped out of the limo as they approached,
trotted around the length of it, and opened the rear door.

Jo Camerata stepped out.

She was as excitingly beautiful as Stoner had remembered
her. Tall, with the long-legged curvaceous figure of a Hollywood star. Thickly lustrous black hair. Blazing dark eyes and
rich full lips. And best of all, a mind, a spirit, as driving and
demanding as Stoner's own had been. An intelligence behind
those midnight eyes that had made her more challenging than
any woman he had ever known.

Eighteen years ago. She had been a child then, a student.
Now she was a woman. She stood before Stoner, dressed in a
simple sleeveless blouse of light blue and a darker wrap-
around skirt. Her throat was adorned with a choker of gleaming rubies and diamonds; a matching bracelet on her wrist.

"You've become a woman," Stoner said to her. "You're
even more marvelous than I thought you'd be."

For a moment she said nothing, then she turned to Richards. "Thanks for bringing him, Gene. I'll see you back at
the lab."

The psychiatrist took her dismissal wordlessly, turned, and
started back for his car.

"I thought we would picnic on the beach, Keith," Jo said.

His memory wrenched back to Kwajalein, to the long hot
frantic days and cool windswept nights on the beaches there
when an eighteen-year-younger Jo Camerata drove the atoll's
male population wild in her cut-off jeans and skimpy halter
tops, laughing as she splashed into the surf, knowing that
every male eye was on her but wanting only the one man
who was too busy to pay attention to her: Keith Stoner.

"A picnic would be fine," he said.

The chauffeur was already pulling a wicker hamper from the limousine's trunk. Stoner took it from him and followed Jo to the edge of the hard-topped parking area and out onto the clean white sand.

"Pretty empty for a public beach," he said.

"It's not a public beach. This is Vanguard Industries property," Jo replied.

He looked at her, more carefully this time. In the flat leisure shoes she was wearing, she came just about up to his chin. "There's something different about you, Jo."

She glanced up at him. "Eighteen years. It's a long time."

"No, not that. If anything, you look better than you did then. More sophisticated. More adult."

"You mean older."

"It's your hair," he suddenly realized. "You used to wear it much longer."

She almost grinned. "Long hair is not highly regarded among corporate executives. Keep it short and simple, like a memo."

"You're a corporate executive now."

"I'm the president of Vanguard Industries."

"The president! I'm impressed."

She stopped and turned to face him. Stoner knelt slightly to let the hamper down onto the sand.

"You've changed, too, Keith," she said.

Nodding, "I'm sure I have."

"Your eyes . . . they're different. The same color and everything, but . . . different."

"In what way?"

She studied him for a long moment, then shook her head. "I don't know. It's there, but I can't tell exactly what it is."

They opened the hamper, took the blanket fastened inside its lid, spread it on the sand, and sat down.

"Chilled wine, caviar, sandwiches, brie . . . you pack quite a lunch," Stoner said.

But Jo took a small black plastic oblong from the pocket of her skirt and ran it over the open hamper.

"You're afraid of being bugged?"

"Goes with the job," she said. "Industrial espionage, corporate politics—it can get pretty cutthroat."

"And the government? The Russians?"

She tucked the electronic device back into her skirt and

reached for the wine bottle. "The Cold War's ancient history, Keith. It's a very different world, thanks to you."

"To me?"

"One of the bits of technology we found on the spacecraft transmutes matter into energy and back again quite easily."

"I know. The door to my room . . . Richards's convertible roof."

She handed him the bottle and a corkscrew. "The same technology has made nuclear bombs obsolete."

"How?"

"We've learned how to create a dome of energy large enough to cover a city. When it's turned on, it protects the area inside from the blast and heat of a nuclear explosion."

"And the radiation?"

Nodding, Jo said, "Radiation, too. All the energy from the nuclear explosion is absorbed by the screen."

Stoner thought for a silent moment as he wormed the corkscrew into the cork, then pulled it out with a satisfactory *pop!*

"That means that nuclear weapons are useless against American cities. . . ."

"And Russian cities, too," Jo said. "We sold the information to the Russians."

"The American government didn't object?"

She held out a glass that sparkled like crystal in the hot sun. "Lots of people objected. The President who okayed the deal was almost impeached. He lost his bid for reelection—never even got his own party's nomination."

"Jesus," Stoner muttered.

"But the world is safer now," she said. "The U.S., Russia, all of Europe, even the major cities of China and India are protected by energy domes."

Stoner poured the wine. They touched glasses with a pure crystal ring and sipped. The wine was cold and dry, with just a hint of muskiness.

"So we're safe from nuclear war," Stoner said.

"Vanguard's making billions, setting up energy domes all over the world."

"Have you seen Kirill lately?"

"Not for years."

They sat on the blanket spread over the beach sand, facing each other, sipping wine. Thoughts raced through Stoner's mind. Richards had been right: there was a lot he would have to adjust to. He watched in silence as Jo took out the tray of iced caviar and warmed brie, then set out a platter of thin crackers between them.

"If the Cold War is ancient history," he asked, "and we're safe from nuclear attack, what's causing the tensions in the world?"

Jo glanced up sharply at him. "Tensions? What do you mean?"

"It's not a peaceful world, Jo. I can feel it. The way your eyes moved away from me when I asked you about Kirill. The idea of meeting here on the beach. What are you afraid of, Jo? What's wrong?"

She opened her mouth to speak but hesitated. For an instant she had been ready to tell him the truth. But something had stopped her, Stoner realized.

"It's a better world than it was eighteen years ago, Keith," she said. Her voice was low, barely strong enough to hear over the gentle murmur of the surf.

"You mean that *in some ways* it's better," he replied. "But in some ways it's worse, isn't it?"

"We've almost solved the drug problem."

He felt a ripple of skepticism. "Don't tell me the alien's technology has turned people off drugs."

"No." She smiled slightly. "Our own technology. Although the new political alignments in the world have helped."

"In what way?"

"We're using sensors on satellites to spot the areas where the raw product is grown. You know, poppies and marijuana and all."

"You spot them from satellites."

"Right. And we destroy them. Send in troops and wipe the fields clean."

"You just invade a nation. . . ."

"No, no. The Peace Enforcers do it. They're an international entity."

"And a nation like Turkey or Colombia just allows them to come in and rip up the poppy fields?"

Jo nodded and took another sip of wine. "They finally realized—oh, a half-dozen years ago or more—that the drug trade was destroying their governments. The drug dealers were taking over whole countries, Keith! I think it was to deal with the drug trade that the Peace Enforcers were really created, as much as to deal with stopping wars."

"Peace Enforcers," Stoner murmured. "My daughter's married to somebody who's a Peace Enforcer, according to what Richards told me. Tell me about them."

"I will tell you about them," she said. "But not now. It's too soon."

He smiled. "I'm not a child. I want to know about the world, Jo."

And she smiled back, but it was tinged with sadness. "Keith, in many ways you *are* a child. A newborn. Don't try to gobble down everything at once. Let us help you to learn about this new world that . . ."

She stopped herself.

"That I've helped to create," he finished for her.

With a nod, she admitted, "Yes, that you've helped to create."

He realized he had been leaning forward tensely. Taking a deep breath, he relaxed and stretched himself out on the blanket, squinting up at the brilliant sky.

"There must be a lot of people out there who want to thank me," he said.

Jo leaned over into his view, blocking out the sun. "Yes, there are."

"And there must be others who hate me."

He heard her breath catch in her throat. But she managed to recover swiftly and say, "There are plenty of others who would like to get their hands on you. You are a very valuable piece of property."

"Property?" He laughed.

She stared down at him. "God, Keith, you *have* changed."

"In what way?"

"Eighteen years ago you would have gone berserk at the idea that we were keeping you under wraps . . . that we regarded you as our possession."

He propped himself up on both elbows, his face close enough to Jo's to kiss her. She edged back away from him slightly.

"I'll let you in on a secret, Jo," he said.

"What is it?"

Grinning, "Richards thinks I'm schizzy, doesn't he?"

She tilted her head slightly. "He's worried that you might be."

Stoner's grin widened. "The secret is this: I *was* a madman—eighteen years ago. I'm sane now. Maybe for the first time in my life, I'm completely sane."

Jo started to reply, but her words were drowned out by the sudden roar of jet engines. A sleek twin-engined plane flashed low across the beach, turned out over the ocean, and as Stoner and Jo watched, came straight back toward them. Its engine pods swiveled and it hovered in midair, then settled slowly down onto the beach, jets screaming, kicking up a maelstrom of gritty sand.

Jo jumped to her feet and yanked at Stoner's hand. "Come on!" she yelled over the noise of the shrieking engines.

Surprised, Stoner got to his feet and ran with her to the plane. It was painted all in white, except for a stylized green V on its tail. A hatch near the rear popped open, and a lean, lithe man in olive-green coveralls jumped down onto the beach. Jo ran to him, almost dragging Stoner behind her.

"*Buòn giorno, signora!*" said the man.

Jo nodded at him as she motioned Stoner to climb up into the plane. He did, and she followed him.

The crewman got inside and pulled the hatch shut. The screaming noise of the jet engines suddenly dwindled to a muted whine. Stoner had to bend slightly to stand in the aisle, but the interior of the plane was ultraplush: massive leather chairs, deep carpeting, rich paneling along the curving bulkheads.

Jo gestured Stoner to a seat, then sat alongside him. As they clicked their seat belts, the crewman hurried up forward and through the hatch that opened onto the cockpit. Within a second the plane was lifting straight up. Through the window on his left Stoner saw the beach disappearing below them, the chauffeur gathering up the remains of their unfinished picnic lunch and hurrying back toward his limousine.

He turned to Jo. "Where are we going?"

"Where we won't be bothered for a while," she answered without the slightest hint of a smile.

CHAPTER II

"It was very good of you to see me," said An Linh Laguerre.

Everett Nillson's long, high-domed face slowly unfolded into a craggy smile. "I apologize for not having taken the time earlier. As the new director of corporate public relations, you should have ready access to me."

"Oh, really?" An Linh made herself smile back at him. "I was told that you avoid the media—that you're a very secretive person."

Nillson laughed, a surprisingly hearty, booming laughter coming from this pale, lean man. "But that's your job, don't you see? You've got to keep the media away from me."

"Ahh," said An Linh.

"And still keep Vanguard's image shining brightly," Nillson added. "Not the easiest task in the world, I know. But if I didn't think you could do it, you wouldn't have been offered the position."

They traded small compliments for several more moments. Nillson's office was a duplicate of his offices in New York, Berne, and Osaka. Every detail was identical, so that he could reach out a hand and find precisely the same pen or communicator keypad or display screen at precisely the same spot on his desk. It was an imposing room, built large and designed to impress visitors. The walls were paneled in rich dark wood, the floors thickly carpeted. Portraits of placid English ladies by Reynolds and Gainsborough hung in elegant gilt frames, flanking a grotesquely tortured crucifixion scene by an unknown medieval primitive.

To get to Nillson's desk from the outer office, a visitor had to stride past a long marble table bearing gifts presented to Nillson by the chiefs of sovereign nations: an exquisitely carved sperm whale from Norway, a delicate porcelain floral arrangement from China, a miniature golden madonna from

Italy, lacquered bowls from Japan, even a crystal American eagle. And many more. There were duplicates of each in Nillson's other offices. No one but he knew which were the originals and which the copies.

Even the windows of the office looked out on the same scenes. At the moment they showed holographic views of a Norwegian fjord: massive stone cliffs dropped precipitously down to deep blue water. Like the owner of this office, the water looked deceptively placid. Beneath its calm surface it was treacherously deep and fatally cold.

His desk itself was a massive fortress of ebony inlaid with ivory and fixtures of highly polished stone from Vanguard's mining operation on the moon. Dressed in a Wall Street cardigan of royal blue, Nillson sat on an elevated platform behind the desk like a general observing approaching visitors from the battlements of his castle. The entire desktop could light up and become a display screen: like a completely modern general, Nillson could survey any battlefield he wished to, at the touch of a finger or the whisper of a command.

An Linh sat in front of the desk, feeling like a wandering beggar at the gates of Nillson's castle. She had carefully chosen her costume: a worker's one-piece jumpsuit of burnt orange, tightly fitted along the torso, loose and blousy along the limbs. Both the sleeves and pantlegs were slitted; when An Linh sat quietly they were demurely modest, but when she moved they revealed bare flesh.

She crossed her legs and leaned back in the comfortable leather chair. It seemed to mold itself to her body, almost as if it were alive.

"Actually," she said to Nillson, "I was going to suggest that you and Mrs. Nillson allow my staff to write an interview of the two of you together—you know, the husband-and-wife team. It's trite, but the viewers like it."

Nillson's face froze for just an instant, then he pursed his thin lips. "That will be impossible."

"Perhaps later? . . ."

He shook his head. "No. No interviews with either of us, now or later."

An Linh made her best smile. "No one will actually have to ask you questions. We have all the information we need in the files."

He showed his teeth. "No interviews. Not of me. Not of my wife. Ever."

"Is that a rule?"

"Yes. Corporate PR will have to concentrate on the company, not personalities. I won't have it any other way."

She hesitated a moment, then plunged. "I consider it part of my job to explain what works well in public relations and what doesn't. Personalities sell."

"I understand. And I appreciate your persistence," Nillson replied slowly. "But the rule still stands. If you need personalities, concentrate on the division managers' level."

"On the other hand," An Linh said, "some of the work that Vanguard is involved with would be fascinating to viewers."

Nillson closed his eyes briefly, then opened them again. "That's better. I prefer concentrating on what we do, what this company actually accomplishes. Which lines of our work do you think have the best PR potential?"

An Linh tried to keep her voice calm, to betray no emotion whatever. "Oh, I suppose the one that would be of the highest interest to the general audience," she said, "would be the subject of life extension."

Steepling his fingers and resting his chin on their tips, Nillson let her talk. His glacier-blue eyes stayed riveted on her; his face became an immobile, impenetrable mask. As she prattled on, An Linh thought that he might as well be frozen himself, a cold and lifeless slab of ice sculpted into the shape of a man.

Finally she ran out of things to say. She ended with, "And, naturally, we should include some mention of the possibilities of cryonics."

He made a small sound that might have been a grunt or merely the gift of life returning to his body.

"You mean the frozen astronaut business."

She almost bit her lip to keep herself from appearing too eager. "I suppose that's part of the story, yes."

Without any change of expression or tone of voice, Nillson said, "Your mother's been frozen for more than five years now."

Madigan had warned her that Nillson would investigate every aspect of her life before agreeing to promote her.

"Yes. In France," she replied.

"Cancer is on the increase," Nillson muttered, almost to himself. "Despite everything we've done, it's becoming more prevalent, not less."

"Do you think cryonic suspension could become inexpensive enough so that all cancer victims might use it?"

He looked at her for a long moment, peering at her as if he had not really seen her before. A thin smile crept across his lean face.

"May I call you An Linh? I understand that's what your friends call you."

"Yes, of course."

"Good. And you may call me Everett."

An Linh knew that only a handful of older men, his former teachers and mentors, were allowed to call him "Ev." She had done her research, too, and knew that he detested the abbreviation.

"Thank you, Everett," she said.

Nillson got up from the desk and walked around it, his eyes never leaving An Linh. He stretched out his hand and she rose to her feet and allowed him to clasp her hand in his.

"An Linh, I know why you're here. I want to help you."

"Help me?" Alarm tingled through her.

Nillson led her to the wall between two holographic windows. The solid wood paneling glowed and vanished, opening a doorway into a smaller room. They stepped through, Nillson leading her by the hand, and An Linh saw that it was a private dining room, its table set for two. There was a real window, and it looked out onto the beach and the brilliantly sunny afternoon. Somehow that made An Linh feel better: less trapped.

Nillson held a high-backed chair for her, and An Linh sat in it.

"Archie Madigan tells me you're ambitious," he said, pulling up the other chair. "I think he's right, but not in the way he thinks you are. What is it that you really want?"

"To be the best public relations director that you've ever had."

"Really? And what else?"

She said nothing.

"You want help for your mother, don't you?"

She hesitated just long enough to let him think he was

forcing the truth from her. "Is there anything that you can do
for her that isn't being done in France?"

"She's at the cryonics facility in Avignon, am I correct?"

"Yes."

"According to my information she is as well off there as
she would be here."

"Is there . . ." An Linh looked away from him, to the
window and the beach beyond it. "Is there any hope of
reviving her?"

Nillson smiled thinly. "You mean, now that we've revived
the frozen astronaut."

"Yes."

He replied, "Eventually, I'm sure."

"But not yet."

"I'm afraid that's right. It's too soon to say whether what
we did with the astronaut can be done for everybody."

An Linh said nothing, kept her eyes focused on the beach
and the sun-glittering sea.

"Besides," Nillson added, his voice slightly tighter, tenser,
"there's no point in reviving cancer victims until we can cure
their disease."

Turning back to face him, An Linh leaned forward slightly.
"There are people who believe you *have* developed a cure,
but are keeping it a secret."

Nillson's face clouded. "Why would we keep it a secret?"

"For power. It would be an enormously powerful tool for
Vanguard, to give the cure to those who will help the corporation and refuse it to those who will not."

"Nonsense," Nillson muttered. But he dropped his gaze
from her face and stared down at the dish set before him.

"There's something else," An Linh said.

Nillson looked up at her, his pale brows arched.

"A priest that I know. In Hilo. He has an inoperable brain
tumor."

Nillson leaned back in the comfortable leather-covered
chair. Using a dying priest. Clever of her. He eyed her with
new respect.

"If you would allow the labs to take his case, we could
tape his final days and his freezing," An Linh went on. "It
would make a spectacular documentary."

He nodded and murmured, "I see."

"The public relations value to Vanguard Industries would

be enormous. I could make an arrangement with an organization like Worldnews to distribute the documentary to its outlets all around the globe.''

Nillson steepled his fingers again and pursed his lips, as though giving her request deep thought.

A human waiter appeared at the far door to the room, pushing a rolling cart bearing dishes covered by silver domes.

Straightening in his chair, Nillson asked, ''You do like French cuisine?''

''Oh, yes. Certainly.'' The aromas were delicate and delicious. An Linh closed her eyes for an instant and saw herself a little girl again in her mother's kitchen.

The waiter placed the dishes before them, poured a light Beaujolais into the tulip wineglasses, then left as silently as a wraith.

Nillson held his glass to the light, then said, ''You'll have to spend a lot of your time on such a project, I suppose.''

An Linh tried to clamp down on the rush of eager expectation that flooded through her. ''Several weeks, at least.''

''And bring in a camera crew from outside.''

She thought a moment, then answered, ''We could use our own company crew, but if you want the absolute best kind of work, a professional documentary team would be best, yes, I agree.''

Of course you agree, Nillson said silently. That's what you're after, obviously. An outside camera crew; probably her boyfriend from Worldnews. She's already told him that the astronaut's been revived, no doubt of that. It will be like inviting a team of espionage agents into the laboratory. Still, what better way to fend off spies than to invite them into your parlor and let them think they are seeing everything? But I mustn't appear to give in too easily. She's clever enough to see through that.

''If I agree to what you want,'' he said slowly, picking up a salad fork and toying with it, ''what will you do for me?''

''I don't understand. . . .''

Nillson smiled at her again. ''It's very simple, An Linh. A life for a life.''

She sat in this preciously appointed private dining room, staring at one of the richest and most powerful men in the world, and hoped desperately that he would not say what she knew he was going to say.

Enjoying the uncertainty in her eyes, Nillson said, "I'm not trying to seduce you, although you are a very beautiful young woman. Surely you're aware of the effect you have on men."

An Linh made herself smile.

"I . . . need"—the word twisted Nillson's face into a pained scowl—"a woman to bear a son for me."

She felt her mouth gape with shock.

Nillson held up a long, bony-knuckled hand. "It's not what you think. I want a host mother to carry a fertilized zygote which I will provide."

An Linh began to breathe again. "A host mother. Mrs. Nillson does not want to be bothered with an unsightly pregnancy."

"Mrs. Nillson has nothing to do with this, other than providing an ovum."

Forcing herself to be calm, An Linh asked, "But I thought that Vanguard had developed artificial wombs for cases where . . ."

His white brows knit again. "I will not trust *my* son to a glorified test tube. I want a human mother to carry him to term."

"I see."

"Naturally, I will see to it that you are taken care of extremely well."

"And if I refuse? What then? Do I get fired?"

"No! Of course not." He gestured with the hand that held the fork. "I'm rather clumsy about these things. I didn't mean to suggest that I expect payment in return for helping your priest."

"Then? . . ."

"Allow me to take you to dinner now and then. Perhaps we could go sailing together. I'm really a very pleasant fellow, despite what you may have heard."

"And your wife?"

His lips pulled back in a smile, but his eyes went hard. "My wife has nothing to do with this. She leads her life and I lead mine."

An Linh heard herself reply, "I'll have to think about this. I can't make a decision right away."

"I understand."

"I have a very jealous boyfriend," she blurted.

Who wants to bring a Worldnews camera team into my laboratories, Nillson told himself.

"I'm sure you can explain this to him," he said.

"Then you'll accept Father Lemoyne and allow us to tape?"

"How could I refuse such a request?"

"Thank you." It was all she could think to say.

"My pleasure." Nillson smiled. "After lunch, I'll have my legal people work out the details with you."

He turned his attention to the salad, while contemplating the possibilities of the future. An Linh would bring her boyfriend and his camera crew into the labs and they would snoop around for weeks. They would find nothing about the astronaut. Nothing at all. Everyone who had been involved in the matter or even heard that the man had been revived would be moved to other locations. Vanguard would get a very sympathetic documentary out of Worldnews and he would get a woman to carry his son. And undoubtedly he would get the lovely Oriental girl into his bed in the bargain. How could she refuse? He pictured her naked, just a little frightened when she realized what he had in store for her. No, more than a little frightened. He felt tiny beads of perspiration dotting his upper lip as he contemplated the fear he would see in those long-lashed almond eyes.

He watched her eating while he dabbed at his lips with his napkin. If only I could grow a mustache, a full handsome Viking's mustache!

The communicator on his wrist chimed delicately.

"What is it?" he snapped.

The voice from the communicator was a thin, weak piping. "An urgent message, sir. Private."

Nillson forced himself not to frown. To An Linh, he said softly, "Would you excuse me for a moment?"

"Of course."

He got up from the table and went through the open portal to his desk. Taking up the phone handset, he growled, "This had better be important."

The face that appeared on the screen set into the desktop was Archie Madigan's. His normal grin had vanished. He looked worried.

"She took Stoner aboard the jumpjet."

Nillson lowered his voice. "They're headed for Maine, then?"

No reply for the span of a heartbeat, then, "That's what she wants you to think. She switched planes at the refueling stop in Nebraska. Two people who look like her and Stoner will go to the house in Maine, but it won't be them."

Nillson felt anger flaring hot inside him. "Where's she going, then?"

"We're not certain. . . ."

"Then find out, damn you! Find out quickly!"

"Yessir."

He slammed the phone back into its cradle. His breath snorted out of him in furious gasps. *She's taken him off to some secret hideaway, has she? The bitch! I knew she'd run off with him. After all I've done for her, she's still got the hots for her childhood sweetheart. Well, she'll regret it. They'll both regret it. By the time I get finished with them they'll both be happy to be dead.*

Then he looked up and saw An Linh staring at him from the dining room.

CHAPTER 12

Everett Nillson had lived with fear all his life. Fear, and anger.

As he replaced the phone in its cradle, watching An Linh's eyes following him, he struggled within himself to keep his fury from boiling out, to keep himself under control. From childhood he had fought this battle. *Never let the anger show. He knows that the anger is born out of fear.*

"You must never be afraid," he heard his father's booming voice. "Fear is a sign of cowardice, and I will *not* have a coward for my son!"

Nillson had been born to great wealth. Vanguard Industries had been his father's creation, and from long before he had been old enough to understand, he had been told, by his mother, his governess, his tutors, and especially by his father himself, how Lars Nillson had fought his way up from the grimy coveralls of a factory grease monkey to the elegant dinner jacket of a successful industrialist.

"And I did it all for you!" his father constantly reminded young Everett. He would pick up the child in his beefy hands and swing him dizzyingly around the huge, opulent drawing room of their home outside Stockholm. "All for you! Someday all this will be yours!"

Everett was an asthmatic baby, a frail child who preferred hiding in his room and watching videos to playing with the bullies and sadists of his own age. His father raged at his weakness, blamed his silent and suffering mother, and swore that he would never leave the industrial empire he had created to a weakling.

But there was no one else to leave it to, and in the end, when a microscopic blood vessel in Lars Nillson's brain exploded and killed him, Everett Nillson became the chairman of the board of Vanguard Industries. He was barely twenty.

And terrified. But for the first time in his life he held in his thin, bony hands something that almost compensated for his fear: power.

The two were an awesome synergy. The more Nillson feared someone or something, the more he wielded his power against it. He sought power constantly, more power always, to keep the fear that ate at his innards under control. Vanguard Industries was slipping when Everett Nillson assumed control. An economic recession racked the industrial world, and his father's generation of managers seemed unable to fend off the politicians who were intent on nationalizing the company. Everett Nillson bought politicians with money, drugs, women, flattery, and the most dazzling bribes of them all: visions of higher political office. He fired managers ruthlessly and put men his own age in their places. And women.

For the first time in his young life, Nillson found women pursuing him. And he quickly learned that no matter what he wanted from them, no matter how dominating or cruel or outright sadistic he might be, there were always women willing to submit to him.

He watched one woman with a special fascination: an

American who burned with an unquenchable determination to
reach into space and recover the alien spacecraft that had
briefly passed by the ball of dirt and blood called Earth. He
watched Jo Camerata climb up the corporate ladder of Vanguard Industries, watched her in her office and in the bedrooms of the men who could help her. He began to help her
himself, and finally he married her. He knew that he could
not dominate her in bed, or even in the office. She would
never willingly submit to him. But he would break her spirit,
sooner or later. One day she would drop to her knees before
him. And that day was approaching quickly.

But now she had flown off with her former lover, and
Nillson felt again the burning fury that was born of fear. Jo
was trying to escape him, trying to best him at his own game
of power. She was smart enough, and tough enough, to win.
That was what frightened Everett Nillson. That, and the
gnawing pain that clawed at his innards.

She had to be humbled. Only victory would silence the
fear that tortured Nillson. Complete victory. A victory that
had to end in death.

An Linh could see that the phone call had enraged Nillson,
but he fought to maintain his self-control as he returned to the
dining room and finished his lunch with her.

"A business problem?" she asked.

He glared at her momentarily, then composed himself.
"Yes. Strictly business."

She thought otherwise. They finished lunch with hardly
another word. But as An Linh was leaving Nillson's office,
he asked her:

"How familiar are you with the labs?"

She blinked at him, surprised by the question.

"Have you gone through them? Do you know what they're
like?"

"Not in any great detail," she admitted. "I've been working at the corporate level, not . . ."

"Not down at the level where the real work is done," he
finished for her.

Picking up his desktop phone, Nillson said, "I'll get someone from the labs' PR department to give you a tour of the
place. If you're going to film a documentary, you ought to
know what's going on there."

Nillson turned An Linh over to a secretary, who led her through the quiet, paneled corridors of the executive office area to a public relations woman who was to "show her around the labs."

After two hours of being toured around the Vanguard facilities, An Linh felt the numbing dizziness of sensory overload. Chemistry labs sparkling with glass apparatus, bubbling and chuffing, odd smells and wary glances from intense-looking men and women in white smocks. A microsurgery room that looked like the control center for a space mission, crammed with beeping electronics and row upon row of display screens. A full-fledged zoo populated by barking dogs, ponderous minihogs whose bare pink skin looked strangely repulsive, and sad-eyed, pensive chimpanzees and gorillas who looked out through the bars of their cages at An Linh as if they knew what was in store for them.

The tingle of alarm that she had felt during her lunch with Nillson faded from her mind as she walked through corridor after corridor, laboratory after laboratory, through offices and workshops and what seemed to be a small but very modern and highly automated hospital section.

Her guide finally detoured into a minicafeteria, saying to An Linh as she pushed through its swinging door, "I'll bet you could use some caffeine."

"And a pair of roller skates," she replied.

An Linh sank gratefully into the closest chair at the first table in the little cafeteria and let her handbag clunk to the floor. It seemed to have gained half a ton since lunch. The cafeteria was actually nothing more than an extended alcove in the corridor, walled off by translucent plastic partitions and lined with automatic food and drink dispensers. There were only six small round tables, with four plastic chairs at each. The walls were pale green, the floor tiles slightly darker.

Almost like a sidewalk bistro in Avignon, An Linh thought, except that this is indoors and automated and serving preprocessed garbage instead of good coffee and real bread and cheese.

"Coffee or tea?" her guide asked.

"Tea, please. With milk."

The woman was about An Linh's own age, pencil slim, with the kind of tightly curled auburn hair that could only be produced by the cosmetics industry. She wore a mannish suit of gray, the blouse unbuttoned down to where it disappeared behind her vest. Not that it mattered, An Linh thought; her chest was just as skinny as the rest of her. Her face was long and narrow, too. She wore eyeglasses as a decoration; no one her age needed them, not with monolayer lenses that you sprayed on and washed off.

The nametag on her jacket read Rebecca Parker. As she sat down and placed two cheerfully decorated plastic mugs on the little table, she sympathized, "It's a lot to take in the first time around."

An Linh sipped at the tea. It was tepid. "I appreciate your taking the time to show me everything."

Rebecca shrugged. "It's my job."

"You do this all the time?"

"A lot of the time. It's the way I keep my girlish figure."

An Linh nodded and took another swallow of the luke-warm tea.

"It must have been great being on television," Rebecca said.

"It's like anything else. Mostly hard work."

"I suppose you have to have the looks for it."

"Sure." Seeing the question in her eyes, An Linh added, "You could do it. You'd be fine."

"Really?"

"Well . . . maybe you'd have to think about redoing your hairstyle. I think something longer and more natural would complement your facial structure better."

"Oh, do you think so?"

"Of course."

"But you've got such great looks—you're a real natural beauty."

An Linh broke into a grin. "Then why do I have to spend so much time fixing my face and hair?"

They both laughed.

An Linh took another sip of tea, then said, "There's a professional service in Honolulu, you know. Send them a hologram of yourself and they'll send you a complete analysis of hairstyles, makeup—everything."

"Must be expensive."

"The company should pay for it. After all, it's important for anyone in PR to look their best."

Rebecca frowned sadly. "My boss would never okay it. He's a real . . . well, he wouldn't okay it, I know he wouldn't."

"Then I will," An Linh said. "You come over to my office tomorrow and I'll approve the request. If your boss complains, tell him to call me."

Rebecca's mouth dropped open. An Linh thought, I'm going to need a friend inside the laboratory complex. This girl could be helpful, especially if she thinks there's a job opening at the corporate level waiting for her.

Now they were friends, and they both leaned forward slightly, toward each other, their heads coming closer as they began to talk about clothes and apartments and, inevitably, men. Slowly, slowly, An Linh steered the conversation toward Rebecca's job, the work she did for the labs, the responsibilities she had, the tours she led for visitors.

"You got the ten-dollar tour," Rebecca told her. "That's just about the best one. Mr. Nillson himself wanted the red carpet rolled out for you."

"He's a very"—An Linh deliberately put a hitch in her voice—"different kind of man, isn't he?"

"Nillson? I've never been privileged to meet him. He's too high up on the totem pole for menials like me to actually be introduced to."

"He seemed kind of . . ." She let the thought dangle.

"Strange?" Rebecca suggested. "A little on the weird side?"

"I don't know. What do you think?"

"There've been rumors. Stories. They say he's a little kinky."

"Really?"

"Maybe a lot kinky." Rebecca giggled.

An Linh looked down into her tea mug, then back at Rebecca. "Well, anyway, he ordered the ten-dollar tour for me."

Rebecca glanced at her watch. "Yeah. I guess I ought to give you the rest of it before quitting time."

"Will we see the cryonics facility?"

She nodded as she pushed herself up from the table. "That's next on our itinerary."

"And the frozen astronaut?"

Behind her lensless glasses, Rebecca's eyes widened for

just the flash of a second. "No, not that. Off limits, even on
the ten-dollar tour. You need a special written pass to see
him, approved personally by Mrs. Nillson."

Picking up her handbag and getting to her feet, An Linh
asked, "But he's well, isn't he? Nothing's gone wrong with
him?"

Rebecca gave her a troubled look. "I'm not supposed to
say anything about him. Really, I don't know a thing. You
must know a lot more about him than I do."

An Linh nodded. She's afraid to talk about him. The
word's gone out that the frozen astronaut is to be kept secret.
No news is good news, as far as his case is concerned.

She dropped the subject and allowed Rebecca to lead her
into the cryonics laboratory. To An Linh, the place looked
and felt like a combination of a morgue and the butcher's
section at the supermarket. It was cold, the kind of cold that
seeps into the bones. Stainless-steel cylinders that they called
dewars, big vaults with heavy steel doors, bare tiled floors.
The technicians here worked in heavy coveralls and rubber-
ized gloves. All of the bodies An Linh saw were animals,
from baby mice to a full-grown chimpanzee lying on a cold
slab, faint traces of frost glistening on the hairs of its face.

With a sudden shudder, An Linh thought of her mother
lying inside one of those gleaming steel cylinders, frozen,
trusting her daughter to watch over her and bring her back to
life.

"Have you seen enough?" She felt Rebecca's hand on her
trembling arm. The woman's voice was sincerely concerned.

"Yes," An Linh said. "Thanks."

Rebecca led her in silence out of the cryonics lab. They
walked slowly down a long corridor. One entire wall of it
was windows, and An Linh felt the warmth of the life-giving
sun soaking into her.

"One more stop," Rebecca said. "Legal department. They
want to talk to you about something; I don't know what."

"I'm going to bring a man here for freezing," An Linh
said. "We're making a documentary of it."

"Super*sonic*!" Rebecca said. "What a great idea!"

"He's a priest," An Linh added.

"Oh, for . . . You'll get an Emmy easy."

An Linh made herself smile. Easy. To Rebecca the priest
was an object, a prop in a TV show, a character to be

photographed. Then her smile faded. *And what is Father Lemoyne to me? I know him, I even love him like the father who never loved me, and I'm the one who's using him.*

"One warning," Rebecca whispered as they turned into a corridor that was suddenly carpeted and decorated with potted plants and paintings on the walls.

"Oh?"

"I'm supposed to bring you in to see Archibald S. Madigan, the head of our legal department."

An Linh waited for the rest of it.

"Be careful with him," Rebecca advised. "He's got a poet's tongue and a policeman's hands."

Grinning, An Linh said, "I know Archie. He's got a lot more than that."

It was late in the evening before An Linh finally got back to her apartment in Hilo. Baker was waiting for her.

She was only slightly surprised when she opened her apartment door and saw him sitting tensely on the sofa. A pair of candles flickered on the coffee table. She saw a bottle of wine and a dish of cheeses and a real baguette already sliced and waiting.

The Australian hopped to his feet and greeted her with a kiss.

"I thought you'd like some real food after a hard day at the office."

She patted his cheek. "You're a mind reader."

An hour later, the wine was gone, the cheeses reduced to a few morsels, and nothing was left of the bread but a scattering of crumbs across the coffee table, sofa, and carpet.

And for some reason, Cliff Baker was as tense as a hunted animal. An Linh could not find out why. She had asked him a half-dozen times why he was so wound up, but he had merely brushed her questions away and asked for more details about her lunch with Nillson.

"He'll let us bring Father Lemoyne in for freezing," she said.

"And tape it?"

"Yes." She did not tell him about Nillson's demand for her to be a surrogate mother and his clumsy, almost half-hearted flirtation.

"That's good. That's really good."

She had never seen his sky-blue eyes look so troubled. If
he had been skeptical, even mocking, An Linh could have
accepted it. Cliff always played the cynic. But he was strangely
tense, almost as if he were terribly afraid of something that
he refused to talk about.

"Cliff, you're going to have to be very careful," An Linh
insisted. "They're keeping the astronaut under very tight
security. They don't want any premature publicity. No
leaks. . . ."

"I understand that!" he snapped. "You don't have to
repeat it twenty times!"

"But I think they're moving him to another location.
That's what Nillson's phone conversation was all about."

"And you don't know where?"

Is that what's bothering him? That they're moving the
astronaut, and now it doesn't matter whether they let Father
Lemoyne into the labs or not?

"I don't think even Nillson knows where. He seemed
terribly angry."

"But that phone call," Baker said. "You think it had
something to do with his wife?"

"Yes, his wife," she replied slowly, uneasily. "Every
time I mentioned her he sort of bristled. And he was really
furious over the phone call. I don't think he'd get that angry
over just a business matter; he's not the type. It had something to do with his wife, I'm sure of it."

"His wife worked with the astronaut before he was frozen."

"I know."

Baker ran a finger absently along his broken nose. Then,
"Lemme make a phone call."

"To who?"

"Whom." Baker got up from the sofa and went to the
delicate escritoire in the corner of the living room. It was the
one piece of furniture that An Linh had brought with her
from Avignon: her mother's writing desk. Now it served as a
base for the phone terminal.

As Baker tapped out the phone number he wanted and
lifted the receiver to his ear, An Linh stretched out wearily
on the sofa and gazed through half-closed eyes at the view
through her terrace window. The moon sat poised above the
rim of the Mauna Loa's dark volcanic bulk. A cloud glided
across its softly glowing face. An Linh closed her eyes. The

excitement of the day had worn off. Fatigue and the wine were catching up with her.

She woke, startled. Baker was tugging at her sleeve.

"Come on, love, we've got to go," he said. His face was set in a strangely determined scowl. He looked grim, frightened.

"You can sleep here. . . ."

"No, you don't understand. We're leaving for London."

"London? When . . . why? . . ."

"Tonight. There's a flight leaving at eleven. We can just catch it if we hurry."

An Linh swung her feet to the carpet and stood up. "Tonight? You're going to London *now*?" She felt stunned, bewildered.

"Wake up!" he snapped almost angrily. "We're both going to London. Right now. Not a moment to lose."

"Cliff, you can't just—"

"Start packing, dammit! I'm not kidding!"

She felt her head swirling.

Baker grasped her by the shoulders as if he wanted to shake her into obedience.

"Listen to me," he said urgently. "I just did some checking with a friend of mine who's got a pipeline into Vanguard Industries. He said you overheard a very sensitive phone conversation he had with Nillson, and now Nillson's afraid that you might have heard too much."

"But what . . ."

"There's no telling what a man with Nillson's power might do," Baker said. "My source was warning me to get you to someplace safe until Nillson calms down."

An Linh felt stunned. She heard herself arguing, "We can't just run away because of a phone call! I've got my job, you've got yours. . . ."

"We're going," Baker said firmly. "I know some people in London who'll take us in for a while."

He pushed her toward the bedroom and helped her pull a garment bag from her closet. An Linh began stuffing it with clothes, her thoughts spinning madly.

"Aren't you going to pack?" she asked as she rummaged through a bureau drawer.

"Already have. My bag's in the car, downstairs."

"Cliff, are you sure we've got to do this?"

The fear in his eyes was real, but there was something

more than fear there. An Linh could not determine what it was.

"I'm sure, pet," he muttered earnestly. "There's no other way."

"But . . ."

"You've got to trust me, An Linh. Please. It's for your own good."

Filled with foreboding, she finished packing and zipped up the garment bag. Baker took it from her and hurried her toward the door.

"Shouldn't you call the airport?" An Linh asked.

"We're already booked for the flight," he said, opening the front door for her.

He did not mention that their reservations had been made by Archie Madigan's secretary, or that Vanguard Industries was paying for their flight.

EUROPE

**And mine has been the fate of those
To whom the goodly earth and air
Are banned, and barred—forbidden fare**

CHAPTER 13

Keith Stoner stood at the stone balustrade and looked down at the city of Naples spread out before him, half-lost in morning mist. Statues of stern old Romans and scheming Renaissance opportunists scowled at him disapprovingly along the length of the railing. Far off to his left, Vesuvius smoldered sullenly, a thin, whitish cloud rising from its dark peak. The Mediterranean was gray and sulking beneath low clouds.

"The land of your ancestors," he said to Jo.

She was sitting at the white wrought-iron table next to the fountain. It splashed softly while she poured morning coffee, strong and black and steaming, into two delicate demitasses. She was dressed in dark blue shorts and a sleeveless white top cut off at the midriff. Stoner still wore the same slacks and short-sleeve shirt he had arrived in the night before.

"The home of my family," said Jo. "How do you like it?"

Stoner turned to survey the fountain and its sculptured cherubs, the gnarled old olive trees lining the pool, the flowering shrubs dotting the patio, the handsome stone villa. It spread across the hilltop, straight and clean-lined, walls glistening white, slanted roofs covered with red tile.

"I don't see why your family would ever leave a place like this to come to America," he said.

She laughed. "It wasn't in my family then. My people came from down there"—she pointed vaguely toward the city—"in the slums. I bought this place for a couple of distant cousins of mine. They keep it for me. It's a good retreat, a place to get away from it all."

"And nobody back in Hawaii knows that it's yours."

"Nobody."

"Not even your husband."

The smile stayed on her face, but her voice became brittle. "No, not even Everett."

"Like a Mafia hideaway," Stoner muttered.

Jo's smile brightened. "That's right. I'm with my family here. They protect me and stay quiet about it."

"And how long do you expect to keep me here?"

She patted the cushioned chair beside her. "Come and have some breakfast."

He sat while she touched a button on her wristwatch. The patio doors swung open and a squat little robot trundled out across the marble terrace. It stopped a precise thirty centimeters from the table's edge and its top slid open to form a serving surface, while a tray of croissants, pastries, butter, and jams rose silently from its innards. Below the tray were dishes and tableware.

Stoner watched Jo transfer the breakfast things to their table. He sipped at the coffee; it was as powerful as it smelled and even hotter than it looked. Darkly rich without being bitter. He recalled someone telling him once that coffee should be black as night, hot as hell, and strong as the love of a good woman. Closing his eyes, he tried to remember who it had been. That Naval Intelligence agent, Dooley. The man who had kept him under house arrest in the name of national security, back when he had first detected the alien spacecraft approaching Earth.

"How long will I be here, Jo?"

She looked at him, her eyes probing his. "I can't say, Keith. A few weeks, at least."

"Is Richards coming here?"

"Perhaps."

"Why all the secrecy? What's going on?"

A hint of fear flashed in her eyes, but it was immediately replaced by stubborn determination. "A lot's going on, Keith. Corporate politics. I've got to get rid of the corporation's public relations director, for one thing. And we've got to figure out why you're not sleeping."

He pushed aside the dish of pastries as he leaned forward urgently. "Jo, has it occurred to you that my revival might have something to do with the fact that I've been"—he groped for a word—"*influenced* by the alien?"

"Influenced?"

"I was aboard that spacecraft for more than six years, wasn't I?"

"But he was dead. How could—"

"The spacecraft was still functioning. The computer aboard it was still working. I'll bet it was damned far ahead of anything we've built here on Earth."

She nodded. "It's still so far ahead of us that no one's been able yet to figure out how it works."

Eagerly, feeling the excitement bubbling up inside him, Stoner said, "Suppose the alien's body is dead, but his *mind*, his *personality,* is inside that computer?"

Jo stared at him, her eyes widening.

"Suppose he was in contact with my mind—all those years, talking to me, merging with me . . ."

"That's . . . No, that can't be. . . ."

"Can't it? I get flashbacks, Jo. I see things that aren't from my own life. Not from Earth. What Richards calls hallucinations are scenes from another world, another life. *His* life, Jo. The alien's."

"That's impossible!"

"It would ruin your business plans, wouldn't it? I mean, maybe the only reason I survived freezing was because the alien helped me in some way you aren't even aware of."

"No!"

"But it might be true!" he insisted. "I'm the first person to be brought back. Richards told me so. You haven't . . ."

Then he saw the look of agony on her face and realized that not everything the psychiatrist had told him had been true.

"Oh, my God, you *did* try it on other human beings."

Jo did not answer. She didn't have to. Stoner saw it on her face.

"And none of them came through."

She reached for the demitasse and took its whole contents in one long, swift gulp.

"They were all volunteers," Jo said at last. "From overseas. Asians, mostly. Two Filipinos, several Chinese, a dozen or so Indians and Pakistanis."

"And all of them poor," Stoner added. "So poor that whatever you offered them for risking their lives was enough to get them to volunteer."

She nodded wordlessly.

"And none of them made it."

"It was pretty gruesome," she admitted. "Horrible, really."

"Then why did you decide to try to bring me back? I mean, if none of them made it . . .''

''I had no choice, Keith,'' she said, almost pleading for his understanding. ''The board insisted. They refused to keep funding the project. It was Everett's doing, really. He demanded results or termination.''

''Your husband.''

''And the rest of the board went along with him. Healy—my chief scientist—he felt we had a chance. You had been in good physical condition when you were frozen. And he had revived two of the volunteers, briefly. One of them had lasted several days, but her brain was damaged too badly. . . .''

Stoner said nothing. The soft Mediterranean breeze touched his cheek, played with Jo's dark hair. The fountain splashed happily.

''Even when we restarted your heart and your body functions, you stayed in a coma for almost a week. I thought you might never come back to consciousness.''

He turned in his chair and looked out toward the city sprawling below this hilltop villa. Millions of human beings were busily at work there, building and destroying, coupling and killing, brimming with joy and hate and tenderness and pain. And each of them, every individual one of them, fearing death. Hoping for immortality.

He said slowly to Jo, ''It might be that the only reason I was able to be revived is that the alien somehow brought me through. It might be that my success has nothing to do with the rest of the human race.''

Jo stared at him as though seeing him for the first time in her life.

An Linh stood in a crumpled daze in the busy lobby of the Savoy while Cliff Baker waited beside her for the registration clerk to check his credit number on the hotel's computer.

The flight from Hilo had taken little more than half an hour, once the rocket plane had started rolling down the long airport runway. It angled up into the sky and boosted into a high ballistic arc over the Pacific, then the rugged Kolyma range on the eastern tip of Siberia, across the frozen Arctic, and down the Norwegian and North seas to the British Isles.

An Linh had dozed fitfully during the brief flight, stirring when the jarring vibration of returning to subsonic flight rattled the rocket plane and awakening fully when the landing gear went down with a loud roar and a thump.

Now she stood befuddled, tired, aching in every joint of her body, longing for nothing more than a good night's sleep—even though bright daylight poured through the revolving doors of the hotel lobby.

No ordinary bellman showed them to their room. A tall, soft-speaking assistant manager in morning coat and elegant bowtie picked up their two scruffy travelbags and escorted them to the elevator, speaking quietly, proudly, of the Savoy's illustrious history.

"Bloody pom," Baker whispered in An Linh's ear as the assistant manager led them down a quiet corridor. "They teach 'em that phony queer accent, y'know."

An Linh was too tired to care about the Australian view of Englishmen. Through her haze of weariness, she thought she heard their man say that the hotel had been built by Messrs. Gilbert, Sullivan, and d'Oyly Carte. That sounded odd to her, but she felt too muddled to press the matter.

The assistant manager ushered them into an elegant suite. The sitting room was a spacious expanse done in art deco, with walnut paneling and big couches covered with boldly striped fabrics. The bedroom was smaller, decorated in blue and white, with bureaus and a vanity that looked like a poor imitation of French Provincial style. But the bed was large and looked irresistibly inviting to An Linh.

"Look!" Baker called to her from the sitting room. "You can see Big Ben!"

"And in this direction," the Englishman said ever so politely, "one can view Saint Paul's Cathedral."

Neither impressed An Linh so much as the wide, high, blue-covered bed. She ignored both the men and dropped herself onto it. Closing her eyes, she was asleep almost immediately. Her last thought was a nagging worry about why she should be so utterly exhausted.

The thought was still in her mind when she awoke.

She sat up on the bed, fully alert the instant her eyes opened. Her head was clear. She felt rested and fine. Daylight still brightened the windows. And she could hear voices coming from the adjoining room.

An Linh took a deep, testing breath. Yes, she felt fine. What had hit her? she wondered. It had been a tense day,

meeting Nillson and having lunch with him, touring the labs
and taking the first steps to set up Cliff's documentary. But
no more hectic than plenty of other days she had put in. Half
a bottle of wine and some cheese and bread with Cliff—and
his sudden wild urgency about getting away from Hawaii.

Why had she spun into such a downer? It was almost as if
the wine had been drugged.

The entire wall next to the bed was a set of mirrored doors;
clothes closets behind them, she guessed. Her reflection showed
dark lines under her eyes, hair tangled and matted, jumpsuit
hopelessly wrinkled. She felt unwashed and sticky. For a few
moments more she sat on the bed, listening to the voices
from the next room. She easily recognized Cliff's and knew
that the other was not an Englishman speaking. The voice
sounded almost American, but not quite. Male. Tantalizingly
familiar.

Glancing at her wristwatch, An Linh saw that it was still
on Hawaii time. She tapped the reset button and whispered,
"London," into the watch's miniaturized microphone. The
glowing red numerals on the readout shifted by ten hours.

She estimated that she had slept for several hours. Whatever
it was that had so disoriented her had worked its way out of
her system, and she was grateful for that. It frightened her to
have her body fail her.

An Linh got up carefully from her bed, left her shoes on
the carpet exactly where she had dropped them, and tiptoed
to the door that connected with the sitting room. She cracked
the door open half an inch.

Baker was sitting on the couch nearest the wide, sweeping
windows that overlooked the Thames, the stately tower of
Big Ben behind him in the distance.

"I don't like any of this," he was saying, his voice low
and intense, his face grimly serious. "And I especially don't
like dragging her into it."

His visitor sat in a wing chair, his back to An Linh. She
could not see his face, but she was certain she knew the voice
and had heard it only recently.

"She's in it, my boy, whether either one of us likes it or
not. And you're the one who brought her in."

"I still don't like it."

"I'm trying to protect her—to protect you both. Nillson's
no fool, you know. He sees what you're after."

Baker shook his head. The grinning mask of cynicism that he usually presented to the world had disappeared. He looked truly concerned, almost angry.

An Linh hesitated. She realized that she had been in this slitted jumpsuit for nearly twenty-four hours. She needed a shower, fresh clothes, and some attention to her makeup.

"We're trying to save a man's life," Cliff said. "A priest."

His visitor chuckled. "You're after the frozen astronaut, and we all know it."

"You mean the thawed astronaut, don't you?"

No reply.

An Linh smoothed her suit and ran both hands through her tangled hair, then pushed the door fully open.

"He's been revived; there's no use pretending he hasn't," she said, stepping into the room.

Baker's grim face eased slightly into a worried smile as he got to his feet. Walking around the wing chair, An Linh saw that the other man was Archibald Madigan, Vanguard Industries' chief counsel.

Madigan smiled, too, and stood up. "It's good to see you again."

"What's going on?" An Linh demanded. "Why are you here?" Turning to Baker, "Why are we here?"

Cliff looked to Madigan. The lawyer grinned broadly at An Linh, and she realized that his light hazel eyes could look greenish, or gray, or even almost blue, depending on the circumstances. Changeable eyes. Traitor's eyes. This was a man who could not be trusted, An Linh knew.

"Let me show you something," Madigan said, fishing in the pocket of his shirt jacket. Like both of them, the lawyer was still wearing clothes more appropriate to Hawaii than London. He must have rushed over here just as fast as we did, An Linh thought.

He pulled a slim black rectangle from his pocket, then shook an even thinner disc from inside it. The disc coruscated in the light from the window, shimmering with all the colors of the rainbow. Wordlessly, Madigan went to the TV set built into the walnut wall paneling and slid the disc into its video recorder slit.

Baker stepped around the low coffee table to stand beside An Linh. She wanted him to put his arm around her shoulders and make her feel protected. But he had moved toward her merely to get a better view of the TV screen.

Stepping back, Madigan told them, "The picture quality won't be too good, and there's no sound. This was taken through a *very* long-range lens."

The screen showed a pair of people sitting on a blanket on a beach, a picnic basket opened beside them. An Linh thought the scene looked like Hawaii.

The camera zoomed in. The picture was blocked momentarily by a truck passing by. Heat waves made the image dance and flicker. But as the focus tightened, An Linh recognized the woman.

"That's Mrs. Nillson, isn't it?" she asked.

Madigan nodded.

"And who's that with her?" asked Baker.

An Linh already knew. She had studied that face, too, for many years and seen it briefly on another videotape.

"Dr. Keith Stoner," she said, her voice weak from the sudden breathlessness that assailed her.

"Stoner! The astronaut!"

"He's really alive," An Linh said. Somehow, seeing him outside the laboratory setting made his revival seem more genuine to her. And she knew that if Stoner lived, her mother could also.

"He is indeed," Madigan said. The grin on his face seemed faintly mocking.

They watched in silence as the man and woman sat on the beach, talking. An Linh wished she could read lips. Abruptly, the camera zoomed back. An airplane swooped in from over the water, hovered above the beach, then settled gently onto the sand. Stoner and Mrs. Nillson jumped to their feet and ran to the plane.

The screen went dark.

"That's it," Madigan said. "They took off for parts unknown."

"Unknown?" An Linh echoed.

Baker frowned at the lawyer. "D'you expect us to believe that Vanguard Industries doesn't know where its own president is? Or where Stoner is?"

"Not only that," Madigan replied easily, "but I expect you to help us find him."

"Now wait—"

But Madigan was already saying, "We know they flew off to the mainland. At a refueling stop there they switched planes—after putting a pair of actors who physically resembled them into their own plane. The actors are at Mrs. Nillson's summer home in Maine right now, going through the motions of pretending they are her and Stoner."

"But where did the real ones go?"

Madigan retrieved his video disc from the TV and slipped it back into his pocket. He pointed an index finger at the bar in the corner of the sitting room.

"Do you mind? After all, this suite is coming off my expense account."

Baker shrugged, then said, "I'll join you. Anything for you, love?"

She shook her head, remembering how the wine of the previous night had affected her. She still felt rather weak, whether from the aftereffects of whatever it was that had knocked her out or the excitement of the past twenty-four hours. She went to the couch along the far wall and sat in it.

Sliding behind the bar with the ease of long practice, Madigan found a bottle of Scotch and poured himself a generous dollop into a cut-glass tumbler.

"Ahh," he sighed after a long swallow. "God bless those kilted sonsofbitches."

An Linh insisted, "Where are Mrs. Nillson and Dr. Stoner now?"

"We really don't know," Madigan said lightly. To Baker, "Scotch for you?"

"Is there any beer back there?"

Madigan ducked down for a moment and came up with a bottle. To An Linh he said, "Their plane crossed the Atlantic, refueled in Madrid, and went on to Italy. We bribed enough air traffic controllers to find out that they landed at Rome. We lost track of them there."

"Lost track of them?"

"It's a huge airport. Of course, if we had known ahead of time that they were going to Rome, we would have had people there to observe them. But as it is . . ." He spread his hands in a gesture of helplessness.

"So what do you expect us to do about it?" Baker asked, the beer bottle tight in one fist.

"Help us to find them."

"Us? You mean Vanguard Industries needs help?"

Madigan's face turned slightly sorrowful. "All right, the one who needs the help is me. Yours truly."

"I don't understand," said An Linh from the couch.

"It's not too complicated," Madigan answered. "Jo—Mrs. Nillson—has run off with Stoner. Why, I can't say. Her husband thinks she's been in love with the man since they worked together eighteen years ago."

Baker gave a low whistle. "There's a bloody human-interest angle for you!"

"Don't count on it," Madigan snapped almost angrily. "I know Jo. She doesn't act on impulse, and she *never* lets her emotions overrule her intellect. She's hidden Stoner away for some reason of her own."

"And not told her husband about it?" An Linh marveled. "The chairman of the board?"

"Corporate politics can get rather Byzantine," Madigan said.

"But how the hell do you expect us to do anything about it?"

Madigan's smile returned. This time it looked impish, An Linh thought.

"Jo knows Vanguard inside out. She knows how her husband thinks, she knows how I think. She's prepared for whatever we might do, I'm sure."

"But she doesn't know me."

"You've got it! Within a day or so, my operatives around the continent will pin down her location. But once they do, I'm going to need somebody she doesn't know—somebody she won't be on guard against—to make contact with her and find out just what in the seven tiers of purgatory she's up to."

An Linh saw that Cliff was intrigued by the idea, and Madigan was playing him like a master programmer works a computer.

"Why should we help you?" she demanded. "What do we get out of it?"

Madigan took another long pull of Scotch. Then, leaning his forearms on the bar, he smiled his most wickedly at her.

"First, there is the matter of Mr. Nillson. He's certain that you're prying into his private business, and he does not take kindly to spies. I can protect you from him."

"Protect . . . ?"

Raising a hand to stifle her question, Madigan said, "You have both been fired from your jobs, you know. He ordered me to do it, and I did."

An Linh looked at Baker. He did not seem surprised or particularly upset.

"I can see to it that you get your job back, Cliff, or even a better job elsewhere. And you'll be able to do the documentary you want to do, about the priest." Turning to An Linh, "You're a tougher problem, I'm afraid. He's really furious with you."

"But why? . . ."

"He saw through your little scheme about the priest, that's why! He's not stupid. He knows you were just kidding him along. Apparently, he's hot for your body, as well. A bad combination—for you."

"What can we do to protect An Linh?" Baker asked.

"Damned if I know, except to keep her hidden from him. Right now, he wants her strung up by her thumbs."

An Linh felt a surge of fright race through her.

Madigan's smile turned darkly threatening. "Not literally, An Linh. Not quite. But he's a man who likes to combine punishment with pleasure."

Baker started, "There's no way—"

"No way you can protect her," Madigan interrupted, "once he sets his mind on having her."

An Linh felt the panic within her subsiding. She thought she understood what the lawyer was saying.

"You're offering to protect me if we help you to locate Mrs. Nillson and Dr. Stoner."

As graciously as a cavalier of old, Madigan bowed and replied, "I am *promising* to protect you."

"If we help you."

"Oh, I know you'll help me. You really have no choice, have you?"

CHAPTER 14

For two days Stoner prowled through the hilltop villa and its lovely grounds, growing more uneasy with each passing hour. Richards did not show up. But someone was out there, beyond the fence that marked the edge of Jo's property. More than one person. Watching. Waiting. Stoner saw no one: heard nothing. But he knew they were out there. He felt it in the tightness of his stomach, in the prickling sensation along the back of his neck. A premonition of danger.

Jo left and stayed away overnight. When she returned she seemed grim, almost haggard, preoccupied.

That evening they dined together on the patio, served only by robots, unfeeling machines whose loyalty was built into them.

"That was a magnificent dinner," Stoner said, pushing his nearly polished dish slightly away from him.

"I'll tell the cook you enjoyed it."

"What was the pasta?"

"Fettuccine Alfredo. And the veal was a local specialty, vitello Napolitano."

He drained the last of the dry red wine and put the wine-glass down carefully on the tablecloth, precisely flat on its base, like an astronaut landing a spacecraft on the surface of an alien planet.

The moon had not yet risen. The only light on the patio came from the candles on their table and the soft glow from the distant lights of Naples. Even this late at night, it was warm and lovely. Fireflies winked in the shadows of the shrubbery. The air bore the tang of the sea and the lingering scent of daylight's flowers. Jo wore a floor-length hostess gown of Egyptian motif, royal blue edged with hieroglyphic symbols in gold, her arms bare. Stoner had found fresh clothes waiting in his room. On a hunch, he had dressed up for dinner: white turtleneck shirt, navy-blue slacks, maroon double-breasted blazer.

"How did things go in Hawaii?" he asked.

Jo blinked and focused her eyes on him, as if seeing him for the first time since dinner had started. "I didn't go to Hawaii."

"Oh? Then where . . ."

"New York. Connecticut, actually. The corporate offices are in Greenwich."

"Is that where your PR director is?"

A small smile crept across Jo's face. "No, she's gone."

"She's quit?"

"She was fired by my . . . by the chairman of the board. I don't know exactly why, but it saves me the trouble of getting rid of her."

Stoner grinned back at her. "You're a tough broad, aren't you?"

"I have to be."

"And what did Healy say about me?"

She looked startled. "How did you know . . ."

"It's obvious that you'd talk to Healy and the other scientists who've been involved in my case. What about Richards? Is he coming here or not?"

"He's asked to be taken off your case."

Stoner blinked with surprise. "He . . . what?"

Jo's smile changed into an expression of reluctantly amused respect. "Dr. Richards told me that he realizes you've been manipulating him—something about riding in his car to the beach."

"Oh, that."

"He doesn't think he can deal with you. He's frightened of you, Keith."

For a moment Stoner felt slightly like a teenaged boy who'd been caught peeking into girlie magazines. But then he realized the irony of it: Richards, the psychiatrist, was afraid of dealing with an equal, afraid of confronting his own psyche, afraid of revealing himself to another human being. A wave of sadness washed over Stoner.

"I could have helped him," he murmured.

"*You* could have helped *him*?"

Stoner nodded.

She frowned slightly. Touching the button on her bracelet

that summoned the robot, Jo said, "I'm going to have to find another psychiatrist to deal with you. And that means a security risk."

"I'm sorry to be so much trouble."

The robot glided across the marble patio and began taking the dishes off the table with its clawlike metal hands. Stoner saw that they were gentle, almost delicate, despite their mechanical nature. And there was a video lens built into the "palm" of each hand, between the gripping claws.

"Will the new man be coming here?" Stoner knew Jo would pick a male psychiatrist.

"Not here. I'll set up a video phone link, so the two of you can talk face to face. But he won't know where you are, and I don't want you to tell him."

Stoner thought it over for a few moments. He turned slightly in his chair and looked out at the city, a sea of twinkling lights arching along the crescent of the bay, outshining the stars in the dark night sky. A soft breeze wafted in from the sea, carrying the piercingly sweet song of a distant bird.

"Is that a nightingale?" he asked.

Jo cocked her head slightly, listening. "I think so. There're plenty of them around here."

"I've never heard a nightingale before," Stoner said, feeling as pleased as a child who's found that storybook tales can come true.

He listened for several minutes to the breathtakingly beautiful warbling.

Finally Jo broke in, "Respighi wrote a nightingale passage into one of his tone poems."

Stoner felt his face knit into a disapproving frown at the interruption.

She took it as puzzlement. "Not a live bird. A recording. One of the musicians plays the recording in the middle of the orchestra."

He looked into her beautiful face, so serious, so preoccupied with other matters. In the flickering light cast by the candles, Jo's dark eyes gleamed.

Stoner reached out his hand toward her, and she took it in hers. He got to his feet, she rose also, and he led her to the balustrade, where the grim-faced statues kept their backs resolutely to the teeming city below.

"Jo," he said softly, "you've got everything that a human being needs for happiness. Why are you pushing yourself? What are you trying to accomplish?"

For an instant, she almost smiled. "You expect me to say that I've got everything except love, don't you?"

He shook his head. "I'm not expecting anything, Jo. I just want to know why you're driving so hard. Why you're so unhappy."

"Do you love me, Keith?"

"I did, eighteen years ago. I was too tied up inside my own soul to know it, but I did love you, then."

"And now?"

He gazed deep into her eyes and saw there what he had seen in Richards and in every human being he had looked into: Fear. And pain.

"We're both different people now, Jo," he said gently.

"I see."

"No, I don't think you do."

"Don't I? What we had eighteen years ago, whatever it was—that's dead. You froze it when you went off into space, and nothing we can do will bring it back to life."

"You're probably right. . . ."

"Probably?"

"But *we're* alive, Jo," he said. "Something new can be born between us."

"You think so?" The smile on her lips was scornful, distrusting.

Taking both her hands in his, Stoner told her, "I don't blame you for trying to protect yourself. I know I've hurt you, even though I never meant to."

Jo's bitter smile faded. The hardness in her expression thawed. Now there was a question in her eyes.

"Give it time, Jo. Don't you understand what this business of immortality really means? We have all the time we need. All the time in the world!"

"Time . . . for what?"

"To learn. To grow. To understand."

She leaned her cheek against his chest. He slid his arms around her.

"Keith, I don't want to be alone."

"I know," he said. "Nobody does. We're warmblooded

creatures, Jo. We need each other. We can't survive by ourselves.''

And while he said it, he suddenly seemed to be looking down at the scene, watching a man and a woman embracing on the marble-floored patio of a hilltop villa while the fireflies danced around them, and down below an ancient city reeking of human passions and blood. Stoner felt himself trembling as he clasped Jo to him. He held her tightly, as if afraid to let go, afraid that he would tumble out of her grasp and fall *upward,* into the dark night sky, as if Earth's gravity no longer could claim him, and he would plummet farther and farther into the star-filled sky, never to return, lost to the world of his birth forever.

But I *am* lost to the world of my birth, he told himself. I left that world willingly, knowing I could never return. I commanded my heirs to set my sarcophagus adrift on the sea of stars.

He squeezed his eyes shut and tried to blot out the vision of the long, stately, somber procession bearing his coffin to the tower that stretched beyond the clouds.

''Listen,'' Jo whispered.

''Another nightingale?''

''No.''

He heard it. A man's tenor voice, far in the distance, singing into the night air.

''A Neapolitan love song,'' Jo said. ''He's singing to his girlfriend.''

Stoner grimaced in the darkness. ''Like the fireflies,'' he muttered.

''What?''

''He's trying to attract a mate. Like the fireflies with their lights. Or the nightingale's singing. Like bullfrogs croaking or peacocks displaying their finery. Males attempting to attract females.''

''That's about as romantic as a computer program,'' Jo said.

Shrugging, Stoner replied, ''Romance is a human invention, the overlay of intelligence to the mating urge.''

''Oh, really?'' She clutched at his hair, her mouth seeking his, her body pressing against him. He held her while that distant part of his mind watched two alien animals entwined in their mating embrace. He felt a wrenching, tearing agony flame through him, as if he were being torn in two, every nerve ripping apart, severing, splitting like a cell fissioning under a microscope. He clutched Jo even tighter, holding on to her as a drowning man hangs on to a floating scrap of wood. Even so he felt himself being pulled away from her, his mind fleeing from the animal closeness, revolted by the heat of her body, the scent of her hair, the touch of her flesh. He wanted her, yet he was repulsed by the very idea.

And then every sense of his being suddenly focused on a brief glimmer of light down below the balustrade, in the tangled, half-wild garden that sloped down the hillside beyond the villa's fences.

He jerked away from Jo, part of him enormously grateful for the excuse.

"What is it?" she asked, her body tensing.

"Someone's down there," he whispered, still holding her, but not so close.

"Where? What do you mean?"

"I saw something down in the shrubbery there."

He felt her relax. "Probably Paolo or one of the other men. They patrol around the place every night."

Stoner shook his head. "It's not one man. There are three of them."

"How can you—"

"And they're armed. I think we'd better get inside."

She peered into the dark garden. "Keith, you can't possibly—"

"Yes, I can," he said. Taking her by the hand, he started for the patio doors. "Come on, we'll be safer inside."

Jo let him lead her inside, then called her majordomo, as dark and slim and evil-looking as a twisted, deadly Neapolitan cigar. She told him to have the hillside searched thoroughly. He looked more annoyed than alarmed but bowed stiffly and left as silently as a shadow.

"This is crazy," Jo said as they stood alone in the villa's central hallway.

"Is it?"

She grinned ruefully. "Maybe not. There are plenty of people who'd like to know where you are."

"Corporate competitors?" Stoner asked. "Or people within your own company?"

"Some of both."

"And others?"

She started to answer, then thought better of it. Finally she said, "You can see why security is important."

He looked around at the stone walls of the hallway. They had been built centuries ago to withstand sudden attack or long siege.

"I think it would be best if I went away for a while," Stoner said.

"No," Jo replied firmly. "You've got to stay here. For your own safety."

"If there are others trying to get at me," he reasoned, "then you're in danger as long as I'm near you. Isn't that true?"

"But I'm protecting you, Keith. You're safe as long as you're under my protection."

"You don't mind being in danger because of me?"

She shook her head silently. Looking deeply into her dark eyes, Stoner saw that she was telling him the truth—as she saw it.

Without thinking further about it, he lifted Jo off her feet and carried her to the sweeping staircase at the end of the hallway. She nestled her cheek against his shoulder, her arms locked around his neck. He knew without asking where her bedroom was. Up the broad, winding staircase, along the corridor to the left. The door opened at his touch. Her bed was wide and high, covered with satin, a gold-inlaid canopy above it, hung with silken draperies.

He placed Jo gently on the bed, bent over her, and kissed her once, lightly, on the lips.

"Sleep," he said softly. "Sleep without dreams."

Her eyes closed languidly and her head turned slightly on the satin pillow. He could see her arms go limp, her body relax. Her breathing slowed to the placid regular rhythm of deep slumber. He stood at the edge of the bed and gazed silently at her, a beautiful human animal, and part of his mind saw her as an alien creature, like an exotic specimen in an exhibit.

"I've got to leave you now," Stoner whispered to her sleeping form. "You'll be in no danger once they know I've gone. And there's so much I need to learn, so much I've got to see and understand, before I can come back to you."

Still, he lingered. Part of him wanted, more than anything, to stay with her and forget everything else. But he knew that could not be. There was too much to be done, too many dangers to face and questions to answer, and it was time that he started on his quest.

"I'll come back to you, Jo," he whispered. "I promise you that."

CHAPTER 15

Getting away from the house was easier than Stoner had anticipated. He went down to the garage, which was underneath the patio. Electronic alarms guarded the doors and windows, and infrared motion sensors kept watch against any movement inside the shadowy garage itself. Stoner walked calmly to the smallest of the five autos in the garage, a sleek red Ferrari, not too different in styling from Richards's convertible.

The overhead lights snapped on, and a man's deep voice challenged, "Who's there?"

Stoner looked over to the door that connected with the house and saw a young, lean Italian in shirt-sleeves framed by the doorway. He held a heavy-looking pistol in his left hand.

"It must have been the cat," Stoner called to him. "The alarm's very sensitive, isn't it."

The youngster stepped down onto the cement floor and walked slowly between two of the cars toward Stoner. The hand holding the gun slowly dropped to his side.

"The cat?" His lean face had a day's stubble across its jaw. His dark eyes were flinty with suspicion. "There are no cats in here."

Stoner smiled at him. "Oh. I must have been mistaken."

"What are you doing down here?"

"I need the Ferrari. Do you know the combination for it?"

The guard squeezed his eyes shut, like a schoolboy strug-

gling in a spelling contest. When he finally opened them, the
suspicion was gone.

"Four fours," he said.

"Thanks," replied Stoner. "Could you open the door for
me?"

Slowly, like a man at war within himself, the guard backed
away from Stoner. He tucked the pistol into the waistband of
his pants, then turned and went to the plate on the wall that
held the door controls. Stoner slid in behind the Ferrari's
steering wheel and punched the number four on the dashboard keypad four times. The electric motor hummed instantly.

The garage doors swung up. Stoner turned on the car's
headlights and put it in gear. He waved to the guard as he
drove out onto the gravel driveway. The guard touched one
finger to his brow, his face a picture of confusion and worry.

Not bothering to figure out if the car's roof could be
dissolved, Stoner drove out into the night, swift and silent.
Wrought-iron gates loomed ahead in the glare of his headlights, but they opened silently, automatically, as he approached, then swung shut again behind him. There were no
direction signs on the hillside, but he simply kept pointing
downhill, toward the sea and the city hugging its shore. As
he expected, a dark car bearing three men swung out behind
him as he negotiated the first curve in the road beyond the
villa's gates.

It surprised him a little that the city was far from asleep.
The lights that had looked so romantic from the villa's patio
blazed along Naples's main thoroughfares. The streets were
clogged with cars, all of them dodging impatiently through
the traffic like a flotilla of New York taxi drivers, horns
bleating angrily and brakes screeching constantly.

Stoner reveled in the people's voices. Bel canto. He remembered that Naples was the city of song. But here the
tenors and baritones and occasional bassos were the drivers
of the cars, bellowing angrily at each other as they raced
aggressively to be the first ones to reach the next stoplight.
Even the women drove like maniacs. Stoner laughed and
pulled the Ferrari up to the curb next to a sidewalk cafe. The
black car that had been following him went by slowly; the
men inside got a good long look at him. Stoner smiled at
them. This late at night, they still affected dark glasses.

He got out of the car and studied the layout of the tiny

tables and the people sitting at them. There were couples along the front windows of the cafe, most of them turned to face each other, not the traffic strolling by along the sidewalk. The tables nearest the curb were all occupied by men, some of them young and sleekly handsome, some of them balding and portly, all of them openly ogling the women who sauntered past. The men all seemed to be in groups of at least four, clustered around their little tables. None of the women were alone, either; they came in pairs or larger groups.

Grinning, Stoner marveled at the game they played, the men eyeing the girls and calling after them, but seldom leaving the protection of their comrades; the women parading by, but pretending either to be deaf and blind or to be insulted by the men's attentions.

He found an unoccupied table off at the far end of the cafe's stretch of sidewalk and ordered an espresso. The waiter was a human being, an old man, lean and gnarled as an olive tree, with a complexion the color of a tobacco stain.

"And bring an anisette with it," Stoner added.

The waiter bowed.

Three men in sleek black windbreakers and skintight chinos came walking slowly along the sidewalk, peering through stylish smoked glasses at the people sitting at the tables. All three of them stared hard at Stoner, suddenly uncertain of themselves, then slowly walked on past. Stoner turned and watched them go down the street, knowing that they would not find him now.

The old waiter returned moments later with the demitasse of frothy black coffee, a sliver of lemon rind on the saucer, and a thimble-sized glass of clear liqueur. Stoner watched the byplay among the men and women as he sipped alternately at the espresso and the anisette. They made a good combination. One of the young males got to his feet, grinning at his companions, and started to follow a trio of girls down the street. In a few minutes he came back with one of the girls on his arm. He waved disdainfully at his erstwhile companions as he escorted the girl inside the cafe to find a table for themselves.

Stoner finished, and the waiter came to him with a scrap of paper. Smiling, he borrowed the waiter's pen and wrote his name on the flimsy bill. The waiter frowned, stared at the signature, then looked sharply at Stoner. Stoner shrugged.

The waiter shrugged. Stoner got to his feet and went back to the Ferrari.

It was almost dawn when he reached the airport. Parking the car at an empty taxi stand, where the police would quickly find it and track down its owner, he went inside and located the next flight out to Paris. It wasn't for several hours, so Stoner strolled through the empty, echoing terminal, looking for an open newsstand. There were none. But he found the Alitalia lounge for first-class passengers. The sleepy-eyed woman at the reception desk made a smile for him and didn't bother to ask to see his ticket.

A television set was flickering silently in one corner of the lounge. Stoner went to it and saw that it was tuned to an all-news channel. Next to the TV set was a rack of head-phones with a dial control that offered translation into six different languages. Stoner took a pair of headphones, set them to English, and plopped into the deep, soft cushions of the chair directly in front of the screen.

The commentator's voice was female, BBC English, dry and clipped. Stoner sat in growing horror as for three solid hours the television set showed nothing but disaster and tragedy.

The Central African War had spilled into Kenya as Zairian troops crossed the border in a series of coordinated attacks. Stoner watched jet planes swooping down to drop eggs of flaming death on villages and towns. Buildings exploded and burned, people ran in terror, clutching whatever meager pos-sessions they could carry, children crying and stumbling as the planes wheeled and dived overhead like hunting falcons. Soldiers appeared on the screen, black men in helmets and mottled camouflage uniforms, firing automatic weapons into thick clumps of bushes. Rockets flashed and roared toward distant hills. Explosions of dirty black smoke sent back faint echoes.

The scene shifted. Grim-faced men in business suits seated around a polished table. The Englishwoman's calm, flat words explained that the government of Nigeria was negotiating with representatives of Vanguard Industries and the Interna-tional Peacekeeping Force for purchase of an energy dome to protect the city of Lagos from possible nuclear attack.

Another shift. Three young white people, two men and a woman, lay sprawled stiffly along the side of a dirt road.

Peace Enforcers, the commentator's voice told Stoner, ambushed by Ethiopian guerrillas in the hills of Eritrea. Stoner felt a pang of alarm. Hadn't Richards told him that his daughter was married to a Peace Enforcer? Just what were they, anyway? he wondered.

But the images on the TV screen did not linger to explain. Famine and disease were sweeping the vast Indian subcontinent again, and an angry dark-faced man in Delhi charged that Vietnamese experiments in genetic warfare had caused the blight that had ruined the rice harvest and sent millions to their deaths. An equally angry Vietnamese stridently denied the charge and insisted that India was preparing to attack Vietnam to take the world's attention away from the failure of the Indian government to feed its own people.

In Switzerland a special international conference of scientists announced that the growing incidence of cancer deaths worldwide was merely the result of modern medicine having all but eliminated the previous leading killers: heart disease, stroke, and viral infections. But demonstrators on the street outside the conference hall insisted that the scientists had discovered a cure for cancer, which they refused to share with "the ordinary people."

Terrorists of the World Liberation Movement had struck at three separate places across the world during the previous twenty-four hours: A food-processing plant in Morocco had been gutted by an incendiary bomb. An electric power dam in the Canadian Rockies had been severely damaged by an explosion. And a trio of scientists, one American and two British, had been gunned down in front of their laboratory in Helsinki. A message left at a TV station in New York claimed that these "battles" had been fought by the World Liberation Movement's "freedom fighters" to help "their brothers struggling in central Africa."

And on. And on. Senseless murders and political assassinations. Sensational love affairs among the rich and famous. Pompous pronouncements by commentators who contradicted each other, and sometimes themselves.

Stoner watched it all, listened to every word, every inflection of voice, studied the expressions on the faces of the men and women, the tear-streaked faces of children torn from their homes by the pitiless fury of war, the greed and pride and self-centered stupidity of men and women in offices of high trust. How can they survive? Stoner wondered. How can the human race continue, day after day, year after year, with all this load of misery and hatred weighing it down?

Yet it was a rich world. Despite famines and wars, there was food enough to feed everyone. The human race was drawing resources from space now, mining the moon, smelting down entire asteroids rich in precious metals. But still there were famines. Still there were wars. Still the uncontrolled passions that led to murder and mass slaughter.

As Stoner watched, dawn brightened the sky. Sunlight filtered through the windows of the lounge. The cleaning robots that had been dutifully scouring the floors and polishing the furniture gave way to the morning's shift of receptionists and servers. Travelers came in, some still rubbing sleep from their eyes, others tense and angry even this early in the morning.

Stoner glanced up from the TV screen to the monitor on the wall and saw that a flight was leaving for Paris in half an hour. He noted the gate, then got up and headed for the door, merely another traveler in the growing swell of passengers, completely unnoticed except by the receptionist, who smiled at this tall, rugged-looking man in maroon blazer and turtleneck shirt. He's an American, I'll bet, she said to herself. It wasn't until many minutes after he had left the lounge that she realized that he had been carrying no luggage whatsoever; not even a shoulder bag.

Stoner made his way down to the gate where the Paris flight was departing, explained to the man handing out seat assignments that he had no money, no credit cards, no passport, no identification at all, but he would deeply appreciate a seat on this flight. The ticket agent frowned at first but soon smiled as Stoner spoke to him. He flicked his fingers over his computer keys and whisked out a boarding pass. After all, he admitted, this early flight is almost half-empty.

Stoner thanked him. The ticket agent wished him a pleasant flight. Stoner thanked him again and headed for the jetway that led out to the plane. The ticket agent watched him for a moment, his eyes blinking and an expression of puzzlement on his face. Then another passenger came up to his counter and he turned his attention to her.

The plane's interior was smaller than Stoner had expected, but as he took his assigned seat next to a window near the swept-back wing, he saw that the fuel truck filling the plane's tanks bore the red H_2 symbol of hydrogen, and its cylindrical body was rimed with a thin layer of frost. He remembered Richards telling him that trucks ran on hydrogen fuel now. So the plane did, too, and the extra tankage needed for the bulky fuel reduced the number of seats available for passengers. Hydrogen must be much cheaper than kerosene, he thought. And safer, he added hopefully.

The flight was swift, quiet, and uneventful. Most of the passengers dozed. Stoner ate the breakfast of juice, pastry, and coffee that the steward offered and gazed out the tiny window, watching the Mediterranean glittering under the climbing sun as the coast of Italy curved away and finally disappeared from sight.

The plane landed at Orly at 0715, less than an hour after leaving Naples. Stoner made his way past the French passport inspectors and customs agents with a pleasant smile and a few words. Inwardly he marveled at his newfound ability to get people to do what he wanted, but he was no longer surprised at it. You're not entirely human anymore, he reminded himself as he strode empty-handed through the airport terminal. The question is, are you more than an ordinary human or less? Are these talents really yours now, or are you merely a host for an extraterrestrial visitor?

He wondered briefly why he had left Jo sleeping in her bed. It would have been easy to make love with her. It would have been pleasant for both of them. Pleasant. He mulled the word in his mind. Pleasant isn't enough, he told himself. Not nearly enough. And the alien part of his mind shuddered at the thought of coupling like a primitive animal in heat.

The terminal was still fairly quiet this early in the morning. It looked more like an ultramodern museum of glass and chrome than a busy airport. Looking up through the sweeping windows, Stoner saw that the sky was gray with clouds; the sun had not yet broken through.

Pretty early to phone a friend, he told himself. Still, he made his way to the ticket counter and asked a lovely slim young agent there if he might use her phone. She hesitated only an instant before wordlessly handing it to him. He had to ask her how to get directory assistance. She looked troubled for a moment, then volunteered to place the call for him.

It took a few moments, but at last she handed him the

handpiece. Stoner had to lean across the countertop to see the picture screen of the phone terminal. He heard the reedy beep-beep of the ring at the other end. Twice. Three times.

A sleepy man's voice said, "*Allo!*"

The screen stayed blank.

"Claude? It's Keith Stoner."

A pause, a cough. Then, "Who?"

"Keith. Keith Stoner."

"No! C'est impossible!"

"It's me, Keith. I'm in Paris. At Orly Airport. Can I stay with you for a couple of days?"

He heard muttering and another voice. Nicole's, he was certain.

"Keith"—Claude returned to the phone—"is it really you? Truly?"

"Yes, Claude. I'm alive and well."

"But we have heard nothing about you for years!"

"I'll explain all that when I get there. Is it okay for me to stay with you?"

"Yes! Of course! You are at Orly? I'll drive out to pick you up."

"No, no," Stoner said. "That's not necessary. I'll take a taxi."

"But they are so expensive!"

Stoner grinned. Claude hadn't changed; still the frugal Frenchman.

"It's okay," he said, thinking that the real test of his powers would be when he tried to pay a Parisian taxi driver with a smile and a few soft words.

"I can be there in half an hour."

"No, please. I'll get a taxi. You're still at the same address?"

"Where else?"

"I'll see you in half an hour or so."

The cab driver knew that Stoner was an American even before he closed the door of the taxi.

"Please tell me in English," he said, looking at Stoner through the rearview mirror. "It will be easier for me to understand."

I'm in France all right, Stoner thought, laughing to himself.

The traffic on the road into Paris was heavy, mostly trucks, but far quieter than Stoner remembered from earlier years.

And there was none of the passionate Italian fury on the road. The Frenchmen drove just as fast, perhaps even faster, but with precision and Gallic coolness.

I must have sounded like a voice from the dead to Claude, he thought. They had been students together at the University of Texas, nearly thirty years earlier. Stoner made a mental note to be prepared for a Claude Appert who was now old enough to be his father, almost. And Nicole, he wondered. How have the years treated her?

He was surprised to see a phalanx of tall glass-and-steel towers barricading the view of Paris as they approached. Even here, he thought glumly, they've gone to high rises.

"You are very lucky to come into the city at this time of the morning," the cab driver said, suddenly talkative as they whisked past a row of slow-moving trucks. "The traffic remains light. This is the way Paris was in the old days, before every person had two cars and a truck. You can see the city now. In one hour from now, nothing but cars!"

It was still a city worth seeing. Skyscrapers might surround Paris like a besieging army, but the city itself was the same as it had been. The Eiffel Tower, the Seine and its bridges, the distant white dome of Sacré-Coeur glorious in the morning sun. Stoner craned his neck for a glimpse of Notre Dame, but it was too far down the bend in the Seine to be seen.

The driver threaded his cab through the mounting traffic circling l'Etoile, while Stoner admired the Arc de Triomphe.

They drove up quiet residential streets that grew increasingly familiar to Stoner until the driver stopped in the middle of a narrow way and announced, "Place de l'avenue du Bois," with Gallic finality. Cars were parked bumper to bumper along both sides of the street, halfway up on the curbs to keep a narrow path open for traffic. Six-story stone apartment buildings rose all around them.

Stoner spoke with the taxi driver for several minutes before he finally, grudgingly, yanked down the flag on his meter and muttered a curt, "*Bon,*" by way of dismissal. Stoner got out of the cab gratefully, and the driver gave him a final distrustful glance before putting the taxi in gear and cruising quietly down the narrow street.

Stoner looked around him. The apartment buildings were formidable, well-kept, expensive. Each set of buildings was arranged around a central courtyard. This is the high-rent district all right, he mused. Now which one of these buildings does Claude live in?

"Keith! My God, it is really you!"

CHAPTER 16

He turned to see Claude Appert, bundled in a long gray topcoat against the morning chill, waving to him from the gateway of one of the courtyards.

Stoner loped over to him and grabbed Appert's outstretched hand. "Claude, it's good to see you again."

"Keith . . . Keith . . ." The Frenchman groped for words, then gave it up and clasped Stoner around the shoulders.

They had been classmates. Now Claude Appert was nearly sixty years old. He had turned into the kind of Parisian that American filmgoers expect to see: slim, elegant, silvery hair, pencil-thin mustache, handsome face with expressive brown eyes. Beneath the open topcoat Stoner saw he was wearing a natty beige suit with an open-necked shirt and a neatly knotted silk foulard of paisley browns and tans. But that handsome face was sagging now; gravity was pulling at it, spiderwebbing it with wrinkles. The eyes had lost the luster Stoner remembered from years earlier. His old classmate was visibly crumbling with age.

Appert held Stoner at arm's length and studied his face for several moments. "You haven't changed a bit. You are exactly the same as the last time we saw you."

Stoner cast back in his memory. "At the astrophysical congress in Vienna."

"Yes. You were working on the telescope in orbit then."

"Big Eye." Stoner nodded. "That was just before we found the alien spacecraft."

"Nearly twenty years ago."

"I've spent eighteen of those years sleeping."

Appert smiled. "No wonder you look so refreshed!"

He clapped Stoner on the back, and they walked side by side toward the entrance to his apartment building.

"It's good of you to take me in like this," Stoner said. "Especially on such short notice, and this early in the morning."

The Parisian shrugged. "I am an early riser always. But Nicole is not. Yet even she is up and around, preparing a good breakfast in your honor."

"I am overwhelmed."

The two men laughed as they strode through the apartment building's tiny lobby and squeezed into the small, open cage of the elevator. The Apperts' home was on the top floor, a large set of spacious, high-ceilinged rooms filled with antique furniture and family heirlooms. Claude Appert, a student at the Sorbonne studying astrophysics on a merit scholarship, had fallen madly in love with a wisp of a girl who needed his tutoring in science to pass her first year's exams. It was nearly a year before he discovered that she was the only child of the count de Rochemont. Claude had met his prospective in-laws in this same apartment, which had been the family's Paris home since the building had been erected, at the turn of the last century.

Nicole de Rochemont Appert was small and slight, dark of hair and eye, pale in complexion, and possessed of the utter self-assurance that comes from being the only child of wealthy parents. She greeted Stoner at the foyer of their apartment with a passionate embrace and warm kisses on both cheeks. Stoner kissed her back, gladly, with all the happiness of greeting a cherished friend. Nicole wore a burgundy sweater and light gray woolen skirt. Her short hair was perfectly coiffed, her makeup so well applied that it was unnoticeable. Already she held a cigarette in her right hand.

"Keith," she said in her husky voice. "Keith, you are alive. And still the most handsome scientist in the world." She bussed him again on both cheeks.

He squeezed her waist and said, "The most jealous scientist, you mean. Because you found Claude before I had the chance to find you."

She laughed, low and throaty. "Keith, you are so gallant. I am old enough now to be your mother, almost."

"Almost doesn't count."

"And you have learned to speak French," she said, pleased. "With a good accent, too."

"I didn't even notice," Appert said. "Yes, you never spoke French before. . . ."

Stoner hadn't realized it himself. It seemed perfectly natural to him. Shrugging almost like a Parisian, he said, "I'm glad you approve of the accent."

"Come." Claude took his arm. "Let me show you to your room. You can wash up while breakfast is put on the table."

Stoner let Appert lead him from the foyer down the hallway that bisected the apartment. The rooms were just as he remembered them, with magnificent high ceilings and long, airy windows covered by delicate curtains of Belgian lace. There were four bedrooms in addition to the parlor, dining room, and what looked like an office. The furnishings were quietly luxurious: dark woods and tasteful fabrics. Oriental carpets. The place smelled of old wealth.

"The children have all gone off on their own?" he asked.

"Ah, yes," Appert said with a sigh. "Scattered to the four corners of the globe. All of them married, except Philip, who is managing the tourist hotel on the moon. I think he is his own best customer, you know, as far as women are concerned."

Stoner laughed. "You're a grandfather, then."

"Yes, of course. Three granddaughters—not counting anything Philip might have accomplished accidentally."

They entered the rearmost bedroom. It was smallish, but very comfortable and quiet. A massive mahogany wardrobe stood against one wall, nearly reaching the ceiling. An exquisitely delicate chiffonier was on the other side. Somehow the two pieces blended perfectly. The bed was large and stood high off the floor on heavy carved legs. A pale blue silk throw covered it.

"They will be coming here for Christmas, all of them, except Philip, who cannot get away for the holidays," Appert continued. "It will be wonderful to see them." He tapped a finger against the side of his nose. "And even more wonderful when they all leave."

Stoner grinned at him as he headed for the bathroom. "I don't have any luggage," he said. "I suppose I'll have to buy some clothes."

Appert called through the half-open door, "Look through

the armoire. Perhaps some of Denis's clothes will fit you. He grew rather tall.''

Stoner rummaged through the clothes hanging in the wardrobe and found a pair of jeans that were long enough for him and a shirt that was only slightly tight across the shoulders.

"What do you think?" he asked as he examined himself in the full-length mirror on the back of the wardrobe's door.

"Like a young cowboy," said Appert.

As they headed toward the dining room, Stoner asked, "Three granddaughters? Are you hoping for a grandson?"

Appert arched a silver eyebrow. "Nicole and I are, but our two married sons and our daughter have each opted for daughters. If they decide to have second children, I suppose they will have sons."

"You can choose?"

"Of course!" Appert looked mildly surprised. Then he remembered. "Ah, you have been sleeping for eighteen years."

Nicole's idea of preparing breakfast was to give the cook detailed instructions on what she desired. She was waiting for them at the dining room table, staring out the curtained window at the cloudy sky, chin in hand, cigarette dangling from a corner of her mouth.

"I don't think I've been up this early in the morning since I am a child," she said as Stoner and her husband entered the dining room.

"I'm terribly sorry," Stoner said. "I didn't stop to think. . . .''

"If it were anyone but you, Keith, I would have stayed in bed."

Stoner bowed slightly, then took one of the heavy high-backed chairs and sat between her and Claude.

"She's telling you the truth, you know," Appert said as he sat down. "Last summer she slept through a visit from the president of France."

"No!"

Nicole shrugged. "He is only a politician."

"And you got up for me?"

"Of course. You are an old and dear friend whom we thought we had lost forever. You have returned from the dead, Keith, and I want to hear all about it. Every detail."

"Okay. But do you have to smoke?"

"It bothers you?"

"Only because it's harming you," he said.

She laughed. "No, no. It is perfectly safe now. Harmless. Like eating candy."

Stoner frowned. "I understand that cancer is not only the number-one cause of death worldwide, but that its incidence is growing."

"Pooh!" said Nicole. "That may be so, but it is not from cigarettes. Not anymore. We have developed synthetic tobacco—all the pleasure of the real thing but none of the risks. No carcinogens. None at all."

"I don't believe—"

"It's quite true," Appert said. "A breakthrough from the biologists. I have even returned to my pipe."

"So you see, my dear Keith," Nicole teased, "you must give up your prejudice against smoking. It is a harmless pleasure now, like eating candy."

Stoner felt suspicious. "Candy can give you cavities," he muttered.

"Not anymore," Appert corrected. "We have had vaccines against tooth decay for more than ten years."

Nicole blew smoke languidly toward the recessed paneling of the cofferwork ceiling. Appert smiled at him like a Cheshire cat.

Finally Stoner broke into a grin. "What do you people do for vices, then?"

They laughed together. "There is still greed and avarice," Nicole said. "And gluttony, I suppose, although the biologists have also produced a reducing pill that actually works."

"Lust!" Appert said firmly. "When all else fails, there is still lust."

At that point the maid pushed through the door from the kitchen. She was a heavyset girl with a round, pinkish face and brawny arms. She bore a laden silver tray in her hands and a pained expression on her face. At Nicole's order she placed the tray on the sideboard, then served the breakfast of fresh juice, delicate, feather-light crepes, croissants, jellies, and coffee. Both Nicole and her husband added milk liberally to their cups. Stoner took his coffee black.

The maid left the room, pushing a stubborn wisp of hair away from her eyes.

"She's Spanish," Stoner said.

"You can't get good help except for the Spaniards," Nicole answered.

"Or robots," said Appert.

"I will not have one of those mechanical creatures in my home!" she snapped.

Appert raised a hand tiredly. Stoner realized that they had argued over this many times.

Nicole came to the same realization. The fire in her eyes calmed, and she smiled at their visitor. "Please," she said to Stoner, gesturing toward the food, "help yourself."

For a few minutes all three of them concerned themselves with getting breakfast onto their plates. Finally, though, Nicole asked again:

"Now, you must tell us *everything*."

Stoner smiled at her. Not everything, he thought. There's so much that I don't understand myself.

But he began to talk, starting with the frantic days so long ago when he had first discovered that a spacecraft from another star had entered the solar system and was heading toward Earth.

"And the alien creature inside it," Nicole asked, "he was dead?"

"Yes. For God knows how many centuries. The spacecraft was his sarcophagus. He had his body sent out drifting among the stars."

"But why?"

"An interstellar gesture of goodwill," Stoner said, absolutely certain of it. "A one-way wanderer, preserved for the aeons. If his spacecraft happened to drift into a star system that had habitable planets, the computer on board was smart enough to steer it toward those worlds."

Appert shook his head slightly. "A computer that can still function after thousands of years."

"Millions, more likely. He left his world before there were any human beings on Earth." Turning back to Nicole, he went on. "The alien was offering himself—his body, all the knowledge that he could cram into the spacecraft—as a gift from the stars. It was his way of telling whoever he stumbled across that there are other intelligent races in the universe, and they mean us no harm."

"Fantastic."

Stoner nodded. "I suppose it is fantastic, at that."

The morning lengthened into noon as Stoner told them how he had literally forced the United States and Soviet Russia into a cooperative mission to reach the alien's spacecraft. And how he had decided to remain aboard it rather than return to Earth.

"It was a crazy thing to do," he told them before they could ask. "After all the work and struggle to reach the spacecraft, things turned out so that we only had a few minutes to inspect it. There had been political problems, even sabotage. I knew that if I left the spacecraft, we would never get back to it again. It would drift out of the solar system while the politicians argued about it. So I stayed aboard. I turned off my spacesuit heater and joined the alien. . . ." He halted, realizing that he had joined the alien in a literal sense. "We both became frozen."

"But you were not dead," Nicole said.

"No. Not dead."

"You offered your body as a hostage," Appert realized. "The world could not allow you to drift away on the alien ship. Someone had to rescue you."

Stoner nodded. "And to rescue me, they had to go out and get the alien spacecraft before it drifted out of the solar system altogether."

"I see," said Nicole. "So you forced them to bring the alien ship back to Earth."

"It's in orbit a couple of hundred miles above us," Stoner said.

"And you are back among us." Nicole smiled at him.

"Yes, but . . ." The words almost froze on his tongue. "But I feel almost like an alien myself. This world has changed a lot since I left it."

Appert glanced at his wife, then turned back to Stoner. "There have been many changes, that is true. Most of them have been very good. We no longer live under the threat of nuclear annihilation."

"So I understand."

"And we have the energy of the stars now," Nicole said.

"Fusion power, you mean."

"Yes, fusion," said Appert.

Stoner saw that his old friend looked uncomfortable. "What is it, Claude? What's bothering you?"

"You won't mind if I ask a personal question?"

"Of course not."

"We are delighted to have you here, Keith. Delighted that you are alive and well. But—you call suddenly at an early hour, you arrive without luggage, without even a razor or toothbrush. You give every appearance of being a fugitive."

"We are concerned for your safety," Nicole added. "Are you in trouble? Can we help?"

Stoner laughed softly and saw the Apperts go from concern to surprise to relief, all in the flicker of an eye.

"I'm not a fugitive from justice," he told them. "I merely ran away from the people who wanted to hold on to me so that they could study me. I got tired of being a laboratory specimen."

"Ah." Appert leaned back in his chair, understanding.

"These are the same people who revived you?" Nicole asked.

"Yes. They have the feeling that they own me. I feel differently."

"I see."

"Who are these people?" Appert asked.

"A research group—part of Vanguard Industries."

"Vanguard." Appert seemed impressed.

"You know of them?"

"Perhaps the largest multinational corporation in the world," Nicole said. "Bigger even than Eurogenetics or Philips/Nestlé."

Now Stoner felt impressed. "I didn't know that."

Appert gestured with one hand. "Vanguard has an annual budget that is almost as large as that of the government of France. It is a huge corporation."

"They will be looking for you very hard, I think," said Nicole.

"I suppose they will," Stoner admitted.

"You will be safe here, though," Nicole assured him. Her husband nodded.

"But I can't stay for long," Stoner blurted.

"Why not?"

The idea formed in his mind as he spoke the words, as if the information were being transmitted to him from some distant point of origin.

"I've got to see one of the men who worked with me, eighteen years ago. A Russian. His name is Kirill Markov."

CHAPTER 17

Jo awoke knowing that Stoner had gone.

She sat up in her bed, still dressed in the long gown she had worn at dinner. She felt more rested and refreshed than she had in years. And she knew that Stoner had left her.

For nearly half an hour she sat there, waiting for the fury that would inevitably rise up inside her. But instead she felt a different emotion. She looked into the mirror above the dressing table on the wall opposite the bed and saw that she was smiling cheerfully.

"He's free," she said aloud. "After all these years, he's free. On his own, like a boy playing hooky from school."

A boy worth a billion dollars, she reminded herself. The smile faded from her lips. Jo slouched back onto the pillows and started thinking about how she should deal with her husband and the others in Vanguard Industries who would try to destroy her.

She showered quickly and put on a business suit, planning ahead as she dressed, picturing the attitudes of Nillson and the other board members. After a quick breakfast of coffee and fruit juice, she phoned Rome and instructed her office there to send a plane to Naples for her, then had her darkly brooding majordomo drive her to the Naples airport.

Security at the villa is gone, she thought grimly. They know about the place now.

"Salvatore," she called to her majordomo, who was driving the limousine.

He glanced up at the rearview mirror to see her. "*Sì, signora?*"

In Italian, Jo instructed him to sell the villa and find a different one, farther south, in Calabria, perhaps, or on the Adriatic coast of Apulia.

Salvatore said nothing. He was a man of few words, a

distant cousin of Jo's whom she trusted with the faith of blood.

She watched his eyes in the mirror, then got a better idea.

"Salvatore, don't sell the villa. Keep it for yourself and your family as your own home. But find me another place farther south. And on the sea."

Salvatore actually turned to look at her over his shoulder. "For myself and my family, signora?"

"In appreciation of your loyal service," Jo said.

The limo wavered slightly, and he turned back to give his full attention to driving. Jo smiled. *That had surprised him; even broken through his rigid self-control a smidgen. But he deserves the villa, especially if it helps keep him loyal. And besides,* she thought, *if I don't sell it, everybody will think that I still use it.*

When they got to the airport and threaded their way through the maze of roads to the area where private planes were hangared, Jo saw a sleek, swept-wing jet painted gleaming white with the stylized green V of Vanguard Industries emblazoned on its tail already waiting for her. Salvatore actually kissed her hand as she left the limousine, a thoroughly unusual burst of emotion, for him.

The supersonic flight to New York took three hours, which Jo used the way she would use any ordinary morning in her office. With a phone terminal and access to her computer files, she conducted business as usual. And ordered Archie Madigan to meet her in Greenwich. His private secretary said he was in London, but she would reach him and have him in Jo's office before the end of the day.

It was not quite seven A.M. when the jet taxied up to the Vanguard Industries' hangar at Greenwich Airport. Another limousine was waiting for Jo, and she was whisked quickly and silently to the Vanguard corporate headquarters, an imposing black tower of anodized meteoric steel, processed in Vanguard's zero-gravity orbital mill, and long columns of smoked glass, set back on the wide, tree-lined lawn of an old estate.

It was still officially the corporation's headquarters, although Nillson had moved all the officers to the laboratory complex in Hilo. For the sake of security. Demonstrators could picket this brooding tower in Greenwich, but terrorists would not find any of the corporation's key people there to be kidnapped. The Hawaii site was easier to defend. Hilo was six thousand miles away from teeming New York City; Greenwich a mere ten.

Having spent the flight across the Atlantic tending to ordinary business affairs, the first thing Jo did once she got into her office was to phone Gene Richards in Hawaii. The psychiatrist was not at the lab complex, said the computer voice of his telephone terminal. Jo instructed the computer to find him and have him call her.

Her office here, near the shrine of Wall Street, was more orthodox than the one she had in Hilo. It was a large room, big enough for a long conference table surrounded by eight high-backed leather chairs, a wide couch flanked by end tables, and four armchairs. Jo sat behind a desk of dark Brazilian cherrywood, in a custom-fashioned leather swivel chair that she always found just the slightest bit uncomfortable. The floor was covered with an exquisite Persian carpet, made to order and a gift of the new Iranian government, which owed its rise to power to Vanguard Industries' generous financing and paramilitary assistance. The walls were hung with neomodernist paintings: mostly abstracts, which Jo abhorred. Doors led to a fully stocked bar she never used, a mirror-walled bathroom, and a small but comfortable bedroom complete with a waterbed.

On the other side of the room there was a single door that connected with the office of the chairman of the board. As Jo leaned back in her chair, waiting for the phone's computer system to track down Richards, that door opened and Nillson stepped through.

"Ah. You *are* here."

Jo nodded to him. "I'm here."

"Finished your fling with the astronaut?" Nillson walked slowly across the office and settled himself in one of the armchairs facing her desk, lanky legs and arms folding like a giraffe settling down on the ground. The expression on his face was unreadable: a slight, twisted smile that might have been anything from mild amusement to buried rage.

"It wasn't a fling," Jo said, suddenly feeling weary. "I took him out of the labs for security reasons."

"Security?" Nillson's white eyebrows rose a centimeter.

"I found out about the television project you okayed."

"Did you?"

Deliberately keeping her voice casual, Jo asked, "Your ex-director of corporate public relations—did she find out you're impotent?"

Splotches of angry red appeared on his pallid cheeks. "I am not impotent!"

Smiling sweetly, Jo said, "Medically, maybe. But what they have to go through before you can get it up . . ."

Voice trembling, Nillson said, "I didn't come in here to discuss my sex life with you."

"Nor mine," Jo snapped. "I took Stoner out of the labs because the place was starting to leak like the *Titanic*. And I don't like you playing at being the jealous husband."

With an obvious effort, Nillson fought down the anger that had seized him. His hands unclenched, his face lost its color.

"All right. So you took Stoner off to a safe house," he said, his voice barely under control. "Why didn't you tell me about it?"

"I was going to—but not over the phone. I made a special trip here to see you, but you chose to stay in Hilo."

"I had special business to take care of."

Shrugging, Jo said, "Who was she?"

He ignored that. "So where is the illustrious Dr. Stoner now? Where have you got him hidden?"

Jo hesitated while several different possibilities whirled through her mind. Finally she chose the only one that she could.

"He got away," she said.

Nillson blinked.

"I don't know how he did it, but he walked out of my house last night and disappeared."

Through clenched teeth her husband grated, "That's . . . not . . . possible."

"Were you having my villa watched?" Jo asked.

"Of course not. You've never seen fit to tell me where it is, remember?"

"You never even tried to find out?"

"Where is Stoner?"

Jo shook her head. "I don't know. That's why I've come back here, to organize a search for him."

"I don't believe you."

"And I don't believe that it wasn't your people who were

watching the villa—'' She stopped abruptly, then realized, ''Unless it was the Russians.''

''Russians? Why would they . . . ?''

''For the same reason we want him. The same reason the competition wants him. God knows how much of the alien's secrets he's got locked inside his brain.''

''And you let him just walk away from you?'' Nillson's voice was rising, the angry color coming back to his cheeks.

Jo felt glad that there was a desk separating them. She knew how violent he could be.

''Ev,'' she said as soothingly as she knew how, ''he's not an ordinary human being. You have no idea of the''—she groped for the word—''the *power* he has.''

''Power? What are you talking about?''

''Ask Richards, back at Hilo. Something happened to Stoner while he was in the alien spacecraft. He's different now . . . different from any human being you've ever met.''

''Where is he?'' Nillson repeated.

''I don't know!''

''Why are you hiding him from me? What are you trying to pull?''

''I'm not hiding him,'' Jo said, hearing her own voice rise. But not with anger. It was fear that was moving her now. ''I'm trying to find him!''

Nillson got to his feet and glared down at her. ''We'll see. We'll just damned well see!''

And he strode out of her office. Jo slumped back in her chair. She knew what he was capable of, and she knew she had to take steps to protect herself from him.

The Russians. Could they have been snooping around the villa? It had been months since she had talked with Kirill Markov. More than a year, she thought. She touched the phone terminal's keypad and asked the machine to connect her with Markov, wherever he was.

It wasn't until well after lunch hour that Jo realized neither Markov nor Gene Richards had answered her calls. Checking with the phone, she heard the same computer answer to both her queries:

''Unlocated as yet. Still trying to reach him.''

At least Archie Madigan showed up, late in the afternoon. The lawyer looked as if he had just showered, shaved, and put on his best Wall Street high-collared imitation Mandarin tunic.

"Jo, my dear, your message sounded urgent," he said as he dropped onto the couch by the bedroom door.

Staying behind her desk despite its distance from the couch, Jo replied, "Have you heard that Stoner's disappeared?"

"Got away from you, did he?"

"He certainly did."

Madigan shook his head as if in disbelief. "I thought you'd have him all buttoned up in a well-guarded place."

"I did. But he just walked out."

"Walked?"

"Actually he took one of my cars. It was found at the airport."

"In sunny Napoli?"

She nodded wearily. His affectations could get tiresome.

"You've started a search for him?"

"Yes. Of course. But it isn't going to be easy."

Madigan's brows knit slightly. "How far can he get? He doesn't have any money on him, and no credit, no ID. He's practically naked as a newborn baby."

Briefly, Jo debated telling Madigan about the strange power she sensed in Stoner. Instead, she said, "If he's been kidnapped by the competition—or by the Russians . . ."

"You think so?"

"I don't know! Apparently he just talked his way past my own guards and drove my car to the airport. But I don't know if he's acting by himself or if he had help."

"You think he might have deliberately gone off with somebody?"

"If he did, it's with Markov."

"The Russian."

"They were friends back at Kwajalein."

"But you don't really believe that, do you?" Madigan probed. "From the look on your lovely face, I'd say you think he went off by himself, and that scares you."

She stared at Madigan for a moment, then admitted, "You're right. And it does scare me. I want to get Gene Richards in here. He's the one who's worked closest with Stoner. I want a complete report on what he's found, and I want him to give it to me in person."

Madigan put on his most doleful expression. "That's not going to be possible."

"Why not?"

The lawyer sighed. "Dr. Richards met with an accident this morning. On the highway. Jumped the lane divider and ran into a truck at extremely high speed."

"He's dead?"

Madigan nodded.

Jo immediately said, "Then I want his notes, his tapes, his entire files—everything! I want them *here,* by tomorrow morning."

"That might not be so easy to do."

"What do you mean?"

Getting slowly to his feet and walking toward Jo's desk, Madigan said, "Your husband ordered all of Richards's files be sent to him, as soon as he heard about the accident."

Jo felt her lips compressing into a tense, hard line.

"Strange thing," Madigan went on. "Your husband had a long meeting with Richards yesterday. Hours and hours, they were closeted in Ev's office together. Then this morning Richards goes out, gets into his car, and takes off. An hour later we got the word that he had been killed."

"And Everett has his files."

"Everything."

So he knew whatever Richards knew, Jo realized. Or he will as soon as he reads the files. He'll know more about Keith than I do.

"The truck that killed Richards . . ." she started to ask.

"It wasn't one of ours," Madigan answered before she could frame the question. "And there was no mechanical foul play with the poor man's car, either."

None reported, Jo corrected silently. Everett had him killed. And he's furious enough now to do the same to me.

CHAPTER 18

The airport was shrouded in fog, and Stoner doubted that a small plane would be able to land safely. He glanced at the wristwatch Claude Appert had loaned him. Almost midnight. Markov's plane was probably already overhead, circling.

But Stoner could hear nothing. The little airport seemed deserted, empty. The lights marking the edges of its one paved runway gleamed weakly in the cold gray fog. The cement ramp on which Stoner stood, just outside the airport's brick administration building, was slick and puddled. The bricks dripped moisture.

Stoner pulled the collar of his trench coat closer around his throat. The fog's cold fingers reached for him, wormed their way to his skin, chilled him. He shivered slightly, remembering the cold that had ended his earlier life. He did not like the cold. Or the darkness of this night.

Yet he smiled. How like Kirill, he thought. As melodramatic as a Victorian temperance play. Markov the romantic, picking midnight at a fog-shrouded airport miles out in the French countryside for their first meeting in eighteen years.

The night was absolutely still. The few men and women working at the airport stayed sensibly inside the administration building. In the misty distance, Stoner could make out the ghostly forms of private planes, single-engined, most of them, sitting in a line like sleeping birds. Their wings gleamed with wetness as they waited for the warmth of the morning sun.

A faint tendril of sound. Stoner turned his eyes skyward, trying to penetrate the fog. Yes, the purr of an engine, coming closer. Straining every sense, as if he could force the plane to appear, Stoner stood locked in place, waiting tensely.

Markov's voice, over the phone, had not sounded surprised. Strained, worried, perhaps even afraid. But not surprised to hear from the man who had been his friend eighteen years ago; a man who had ended his life aboard an alien spacecraft, more than a million miles from Earth.

Like a supernatural apparition, the plane seemed to take shape out of the fog, its single engine buzzing quietly. Or perhaps the fog's muffling the sound, Stoner thought.

It touched down on the wet concrete and rolled along on three wheels, then turned neatly and stopped. Stoner remained where he had been standing. A hatch on the plane's side opened, and a short, solidly built man stepped lightly to the ground. That's not Kirill, Stoner realized. But he took a step forward toward the plane, then another.

Watching as he walked forward, Stoner saw the Russian reach up to the hatch and help another man down to the concrete. An old man, rail thin and bent, bareheaded but wrapped in a long dark overcoat and muffler. He carried a cane, and once the younger Russian removed his helping hands, he walked slowly, hesitantly, like a man on a high wire, fearful that the slightest misstep would plunge him to his death.

But Stoner was moving faster, almost loping toward the slowly advancing Russian. Squinting through the fog he saw that it truly was his old friend. Stooped, aged, his face lined, his hair and beard gone completely white. But it was Kirill Markov.

"Kir!" he called out. "It's me, Keith!"

Markov stopped and leaned on his cane. "Keith . . . my friend, my dear, dear friend."

Stoner reached him at last and wrapped his arms around the old man's frail frame. Markov clasped Stoner, too, and they held on to each other for long moments.

It is customary, a voice in Stoner's mind whispered, as if explaining the gesture to a visitor. It is a show of affection to hold someone in one's arms. Also, the ritual symbolizes peaceful intent, showing that one holds no weapons in one's hand, nor has any concealed upon one's body.

He waited for Markov to pull himself loose. The Russian seemed to be leaning on Stoner for support. Finally Stoner disengaged and, holding the Russian by the shoulders, looked deeply at him.

The years had not been kind to Markov. The blue eyes that once had twinkled with boyish mischievousness were now watery and lined with dark pouches. His cheeks were hollow, and even his smile tinged with grief.

"Kirill, it's good to see you again." Stoner meant it, even though he was saddened to see how his friend had aged.

Markov nodded, eyes closed. "I knew you would come back someday. I only hoped that I would live long enough to see it."

His voice was soft and slightly quavering.

"Come on now," Stoner said, sliding one arm around Markov's narrow shoulders. "How old are you, sixty?"

"I will be sixty-six by the end of this year."

"Ready for retirement?"

Markov laughed softly, but there was bitterness in it. "In the old days I would be just getting started on my career. The Soviet Union was called a gerontocracy, remember?"

They were walking slowly back toward the administration building. Stoner had no idea of where they would be going from there, but he instinctively headed for light and warmth. This damp cold can't be good for an old man, he told himself, knowing that he wanted to be out of it himself.

"In the old days?" Stoner echoed.

"The Soviet Union has changed enormously, Keith," said the Russian. "Because of you."

"Me?"

"In a sense, my dear friend, you have destroyed the Soviet Union. There is little left of it, today, except the wreckage."

Stoner looked into Markov's eyes. The pain that he had seen elsewhere was in them, but sharper, deeper.

"Your wife." It was not a question. Stoner knew.

"Maria Kirtchatovska is dead. Part of the turmoil that has racked my country for many years now. She was a casualty in the battles that have shaken the KGB and the Kremlin."

"I'm sorry." It sounded pathetically weak, even to Stoner himself.

"She went peacefully enough. They allowed her to take a painless drug."

"But you're . . ." How to phrase it? "You're not in any danger?"

The bitter smile returned to his old friend's bloodless lips. "I am a high official of what's left of the Soviet government. I am general secretary of the National Academy of Sciences."

"You?"

Markov's smile broadened, and Stoner could feel the pain radiating from him. "Yes, me. You see how much Mother

Russia has changed? A half-baked linguist known chiefly for chasing after his female students has become top dog at the academy. Thanks to you.''

They had reached the door to the administration building, but Markov showed no inclination to go inside.

"The strange thing is," he said, "our marriage was finally beginning to go well. Maria and I were just starting to understand each other, after all those years, when the storm struck.''

"I really don't know what's happened," Stoner said. "No one's told me anything about it.''

Markov looked up at him, the gaunt, aged shell of the man who had once befriended Stoner and worked beside him on the distant atoll called Kwajalein.

"You remember Jo Camerata, of course," he said.

"Sure.''

"Yes. She was in love with you.''

Stoner nodded.

"Once you decided to remain aboard the alien spacecraft, Jo returned to America. We communicated back and forth. At first she phoned almost every week, or I phoned her. Then the interval between calls grew longer. She went for months without calling.''

"And?" Stoner prompted.

"Ah, forgive me." Markov smiled, almost shyly this time. "One of the attributes of old age. I tend to wander.''

"That's all right. I want to know everything that happened.''

"She fought her way to the top of one of the largest corporations in the world," Markov said, his voice taking on a new crispness. "She acquired the power she needed to send an expedition out to the edge of the solar system, to retrieve the alien spacecraft.''

"With me in it.''

"Yes, you and the dead alien.''

"And she brought us back to Earth," Stoner said.

"Not without Russian help. The Soviet government insisted that we take part in the rescue mission and that all scientific knowledge gathered from the alien spacecraft be shared through the United Nations.''

"I see.''

"Jo's corporation still reaped fantastic profits from what has been learned from the alien ship.''

"Yes, I know."

"The two most important discoveries, so far, have been the energy shield and the fusion power generator."

"Which have made the world safe from nuclear war," Stoner said.

"And destroyed the Soviet Union."

"What? How can . . ."

Markov shrugged, and the bitterness that Stoner had felt seemed to return. "Without the threat of nuclear weapons, the power of both the Soviet Union and the United States has dwindled enormously. For America, this has not had very bad repercussions. But for Russia, the change has been very painful."

"I don't understand."

"It happened at a time when the old leadership—the gerontocracy of earlier years—had died away and a new generation of younger men was in charge of the Kremlin. Suddenly the threat of nuclear attack disappears. The world turns upside down. Eastern Europe goes into turmoil. Poland, Czechoslovakia, Hungary all renounce the Warsaw Pact. The Germans reunite themselves and tell both East and West to go to hell. The Soviet Union itself is split. The Ukrainians want independence. Moslem fanatics want to split the Kazakh and other Asian republics away from the USSR. Riots break out in Moscow—over television broadcasts from the West! The people suddenly demanded Western television shows and an end to shortages and restrictions of all kinds. The government tottered."

"And that's when Maria . . . ?"

"She was a victim of the turmoil, yes. That was part of it. The situation is still volatile—like a bottle of nitroglycerin. Russia may explode at any moment."

"And it's my fault," Stoner said.

Markov hesitated, then gave a weary sigh. "Yes, my old friend, it is at least partly your fault. But don't be dismayed. Some of us are trying to build a new Russia, a stronger country, with the freedoms that we have yearned for over all these long centuries."

"I wish you luck."

"It will take more than luck," Markov said. "We face civil war. Even the Baltic republics have declared their inde-

pendence. And there are still plenty of enemies in the West
who would be delighted to see the USSR dismembered.''

"At least you don't have to worry about a nuclear
holocaust.''

"No," Markov agreed. "But there are poisonous gases
and biological agents that can kill just as many people as
hydrogen bombs would. The energy screens can't stop them.''

For the first time, Stoner felt a shudder of alarm race
through him. "Kirill, you don't think anybody would use
such weapons, do you?''

"They exist. In plentiful numbers. They can even be
attached to the missiles that once held the nuclear warheads.''

"But that's insanity!''

Markov's sad eyes regarded him wearily. "Yes, once I
thought so, too.''

"You still believe so," Stoner said firmly. But he realized
that Markov's sadness was more than personal grief. The
Russian bore the yoke of responsibility now, and it was
crushing him.

"Keith, my first loyalty is to Mother Russia. Can you
understand that?''

"Not to the Soviet Union?''

"Russia," said Markov. His voice was soft, but all the
strength of his heritage and his people was in it. "I must do
what is best for Mother Russia.''

"Of course," Stoner said. "I understand.''

"Then you know that you must come back to Moscow
with me.''

Stoner felt no surprise at all.

"I would not do this for myself, Keith," Markov said,
"but it is necessary for my nation. There is knowledge in
your mind, Keith, fantastic knowledge that not even you are
aware of.''

"You think so?''

Markov nodded slowly. "We know everything about you,
Keith. We have all your medical records, transcripts of all
the conversations you've had with Dr. Richards. Our best
scientists have studied you like astronomers studying a distant star.''

"And now they want to study me at first hand.''

"Yes. I'm afraid so.''

"But what if I refuse to go with you, Kirill?''

The Russian took a breath, then let it out in a slightly wheezing sigh. "Keith, I ask you to do this for me, for the sake of our old friendship. I need your help."

Stoner looked past the white-haired old man, out into the cold night fog. Half a dozen men were waiting out there, he realized. Not merely the two that had accompanied Markov in the plane, but others who had come to the airport silently. Armed men, prepared to follow the orders they had received.

"If I refuse, you'll be in trouble? In danger?"

"No," Markov snapped. "We have progressed beyond that primitive stage. I will not be sent to Siberia for failing my mission."

Eighteen years ago, he would have said that as a joke, Stoner remembered. Now he's completely serious.

Markov went on. "You are the most important man on Earth, Keith. Your mind holds untold treasures of the alien's technology. The secrets of their civilization are locked inside your brain."

Stoner closed his eyes and pictured the interior of the alien spacecraft. The strange swirling writing that was engraved around the base of the alien's bier was clear to him. He could understand the craft's engines, how they converted gravitational field flow to directed thrust. He could see how to convert a handful of dust into enough energy to heat and light a mighty city.

But when he opened his eyes and looked at his old friend again, he realized that none of this was as important as the fact that a human being had been returned from frozen death.

"How old is the head of your government, Kirill? What's the average age of the Central Committee? It may not be a gerontocracy anymore, but they're all older than you, aren't they?"

"Keith, you must come with me. Neither of us has any choice."

Markov fumbled in the pocket of his overcoat and pulled out a strange-looking pistol. Stoner sensed the six other men moving through the fog toward them.

"Would you really use that on me, Kirill?"

"It isn't lethal. It fires a dart that puts you to sleep." But there were tears in the Russian's eyes.

"You won't need it," Stoner said.

"You'll come with me?" The surprise on Markov's face was obvious.

"Yes, of course," Stoner said. "But not now."

The Russian blinked with confusion.

"I'm not ready to meet your leaders in Moscow. Or your scientists. I don't really want to be dissected just yet—even if it's just my mind they want to take apart."

"But—"

"I'll see you again, Kir. I'll come to Moscow on my own power. But not tonight."

Markov raised the pistol to the level of Stoner's chest. Stoner did nothing, said nothing. *If his finger starts to tighten on the trigger, I can knock his hand away,* he told himself.

"You can't get away," Markov said. "There are—"

"Six of them, I know. And more parked along the access road, if they're needed."

Markov's eyes widened.

"Your scientists are entirely right, Kir. I'm no longer exactly human."

The gun wavered. Markov took half a step backward, leaning heavily on his cane. Then he raised the hand with the pistol in it and wiped his sleeve over his tearing eyes.

"Can you get away?" he asked.

"I think so."

Markov let the gun drop to his side. "Then go, if that's what you want. Go! Quickly!"

"You'll be all right?"

"Yes."

"I promise, Kir. I'll come to you in Moscow."

The Russian nodded. "I believe you, Keith. I will wait for you."

Stoner could make out the bulky shapes of six dark-suited men in the drifting fog. Without another word, he turned away from Markov and started walking rapidly toward the corner of the building.

CHAPTER 19

He heard a shout from behind him, but Stoner strode quickly to the corner of the administration building, stepped around it, then flattened himself against the wet brick wall. Rapid footsteps approached, and a burly man ran past him, a gun in his hand just like the one that Markov had failed to use. Another man followed him, dark coat flapping as he ran.

Their footsteps died away in the distance, muffled by the fog. Stoner could hear deep, intense voices arguing in Russian.

"You let him get away!"

"There was nothing I could do," Markov answered.

Stoner no longer marveled that he could understand their language. Or that he could make himself unnoticed by men whose profession was to hunt down other men.

"It was your task to detain him if he would not come willingly," one of the Russians was complaining.

"I'm an old man," Markov replied, "and he's a black belt karate fighter. Do you have any idea of how easily my bones can be broken?"

Stoner grinned to himself. That sounded more like the old Markov.

"Moscow will not be pleased about this."

"I know that. There was nothing I could do."

So Kirill wasn't being totally honest about how things had changed in Moscow. Stoner debated swiftly about the possibility of snatching Markov from his strong-arm friends. It would be fun having Kirill along, he thought.

But then an overwhelming flood of revulsion engulfed him like a tide of icy cold rolling over his head and drowning him in freezing water. He saw himself and Markov like two little boys playing at the beach, building sand castles that the waves washed away.

No, a voice within him warned. What you must do must

be done alone. There is no time to spare. You cannot bring a weak old man with you.

Stoner squeezed his eyes shut and leaned his head back against the wet bricks. No time for human friendship, he told himself. No time for human warmth.

He stood there, alone, in the cold, clammy fog and waited for the Russians to leave the airport. It seemed like hours that they searched through the darkness. Each time Stoner felt the urge to go out and take his old friend by the hand and lead him to safety, the coldly unemotional logic of his situation forced him to remain still.

Finally he heard the engine of Markov's light plane whine into life. He stepped out from the shelter of the administration building's wall and watched the plane taxi into the mist, its whirling propeller shredding the fog and sending spinning tendrils back toward him.

No time for friendship, Stoner told himself again. He knew he should feel sad about that, but there was no emotion inside him; nothing except glacial self-control.

Self-control? He smiled grimly. You know better than that. Whatever's controlling you is not Keith Stoner. But it's *becoming* Keith Stoner. It's taking over my mind. It's becoming a part of me—or maybe I'm becoming a part of it.

He went to the door of the building, footsteps clicking on the wet cement, and stepped into the small, spare waiting room inside. It was bright and warm. And empty. The lone ticket counter was closed for the night, and there was no one else in the room, not even a floor-sweeping robot. Stoner sat in one of the cheap plastic-covered couches to await the morning and the bus that would take him back to Paris. Leaning back in the creaking imitation leather, he desperately wished that he could sleep, close his eyes and drift into peaceful oblivion, forget everything for a little while.

What is it that I'm supposed to do? he asked himself. Why have I been driven to leave Jo and turn my back on Kirill? Where am I heading, and why?

He stared up at the plastic tiles of the ceiling, smudged with gray around the heating ducts, and tried to fathom it out on sheer willpower. Then he remembered that there was something he had been wanting to do. Like a deep-sea diver surfacing after a long time underwater, the memory of his children made its way up to the level of his conscious mind.

Looking around, Stoner saw a single phone booth off in a corner of the waiting room. He went to it, sat on the padded bench, and closed the curved glass door. The phone screen immediately lit up, and a prerecorded Frenchwoman smilingly offered instructions on how to make local and long-distance calls.

He needed a credit number, and there was no way to fool the phone's computer into allowing him to make the call without one. Unlike human beings, the computer recognized only numbers and voice prints; Stoner could not talk it into doing what he wanted. Reluctantly, he asked the phone to make the call collect, to Mr. Douglas Stoner in Los Angeles, address and phone number unknown.

Almost instantly the screen showed a young man's face.

"Doug?"

But the man's image ignored his question and said, with a fixed smile, "The Los Angeles-area directory lists seventy-three Douglas Stoners. Unless you can tell us the address or phone number of the particular Douglas Stoner you are seeking, I am afraid that the system cannot complete your collect call."

The young man looked nothing like Douglas, Stoner realized. His hair was light brown, his features so smoothly perfect that Stoner realized it was a computer simulation that was talking to him, not a real person.

He stared at the smiling image for several moments, then tapped the key on the phone terminal that ended the connection.

Elly, he thought. Richards told me she was married and living in New Zealand. He pictured the psychiatrist and the conversation they had had about his children. Then he touched the phone's keyboard again.

"A collect call to Mrs. Eleanor Stoner Thompson, in Christchurch, New Zealand."

In the flicker of an eye the screen printed: MESSAGES FOR WALLACE AND ELEANOR THOMPSON MAY BE FORWARDED THROUGH THE INTERNATIONAL PEACEKEEPING FORCE REGIONAL OFFICE IN SYDNEY, AUSTRALIA, OR THROUGH IPF HEADQUARTERS IN OSLO, NORWAY.

His jaw clenched with frustration, Stoner asked the phone to connect him with the Peace Enforcement headquarters in Oslo. After several minutes of talking with computer images, he finally got a dour-looking woman on the screen. Her hair was iron gray, her jaw long and stubborn. But she listened to Stoner's plight.

"It's been twenty years since I've seen her," he finished his story, "and now I can't seem to track her down."

"Divorced twenty years ago?" the woman said, a glare of disapproval in her stern look.

"That's right."

"It took you long enough to decide you wanted to see her." The woman's English was excellent, with hardly a trace of Scandinavian twang.

Stoner decided to accept her rebuke and look sheepish, rather than trying to explain. He had not mentioned Elly's maiden name or his own. He had not told this austere woman that he had not been alive for eighteen of those twenty years. The woman's expression softened a little, and she glanced down as she worked her computer keyboard.

"Eleanor Thompson," she read off a screen that was out of Stoner's view. "Volunteer medical officer. Serving in Tanzania with husband, Major Wallace Thompson, International Peace Force."

"Tanzania," Stoner echoed.

"That's in east Africa," the woman said.

"Thanks."

"I'm afraid I can't put you through to her. These circuits are for IPF calls only, not personal. And she's probably out in the field somewhere, not at the regional headquarters in Dar es Salaam."

Nodding, Stoner thanked her again and cut the connection. He stepped out of the phone booth and walked slowly back to the couch where he had been sitting.

Tanzania. The Central African War. It all clicked together. Now he knew where he was going, and what he had to do.

"I don't trust him," An Linh said. "I don't believe a word of what he says."

Her garment bag was spread across the bed, and she was packing the few bits of clothing she had brought with her from Hilo.

Cliff Baker leaned against the doorjamb, watching her with a worried little smile on his face.

"I don't trust Madigan, either," he admitted. "But I don't see where we have much of a choice in the matter."

"Well, I do," An Linh said. "I'm going back home and beg Nillson to give me my job back. It's only been four days. . . ."

Baker crossed to the bed and sat on its edge. "You can't do that, pet."

"Who says I can't?"

"Everett Nillson," Baker replied, his voice low, almost as if he were afraid that the room had been bugged.

An Linh thought of her meeting with Nillson and his strange request that she become a surrogate mother for his son. I can deal with that, she told herself. I can work it out with him—especially if he'll help to revive my mother.

Defiantly, she said to Baker, "Do you expect me to believe that line of organic fertilizer that Madigan handed us?"

"That Nillson's after your body? Yes, I believe it."

She tried to scowl at him, but he looked totally serious. He really cares about me, An Linh told herself. He's really scared for my safety.

"And he's got the power to take what he wants," Baker added. "You won't get your job back unless you give Nillson what he wants. We're both working for Madigan now, whether we like it or not."

"You, maybe," An Linh insisted. "Not me."

He reached for her wrist. "Will you listen to me? You're in danger."

"Nillson's going to throw me into a dungeon and make me his slave, huh?"

"If he wants to."

"And Madigan's protecting me from that?"

Baker nodded.

An Linh pulled her hand away from him. "I don't trust Archie Madigan," she said. "Not for a second! And the worst part of this, Cliff, is that you do. You're going along with him. Do you really believe all his bullshit?"

He made himself grin at her. "Is it so bad?" Sweeping an outstretched arm around the blue-and-white bedroom, he asked, "I mean, even if it is bullshit, it's a lot better than Hilo. All our bills are being paid, aren't they? And we're on the track of the biggest story of the century!"

"While Father Lemoyne is dying in Honolulu."

"Madigan's taking care of that. He promised us. . . ."

"Sure he did."

"We'll do the documentary for Vanguard and auction it off to the networks."

"That's fine for you, Cliff. But what about me?"

"You'll be part of it! The most important part! You'll be the on-screen personality, the commentator. It'll make you internationally famous! We'll make a fortune!"

She stared hard at him. "Cliff, if I didn't know you better, I'd think that all you're after is the money."

"I'm trying to protect you, love," he said. "Whether you accept the fact or not, you're in real danger."

She shook her head again, but it was more out of stubbornness than conviction. He was utterly serious, and Nillson *had* come across to her as—as what? An Linh asked herself. Threatening? Deviant? Maybe. But what she had seen in Nillson had been something else. Anger. And frustration. The kind of anger that a little boy feels when his mother thwarts him. Rage, that's what it was. Barely controlled rage. In a man of Nillson's power, such a passion could be dangerous.

And what of Cliff? she asked herself. What of this man I love? Is he really trying to protect me, or is he so hot to get at the frozen-astronaut story that he'll use me and Madigan and anyone else who can be manipulated into helping him? No, she told herself. I can't believe that. I mustn't. Cliff loves me. He wants to protect me. He's afraid of Nillson, and he's playing off Madigan to protect me.

But she heard herself say, "I can't believe all this, Cliff."

Baker leaned back and stretched himself out on the rumpled bed. "Then just what do you believe, pet?"

"I don't know what to believe!" An Linh said. "It's all been too much, too many things happening all at once. . . ."

His face took on a curious, quizzical expression. Hauling himself up off the bed, he glanced around the room, then held his hand out to her.

"Come on," he said. "Let's take a walk. The fresh air will do us both some good."

She saw his brows raised pleadingly and realized that Cliff wanted to be out of the hotel suite, out on the streets where they could not be overheard. With a nod, An Linh took the only jacket she had with her from the garment bag and threw it across her shoulders.

They walked up the Strand to Trafalgar Square, where

Nelson's column stood against the clean blue sky, flanked by proud British lions and thronging crowds of tourists from every corner of the world.

"Remember when kids used to paint graffiti on monuments like that?" Baker asked over the hubbub of street vendors and hissing steam-powered busses.

"I haven't seen any for years, now that you mention it," said An Linh. "A passing fad, I guess."

"It's more than that."

"Those new polymer coatings that they spray onto the walls of buildings make it impossible for paint to stick to the surfaces."

He smiled tightly. "Don't you believe it! The real truth is that there aren't so many poor kids running around with nothing better to do."

"You think so?"

"I know it," Baker said.

They crossed the square, dodging the steam buses and honking black taxis, then pushed through the crowd sitting on the steps and enjoying the afternoon sunshine. An Linh wanted to sit for a while, too, but Baker insisted that they keep moving. He constantly glanced back over his shoulder as they made their way through the streets toward Piccadilly Circus.

"Are we being followed?" An Linh asked him.

"I don't think so. Not close enough so they can pick up what we say, at least."

"And what is it that you want to say, Cliff? What do you want to tell me that couldn't be said back in the hotel?"

He hesitated, as if trying to form the right words in his mind before speaking.

Finally, "There's still plenty of graffiti in Africa, An Linh. And India. All through Asia and the poor island countries of the Pacific."

"In Cambodia, too," she agreed.

"Yes, in your homeland."

"France is my home, Cliff. I have no childhood memories of Cambodia."

"But it's your real home, An Linh," he said, his voice low and urgent. "It's the home of your blood, your ancestry. You can't stand there and tell me that it means nothing to you."

"When I was in Cambodia, doing the documentary, it was like . . ."

"Yes?"

She made a little shrug. "Well, it was sort of like visiting distant relatives. I knew everybody there was sort of related to me, but I had no real ties to them. No emotional ties, I mean."

"But you must have felt something," he insisted.

"I felt guilty, I guess."

"Guilty?"

"Because I had so much and they were so poor. Because I knew I was going back to Paris in a couple of weeks, while the people I was taping would have to stay in their villages and their poverty."

"That's just it," he said, quickening their pace as they approached the heavier traffic of Piccadilly. "We have so much, and they have so little."

An Linh asked, "What's all this got to do with . . ."

He clutched her arm, almost hard enough to hurt. "There are people in this world who are working to change the balance of power, the balance of wealth."

"People? Who?"

"Why should Nillson and Vanguard Industries have such enormous wealth? Why should the people of equatorial Africa be plunged into starvation and war?"

He was practically dragging her along the street. An Linh pulled her arm free of his grasp and stopped walking. She saw a doorway with a small sign hanging above it that read "The Lion's Roar." Next to the door was an advertising poster urging, "Take COURAGE."

"I'm hungry," An Linh said. "Buy me lunch."

Baker frowned.

"This conversation is going to need Courage," she insisted.

Reluctantly, he pushed the door open and they stepped into the smoky, noisy pub. Finding an empty booth toward the rear, An Linh slid herself in on the wooden bench while Baker went to the bar to order sausages and two pints of Courage lager. The pub was crowded with late afternoon customers, dozens of conversations buzzing simultaneously, good-hearted laughter, and a constant flow of people in and out the front door. In an American bar, An Linh knew, there would always be at least one man who would try to pick her up. Here in the pub, none of the men paid her any attention.

Behind her relief at that, she felt a slight twinge of annoyance, but she knew that Cliff would see things very differently.

He struggled through the crowd to their booth, holding the plate of sausages and two mugs of beer high over his head as he squeezed past the men clustered around the bar.

Sliding in next to An Linh, he grinned boyishly.

"I guess nobody's going to eavesdrop on us in here," he admitted.

She smiled back and took a sip of the beer. "Now what's all this about poor people and rich people?"

Baker glanced around the crowded pub before answering. Hunching even closer to her, he dropped his voice to a husky whisper. "There's an organization . . . it's international in scope, made up of people from every part of the world. . . ."

"Including Australia?"

He nodded. "Including me. We need your help, love. In return, we can protect you from the likes of Nillson and Vanguard Industries."

He was serious, she saw.

"You need my help to do what?"

"To find the frozen astronaut," said Baker. "We want him."

"But why?"

"Do you realize the knowledge he's got stored in his brain?" Baker's voice did not rise in volume, but it grew more intense, agitated. "I've listened to the tapes of his conversations with a psychiatrist. . . ."

An Linh felt a shock of surprise. "Then you *knew* he'd been revived!"

"Yes. We did."

"When you hatched the idea to do a documentary on Father Lemoyne—you knew?"

"We had the tapes. We had to make certain they were authentic. The psychiatrist might have been a double agent."

"What is this organization?" she demanded. "Who belongs to it? Where does their money come from?"

Strangely, he seemed to relax. Grinning at her, Baker said, "The reporter's instincts come right to the front with you, don't they?"

"I need to know about this, Cliff."

Baker lowered his voice even further. "You've heard of them. It's called the World Liberation Movement."

"But they're terrorists!"

"No they're not," he snapped in a hissing whisper. "Not entirely. They've performed a few acts of sabotage and some assassinations, yes. But not as many as the media claims they've done."

"A few? . . ." An Linh's mind was spinning. "Cliff, they blew up that shopping complex in Madrid! And the airliner . . ."

"We get blamed for a lot of things that we never did," he insisted. "And nobody gives us credit for the good things we have done."

"What good things?"

"In the Central African War, for example. We saved the Ebos from being exterminated by the Nigerian army. We supplied the weapons the Ugandans needed to defend themselves."

"But how? Why?"

"I can't tell you. A lot of it I don't know myself. They keep a very tight security wrap over everything, for obvious reasons."

"But what is the World Liberation Movement trying to accomplish?"

"A redistribution of the world's wealth."

An Linh leaned her head back against the wooden wall of the booth. "Is that all?"

"It's no joke, pet. This is for real."

"A redistribution of the world's wealth," she echoed.

"And power," Baker added.

"And power. Of course power. Power is what it's all about, isn't it?"

CHAPTER 20

All that day Stoner wandered the streets of Paris, thinking, questioning, asking himself if the decision he had made was the right one.

He walked the broad avenues in the morning hours, down

the Champs Élysées to the Tuileries and into the Louvre. He edged his way through the early throng that crowded around La Giaconda, the Mona Lisa, and stared long at the enigmatic smile of that immortalized young woman. He listened to people speaking in a dozen different languages, chattering like the monkeys they so closely resembled. He saw that the painting was sealed behind thick plastic and roped off so that no one could get close to it. Stern-faced guards flanked the serene portrait. Like monkeys, the people had an innate urge to stretch out their hands and touch the picture.

He understood all their simian gibbering, no matter what the language.

In Japanese, "Why does she smile so?"

"She's pregnant."

"Nonsense! Is that all you women think about?"

"I read it in a book."

Another voice, in German, "How much do you think it's worth?"

"It's priceless."

"Yes, I know, but how much money would it take to buy it from these Frogs?"

"Don't be so crass."

"They must have it insured. How much is the policy for?"

"You're impossible!"

And another, in New York American, "It oughtta be in Italy, not France."

"Leonardo was employed by the French king, wasn't he?"

"Not when he painted this."

"How did it get to Paris, then?"

"How do you think? The French invaded Italy and stole it."

"Oh, I don't think so."

"No? How much ya wanna bet?"

With an effort of will, Stoner tried to shut their chatter out of his mind and concentrate on the painting itself. What was Leonardo trying to tell me when he painted this? What was the message he put onto this canvas? The shadings of the woman's eyes, the subtlety of her smile, the fantasy landscape behind her—the scene past her right shoulder did not match the scene behind her left.

For nearly an hour Stoner studied the painting, while tourists pushed past him, glanced at it for a moment or two, and then hurried on.

Finally Stoner understood. He smiled back at young Lisa Giacondo. Leonardo had created a masterpiece because he had the genius to recognize the goal of human aspirations and then capture it with his pigments. The serenity of a young woman's smile. The placid pose, the calmly folded hands. This was what every human soul longed for: serenity, calm, the peace that passeth understanding. Despite the fantastic landscape beyond her window, Mona Lisa had achieved that elusive quality that humans call happiness. For six centuries, all who saw the painting were tantalized by that, yearning to understand what they were seeing. So few did. So few recognized happiness when they saw it.

He walked out of the Louvre at last, past the old Palais Royal and up the wide avenue to the magnificent Opera House. Then farther, into the narrow streets of Montmartre, where children ran along the alleyways in which Piaf had once sung for pennies. The labyrinth of dark, winding streets echoed with children's shouts and laughter. Hardly an adult in sight: this was a working day. No tourists here, although an occasional steam bus huffed by, squeezing through the tight lanes left by the cars parked half up on the sidewalks, heading up the hill toward Sacré-Coeur.

Stoner hiked up to the basilica, his long legs plodding up the steeply rising streets. He watched a robot street cleaner patiently scooping up litter from the gutters. There was no graffiti on the walls. No loungers hanging around the neighborhood bistros. The economy must be good, Stoner thought; very good. The children he saw scampering through the streets were as much Algerian and Moroccan as French. But they played together without any noticeable antagonisms. They've been absorbed into the French culture, accepted by the Parisians. It took a few generations, but it's happened at last.

Tourists swarmed around Sacré-Coeur. Stoner ignored them like a man turning his back on an exhibit at the zoo and looked out from the hilltop at the rest of Paris spread out before him. Far in the distance he could make out the spires of Notre Dame, the medieval cathedral where Quasimodo had held off the besieging army of beggars.

Where are the beggars today? Stoner wondered. Has poverty really been beaten, or am I merely seeing the best side of a rich nation?

He leaned both hands on the stone parapet and let the wind tousle his hair. It was a beautiful day, in a beautiful city. But Stoner knew what he had to do. His decision of the previous night had been the correct one. It had nothing to do with Elly or the life he had led eighteen years ago. Nothing to do with his personal desires or emotions. He had no emotions, they had been removed from his inner being, leaving an emptiness as deep and cold as outer space itself.

He nodded to himself. The purpose he had sought was now clear to him.

He found a pay phone and called Claude Appert, collect. Nicole answered, the inevitable cigarette dangling from the corner of her mouth. She recognized Stoner and smiled.

"Keith! We worried about you. Where have you been all night? Did you see your friend?"

"Yes, I met him last night."

"You stayed with him?"

"No, not really."

"Ahh." Recognition dawned on her face. "You made a conquest, eh?"

He made himself grin and let the question go unanswered. But inwardly he shuddered at the thought of embracing some unknown woman, mating the way monkeys mate, furious passion for a moment and then parting forever.

"Claude is at the university. . . ."

"That's all right," he said. "Nicole, I'm going to have to leave Paris."

"Leave? But why? When?"

"Today. This afternoon. I won't be able to get back to your apartment and return everything Claude's loaned me."

"That is of no importance. But why do you have to leave so soon? An affair of the heart?"

"No, I'm afraid not."

Nicole looked disappointed.

"Listen. If anyone comes looking for me, tell them exactly what's happened. Don't hide anything from them."

Her disappointment changed to a disturbed, almost worried, frown. "What are you saying, Keith?"

"I'm taking a trip. South, toward Marseilles. And then to Algeria and on into Africa, where the war's going on."

"But that is madness!"

"I've got to do it, Nicole. I can't explain why right now, but that's where I've got to go."

She shook her head, hard lines etching her brow.

"Thanks for all your help," he said. "And remember, if anyone asks about me, tell them everything. Hold nothing back."

He punched the button that cut off the connection before she could ask another question. They'll be safe enough, Stoner told himself. No one will hurt them.

But he wished he felt more certain of that.

As they turned in from the Strand to the alley that led to the Savoy's front entrance, An Linh asked Baker, "Let me get this straight: you're using Madigan so that you can find the astronaut for the World Liberation Movement?"

Nodding, he took her arm as they walked past a snub-nosed black taxi that was deftly turning around in the narrow circle in front of the hotel's entrance. The uniformed doorman was tooting his whistle for another taxi; a trio of Arabs in Western business suits and checkered burnooses held in place by twisted goat-hair cords stood beside him, gesticulating animatedly as they spoke with one another in their guttural yet strangely musical language.

Baker glanced back over his shoulder as he answered, barely loud enough for An Linh to hear him over the taxi's motor and the noise from the street, "That's right, love. Vanguard's got a helluva lot more resources than we do."

"And Madigan thinks that he's forcing us to help him."

The Australian grinned broadly as they pushed through the revolving door. Inside the hotel lobby, he took her arm and whispered, "He's using us; we're using him. Turn about's fair dinkum, right?"

An Linh kept her silence as they rode up the elevator to their suite. But in the back of her mind she kept thinking, Cliff's right. This *is* the biggest story of the century. Not just the frozen astronaut, though. The World Liberation Movement. If they've penetrated Vanguard Industries, they must be *huge*. What a story it will make!

The red message light was blinking on the phone terminal. Baker went straight for it as An Linh dropped her handbag into the nearest chair and headed for the bathroom. She remembered an old Australian dictum that Cliff had once told her: "Nobody ever owns beer; you just borrow it."

By the time she came back into the sitting room, Baker was hunched forward in one of the armchairs, staring at the image of Archie Madigan's face on the phone screen.

"Okay," Madigan was saying. "I've got the scrambler working. Nobody can listen in on us."

"What's happening?" Baker said.

Madigan cocked an eyebrow as An Linh moved into his view, standing behind the chair in which Baker was sitting.

"The boss has been asking about you," he said, a slight smirk playing across his lips. "I told him he should offer you your job back. He said he'd think about it."

An Linh suddenly felt like a mouse being eyed by a grinning, evil cat. Taking a deep breath to steady her voice, she replied, "Is that why you've called?"

"And scrambled the transmission?" Baker added.

Madigan's smile turned almost apologetic. "No, of course not." He seemed to straighten a little in his chair. "We've run a computer check on every person known to have come in contact with Stoner during his days on Project Jove. . . ."

"Jove?" asked Baker.

"That was the name of the project to make contact with the alien spacecraft, eighteen years ago."

"Oh. I see."

"We've gone through every person on that project, all the people who he knew when he worked for NASA, and as far back as his classmates at college. . . ."

An Linh asked, "All of them? Every single one?"

"As many as we could identify," said Madigan. "We've even checked out his kids and his ex-wife." Madigan's hazel eyes flashed a silent message to her, and An Linh knew that she could never trust this man.

"Find anything?" Baker asked.

"The kids haven't seen him in twenty years. His ex-wife is dead. We've got an army of people checking out everyone we can get to, including one of the Russians from Project Jove that Stoner got particularly friendly with."

"Who's that?"

Madigan glanced down for a moment, probably at the computer screen on his desk, An Linh thought.

"I don't have his name here at the moment," he replied.

"But there is somebody that you two can check out for me. A French astrophysicist named Appert. Lives in Paris."

"He was on the project with Stoner?"

"No. They went to school together."

"That's a long time ago," said An Linh. "The man must be retired by now."

Madigan looked straight at her, and again his changeable, traitorous eyes sent a shudder of distrust through her.

"We are checking out everybody," he said firmly. Then, lightening his tone, he went on, "Besides, we've learned that Mrs. Nillson brought Stoner to Naples, and he left her villa several nights ago. Of all Stoner's former associates and friends, this man Appert is the closest one to Naples."

"We'll check him out," said Baker.

"Do not mention Vanguard Industries," warned Madigan. "I repeat, Vanguard is not to be mentioned."

"Never heard of 'em," said Baker, grinning.

Madigan grinned back at him and cut the connection. The telephone screen went blank.

CHAPTER 21

"Do you mind if I tape our conversation?" Baker asked, beaming his most disarming smile at Nicole Appert.

She stared with obvious distaste at the tiny black oblong that Baker placed on the coffee table. An Linh, sitting on the sofa beside him, looked at it, too. It was unlike any tape recorder she had seen before; a row of tiny white lights were blinking across its back, where Madame Appert could not see them.

A voice analyzer, An Linh realized. Cliff's going to check on whether she's telling the truth or not.

Nicole leaned forward in the dainty Louis XVI chair in which she was sitting and picked a cigarette from the gold box next to the pocket-sized recording machine on the polished wood coffee table.

"You said on the telephone that you are friends of Dr.

Stoner," she said in Gallic-accented English as she put the
cigarette between her lips. Before she could reach for the
lighter, Baker scooped it up and lit the cigarette for her.

"Yes. We're trying to locate him." He was wearing a
casual tweed jacket over his denims. Comfortable clothes.
Leather patches on the elbows. Very British. The outfit
usually put an interview subject at ease.

But not Nicole Appert. "How long have you known Dr.
Stoner?" The suspicion in her low, throaty voice was obvious.
The lights of the voice analyzer turned amber.

In French, An Linh replied, "We are television reporters
seeking to interview Dr. Stoner. We know of him by
reputation."

She noticed that the lights on the analyzer's circuit faded to
cool green as she spoke.

Nicole blew a puff of smoke toward the ceiling and leaned
back in her chair. "Ah. I see."

And the lights stayed green, showing that the stress in her
voice had eased.

"He was here, wasn't he?" Baker asked. An Linh was
surprised to see the voice analyzer's lights turn orange as he
spoke, indicating heavy tension.

Nicole regarded them silently for a moment, her eyes
shifting from Baker to An Linh and then back to the Australian again. She was a petite woman, An Linh thought, small
but elegant. The simple blue frock she wore must have cost a
fortune. This living room was filled with priceless heirlooms.
Nicole Appert was rich, and intelligent, and despite her tiny
frame she seemed to An Linh as delicate as a black widow
spider.

"Perhaps you should come back when my husband is
here."

"We don't have time to spare," Baker said tightly.

"This afternoon. Claude has gone to give a lecture at the
university. You picked the one morning of the month when
he must be there."

"We really need to know whatever you can tell us,"
Baker insisted. "Now."

But Nicole shook her head. "This afternoon. Come then,
and we will both talk with you."

An Linh started to reply, but Baker put a hand on her thigh
to restrain her. He looked around the living room, at the

antique furnishings, the exquisite fabrics, the bookshelves stacked neatly, precisely, the curtains that framed the long windows. Without a word, he got to his feet, stepped past An Linh, and went to the glass-fronted cabinet that held miniature china dolls and delicate fossil seashells.

Nicole half rose from her chair. Baker raised his arm and smashed the glass front of the cabinet with his elbow. The shattering noise made An Linh jump, startled.

"What are you doing?" Nicole demanded angrily. She got to her feet and turned toward the telephone terminal, sitting on a high table against the wall.

Baker picked up a jagged piece of broken glass and swung back toward her, holding it up to her face.

"Sit down!"

An Linh gasped. "Cliff, what—"

"Shut up!" he snapped. Insanely, An Linh noticed that the voice analyzer lights burned hot red now.

Nicole resumed her seat.

Baker leaned over and scratched the sharp edge of the glass the length of the antique coffee table. The sound made An Linh's blood run cold. She stared at the scarred tabletop.

"We don't have time to play games," Baker said, his Aussie accent stronger than An Ling had ever heard it. "Where is Stoner? Where has he gone?"

With cold fury, Nicole said, "It may interest you to know that Dr. Stoner instructed me to tell everything to whoever inquired about him."

"Did he now? Then start telling!"

Nicole spoke swiftly, in English, her voice murderously low and enraged. The voice analyzer's lights flickered red and amber, but Baker was not watching. He stood over Nicole, staring at her, the shard of glass in his upraised hand. An Linh sat there on the sofa feeling more terrified of him than the Frenchwoman apparently did.

Finally Nicole stopped.

"That's it?" Baker demanded. "He's going to Africa and that's all he said?"

"That is all."

"I don't believe you!"

"I do," said An Linh, rising from the sofa.

"There's got to be more," Baker insisted.

"There is one thing," Nicole said.

"What?"

"Yesterday Keith told me that his daughter is married to a Peace Enforcer."

"In New Zealand," said Baker.

With a hating smile, Nicole said, "The largest contingent of Peace Enforcers in the world is deployed in central Africa, trying to keep the war there from spreading further. Perhaps he learned that his daughter is there, with her husband."

Baker rubbed his chin with his free hand. "Right. Maybe so."

Nicole seemed perfectly calm, not the slightest bit afraid of Baker. An Linh saw her glance at the cabinet, as if checking to see if anything more than the glass had been broken.

"What's her name?" Baker asked.

"Eleanor, I think." Nicole reached for a fresh cigarette. An Linh realized that the one she had been smoking had fallen to the floor when Cliff smashed the cabinet. "Yes, Eleanor is his daughter's name."

"Her *married* name!"

Shrugging, Nicole replied, "That I do not know. I have not seen her since she is ten years of age."

"He didn't mention her husband's name to you?"

"No."

"You're sure?"

"Cliff, she's telling the truth," An Linh said. She bent down and picked up the recorder/analyzer. "She's told us everything she knows."

Baker looked from An Linh to Nicole and back again. Then he broke into a boyish grin.

"Yeah, I suppose so." Gently he laid the glass shard on the scratched coffee table. "Sorry I lost my temper."

Nicole nodded curtly, then got to her feet. "There *is* one other thing that might be of interest to you."

"Really?"

"A notebook that Keith left here."

"Notebook?" An Linh echoed.

"Where? What's in it?"

Nicole stepped around the coffee table and went to the desk next to the windows. "I believe Claude put it in here. . . ." She rummaged through the top drawer for a moment.

Turning back to face them, she pointed a small onyx-plated automatic pistol at Baker's chest. An Linh's breath caught in her throat. Baker's grin vanished.

"Now, you swine, you will put your hands above your head while I call the police."

Baker remained utterly still. "You're not going to use that thing. It's probably not even loaded."

Perfectly calm, her eyes flaming, Nicole said, "It is fully loaded, I assure you. And I know very well how to use it."

The Aussie's grin returned slowly to his face. It looked more than a little forced to An Linh.

"No," he said. "I don't think you'll shoot us. Come on, love. Time for us to go."

He turned slowly and started for the door. An Linh followed him, feeling the gun and Nicole's eyes focused on her back. Baker hesitated at the door and turned back toward the Frenchwoman.

"I'm really sorry about this. G'bye now."

He opened the door and allowed An Linh to go out into the hallway first. Nicole raised her arm and fired once. The shot sounded enormous in An Linh's ears, like a cannon blast. Baker lurched through the doorway and stumbled against her.

"Sonofabitch!" he screamed. "The damned cunt shot me!"

An Linh staggered under his weight. Blood was spurting from his shoulder. Past his half-collapsed form she saw Nicole Appert coolly surveying them, her lips almost smiling.

"*Bon,*" she said. "*Et maintenant la police.*" And she slammed her door shut.

Fortunately the elevator was still at this level; no one had used it since they had come up in it. An Linh tottered toward it, with Baker in her arms, and let him fall in a heap to its floor. She slid the cagework door shut and punched the down button. The elevator whined to life while other apartment doors popped open and nervous, curious, suspicious faces peeked out.

"Come on," An Linh said when they reached the street level. "We've got to get out of here before the police arrive."

Tugging him up to his feet, she hauled Baker out of the elevator, across the marble-floored foyer, and out into the rainy street where their rented car was parked.

"She shot me," Baker kept muttering. "That crazy old lady shot me."

An Linh nearly slipped in a curbside puddle as she dumped him into their compact sedan. She could hear the singsong wailing of approaching police cars. She slid behind the wheel and drove out of the narrow street, heading for the Champs Élysées and the hotel that Madigan had booked for them. Two police cars passed them, sirens blaring, as she swung out onto the broad avenue, windshield wipers flapping. Baker gripped his shoulder and swore through clenched teeth all the way to the hotel.

By tugging his raincoat over his shoulders, An Linh got the Australian through the hotel's minuscule lobby and up the tiny elevator to their room. It was also small, with barely enough space for a double bed and a bureau.

Baker collapsed on the bed, groaning. An Linh pulled the raincoat away and saw that his tweed jacket was soaked through with blood. She reached for the phone terminal on the night table beside the bed.

"Who're you calling?" Baker asked weakly.

"Madigan . . . he'll get the local Vanguard people to take care of you. . . ."

"No. Not Madigan." He propped himself up on his good arm, wincing. "Gimme the phone."

An Linh swiveled the picture screen toward him and lifted the keypad from the terminal. Handing it to Baker, she watched him tap out a twelve-digit number.

The phone screen stayed blank, but a voice said, "Yes? May I be of assistance?"

"Blood," said Cliff Baker. "Blood."

Immediately the voice replied, "Keep this link open for thirty seconds."

"Aye."

The voice sounded strangely flat and sexless to An Linh. A computer's synthesis, she guessed. And the single word "blood" was probably a code signal that the computer recognized as an emergency.

"Terminate link," said the voice.

Cliff leaned a thumb on the phone's off button.

"What was that?" An Linh asked. "Whom did you call?"

"Those friends I told you about. They'll have a medical emergency crew here inside of an hour."

He sank back onto the pillows and closed his eyes. "Christ, it hurts!"

"Let me call a doctor," An Linh said.

"No! We'll both end up in a Frog prison. And don't call Madigan, either. What we learned isn't for Vanguard. It's for the movement."

An Linh sat on the edge of the bed and watched the pain scribe his face with deep lines.

"Cliff," she blurted, "I'm scared."

"You'll be all right."

"Not me! It's you that I'm worried about."

"They'll take care of me."

"But you're still bleeding. How long should we wait—"

The phone chimed.

An Linh started to reach for it, but Baker stopped her with an upraised hand. "Keep the picture off. If it's Madigan, stall him. Don't tell him what that trigger-happy old lady did, and above all don't tell him what she told us about Stoner!"

It was the concierge, not Madigan. A gentleman and a young lady were downstairs, asking to see them.

"What's their names?" Baker whispered. An Linh asked the concierge.

"*Monsieur Van et Mademoiselle Gard,*" the concierge's raspy voice answered.

Baker grinned against the pain of his shoulder. "They're okay. That's the code."

Van and Gard. As An Linh told the concierge to allow them to come up, she thought, At least somebody in the World Liberation Movement has a sense of humor.

Van was an Oriental. Chinese or perhaps Korean, An Linh judged, from the size of him. He looked like a professional athlete, a football player, perhaps, or a boxer. He said nothing at all, simply took a position by the window and watched the street as silently and intently as a robot would.

Mlle. Gard was very French, younger than An Linh by at least five years, and talkative enough for all four of them. She was pretty, too, except for the misfortune of a Gallic nose. Nothing that a bit of plastic surgery could not fix, though. She was the paramedic, and she jabbered and clucked and *tsk*ed as she worked on Baker's shoulder. An Linh helped her to ease Cliff's jacket off. Then she cut away his shirt, jabbed him with an anesthetic, and probed for the bullet—blathering blithely away all the time. An Linh decided she was covering up her nervousness, although the young woman's hands were as steady as her flow of chatter.

"How did you get to us so quickly?" An Linh asked, as Mlle. Gard sat Baker up on the bed and started bandaging his shoulder.

"We are your backup team," the girl replied, cocking her head slightly toward the Oriental still staring out the window. "That one and I. We were parked outside the apartment building when you came out. If the police had tried to follow you, we would have cut them off and given you time to get away."

"Then if you saw that he was injured, why didn't you come into the hotel with us?"

"That was not our assignment. We were told to back you up and then await further orders. When we received the command to give him medical attention, we came immediately to the hotel."

Discipline, An Linh realized. And organization. Whoever these people are, they're not amateurs.

"But who gives you your orders?" she asked.

The young woman smiled at her. "If you need to ask such a question, you must not be told the answer."

"Security, love," said Baker, sitting up on the bed. "No one knows more than they need to know."

The Oriental and the Frenchwoman left as swiftly as they had arrived, but only after Mlle. Gard assured Baker that his shoulder would be stiff for a week or more and left him with a small bottle of pain-killers.

"*Adieu*," she chirped from the doorway. "*Bonne chance*."

An Linh closed the door behind them, then turned to Baker. "You've got to tell me more about this organization, Cliff. I want to know . . ."

But he was stretched out on the bed, eyes closed, snoring lightly.

CHAPTER 22

From the landing at the top of the stairs that led into the station's restaurant, the Gare de Lyon looked like a frenetic zoo. Stoner leaned both hands on the metal railing and watched the people rushing to and fro, lining up at the ticket windows, hauling luggage to the gates where the trains departed, knotting in little groups, running, gesticulating, and talking, talking—always talking, incessantly.

The noise was almost painful, and without letup. A thousand voices all going at once. Loudspeakers blaring announcements. Vendors calling out their wares. Even the people sitting at the tables spread out around the foot of the ornate *la belle epoque* staircase did more talking than eating or drinking.

A young couple embraced passionately at one of the gates, while the train—an aging TGV—thrummed with impatient power. Stoner tried to guess which of the pair would run to the train and which would stay behind. It was the man who dashed out along the platform. The woman waved to him briefly, then turned and walked slowly away. Stoner could not tell from this distance, but he guessed there were tears in her eyes.

Stoner's train would not leave for Marseilles for another fifteen minutes. It was one of the new electric specials, gleaming silver as it stood waiting on its track, powered by the cheap electricity generated by the new fusion power plants.

A gift from the stars, Stoner mused. A gift *of* the stars: in the heart of each fusion reactor is an incandescent plasma hotter than the core of the sun, he knew.

And I helped to bring this to Earth, he thought. I did. But which me? The man who was born on this world, or the alien within me?

He blinked his eyes, and the scene before him seemed to shift, change focus. The people crowding the train station were still there, the trains lay stretched along the tracks, the noise and muted light slanting through the rain-spattered glass roof did not change. But now it seemed as if he were examining an exhibit in a museum, observing a strange tribal ritual. Far back in the recesses of his memory, Stoner recalled once as a teenager peering into a microscope for the first time and discovering the teeming world of living creatures that bustled and scurried within a drop of water.

He watched the humans bustling and scurrying through the train station, hyperactive monkeys jabbering away their lives, not a shred of dignity about them, living on their emotions, letting their glands and their mammalian brains dictate the ordinary moments of their existences. It's not fair to think of us that way, said one part of his mind. But that's the way you are, replied another voice within him. You have the power of abstract thought, the capability of comprehending the universe—yet you behave like the monkeys in the forests.

Stoner shook his head, as if to drive the alien voice out of his thoughts. It went silent, but he could feel its presence inside his skull, watching, observing, analyzing. There was no hint of censure in the voice, no anger or disappointment with the human condition. No pity, either. Nothing but precise objective measurement.

Then his eye caught a scene below him, one individual encounter out of the hundreds happening simultaneously in the tumult of the busy station. A woman with three young children and as many pieces of odd-sized luggage—plus a heavy pack strapped to her back—was trying to take a table among those spread out on the floor of the station at the foot of the staircase. She was wrapped in a shabby overcoat that was much too big for her and had a fringed shawl over her head. The children were bundled in old, stiff, quilted winter coats; to Stoner they looked almost like miniature astronauts in space suits that had been pressurized to the point where they could hardly bend their arms.

The waiter was yelling at her in French and waving his arms at her. She obviously could not understand him. The children were very young, the smallest of them barely a toddler. They looked frightened and about to cry.

On an impulse, Stoner hurried down the stairs toward them.

"These tables are for serving cocktails only," the waiter was insisting. "For dinner you must go upstairs, into the restaurant."

"We only want to sit down for a few minutes," the woman was saying in strangely accented English. Her skin was no darker than a good suntan would produce, but Stoner realized from her singsong inflection that she was Indian.

To the waiter, he said, "They are tired. They need to rest for a few moments."

"Impossible! These tables are for paying customers, not charity cases."

Stoner took the man's right hand in his own and held it firmly. "The children are very tired, you can see that, can't you? They'll only be here a few minutes, I promise you."

He released the man's hand, and the waiter immediately slipped it into his pocket. Gruffly he said, "Only a few minutes, then."

Stoner thought about ordering something for them to drink but decided that deluding the waiter into thinking he had been tipped was enough of an imposition on the man.

"Oh, thank you, sir," said the Indian woman. She made a short shooing motion with one hand, and the three children clambered onto the rickety, wire-backed chairs.

Stoner nodded to her. "You're very welcome."

"We have been traveling for three days," the woman said, easing the straps of the backpack off her shoulders. It clunked to the floor heavily. "My husband has left for a new job in Madras, and I am bringing the children and myself to join him."

She would have been pretty if she had not been so tired, Stoner thought. She let her coat sag open and he saw that her clothes were entirely Western. So were the children's. Without an instant's hesitation she told Stoner her whole story: how she had married the man her parents had selected for her, when they had both been teenagers. How they had left India to escape the strictures of their families.

"I would have had six children by now, instead of merely three!" she said. "And a jewel in my nose, and a caste mark on my brow. Yes, for women in my village the age of freedom has not yet arrived."

She was only twenty-two, Stoner discovered. Yet she looked much older. The children were very well behaved. They fidgeted and squirmed on their chairs, but they kept silent and asked for nothing. Stoner saw their huge brown eyes watching the adults around them eating parfaits and drinking from mysteriously shaped glasses.

Her husband had been a textile worker, but robots had eliminated the craft that his father had taught him. So she and their growing family went with him to find work, first in Bombay, then in the construction teams building the solar power arrays in Arabia, and finally in Flanders—where some textiles were still made by hand.

"We were so happy there." She sighed. "He loved his work and I started at the university. I was to be a biotechnician!"

But Belgium is not India, she went on sadly. Her husband grew homesick, especially when the winter cold made them all ill. One winter he stayed. And a second. But by the time spring came, he had made up his mind to return to Mother India.

"I told him I would not go. I would not return to a society that only paid lip service to the rights of women. But he would not listen to me. Finally he told me that he was going home. I could come with him, or I could stay where I was. He was going home."

Stoner did not have to ask what she had decided; she gave him no time to ask before continuing:

"I refused to go with him. But what could I do? I could not remain in the university; I had to find a job to feed the children. I became involved with another man, but he would not marry me even if I divorced my husband. He did not want to support children who were not his own, you see."

The loudspeaker blared the announcement for Stoner's train.

With a painful sigh, the Indian woman said, "So I am returning to my husband, after all. He has found a job in Madras. At least we will not be living in our home village. The city may be better for me."

"I hope it is," Stoner said gently.

"It makes no difference," she replied. Gazing gently at the three silent, big-eyed children, she said resignedly, "They are the important ones. Their life is my life. I must protect them as best I can."

Stoner walked her to the train, carrying the toddler in one arm and the largest of the makeshift suitcases in his other hand. She was taking the same southward-bound train, but her tickets were for the cheapest coach. It won't be so bad for them, Stoner thought. The train will be in Marseilles in less than three hours.

He helped them into the train and saw them settled comfortably in two pairs of facing seats.

"Thank you so much, sir," the woman said. "I am sorry to have burdened you."

Stoner smiled at her. "No, no. I thank you. You have taught me what real courage is."

And he left her, heading farther toward the rear of the train, where the seats were more comfortable and he could watch the landscape blurring past without being interrupted. He needed to think, he told himself; needed to reflect on what the woman had told him. But he was glad to get away from her, happy to find a seat all by himself with no one near him, where he could be alone, isolated from these constantly chattering monkeys.

The train was hurtling through the beautiful countryside, down the Rhone valley, dotted with vineyards and old nuclear power stations. Stoner remembered the furor over nuclear power in his earlier life. The nukes seem peaceful enough now. They haven't harmed the environment. They don't even have smokestacks. He saw his own ghostly image on the window, his face frowning in concentration. The conductor stared at him each time he passed, as if trying to remember something important, but each time he went past without demanding to see a ticket.

I must protect them as best I can.

The woman's words rang in Stoner's mind. Yes, he agreed silently. We must all protect the children as best we can.

Baker was still sleeping when Madigan came into their tiny hotel room. The concierge had announced him, and An Linh was glad to see the lawyer from Vanguard Industries.

The only sign of surprise Madigan showed when he saw Baker stretched out on the bed, naked to the waist, his left shoulder bandaged, was a pursing of his lips and a low whistle.

"What happened?" he asked, his voice low so that it would not disturb the sleeping man.

An Linh said, "Madame Appert shot him. She didn't like being questioned about Stoner."

"Jesus, Mary, and Joseph! Shot him?"

"She refused to tell us anything," An Linh lied. "Cliff

started to get rough with her. She pulled out a gun and shot him. We were lucky to get away without being caught by the police."

Madigan went to the bed. "And who patched him up?"

Hesitating, An Linh improvised, "Why . . . I did. It wasn't a deep wound, really. I . . . uh, I got some bandages and antiseptic from the pharmacy down the street."

"Very professional work."

"Thanks."

He looked briefly around the cramped little room, then went to the only armchair, by the window, and sat in it. Madigan was wearing his corporation lawyer's uniform, a dark gray hand-tailored suit that fit him perfectly; it was in the latest New York style, high-collared Mandarin tunic, razor-sharp creases along the trousers, a small diamond clip in the shape of the corporation's stylized V over his left breast. An Linh's balloon-sleeved yellow blouse and knee-length knit skirt suddenly seemed terribly ordinary to her.

"Sit down," Madigan said. "No need to stay on your feet."

An Linh took the only other chair in the room, a wooden ladder-back that stood by the combination vanity and writing desk.

"The concierge tells me you had two visitors a couple of hours ago, an Oriental gentleman and a French lady. Called themselves Mr. Van and Miss Gard, she claims."

She froze. Trying not to reveal the slightest hint of surprise, An Linh held her breath for a moment, then slowly shook her head. "The concierge must be mistaken. We've had no visitors."

Madigan smiled sadly. "The woman works for Vanguard. Why do you think I put you up in this particular hotel? She didn't make any mistake."

All that An Linh could do was to shake her head again.

"Mrs. Appert told you something, didn't she?"

"No."

"That's a lie, dear girl. You mustn't tell lies. You could get hurt, you know."

He said it softly, almost sweetly, but An Linh's blood ran cold.

Madigan chuckled, low in his throat. "By Jesus, you really are new to this business, aren't you?"

"I don't know. . . ."

"That's just it," the lawyer said almost jovially. "You don't know how to play this game. You don't even know what the rules are."

She sat there silently, waiting for him to go on.

"This is where you offer me your body, darling girl. In return for my protection, you go to bed with me."

"Go to bed with you?"

"Come on now, is that such a repulsive idea?" He was grinning broadly. "Was it so bad the last time?"

The fears swirling through An Linh's mind began to fade a little. She tried to organize her thoughts. Madigan had been a competent lover, nothing extraordinary, but nothing hurtful, either. And he had kept his word: he had recommended her for the PR director's job the following week. She had expected him to demand more from her, but until this moment he had never bothered her again.

The lawyer made a small gesture toward Baker, sedated on the bed. "You do want to protect him, don't you?"

"Yes."

"Do you love him?"

An Linh nodded slowly.

"I want to protect him, too. And you, my dear girl. You need my protection. Very much."

"From Nillson," she said.

Madigan stared at An Linh silently. She felt him stripping her with his eyes. In the light of the rainy day filtering through the window curtains, his eyes were gray green, cold, guarded.

"Mr. Madigan," she said, "I'm not a whore. Don't force me to do something I don't want to do."

His lips curled slightly in a sardonic smile. "I wouldn't dream of it. But if you want to keep him out of Nillson's clutches, you've got to do something for me."

"Do what?" she asked, her insides fluttering at what his answer might be.

"Get Stoner back."

"What?" She gasped with surprise. "What do you mean? How can I—"

"We know he's heading south, toward Marseilles. I've got people watching every train. I want you to go to Marseilles, and on to Africa if necessary. I want you to find him and bring him back to Paris with you."

"To Nillson?"

"No. To me." Madigan's smile turned sphinxlike, mysterious and strangely self-satisfied. "Bring him to me, not Nillson."

"But how can I find him? How can I make him return here?"

With a vague wave of one hand, Madigan said, "Oh, I'm sure you'll find a way. We'll give you all the help you need, of course."

"If you have so much help, why do you need me?"

His smile turning just slightly acid, the lawyer answered, "I put myself in the man's place. If I were on the run, whom would I trust? A stranger who is male, or a stranger who is female? Who could convince me to follow her better than you could, darling girl?"

An Linh shook her head. "I can't do it. I can't just walk up to the man . . ."

"You'll have help, as I said. And if you refuse to do as I ask . . ." Madigan's gaze turned toward the unconscious man on the bed.

An Linh felt her jaw tighten.

"I promise that he'll be well cared for, if you get on Stoner's trail."

"And if I don't?"

"Nillson's people will find your young friend here. They can be very rough when they want to be. Ev enjoys pain, you know."

She saw a small flaw in what Madigan was telling her, a tiny inconsistency, a crack in the wall the lawyer was building around her.

"You say Nillson's people will find him. Aren't you one of Nillson's people?"

Madigan's grin became wider. "Well now, I am and I'm not. So to speak. In the corporation's organization chart, I work for Mrs. Nillson, the president of the firm. Sometimes she and the chairman of the board don't see exactly eye to eye."

An Linh felt suspicion and hope riding side by side within her. "Who are you working for now?"

He actually laughed. "Why, for who else but myself, darling girl? The one all of us works for, every minute of the day. Numero uno."

"You're playing off the president against the chairman of the board, for your own advantage."

"And it could be for your advantage, too, An Linh," he said, suddenly serious once more. "Play your cards well and you will gain from this. A lot."

"You'll see that Cliff is well taken care of?"

"Of course."

She glanced at the bandaged man lying unconscious on the bed, then looked back into Madigan's eyes. They had changed to slate gray, ominous, expectant.

"I'll try to find Stoner for you."

"You'll succeed," Madigan said.

An Linh couldn't tell, from his inflection, whether he meant those words as a compliment to her abilities or as a threat of the consequences of failure.

CHAPTER 23

By the time the train began slowing down as it approached the station at Avignon, the sun was shining warmly while it sank toward the horizon, casting long, slanting shafts of golden light across the green landscape. Stoner saw fields of gorgeously red poppies and bright yellow mustard flowers gliding past, and he recalled that this area called Provence had been a magnet for painters over the centuries.

Briefly he debated getting out here and seeing the ancient city, walking into the soft hills and letting the hot southern sun darken his skin and warm his soul. Then the train slid into the station, and it was a shabby, tired platform with walls covered by fading advertising posters, like train stations everywhere. He decided to stay aboard the train and go straight to Marseilles, as he had originally intended.

Only a few people got out at Avignon. One of them, he saw, was a strikingly beautiful Oriental woman: she was not tiny, but her delicate features and slim figure almost gave her a doll-like appearance. She carried no luggage, only a largish leather shoulder bag. Her dark almond eyes seemed troubled as she stopped on the platform almost directly before Stoner's window and looked up and down, as if in confusion.

Three men hurried off the train behind her, an Oriental and two Westerners. The Oriental was big, barrel chest and fat belly bulging the black T-shirt he wore under an unzipped oily leather jacket. His head was shaved completely bald, and his face was so bloated that his eyes were little more than slits imbedded in fat. He towered over the girl as he spoke to her. She turned away from him, but the two others—younger, wearing blue jeans and windbreakers, but also hulking heavyweights—closed in on her.

The big Oriental grabbed the girl's wrist. She tried to twist away, to no avail. All three of them laughed.

Stoner jumped to his feet and loped to the end of the car, ducked through the door and out onto the platform between cars.

An Linh did not see him. She had realized as the train pulled into the station that she could go no farther. Completely spent emotionally and physically, the sight of the city where she had grown up was too powerful for her to refuse. Something deep inside her told her that safety was there, and the little happiness she had known in her life. Her mother was there, too, waiting for her, waiting for the magic stroke that would bring her back to life so that she could hold An Linh in her comforting arms again.

She had realized as soon as the big Chinese came toward her that Madigan had obviously placed his own team of toughs on the train. She tried to get away from him, but the two other young hoodlums hemmed her in. Desperately, she searched the station platform for someone to help her. No police in sight. Only a few passengers, their backs turned to her as they carried their luggage toward the parking area on the other side of the platform. The train hooted, signaling it was ready to pull away.

"Come on, back on the damned train, don't make a fuss," the Chinese said to her. "You'll only make it harder on yourself."

His grip on her wrist was painful. One of the hoodlums behind her giggled and told his companion, "I'd like to make it hard on her!"

"You'll get your chance," the other said, "after me."

"Hold it. What's going on here?"

An Linh looked up and saw a tall man blocking their way.
The sun was at his back, lighting his long, tangled hair like a
shining halo, making the features of his face impossible to see.
She squinted at the apparition.

"I'm taking my daughter home," said the Chinese gruffly,
"whether she wants to go or not."

"I'm not his daughter!" An Linh was surprised at the
sound of her own voice; it was a nearly hysterical scream.

"I think we'd better find a policeman," said the tall man.

The Chinese made a slight motion of his head toward the
two youths. "And I think you'd better get out of my way
before my friends scramble your face."

Stoner looked them over. The Oriental was his own height,
and although he looked fat he was probably a formidable man
in an alley fight. The other two were younger, no doubt
faster. They were grinning at him, eager for action.

The train hooted once again and began pulling slowly away
from the platform. Stoner registered it out of the corner of his
eye; it did not matter, there would be another train soon
enough. He focused his attention on the scene before him.

He could feel his body tensing, every nerve alert, every
sense so acute that he could count the wispy hairs of the fat
Oriental's eyebrows.

"Let her go," he said quietly.

The Oriental tried to push past him, still hanging on to the
reluctant girl with one hand. Stoner laid a hand on his chest,
fingers outstretched. The Oriental looked into Stoner's eyes,
and his determination began to fade. He looked troubled,
almost frightened.

But the two younger men came up on either side of Stoner,
and he realized that he could not restrain all three of them at
the same time. I won't be able to avoid fighting them, Stoner
said to himself—an explanation for the other presence within
his mind. They're too eager for a brawl, too young and full
of testosterone to realize that they might get hurt. All they
can think of is showing off their muscles in front of the girl.

Is that what I'm thinking of? Stoner wondered, far back in
the part of his mind that watched him laconically, trying to
understand why he did what he did.

Without a word, one of the grinning youngsters reached
for Stoner's arm. He took a step backward, and they both

moved toward him. Stoner waited, hands dropped to his sides.

"You shouldn't butt into other people's business," said the tough on his left.

"Yeah. It's going to cost you a lot of pain, friend," the one on his right added.

They were so sure of themselves that they did not bother with weapons. Stoner knew that they both carried knives. But they advanced on him barehanded.

The Oriental yanked at the girl's arm and headed off toward the moving train as Stoner retreated a few more steps. The youth on his left threw the first blow, a karate kick aimed at Stoner's kidney.

He blocked it, spinning and catching the kid with an elbow solidly on his jaw. Ducking under the other one's charge, he rammed a fist into his groin, then kicked his feet out from under him.

An Linh's shoulder felt as if it were being pulled out of its socket. She turned as the Chinese yanked on her arm and saw a blur of action. Then the two hoodlums were sprawled on the platform's weathered boards and the stranger was stepping over their prostrate bodies, heading toward her.

The Chinese let go of her wrist and pulled a length of chain from inside his leather jacket. He squared off, facing the tall man, the chain yanked taut between his two big hands. The train pulled away and disappeared around the bend of the track. Suddenly An Linh recognized the stranger's face, and a shock raced through her. Her mouth dropped open and her hands flew to her face. It can't be! I'm having a hallucination.

Stoner eyed the chain in the Oriental's heavy fists, then looked into his narrow, fat-enfolded eyes.

"You could get killed," he said. "I'd feel badly about that."

The Oriental wavered. He looked over at his two unconscious aides, then at Stoner, and finally at An Linh.

"Is she worth dying for?" Stoner asked softly, almost sadly.

The chain sagged. The Oriental opened his left hand, and the chain swung limply from his right. He turned abruptly and walked away.

Keith Stoner, thought An Linh. It really is Keith Stoner.

"What were they after?" Stoner asked her.

"I don't know," she heard herself lie. "I was . . . I was just coming back home for a visit and they came after me."

His eyes seemed to penetrate completely through her. She realized that she had no luggage, not even a coat with her, and her profession of innocence was totally unbelievable.

But Stoner merely shrugged and said, "There won't be another train for several hours. I haven't had anything to eat all day. Do you know a good restaurant around here?"

"Yes," replied An Linh, thrown off her guard by his seeming ingenuousness. "Yes, as a matter of fact, I know lots of them!"

He smiled at her and offered his arm. She took it happily, and they walked off toward the taxi stand like two children setting out to explore the world.

"It's the World Liberation Movement," Madigan was saying. "They're far better organized than we ever thought they were."

The lawyer looked tired, Jo thought. I've been sending him back and forth across the Atlantic like a volleyball the past few days, she realized. But there was no alternative. She could not risk talking to him by telephone. Even the tightest laser-beamed satellite links could be tapped. Now that she knew her husband was working against her, Jo understood that ordinary security measures were useless. Like her Italian forebears, she was reduced to relying only on those whose loyalty was unquestionably to her personally, not to the corporation.

But is Archie really loyal to me? Jo asked herself as she studied the lawyer's drawn, sleepless face. Is he telling me everything? Is he working for me or against me? She knew Madigan was ambitious; did he have the courage to try to betray her to her enemies?

The two of them were riding on an electric cart as it rolled noiselessly along a wide, brilliantly lit tunnel beneath Governors Island, in New York Harbor. Ostensibly, Jo was inspecting the nuclear fusion power plant and energy screen that Vanguard had built for the city of New York. She had spent the morning listening to boring briefings by city officials and scientists who fulsomely praised Vanguard's high technology and public spirit. None of them mentioned the fact that although Vanguard Industries shared the scientific knowledge gleaned from the alien spacecraft with the entire world (at Russian insistence), Vanguard also reaped enormous profits from building the machines that this new knowledge had revealed to the human scientists.

Deep underground, in tunnels and shelters originally built to withstand the impact of hydrogen bomb explosions, Vanguard had built a defense against nuclear attack. Thanks to the knowledge from the stars, New York and most of the other major cities on Earth's Northern Hemisphere were covered by invisible, impalpable bubbles of energy which could absorb the fury of a thermonuclear explosion and protect the city within its sheltering dome from the blast, heat, and radiation of any number of nuclear bombs.

Jo had given the luncheon speech, there in the underground facility's sparkling commissary, noting how a shelter originally built in fear of nuclear holocaust now protected the entire city from the threat of nuclear attack. Her audience of politicians and bureaucrats applauded her enthusiastically, while media reporters and photographers duly noted that they were actually applauding themselves. The mayor, a young, handsome, photogenic Puerto Rican with rumored designs on the White House, presented Jo with a plaque machined from the new metal alloy used in building the energy screen generators. It was called Staralloy because the secret of its composition had been wrested from the data banks of the alien's starship.

Now, luncheon over, photographs taken, news interviews finished, Jo was riding back to the surface with Madigan, who had joined her just a few minutes earlier, after landing at the Harbor Skyport on his rocket plane flight from Paris.

They rode up the tunnel toward the surface in the middle of a regular parade of electric carts. Jo had picked this one at random out of the dozens waiting for the VIPs, assuming that not even her husband would be able to have every cart bugged.

"The World Liberation Movement," Jo repeated. She kept her voice low. Sounds tended to echo annoyingly off the tiled curving walls of the tunnel.

"That's right," said Madigan. "They're more than just a scattered bunch of terrorists. They're real, they're apparently well organized, and they're trouble."

The rubber-wheeled cart rolled along the long tunnel, its guidance microprocessor faithfully following the pencil-thin red line painted on the cement floor. Jo mulled over what Madigan was telling her.

"Archie, are you sure you haven't just stumbled onto some little gang of college kids with delusions of grandeur?"

"I don't think so. But we'll find out soon enough. Your husband's pumping this Baker character for every bit of information inside his skull."

"Just make sure you don't kill him."

Madigan made a sickly smile. "Don't worry. The interrogation team has had plenty of practice. They'll squeeze what we want to know out of him."

They had arrived at the end of the tunnel, a large, circular chamber with a wide stainless-steel elevator door at its far side. The cart in front of them swung over to its designated parking space; attendants in butter-yellow coveralls helped the two elderly VIPs off the cart and escorted them toward the elevator doors. There were more photographers milling around, clicking and whirring. Jo smiled prettily for them as she and Madigan walked toward the elevator.

"Where do they get their money?" Jo asked. "Who's financing them?"

"We're trying to find out," said Madigan.

"Just make certain you don't kill him, Archie," she repeated. "He may be our best avenue to finding Stoner."

The lawyer nodded and said nothing about An Linh Laguerre.

Madigan watched Jo climb into a green-and-white Vanguard Industries helicopter and whirl off from Governors Island toward the corporation's offices in Greenwich. He waited for almost fifteen minutes as a buzzing airlift of choppers took the various VIPs up and away to their respective offices. The helicopters were noisy despite their electric motors, the big rotors *whoosh*ing through the air like giant scimitars and kicking up sandstorms of grit and dust. The harsh wind blew wildly at his hair. He clutched his suit jacket with one hand and squinted against the blast.

Madigan's own chopper was small, dark brown, unmarked. He clambered up into the seat behind the pilot and latched his safety belt. The aircraft jerked neatly off the cement landing pad and lifted quickly into the sky. Looking down, Madigan saw that there were only a few people left on the pad.

It was a beautiful afternoon in late spring, warm without being muggy. The skyline of Manhattan sparkled against the clean blue sky. Cheap, abundant electricity had transformed New York City. Electric cars had replaced most of the taxis and private automobiles; those that were not electric-powered ran on hydrogen fuels. No more soot or carbon monoxide was being pumped into the air. The gray smudge of pollution that once hung over the city like a funeral shroud had disappeared for good.

But Madigan had no time to admire the view. His only real thought about it was that the fusion generators that provided the electricity were very profitable for Vanguard Industries.

His little helicopter winged across the harbor and turned south, following the New Jersey coastline past Bayonne and Elizabeth, then swinging eastward out toward Sandy Hook. Madigan saw the near empty runways of the old Newark Airport on one side of him, the green-patined Statue of Liberty standing resolutely on the other side.

Finally the chopper dropped down onto the cracked concrete of the old Fort Monmouth Army Electronics Center. Vanguard Industries had bought the weed-infested base from the government several years earlier. Outwardly, the base still looked abandoned and forgotten. But there were certain Vanguard operations going on inside its dismal gray concrete buildings.

It made sense to turn Baker over to Nillson, the lawyer insisted to himself as he ducked out of the helicopter. It made him look good to the chairman of the board, and by offering to tell Jo whatever Nillson's people pumped out of Baker, he looked equally good to the corporation's president. It was the right move, he repeated. They won't kill Baker. They know what they're doing.

Cliff Baker lay naked on a table, wrists and ankles securely cuffed, legs spread apart. A bank of bright lights blazed overhead, and a team of men and women in green surgical gowns clustered so closely around him that Madigan could barely see his naked, vulnerable body. From his vantage point in the control room, above the floor of the interrogation center, it looked almost like an old-style surgical theater. They had even taken the bandaging off Baker's shoulder wound and inserted a metal probe into the torn flesh.

Wires were attached to Baker's nipples, fingers, scrotum, and toes. His eyes were clamped open, and an intravenous tube had been inserted into his left forearm.

"I don't know where Stoner is," Baker was muttering, his voice so weak that Madigan could barely hear it over the intercom in the darkened control room. "I don't know," he repeated.

One of the green-gowned women bending over him reached out a gloved hand and turned the dial of a gray metal box that stood on a wheeled table next to Baker's outstretched body. She turned the dial ever so slightly, but Baker's spine arched and he gave out a strangled scream.

"Suction!" snapped the man on the other side of the table. "He's vomiting again. Clamp the tongue before he chokes on it!"

Madigan felt his own stomach heave, and he turned away. Sitting in the darkness, leaning forward eagerly until his forehead almost pressed against the one-way glass, Everett Nillson licked his lips and patted at beads of sweat on his upper lip. A woman sat next to him, someone Madigan had never seen before. She was very young, barely a teenager, and she wore a green surgical gown like the workers down in the harshly lit scene below. Her eyes were fixed on the work going on down there, burning bright and hot. Her hand stroked Nillson's thigh, absently, automatically, almost like the reflexive twitch of a cat's tail.

"For God's sake," Madigan burst out, "he's told us everything he knows!"

Nillson looked up at him, his head tilting back slowly, his eyes dreamy. "Yes," he said quietly, "I suppose he has."

"Then let's stop it before we have a corpse on our hands."

Nillson turned from Madigan to the teenager sitting beside him. In the light from the operating room coming through the window, her face looked harsh, heavily painted. Ruby-red eye shadow and lips almost purple. Wild hair, brick orange.

"A little more," Nillson said, smiling at the girl. "You'd like to see a little more, wouldn't you?"

"If you would," she replied.

"Oh, I would. Yes, I surely would."

Madigan started for the door. He needed fresh air and a

soundproof barrier between him and the noises gargling from Baker's throat.

"Stay here," Nillson said.

Madigan's hand touched the cool metal of the door, but Nillson's voice, as soft as the caress of a lover's hand, froze him where he stood.

"Come back here and tell me about my loving wife," Nillson said slowly. "What is she up to? How much does she know about this international gang of terrorists?"

"Jo?" Madigan asked, startled. He came slowly back to Nillson's side, trying not to look out the window, not to hear what was filtering through the intercom. "You don't believe that she knows anything? . . ."

"I do," replied Nillson.

"I don't think—"

"I don't care what you think, Archibald. Or what you don't think. You just make certain that my adoring wife thinks you're still on her side. The instant you stop being useful to me, you know, you could end up on the table down there."

Madigan's stomach twisted. He tried to fight down the bile rising in his throat. And failed.

CHAPTER 24

All through dinner at the sidewalk restaurant that An Linh picked out, Stoner listened to her talking about her childhood in this ancient city, knowing that he was getting a carefully edited biography.

She was stunningly beautiful, with the delicate blend of feminine fragility and lissome allure that characterized southeast Asian women. Lovely flowers, innocent yet knowing. As he studied her almond eyes and high cheekbones, her short-cropped ebony hair and sensuous lips, he realized she could be very seductive. Remembering an earlier life, he thought of how many American males had succumbed to the powerful charms of Indochinese women.

But she was not trying to seduce Stoner. Sex, even the casual flirting games that men and women constantly play with each other, was far from her mind. He could see that she was frightened, and whatever was frightening her was something that she did not want Stoner to know about.

He watched her and listened all through their leisurely dinner. Each time she came to a point that she wanted to keep hidden from him, her breath caught just slightly, her eyes shifted away from him for an instant, her hands smoothed the napkin on her lap or made tiny adjustments on the placement of her dinner plate, her silverware, or wineglass.

Stoner thought, She claims she's a television news reporter, yet she hasn't asked me anything at all about myself. A stranger steps off a train—a foreigner, no less—and rescues her from three thugs, and she doesn't even ask where he's come from or what he's doing in this town. Then he smiled with understanding. Of course! She knows who I am.

He felt his body relax. She knows who I am. Maybe she's been following me. A television news reporter. Who's she working for? And why the scene at the train station? He mulled that over as he worked his way through the trout almondine. There was no need to rush; plenty of time to unravel the mystery. An Linh had recommended the house wine, and it was excellent: a crisp dry white, cold and delicious. For the first time, Stoner leaned back in his chair and surveyed their surroundings. The sidewalk was narrow, and the few pedestrians walking by had to navigate around the little tables or walk out in the brick-paved street. A huge old tree murmured overhead in the soft springtime breeze; strings of lights swung from its branches. A picture painted by Van Gogh, he thought. A scene from a Hemingway story.

He turned his attention back to An Linh and saw that she was truly frightened. It's not just worry that I'll find out she's after a story about me. Those men at the station were real; it wasn't a fake scene just to impress me.

She refused dessert, but Stoner chose a napoleon from the big tray the waiter presented. They both finished with good strong black coffee.

Then came the bill. Stoner watched her glance inadvertently down at the handbag she had left at her feet, and then up at him. He could see the chain of thoughts flashing through her mind: If I use my ID card to pay, they'll trace it and know where I am. But he won't have any ID at all; he can't pay.

Stoner took the check from the waiter, asked the young man for a pen, and signed the back of the check.

"Will that be all right?" he asked.

The waiter blinked and frowned, but finally nodded.

Stoner got to his feet, went around the little table, and helped An Linh up from her chair.

"It's a beautiful night," he said. "Let's take a walk."

The sun still lingered above the horizon, painting the placid Connecticut River orange gold. Dozens of sleek launches and sailboats were tied up at the pier adjacent to the Goodspeed Opera House. Long limousines, black, white, even one of salmon pink, pulled up on the gravel driveway. Men in dinner jackets and women in bejeweled gowns were streaming from their limos and boats, smiling graciously at one another, laughing politely here and there as they headed into the old Victorian clapboard building. It rose shining white among the graceful old trees like a memory of an earlier century, when a man could build an opera house in the middle of the Connecticut hills to his own quirky specifications and then get the best performers in the world to come to it—if he were rich enough.

Jo Camerata Nillson stood at the base of the winding stairway, beneath the ornate chandelier, greeting the theatergoers as they entered. They were her guests. The Goodspeed had fallen on poor times a decade earlier, but Jo had bought the place and revitalized it. In bygone years it had housed revivals of old Broadway musicals. Now she had returned it to its original purpose, and the opera house was presenting a special performance of *Carmen*. The entire cast had been flown in from La Scala in Milan for this one evening.

Everett Nillson stood beside his wife, tall and elegant in a crimson dinner jacket. He wore medals from several nations pinned to its breast, and the French *Légion d'honneur* on a blue silk ribbon around his neck. Jo was in a white floor-length gown, classic Greek in inspiration, which subtly accentuated her tall, elegant figure. Her decorations were diamonds set in platinum at her wrists and throat, and a diamond clip in her thick dark hair.

"Quite a success you've made of this," Nillson said after

the last guest had been greeted and ushered up the stairs to their seat.

Jo surveyed the empty foyer. "It's easy to fill the house when the tickets are free."

"Do you think you'll ever make a profit out of this place?" he asked, offering his arm to her.

"Only if I want to."

As they started up the stairs, the familiar strains of the overture came filtering out to them. Nillson took a deep breath. "I suppose we'll have to sit through the whole damned show."

"Don't you want to?"

"I don't enjoy watching when I know what the outcome will be."

Jo looked into his ice-pale eyes. "But it's different every time. No two performances are exactly the same."

"They both get killed every time, don't they?"

"We all die, sooner or later."

They reached the landing, and he stopped before the double doors that led into the theater. Bizet's music was reaching for a crescendo.

"Jo, why are you fighting me?"

She felt a pang of surprise. "Fighting you? I'm not—"

"About this astronaut, this man Stoner."

Jo's mind raced into overdrive. *Is this another one of his little traps? Is he really jealous of Keith, or is he just playing his usual power game with me?*

"Everett," she said, stalling for time to think, "when I first met you, all those years ago, I told you that the only thing in the world I wanted was to go out and recapture that alien spacecraft."

"With Stoner aboard it."

"He was aboard it, yes. And so was the knowledge that's brought Vanguard billions in profits."

"Tens of billions, actually," he said. "But the real reason you wanted to get the spaceship was because *he* was in it."

"So what?" she snapped. "You accepted the situation. And you made my marrying you the price for what I wanted."

"Did I? You married me to make certain that you'd get what you wanted."

Jo knew she had to control her temper. Everett was no man to face on raw emotion. "We were married at *your* insistence. And you know why."

"Do I?"

"You married me to prove to the world in general—and the nastier members of the board in particular—that you were a real man."

Nillson ran a long, bloodless finger along the side of his lean jaw. "Here I thought that you married me because I was the only male member of the board that you hadn't fucked."

She made herself smile at him. "That's not quite true."

He remained serious. "I thought that our marriage would prove to be a powerful alliance: your strength and vigor combined with my knowledge and wealth."

"And it has been," Jo replied. "Vanguard has grown tremendously."

"Yes, I suppose it has."

Inwardly, Jo reflected, A marriage of convenience. A corporate marriage. You should have known what he was like when he wouldn't go to bed with you before the wedding. You were ready to accept anything, weren't you? Anything.

"But your real reason for all this," Nillson was saying, "is that you wanted to bring Stoner back to life. You're still in love with him."

"That's nonsense."

"Then why are you working against me?"

"I'm not! What makes you think—"

"You spirited him away. You hid him from me."

"And you murdered Gene Richards!"

Nillson backed away from her blazing eyes, almost staggering, as if slapped in the face.

"I'm trying to find Stoner," Jo insisted. "All along I've been trying to keep him safe and protected, so the competition couldn't get their hands on him."

"And you've failed miserably, haven't you?"

She had no answer for that.

The overture came to its climax. The audience applauded.

Still standing between Jo and the door into the theater, Nillson demanded, "Have you made any progress at all toward finding him?"

"Some," she equivocated. "If we both have people out trying to find him, it would be better if we worked together."

He shook his head slowly. "You can beat the bushes looking for him, if you want to."

"And what are you going to do?" Jo asked, suddenly frightened.

Nillson smiled, a faint, ghostly smile on his cold, colorless face. "There's another way to prevent the competition from getting their hands on him. A permanent solution to the problem."

His long-fingered hand closed slowly, tightly, into a fist. To Jo it looked like the claws of a rapacious predator gripping its prey.

Inevitably Stoner and An Linh found themselves at the foot of the ancient stone bridge jutting halfway across the peaceful Rhone River. Moonlight glittered on the water. The stars shone splendidly above.

They walked slowly out onto the bridge, toward the little chapel that had been built there centuries ago.

"My mother is there," An Linh said, pointing to one of the buildings in the city that bulked darkly against the moon-bright sky. Hardly a single light shone from it.

"That's the hospital?" he asked.

"The annex, where they store medicines and bedding and toilet paper and dead bodies whose relatives insisted on their being frozen."

"You'll be able to revive her someday," Stoner said. "You'll be able to return her to life."

"Yes. Someday."

"Why were those men trying to abduct you?" Stoner asked An Linh.

In the soft moonlight she looked even more beautiful. She hesitated, then turned away from him.

"You know who I am," he told her, thinking to himself, But you don't know *what* I am. Neither do I. Not yet. Not fully.

She turned back to him, and he saw that there were tears in her eyes.

"Why don't you tell me the rest of it?" he suggested gently. "I can't help you if I don't know the entire story."

"Will you help me to revive my mother?"

"Yes, of course."

"Now? Tonight? Tomorrow morning?"

He wanted to reach out and pull her to him, not as a lover would embrace her, but as a friend, a father, an older brother might. But something stopped him. There are too many entanglements in the relationship between a man and a woman, he told himself. It's too easy for any gesture, any word or hint of an emotion, to be misinterpreted. Yet he knew that she needed to feel protected, to feel less alone. Poor frightened lonely mammal, so lost and scared without a tribe, a family, a companion to share warmth with her. But he could not move himself to cross the distance between them. It was only a foot or so, less than a meter, wider than the gulf between worlds, a distance he could measure in light-years.

"No," he said softly in the moonlit night. "Not tomorrow or the day after. Not for a while."

He saw the protest in her eyes before she began to speak. "But . . ."

"Why revive her if the cancer is still there, waiting to kill her?"

"They have found a cure for cancer," An Linh said.

"Really? A cure? One that works for all kinds of cancers?"

"It's common knowledge," An Linh said, wishing she felt as certain as her words.

Stoner smiled. "It may be common knowledge, but is it true?"

She glared at him.

"If someone's found a cure for cancer, then your mother will be revived, sooner or later. You have the greatest ally of all, An Linh: time," Stoner told her. "Time is on your side. She will wait. You must be patient."

"For how long?"

"I don't know. Not yet." Then he smiled for her. "But the fact that I'm here means that we'll know how to revive her soon. And if you're right, we'll be able to cure her disease."

"But why not now?"

His smile turned sad. "Because I don't know how to do it. And I'm not sure that the people who revived me could revive your mother—or would choose to."

She understood. He could see that.

Slowly they walked to the crumbling old chapel and sat on its stone steps, still warm from the long day's sun. An Linh began to tell Stoner her true story, the part she had kept from him. About her aborted career at Vanguard Industries and Nillson and Madigan and Cliff Baker.

"I must bring you back to Paris," she admitted finally, her voice so low he could barely hear her. "If I don't, they will kill him."

The moon had set. In the shadow of the chapel's hulking stones it was so dark that Stoner could not see her face. She fell silent at last, and he leaned his head back against the rough wall, thinking. She accepts responsibility for her lover's life as a matter of fact. No scream for help. No railing at the heavens over an unjust fate. He's the man she loves, and she'll move heaven and earth to protect him.

Abruptly, he got to his feet.

"All right," he said. "It's time we got moving."

Looking up at him, she asked, "Where?"

"To Africa."

"Africa?"

"My daughter's there. I want to see her."

"But Cliff . . ."

"Send word to your friends in Paris that you're following me to Africa. Give them a progress report and they'll keep your boyfriend alive."

"But there's a war in Africa!"

"I know," Stoner said. "I need to find out what the war's all about. What's causing it. *Who's* causing it."

"Why? I don't understand."

Reaching out his hand to her, he answered, "I've got to see it firsthand. That's the only way I'll be able to stop it."

AFRICA

Why this is hell, nor am I out of it

CHAPTER 25

The land lay in ruins. Stoner and An Linh walked along a path that had once threaded through a rich forest. Now it was a wasteland, treeless, barren. The hot tropical sun hung high in a cloudless brazen yellow sky, beating down on them like a merciless god.

"The war did this?" An Linh asked.

"No," said Stoner. "These trees were cut down by hand, one by one. There was no battle fought here."

They had changed. For nearly two months now the two of them had been on the move across the width of central Africa. They had lost track of which country they were in. For more than a week they had been trekking on foot; the solar-powered electric jeep Stoner had "borrowed" from a puzzled, darkly suspicious Ghanian major had run over a land mine, blowing off its left front wheel and knocking both Stoner and An Linh completely out of the open car.

So now they walked. Stoner was leaner, tougher, his face taut and hard where it was not covered by the bristly dark growth of a month-old beard, hollows in his cheeks, gray eyes moving constantly, searching, probing, on the alert against hidden snipers or ambushers who would gladly kill him for his boots or the woman or just because he was not one of the local tribesmen. The camouflage green fatigues he wore were caked with dirt, one knee torn slightly, the sleeves rolled up past the elbows. He toted a bedroll and small pack on his back. He carried no weapon of any kind.

An Linh also wore fatigues. They were several sizes too large for her and hung limply on her slim frame. She had cut her hair boyishly short after a week in the bush, and with the dirty green baseball cap she wore, it was not easy to tell that she was a woman—at least, from a distance.

Stoner had lost his hat in a wild firefight they had been caught in a few days earlier. They never saw either side.

They had been working their way down a steep wooded
hillside, treacherously slippery after a sudden downpour, when
automatic rifle and machine gun fire erupted on both sides of
the trail. Stoner had grabbed An Linh and dived for the
shallow cover of a fallen log. Bullets whined and cracked all
around them, chewed up the log and churned up the yellowish mud in which they were both trying to bury themselves.
Then it was over. A minute, perhaps. Or even less. It had
seemed like years. The noise of gunfire still rang in their ears
as Stoner slowly, cautiously, lifted his face from the slimy
mud and took a careful look around. The woods were absolutely silent, a faint wisp of bluish smoke drifting upward and
dissipating like a forlorn ghost, the acrid smell of gunpowder
burning through the humid air.

Then insects began buzzing again, birds cried out, and the
monkeys high in the trees started scolding angrily. Stoner got
to his knees, then to his feet, his boots sticking stubbornly in
the muck. He helped An Linh up. With shaking hands she
tried to wipe the yellowish ooze off her face. She did not
complain about the mud or dirt or heat. She did not mention
how awful she must look, unwashed, without makeup, caked
with days of grime. She just stared at the splintered log,
realizing how close the messengers of death had come.

"It's all right," Stoner said to her quietly. "They've gone,
whoever they were."

She nodded and started down the slippery slope again.
Stoner realized his cap was gone, looked around for a few
moments, then decided it was better to be away from this
spot, even bareheaded.

Now they walked wearily in the blazing sun through a
deforested area. No sound of bird or monkey or even an
insect. The ground was caked dry beneath their boots, pow-
dery dust raised by each footstep.

"Defoliated," An Linh murmured, her voice parched and
strained.

Stoner shook his head. "I don't think so." Pointing to the
stubble of tree stumps on both sides of the trail, "People
have been cutting down the trees. Probably using them for
firewood." He realized that his own voice was harsh, his
throat burning.

"Then there must be a village up ahead," An Linh reasoned.

"Unless the people who did this were from the village we passed this morning."

It had been utterly destroyed. Empty and dead as a desecrated tomb. A village of mud-walled huts scattered haphazardly around a single cinder-block one-story building—the village center, obviously. But the cinder blocks were scorched black, the building's roof caved in by fire. Each hut had been methodically sacked, then burned. Stoner had poked into the still smoking ruins of the central building. Beneath the fallen timbers lay a half-dozen bodies, laid out neatly in a row, charred black. Shot before the fire was started, he realized. They found more bodies in some of the huts. But no living person or animal remained in the village. It had happened so recently that the stench of death was barely noticeable. Yet vultures were already circling high above in the merciless sky.

"Why would someone destroy a village like that?" An Linh asked as they pushed along the dead, dusty, deforested trail.

"Reminds me of Vietnam," said Stoner. "Somebody came in, rounded up the village elders and shot them, did a little raping and looting, moved the rest of the people out, and then burned the place to the ground."

"But why?"

" 'We destroyed the village in order to save it,' " Stoner quoted grimly. "They stole everything they could carry, burned the rest, and moved the people to someplace where they could be protected from the other side—who will one day come into the new village, shoot the leaders, rape the women, steal everything they can carry, and burn the rest."

An Linh stared at him, her eyes red from fatigue and the dust that was blowing through the oven-hot air with every wafting breeze.

The sun was lowering over the hills when they caught their first sight of the village. It was surrounded by a rude palisade of lean poles, lashed together and topped with spirals of barbed wire. Thatched roofs rose above the top of the circling fence, and smoke was drifting up from several of the huts. Something glittered among the roofs, catching the brilliant rays of the sinking sun. It was too bright for Stoner to look at directly or to make out what it was. On the far side of the village Stoner could see cultivated fields and even a few oxen pulling plows. There were several corrals of gnarled poles lashed together, filled with fat cattle. Stoner's nose wrinkled at their smell, but he realized that, by the standards of the war-torn land, this village was rich.

Rich enough to have armed guards posted at the palisade gate, he saw. Two old men in shabby shirts that hung out over their knee-length shorts sat beside the open gate, a pair of automatic rifles leaning against the rickety fence, within arm's reach. The low sun was in their faces, painting them a rich reddish gold, making them squint and hold up their hands to shade their eyes as they saw Stoner and An Linh approaching.

They picked up their rifles and got to their feet. One of the men, the taller of the pair, rested his gun on his hip, pointing it at the strangers. The other tugged a palm-sized flat black object from his ragged cut-off trousers and spoke into it. A radio, Stoner realized.

"Who are you?" shouted the taller villager. "What do you want?"

His dark face was deeply wrinkled; squinting painfully against the sun made even more lines. His hair was grizzled, his bare arms and legs long and lean. But he held the rifle steadily, with the calm assurance of long practice. Stoner guessed that he could fire it quite accurately from his hip, especially at a range of only a dozen meters or so.

"We're not armed," Stoner said in the same language the villager had spoken. "We are looking for the Peace Enforcers."

More villagers appeared at the gate, mostly old men, but some boys and even a few young women were among them. Each carried a gun of one sort or another. They scowled at the two strangers, whether out of suspicion or fear or hatred—or merely having the sun in their eyes—Stoner could not yet tell.

Satisfying themselves that the strangers were not armed, that neither of them was African, that they were indeed alone and not the vanguard of a marauding band of looters, they allowed An Linh and Stoner into their village. Under guard.

Stoner counted twenty-seven armed men, boys, and girls as they walked along the dusty twisting lane past mud-walled huts and a few square cinder-block houses scattered among them. Women appeared at the doorways, most of them hanging back in the shadows, silent, their black faces impassive, but their eyes bright with curiosity. Stoner smiled inwardly.

It was the same curiosity that a scientist would show when he stumbled across a new and unexpected phenomenon. It's built into the human race, he said to himself. Curiosity may have killed the cat, but it's raised human beings up from the level of the apes.

An Linh was taking it all in, just as curious and wide-eyed as any of the villagers. As they trudged along the twisting pathway in a silence broken only by the occasional clink of a gun butt against a bandolier of cartridges, Stoner saw up ahead of them a two-story building, topped by an array of dish-shaped solar mirrors, almost blood red in the reflection of the setting sun. That's what was gleaming so brightly, he realized. This village has solar power. They don't have to cut down the forest anymore.

As their escorts brought them toward the central building, Stoner could hear the clanking and buzzing of open-air workshops. The central square was surrounded by minifactories set up in lean-tos and makeshift sheds. Men and women worked side by side, bent over metal piping, welding in showers of sparks, cutting sheets of bright metal with whirring power tools. They hardly looked up from their work, and Stoner found himself beginning to burn with curiosity. He almost laughed at the human sensation of it. You still have some monkey genes in you, don't you?

Behind the central building, he saw, a power station hummed away, converting the heat energy collected by the rooftop mirrors to the electricity that drove the workers' power equipment and welding tools.

They stopped at the entrance to the cinder-block building, a set of blank double metal doors. The doors, the building itself, all the machinery that Stoner saw looked very new, shining, not yet scuffed and smudged by hard use.

The doors were opened from the inside by another pair of armed men. These two wore merely pistols strapped to their hips. Their sleeveless, buttonless shirts and baggy cut-off shorts, although less shabby than everyone else's, were hardly uniforms. Both the new guards looked as sternly as they could at Stoner and An Linh, but they were too young to seem really fierce. The leader of the band that had been escorting them, the taller of the two old men who had been guarding the gate, spoke up loudly, saying that he and his men (he ignored the girls among them) had brought these two

strangers to the chief's house, as commanded. They had done
their job, and now they would wait outside the chief's house
in case the chief needed them for some further tasks.

One of the young guards frowned and said, "No, no. You
have done your duty. Get back to your post! The south gate
is unprotected."

They argued back and forth over that for a few minutes.
Finally the old man dispatched almost all his people to the
south gate. But he insisted on waiting here by the village's
central building to see what the chief was going to do about
these two strangers. Reluctantly, most of the youngsters and
old men in his charge started walking back toward the gate.
Stoner noticed that the only members of his loose squad who
remained were three of the young girls. The old man ignored
them and sat on the dusty bare ground in front of the double
doors.

The two young guards motioned to Stoner and An Linh.

"We're being invited inside," Stoner said, letting An Linh
step through the open doors ahead of him. She went in
silently, without a trace of fear on her face. Stoner thought
that once she saw the solar energy array and the machinery,
she felt that they were in a civilized setting, and now she was
more curious than afraid.

Stoner half expected the cinder-block building to be air-
conditioned, but it was not. Yet it was insulated well enough
to be noticeably cooler inside. Not really comfortable, by his
own standards, but at least they were out of the searing heat
of the late afternoon. His mind flashed back to the days on
Kwajalein, where the salt air was so heavy with humidity that
clothes, food, everything was always soddenly damp.

The guards shut the door behind them. After the bright
sunlight outside, the building's interior seemed dim and shadowy. There were no partitions, he saw as his eyes adjusted to
the lower level of lighting. Just one large room, with desks
and tables scattered about in no discernible order. The windows were shuttered tightly, although glints of brightness
showed through chinks between the slats, like tiny beams of
laser light trying to burn their way into the big, open room.

An Linh moved closer to Stoner and put a hand on his
arm. But his attention focused on the far corner of the room,
where a desk, a pair of chairs, a long table piled high with
blueprints and other papers, an army cot covered by a single

rumpled blanket, and a smaller table holding a computer and a telephone terminal were jammed together so tightly that a man could sit on either one of the chairs or on the rumpled cot and reach any one of the items there.

A man was sitting at one of the chairs. He got up and edged himself around the corner of the desk, past the narrow strait where the cot and the long table almost met, and then walked the nearly empty length of the room toward Stoner and An Linh.

He was a very tiny man, wizened and snowy-haired. His skin was deeply black, his eyes alert and piercing. Incongruously, he wore a pair of soldier's khaki pants rolled up almost to his knees and a loose-fitting batik vest patterned in bold reds and browns. Over one breast of the vest was pinned a nametag: KATAI. On the other side another plastic tag proclaimed INTERNATIONAL PEACEKEEPING FORCE.

He stopped a few paces before them and looked the strangers over carefully, his hands clasped behind his back. He only came up to Stoner's chest, and he could have weighed no more than a robust twelve-year-old, Stoner thought. His face had the sunken-in look of a man who had lost most of his teeth. He had obviously not shaved in days. Yet his eyes sparkled with undimmed intelligence. Stoner thought of his own appearance, bearded, gaunt, dirty. And An Linh, standing beside him, was equally disheveled and crusted over with grime.

The old man smiled at them toothlessly. "I can speak French, if that will make it easier for you. I have no English."

"French will be very good," said Stoner.

He nodded. "I am called Katai. I am the elder of this village."

"My name is Keith Stoner. This is An Linh Laguerre."

"I am pleased to meet you," said Katai, "although it is a very great surprise to find the two of you at our village gate. What are you doing in this land?"

"We are seeking a detachment of Peace Enforcers." Pointing to the old man's badge, Stoner added, "I see they have been here."

"Oh, yes. This village is under their protection. It is they who taught my people how to use modern machinery."

"They have gone?" An Linh asked.

"Yes, of course. They are few in number, and their task is

a very large one. Like gods, they seek to calm the hearts of men and give them gifts of wealth and peace. Yet there are so many men filled with hatred and fear, so much war and plundering, that even the Peace Enforcers are hard-pressed.''

"Do you know where we could find them?" Stoner asked.

"Yes. I think so. I can call their headquarters on the radio they left and find out for you where their nearest detachment may be.''

"We would appreciate that.''

"Of course! But first you must rest and eat. You must allow us to show you the proper hospitality. I can see that you have come a long way, and you are fatigued.''

"Yes, we are,'' said An Linh.

"Then you must be our guests. We can offer you many of the comforts of modern civilization, even a shower with hot water! You are very fortunate to have found our village.''

Stoner smiled at him. "I can see that. What is the name of this village?''

The old man blinked. "Why, Katai, of course. What other name could it be?''

Katai had the two young guards show them up the stairs, apologizing that his age made it difficult for him to climb. Stoner was pleasantly surprised to find a functional Western bathroom, complete with shower stall and four separate cubicles with army cots in each. The cinder-block walls of the cubicles were bare except for a calendar and a pair of nude photos taken from magazines. They had been taped up so recently that not even the equatorial heat had curled them yet. This must be where the Peace Enforcers sleep when they visit the village, Stoner reasoned.

Wordlessly, he chose one of the cubicles and An Linh another. They had been living together for weeks now, sleeping in the open for the most part, yet the matter of sex had never even been mentioned. An Linh seemed to accept Stoner as a sort of older brother, a guardian and companion rather than a possible mating partner. Stoner knew she was attractive and vulnerable, knew that he could have her if he wanted her, knew even that somewhere deep within him he did want her, just as every male ape wants every available female for himself. But he made no overtures. The alien part of his mind seethed with disgust at the thought of coupling like an animal.

Sometimes, late at night as she slept and he lay on his back staring into the starry sky, he felt frightened that his natural human instincts were under such constraint. Yet even as the flames of fear began to burn within him, he felt them banked down, smothered, extinguished by a presence that enforced calm and suppressed emotion. So he accompanied An Linh across the war-torn wilderness, and they lay together each night without touching.

The guards insisted that they give up their clothes, to be washed by the village women. They offered some of their own spare clothing in exchange. Stoner made the trade gladly, even though the threadbare jeans and sleeveless shirt he wormed himself into were barely big enough to fit him without bursting a seam. An Linh looked beautiful in a long khaki shirt that she belted at the waist and turned into a mini-skirted dress.

"There's still a pretty face under all that mud," Stoner joked when she came out of her cubicle, hair still wetly shining.

"I wish I had some makeup," she said.

"You don't need it."

"Do you think they'll have our own clothes ready for us by tomorrow?" she asked.

He looked her up and down. "I think you look much better this way. I had forgotten that you had legs."

Grinning, she shot back, "You have lovely legs, too. Have you ever thought of shaving them?"

CHAPTER 26

They were both laughing as they went down the narrow wooden stairway to the ground floor. Katai smiled back at them, standing behind a table that had been bare an hour earlier. Now it was laden with an assortment of fruits, dishes of meats and steaming vegetables, and a pile of huge round flat breads that looked as light as gossamer. Candles burned at either end of the table, filling the big room with the pungent odor of incense.

Spreading his arms to take in the whole table, Katai said almost apologetically, "I am afraid that the Peace Enforcers took their eating implements with them and we have none to offer you. We eat with our fingers, of course, and I hope you do not mind doing the same."

Stoner noticed that the old man had teeth in his mouth now. "If you'll show us what to do . . ."

"I will be happy to." But Katai hesitated. "Would you mind if I asked the village council to join us? They are very eager to learn of your story. As I am, also."

An Linh answered, "We will be happy to."

They literally ate off the floor, sitting themselves on a woven grass mat after Katai introduced the twelve men of the village council and they all made their way down the long table. Katai led An Linh and Stoner, showing them how to use the bread puffs as a platter to hold the food they selected from the abundant assortment of dishes that were displayed for them. Over the redolence of the incense candles, Stoner sniffed fragrances hinting of strange, exotic spices.

His mind wandered back to the first time he had been invited to a Mexican fiesta, a lifetime ago when he had been a student in Texas and he and Claude and a gang of the other astronomy students had driven across the border at Laredo. But it wasn't the flat brown Texas back country he saw in his mind's eye. It was a gleaming metallic ring hovering in midair while his entire family, all one hundred of his crèche mates, stood linking hands, completing the circle, reaffirming their bonds of genetic kinship and individual harmony as the orange sun set exactly behind the stele that marked the end of the old year and the beginning of the new. He could feel the tingling of his body fur as he clasped the hands of the mates on either side of him and watched the hundred separate shades of their coats shimmer and shift until they all turned the same golden hue of joy. Before this feast was over they would shed their pelts completely and begin the new year as naked as the moment they had been spawned in the cavern of the sea.

Stoner felt his legs buckling beneath him. He grabbed for the table edge with both hands and leaned heavily, head down, eyes squeezed shut.

"Keith, what's wrong?"

"Are you ill, sir?"

He took a deep breath. The fragrance of the hot food brought his mind back to *here* and *now*, to an African village on the planet Earth, to a world in which he was both a fugitive and a hunter.

"I'm all right," he said, his voice weak and distant. With an effort he straightened up, lifted his bearded chin. "Sorry. I must be more exhausted than I thought I was."

"Food will do you good," suggested Katai.

The old man watched Stoner carefully as they went down the table, then walked across the big room to the mat spread over the cement floor. An Linh followed him and sat at his side. The food tasted good: the meats were hot and spicy, the fruits tangy and refreshing. They drank something chalky white, thick; it had an alcoholic kick to it. Fermented cow's milk, Stoner decided.

While they ate, a group of several dozen children were ushered into the room, escorted by four adult men, and began to serenade the diners. Their high-pitched voices sounded strangely pleasant as they sang, faces serious with concentration, eyes on their leader, about the beautiful woodlands and abundant crops of their country, the lovely animals and the rains that make the land fruitful. Stoner was reminded of a similar song he had learned when he had been a child: "O beautiful for spacious skies,/For amber waves of grain/For purple mountain majesties/Above the fruited plain! . . ."

He saw that An Linh was enchanted by the children, smiling at them and enjoying their performance so much that she had stopped eating. Not so the elders of the council. They smiled encouragingly, too. No doubt some of those boys and girls were their grandchildren. But they kept on eating all through the concert.

When the children had left and the diners had finished eating, a dozen women entered the room and cleared away the remaining food from the table. Except for a few crumbs there was nothing to take away from the circle of diners on the woven mat. One of the advantages of using your fingers, Stoner thought, and eating the dinner plates. There were no insects in sight, no ants or other bugs to bother them. Then he saw a flash of motion, the scurrying of a tiny, long-tailed lizard. And another one, hanging motionless up near the ceiling. Pest controllers.

Katai spread his hands to silence the whispering conversations among the councilmen, then announced, "We have been honored with guests this night." Turning to Stoner and An Linh, "It is our custom to tell guests of the history of our village. Tonight we will give you the short version"—he smiled—"and emphasize recent events. I doubt that our ancient genealogies will be of much interest to you."

He nodded to one of the council members, a frail, withered gnome, totally bald, who leaned on a gnarled walking stick even while sitting on the mat. He was obviously the oldest man there, possibly the oldest in the village. Yet his voice was strong and rich, like an operatic baritone. Despite Katai's assurance, the village historian began his tale with the primeval moment when the gods created the sun, the moon, and the land. Stoner hunched forward eagerly. As an astrophysicist, cosmology had been an intriguing puzzle to him. Now he listened to the villager's ideas of how the world came into being.

The gods created the land but saw that it was dry and lifeless, so they created the clouds that yielded rain. Only when they saw that rain made the land bountiful did they create men. Not one single original man, Stoner heard, but men. Many of them. And women, to serve them. But even with women and land and rain and food growing out of the ground, the men were not satisfied. They quarreled among themselves and killed one another. This displeased the gods mightily, and the gods therefore decided to stop the rain and let the land—and mankind—wither into death. So the rains stopped, and drought turned the land to dust. And the men began to die.

One of the gods took pity on the starving, dying men and stole fire from a volcano's pit and gave it to one tribe of men. The tribe of Katai. The men of this village. Since they were nobler than most men, the men of Katai shared this wonderful gift with other men, and soon all the people of the land had fire. With fire, not only could men warm themselves and protect themselves against the beasts of the forests, they could also make clouds of their own, and the clouds would yield rain. This is why, the village historian said quite seriously, a drought may be broken by building big bonfires and sending clouds of smoke into the empty sky. Naturally, he added, the smoke clouds will yield rain only if the men prepare the fire in precisely the correct way, according to ancient ritual, and placate the gods with gifts and prayers. For if the gods are angry with men, not even the greatest fire will produce a single drop of rain.

An Linh seemed to be nodding off to sleep, chin dropping, eyes closing, while the old villager droned on. Stoner listened, fascinated, as the historian jumped ahead to the time when fierce nomadic warriors swept across the land, converting every village to a new religion that worshiped only one god called Allah. The villagers accepted Allah and added him to their other gods, although to the warriors they pretended to worship only the warriors' god. Generations later a new kind of man came upon their village, offering gifts of steel tools if the villagers would accept a new god whose symbol was a cross. The villagers accepted the gifts gladly, together with the new god. The men of the cross also thought that their god was the only god, yet the villagers knew better. One of their oldest gods died every year, to be reborn in the planting season; this was nothing new. And although the men of the cross said that their god was a jealous god and would have no other gods worshiped with him, the villagers soon found that there were many different men of the cross, who fought against each other, even killing one another while their god of peace and love watched impassively from his cross.

One group of strangers eventually won out over the others and took command of the land. This is why the men of the village, to this day, can speak their foreign tongue. But several generations ago the strangers grew weary of being in a land that was not truly theirs. Although the men of Katai did nothing to harm them, the strangers went away and the authority of the land returned to its rightful owners.

"Our village is part of a great nation," Katai took over. "So we are told. We pay a tax each year to this great nation, yet we see nothing of its greatness."

An Linh was sound asleep, leaning against Stoner, who had put his arm around her shoulders. The village elders said not a word about her; they ignored her presence among them.

He asked, "But didn't your national government build the solar power system for you?"

"We built it for ourselves!" snapped one of the councilmen.

Katai raised a placating hand. "We did build it ourselves, but we had help and guidance."

"From your central government," Stoner said.

"Oh, no." Katai smiled as if the thought of getting help from the national government were something of a joke. "No, we received our help from the Peace Enforcers."

"The Peace Enforcers?"

The village of Katai had been squarely in the path of the war burning through central Africa, Katai explained, when a contingent from the International Peacekeeping Force arrived. For two whole days and two nights the air was filled with huge hovering machines that alighted on the ground and disgorged hundreds of men and women in the sky-blue uniforms of the Peace Enforcers. And their equipment: trucks and crates and tents and machines of every description. All the while the sky far overhead was crisscrossed by aircraft flying so high that nothing could be seen of them except the thin white trails they left behind them.

Far from being warriors, the Peace Enforcers were engineers, medical doctors, and—strangest surprise of all—even farmers. They came from many distant lands. Some of them were as dark as any man of Katai, while others were so milky white that they could not go outside in the sunlight unless they slathered their faces and arms with a liquid that protected their skin against burning.

The village was put under their protection, and Katai was told that a battle had been fought miles away to stop the advancing invaders from coming any closer. A strange battle, from what Katai learned. No man among the Peace Enforcers actually did any fighting; they stayed in their camp just outside the village and sent strange flying machines off to slaughter the enemy.

The Peace Enforcers soon saw that the village of Katai faced a serious problem. Each day the men of the village had to walk miles to find firewood. In bygone years, gathering firewood had been women's work. But the forest moved farther away each year, and now it was so far distant that only men could go out to cut the wood. The villagers knew that they were killing the forest, but what else could they do? Without wood they would have no fires. Without fire, they were little better than the beasts of the field. That was when the Peace Enforcers showed the villagers how to build the solar power station. With help from these strangers, the villagers began to get their energy from the sun itself, and now many of the village men—and even women—were building heaters and stoves for every home in Katai village.

The Peace Enforcers also helped the farmers with medicines for their livestock and new kinds of seed, which, they said, will grow well even in a dry year. Katai had his doubts about that, but since the gods had sent enough rain for a good crop, there was no need to worry about a dry year. Not yet.

Not everything the Peace Enforcers offered was accepted by the villagers, Katai pointed out. The strangers suggested— even insisted—that his people should stop selecting male children over female and return to the old way, where a husband could not choose whether his wife bore him a son or a daughter. By choosing to have so many boys, the Peace Enforcers said, villages such as Katai have created a huge imbalance of men over women, and this is one of the causes of the war. Too many men, they claimed, lead to violence and fighting. Katai himself thought that perhaps the wise strangers were correct, but he knew that any man in his right mind would choose to have sons rather than daughters. How could he, or any of the elders, tell their young men to stop selecting sons?

Except for that, the village benefited and grew rich from the strangers from the sky. The solar array was a sign to all the world that the village of Katai was protected by the Peace Enforcers. High in the sky, up where the stars shine, the Peace Enforcers have a machine that watches over the village night and day. If any invaders should try to attack Katai, the Peace Enforcers will return to drive them away. Thus peace has come to the village. And with peace, abundant crops.

Stoner took it all in. The Peace Enforcers had done a good job here. These people trusted them. In time, they might even make inroads in the areas of birth control and population growth that lay at the heart of the region's troubles. But what about the other villages he had seen, burned out and looted? Had they been under the protection of the Peace Enforcers also? If so, how much did that protection mean? Could a small contingent of men and women actually protect a village, a region, a nation against war? No matter how sophisticated their technology, or how dedicated they were,

Stoner doubted it. There *were* too many young men, too many weapons, too much poverty and fear and anger.

"Now you must tell us your story," Katai said. The men of the council nodded and muttered agreement.

How much should I tell them? he wondered. How much can they understand?

Then he decided that they were human beings, nothing less, and they could understand anything that any human could understand. He decided to tell them the entire story, just as they had told theirs, from the beginning.

"Many years ago," he began, "I lived in the land called America. I was a scientist, a man who studied the stars."

"I, too, study the stars," said one of the councilmen with a bright, eager smile.

Stoner nodded and returned his smile. "In my native land, we have built enormous machines to help us in such studies. And one of the machines we built was placed in space, among the stars themselves, alongside the machine that watches this village for the Peace Enforcers."

An Linh stirred slightly, but Stoner held her and went on with his story. He began to enjoy the challenge of putting his tale into terms that the village elders could understand. They recognized the alien for what he was, a visitor from another star. They saw nothing impossible or fearful in that—at least, nothing more fearful than the various strangers who had invaded their village over the centuries.

Stoner told them about his voyage to the alien spacecraft, and how he was frozen there and eventually recovered and brought back to Earth.

"You slept for eighteen years?" asked an incredulous councilman.

"Yes, I did."

"What did you dream?" asked another.

Stoner paused. "I don't know. I cannot remember any of my dreams."

They muttered among themselves for a few moments before Katai said, "But now that you have awakened, what brings you here to our village? And where did you find this woman?"

Stoner glanced down at An Linh. In sleep her face looked more childlike than womanly.

"We seek the Peace Enforcers," he said. "My daughter married one of them. I have not seen her in twenty years."

"And this woman with you?"

"She was being pursued by evil men. I am protecting her."

That puzzled them, and Stoner had to admit that the situation puzzled him as well. Had he taken An Linh under his protection, or had she sought him out and clung to him? Some of both, he decided. The rare hermit aside, no human being likes to be alone. Even holy men who have shunned civilization end up by creating a monastic order of monks and building temples and castles, transforming their tiny slice of wilderness into an ordered, sheltered habitat with rigid rules of conduct and thick stone walls.

"The Peace Enforcers will come in the morning," said Katai. "I have spoken with them on the radio they left with us. They will send a helicopter for you in the morning."

For a moment Stoner was surprised that Katai knew the word "helicopter." Then, as he grinned his thanks to the old man, he marveled at how supple the human mind can be. Radio, helicopter, Peace Enforcers with remotely controlled drone weapons, modern electronics, observation satellites—all these strange new bits of technology were miracles on the day the villagers first saw them and commonplace a few weeks later. Just like people anywhere. The first space missions were the biggest peacetime media events of the century, but by the time the third team of astronauts reached the moon, hardly anyone cared.

Most of the old men of the council were obviously sleepy. Stoner rose slowly to his feet, lifting An Linh in his arms, and thanked them for their hospitality.

"How can I repay you?" he asked.

The man who studied the stars replied, "If you are not too sleepy, you could come outside with me and we could examine the sky together."

"I'd be glad to."

Stoner carried An Linh upstairs and deposited her sleeping form gently on the cot. Then he hurried down again and, together with the village stargazer and Katai, stepped out into the deeply dark night.

There were no lights at all outside the village's central building. The other councilmen were making their way back to their homes by the faint glow of a crescent moon and fainter glimmerings of the stars. Throwing his head back, Stoner saw the resplendent heavens: Orion and his Dogs, the Bull, the Twins, the shimmering band of the Milky Way glowing against the darkness. He felt a thrill he had not known since childhood as he picked out individual stars, like old friends, and renewed acquaintances.

Hello, Altair, he said silently. Hello, Rigel and old Beetle Juice, Sirius and Procyon, Castor and Pollux. Still in your places, I see. Still as bright and dependable as ever.

One of the points of light was moving slowly from west to east. A satellite. Maybe the alien's spacecraft, Stoner thought. He closed his eyes and saw the stars from a different view, a vantage point deep in space above the alien world, a sky that no human eye had ever seen. Not the velvet softness of Earth's night with its inconstant moon and scattering of stars. This sky was ablaze with stars, hundreds of thousands of them, gleaming and glittering like heaps of multicolored jewels strewn so thickly that no darkness pierced their display. Stars so thick that they dazzled the eye, so close that you could almost touch them.

"Is that the machine that watches our village?"

Stoner snapped his eyes open. He was in Africa, the night was dark, the stars above few and feeble. Insects buzzed and chirruped in the shadows.

"That is an artificial satellite, yes," he answered the stargazer.

"Is it true that the stars influence our destiny?" Katai asked.

Stoner felt himself smile in the darkness. Of course it's true, he told himself. But to the village leader he said, "That depends on what you mean by 'influence.'"

They launched into a discussion of philosophy and astronomy as the stars wheeled slowly above them. Katai grew weary, finally, and bade them good night. Stoner and the stargazer, whose name was Zahed, debated the possibilities of predestination, discussed the origin of the universe, the nature of time, the orbital mechanics of artificial satellites.

Zahed produced a pair of binoculars, a gift from one of the Peace Enforcers, and they took turns studying the slim crescent of the moon. Stoner saw pinpoints of light shining on the darkened part and told his newfound friend that they must be the lights from human settlements on the moon.

"Oh, yes," said Zahed quite matter-of-factly, "there are several villages on the moon now. I have seen them on the television."

The moon went down, and they turned their attention to the stars. The binoculars were not powerful enough to separate Castor into its three binary components. But they could see the shining veils of luminosity that hung among the blazing stars of the Pleiades. As he peered through the binoculars, resting them against a low fence to keep them steady, Stoner wondered if this star cluster might be the home of the alien. No, he decided. The view from the homeworld is clear, not shrouded with nebulosity. And the Pleiades is too poor a cluster to make the heavens glow the way I saw them.

At last the stars began to dim and the sky turned gray, then milky white. A brilliant star rose above the eastern horizon, far brighter than Sirius.

"That is the planet Venus," Stoner said.

"Yes, I know," replied Zahed. "One of the Russians among the Peace Enforcers told me that it is a world like ours, but so hot that the ground glows like burning coals."

Nodding, Stoner agreed. "True enough."

The sun rose, huge and red, its glare overpowering the lesser lights, driving even beautiful Venus from sight. The true jealous god, Stoner thought. He will have no other gods sharing our adoration.

Then he heard the faint whickering sound of a distant helicopter.

Zahed heard it, too. "The Peace Enforcers. Katai said they would be here in the morning."

"They must get up early."

"They are like you," said the stargazer. "They never sleep."

Stoner laughed. "I haven't seen your eyes close all night."

"I will sleep later, during the afternoon, when the sun climbs high and it is too hot to do anything else."

Stoner could see the helicopter now, a dark spot moving fast across the sky to the west of the village.

And he saw a white streak leap up from the wooded hills out in the distance, crossing the sky almost faster than the eye could follow, heading directly for the approaching helicopter.

Before he could say a word, the rocket hit the helicopter and exploded in a blazing fireball. The helicopter blew apart, dark, smoking pieces raining down onto the dusty plain below. One of the pieces looked like a human being, and Stoner imagined he could hear the man screaming to his death.

CHAPTER 27

The shock wave of the explosion took almost a full minute to reach them, and when it did Stoner flinched as if struck in the face. The realization hit him at the same time: someone has destroyed a Peace Enforcer helicopter and killed its pilot.

He stared wordlessly at the dirty black smoke cloud expanding into the clean morning air. Beside him, Zahed gaped as if one of his gods had just been killed. Then he turned and ran toward the village's central building.

Stoner saw flashes of light from the distant hills, rockets being fired from the concealment of the forests miles away. In the moment it took his brain to register that the rockets were being fired at the village, the first of them hit and exploded just outside the rickety palisade. The fence caved inward, spindly stakes bursting apart like so much kindling. Four more hit just behind it, inside the village, blasting apart several mud-walled huts. The roar of the explosions almost deafened Stoner. The dried thatch of other huts' roofs caught fire. People ran screaming from their homes, some of them naked, women clutching babies, older children stumbling, sprawling, crying.

The next explosion knocked Stoner off his feet. A cinderblock house took a direct hit and disappeared in a ball of flame and dust. More shells rained down. Stoner saw one hit in the open area where people were milling about. Bodies flew everywhere, the stench of blood and death carried on the concussion wave that blew stinging dust into Stoner's face.

Groggy with shock and pain, he forced himself to his feet and staggered toward the central building. The solar array on its roof was already coated with dust from the soil churned up by the explosions.

Katai was at the doorway, leaning against the jamb, his eyes wide with terror. Stoner could not see any obvious wounds on him, the central building had not been hit, yet the old man sagged as if mortally wounded.

"But we are under the protection of the Peace Enforcers!" he screamed to Stoner. "We are under their protection!"

A fresh round of explosions shook the ground and knocked him to his knees. Stoner pushed past the dazed old man and went into the building. An Linh was running down the stairs, stuffing the freshly washed shirt of her camouflage fatigues into the waistband of the trousers.

"I thought this village was safe!" she shouted to Stoner.

"So did they."

He put his arm around her shoulders as they rushed toward the door. Another explosion knocked them both to the cement floor. Windows and the display screens of the telephone and computer on Katai's table shattered. Groping, coughing in the gritty dust, Stoner saw that the doors had been knocked off their hinges. A smoking crater yawned just outside, bodies and pieces of bodies strewn bloodily around it. More explosions, air bursts this time, and the ground was churned by thousands of chunks of white-hot shrapnel flaying the flesh of the living and the already dead without distinction or mercy.

The back half of the building blew away, and the ceiling over them groaned hideously, timbers splitting, flames already licking along their length.

"Come on," Stoner said into An Linh's ear.

"Out there?"

There was no time for discussion. He picked her up in his arms and dashed outside, dodging the sprawled bodies. He heard the deadly whistle of incoming shells and dived into the crater, covering An Linh with his own body. More air bursts, spraying the area with singing, lethal shrapnel.

"They're out to kill everybody," Stoner muttered.

"But why? . . ."

The solar array took a direct hit, mirrors shattering into a thousand glittering slivers that twirled and glinted in the early morning light as they blasted outward in every direction. Two more shells flattened the building, cinder blocks pulverized into dust as Stoner buried his face in the blood-hot protection of the crater's freshly dug earth. Another round of air bursts churned the ground, and he felt a hot sliver slice through the meaty calf of his right leg. An Linh cried out. Turning, he saw a rip across the back of her shoulders, blood soaking the green fatigues.

It's death to stay here, he realized. They won't stop until they've killed every living thing in this village.

He scooped her up in his arms and waited, crouching in the crater, while a fresh round of shells blasted into the village. Then he got to his feet and climbed out of the crater. His right leg stung painfully, but it bore his own weight and that of his burden. Sprinting carefully, deliberately, Stoner headed toward the far end of the village. He stepped over the mangled body of an old man. The face was torn off, nothing below the scalp but an oozing red pulp. It might have been Katai. Stoner did not stop to find out. He heard more shells whistling toward them and ducked behind the shattered wall of what had been a cinder-block house a few moments earlier. The explosions seemed to be concentrated near the center of the village now. They were methodically destroying every building, starting at the periphery and working inward.

Running, dodging bodies and shell holes and the burning debris strewn across the ground, Stoner carried An Linh to the edge of the village, where the palisade fence leaned and sagged like a wall built by a drunkard. In several places the fence had been blown away altogether, replaced by craters.

Stoner looked back into the village. Hardly a building remained standing. No one was moving. The shelling seemed to have stopped. He saw several clouds of dust out in the distant hills: trucks or personnel carriers. They're sending in the infantry to finish the job. They want to make certain they've destroyed the village and everyone in it.

An Linh moaned as he lifted her again. He wondered how deeply the shrapnel had cut into her. And where the nearest medical aid might be. But as he wondered, he ran. In a careful, controlled, measured sprint, he ran away from the village with An Linh in his arms, heading out along the dusty deforested barren ground, running for his life.

Is it me that they're after? he asked himself. Did they destroy the whole village just to get at me? Or An Linh?

Shaking his head, he wondered if he wasn't being paranoid. The village was just another victim in a senseless war. A war you were going to stop, he reminded himself. So what have you accomplished? Nothing. Not a thing. With your delusions of grandeur to guide you, you've witnessed the devastation of a peaceful village and perhaps gotten this poor girl killed.

He ran until fatigue and the growing pain in his leg forced him to stop. Placing An Linh down carefully against the stump of a tree, he sat on it and stretched his leg out. The wound did not look serious; it was already clotting. But it hurt.

Pain is the body's communication system, Stoner explained to himself. It informs the conscious mind that there is a wound or an infection that must be dealt with. Yes, the other part of his mind replied. But the system has its drawbacks. It activates hormonal reactions. Pain stimulates the adrenals and other glands. It leads to fear and panic.

He forced himself to stand and survey his situation. No fear. No panic. Stay calm and see just where you are. In the middle of the barren, dusty, blackened area that once was a forest. Picked clean now, like the carcass of a noble gazelle gnawed to nothing but bones by jackals and hyenas. Except that the bones would be gleaming white, a final proclamation against fate, while the dead remains of these trees were blackened by fire. On every side, nothing but scrawny dead sticks or hacked stumps. No life at all; as barren as the moon. Stoner scanned the area and could not even see a termite nest.

He looked back toward the village. It was a smoking ruin, more than a mile away. Not a sign of life there, either, except for the dust clouds of approaching vehicles coming down from the hills. Katai, Zahed the stargazer, those children who sang for us. All smashed to pulp. Stoner knew that he should feel frightened, angry, remorseful or revengeful or more. But it was as if all emotion inside him was smothered. As if something or someone was damping down the glandular secretions that produced emotions. He was a detached observer, as emotionless as an astronomer peering through a telescope. Somewhere deep within him there should be rage, he knew, fury and hatred and overwhelming grief. But he felt nothing; his soul was frozen, disconnected from the rest of the world by a layer of impenetrable ice.

And he was glad of it. He knew, in the gray thinking part of his brain, that if his emotions held sway, he would collapse right here in a mindless heap of blubbering anguish and guilt. He tensed at the thought of guilt. But yes, it was there. Beyond all shadow of a doubt, beyond the need for evidence, Stoner *knew* that the village had been attacked because he had been in it. Whoever had demolished the village had been trying to murder him. Not An Linh, he realized. Me. This attack had nothing to do with the war. Or with her. They were after me.

And they still are. The troops will go in there and try to find my body. When they don't, they'll send patrols out looking for me. Or helicopters.

He bent down to reach for An Linh again, but as he did his eye caught a flicker of something high up in the sky. Looking up, he saw contrails, six of them. Planes flying so high that they could be neither seen nor heard. In two groups of three they came across the sky from the west.

And the ground erupted beneath them. The hills where the attackers' artillery had fired from simply disappeared in a carpet of flame and thundering, earthshaking explosions. Even at this distance Stoner felt the ground tremble. He sank to his knees, his eyes unable to move from the distant scene of destruction. Methodically, dispassionately, the hillsides where the rocket artillery had been hidden were pounded into flaming rubble. Nothing could live through the terrible bombardment. Nothing.

The dust clouds that marked the troop-carrying vehicles began to veer away from the trail that led to the village and scatter madly across the countryside. To no avail. One by one, each vehicle was sought out and blasted into oblivion. Stoner could not see how, or what weapons were being used. It was as if the finger of an angry god reached down from the heavens and snuffed each vehicle out of existence.

The Peace Enforcers, Stoner knew. Too late to save the village, but not too late to avenge it. Were they angry, whoever flew in those planes, whoever directed those devastating weapons? Or were the Peace Enforcers merely technicians who calmly touched buttons on computer keyboards as they flew seven or eight miles above their targets? Did they realize that they were blasting apart human flesh, pulverizing bones and brains, killing men? Or did they keep their eyes and their thoughts focused on display screens that reduced the facts of mass death to bloodless equations and neat graphs?

It was all the same to the troops on the receiving end of the Peace Enforcers' weaponry. In a matter of moments half a dozen sooty black pyres marked the spots where the troop carriers had been. The hills where the artillery had been sited were ablaze.

The six white contrails, so high above in the pure blue sky, circled the area once, then headed back the way they had come. The village was avenged. Death for death.

But how can we give life in place of death? Stoner asked himself. How can we stop men from killing each other?

He looked down at An Linh again. Her eyes fluttered open. She slowly turned her head, scanning the devastation all around her.

"Am I going to die?" she asked in the voice of a frightened child.

Reaching for her, Stoner said with a confidence he did not feel, "No. I won't let you die. I'll take care of you."

He picked her up again, feeling the burden of her life in his arms, and began walking blindly away from the ruins of the village, through the dead land, toward the east.

It was a beautiful summer afternoon in Moscow, one of those rare days when the sun shone out of a clear sky, when people smiled at one another on the streets and the brightly colored onion domes of church towers gleamed brilliantly.

"After all these years," said Kirill Markov happily, "you finally come to visit me."

Jo grinned at him, masking the haunting fears that followed her. "I never realized what a beautiful city Moscow is."

"Ah!" Markov beamed. "The city is smiling for you. Even nature herself is at her best, to honor the occasion of your visit."

They were standing on the balcony outside Markov's office. Across Red Square, the brick wall of the Kremlin stood as stoutly as ever. But the flamboyant domes of the Archangel Cathedral and the palaces seemed like fairyland towers to Jo. She wore a demure doeskin suede chemise of deep forest green, cinched at the waist with a wide leather belt and solid gold buckle. Markov, never a fastidious dresser, was in a rumpled gray suit and darker turtleneck pullover.

"All of Moscow is at your feet, beautiful lady. What can I do to please you?"

"You always knew how to turn a girl's head."

Markov's smile was also a mask. "Dearest Jo, in the old days I spoke to charm you into a horizontal relationship. But now, at my age . . ."

Jo arched an eyebrow. "You're a dangerous man, Kirill."

"Not as dangerous as you."

"Oh?"

"Do you remember the swimming we did at Kwajalein? And the sharks?"

She burst into loud laughter. "And the outrigger that you managed to turn over!"

"I managed?" He feigned outrage. "There were two of us in that canoe. And to this day I'm not certain it wasn't sabotaged by reactionary elements among the natives."

Laughing together, they stepped back through the French windows into Markov's office. It was a modest room, large enough for its purpose but not so big as to awe visitors. Markov had accepted it from his predecessor when the academy had voted him its new director. The furniture was solid and functional, unchanged from earlier days. The gleaming silver samovar was also the same as before. The only things Markov had introduced into the office had been a splendid carpet from Samarkand to replace the threadbare one he had found there when he had moved in, and a small shelf of books he had written while a professor of linguistics at the university.

Markov went to the samovar to pour tea while Jo sat in the cushioned armchair beside his desk. She accepted a delicate china cup and saucer from him; the hot tea steamed deliciously.

"And how fares Mother Russia?" Jo asked as Markov settled himself in the creaking leather swivel chair behind the desk.

He scratched at his scraggly white beard with one hand while placing his teacup down on the desk.

"Russia will survive," Markov said. "The land, the

people—they will endure. But the Union of Soviet Socialist Republics . . ." He sighed heavily.

"Is it really going to break up?"

Markov shrugged.

"After all these years," Jo murmured. "I just don't understand why it's happening, Kir! Now that the burdens of nuclear weaponry have been lifted from our backs, now that your economy finally seems to be doing better."

"This is not America, my lovely one."

"But what's wrong? Why are you having all these upheavals? Can't your people tolerate prosperity? Do they *have* to be miserable?"

With a sad shake of his head, Markov gestured to the gray metal computer sitting on his desk. "There is the culprit," he said. "One of them, at least."

Jo frowned at him. "The computer?"

"We cannot run a modern nation without computers," Markov said, "any more than you can run your corporation without them."

"Yes, but . . ."

"But," Markov went on, "we cannot control the people once they have computers. There are hundreds of thousands of them in the Soviet Union. Perhaps millions. People use them to communicate with each other. The government has no control over what they say, what they learn."

"But how can that cause such problems for you?"

Markov smiled at her, but there was bitterness in it. "Dearest Jo, coming from America it is difficult for you to understand. The Soviet Union has been built on discipline, on order, on control of the people by the government. Suddenly that control weakens, perhaps evaporates altogether. It's like suddenly giving sight to a person who has been blind all his life. He goes crazy!"

"And that's what's happening to your country?"

"Yes. Thanks to computers and communications satellites and all the other miracles that you of the West take for granted, the peoples of the Soviet Union have started running amok."

"How bad is it?" Jo asked. "I mean, really?"

"It seems that nothing will placate the Moslems, short of civil war," he said, sighing again. "The Uzbeks and Kazakhs

. . . all of them want their own separate nations. And naturally, our Baltic friends are making the same demands.''

"But the Ukraine?"

Markov shrugged. "I am merely the head of the Academy of Sciences. I do not deal with politics."

Jo gave him a skeptical look.

"Well, perhaps just a little," Markov admitted.

"The betting in New York is that your government will offer the other socialist republics a commonwealth arrangement—the way the Brits handled their former colonies like Canada and Australia.''

"That is being discussed," Markov admitted.

Jo sipped at the tea. Then, "It's funny. I mean really funny, to laugh at.''

"What is?"

"The way everybody on Wall Street and in Washington is reacting to your problems.''

"I see nothing funny—"

Jo overrode him. "When I was a kid, everybody in the States who made more than the minimum wage was looking forward to the day when the Soviet Union fell apart.''

"Yes," Markov murmured. "They called us an evil empire in those days.''

"But now that the Union is breaking up—they're all scared to death. Especially the Wall Street types. They don't want the Soviet Union to dissolve.''

"Naturally. It would interfere with their markets. They've learned how to deal with Moscow. Let them try trading with the Uzbeks!''

"I'm going to have to try," Jo said. "Vanguard Industries was contracted to build the fusion power station just outside Tashkent. . . .''

"A joint endeavor with the Soviet electrical power commission," Markov pointed out.

"Of course. But now, nobody seems to know who's responsible for what.''

Markov hunched forward in his chair. It made a hideous groaning creak.

"You ought to have that oiled," Jo said.

He cocked a brow at her. "I have. I think it's me, not the chair.''

She laughed as he tapped an outstretched finger on the keyboard of his desk computer several times.

"Call this man," Markov said, swiveling the display screen so that she could read it. "If anyone in Tashkent can make a decision for you, he can."

Jo nodded and spoke the name and number into her wrist communicator. "Would you call him for me, Kirill? Introduce me to him?"

"I would be happy to. But once he gets a look at you, he will be anxious to help you in any way he can. He will be like butter in your hands." Markov thought a moment, then added, "Rancid butter."

"That bad?"

"The political uncertainties have opened the door to unparalleled opportunities for corruption. Our devout Moslem friends may be ready to give their lives for Allah, but they are even more ready to sell anything else to the highest bidder."

Jo took another swallow of the unsugared tea, replaced the cup on its saucer with a tiny clinking sound. Markov leaned back in the creaking chair, smiling bleakly at her. For several moments the room was silent except for the traffic sounds wafting through the French windows from the street below.

"Kirill," Jo began, speaking slowly, hesitantly, "if it became necessary . . . would it be possible for me to come to Moscow . . . to live here for an indefinite time?"

Curiosity made Markov's eyes go round. "Live here? In Moscow?"

"Under your protection."

He blinked twice. Then, "You mean under the protection of the Soviet government?"

Jo nodded.

"Are you in such danger?"

"I may be."

"But from whom? One of the most powerful women in the capitalist world, who would dare to threaten you?"

Smiling bitterly, she answered, "Someone more powerful than I am, of course."

"I see. You prefer not to tell me."

"It's my husband," Jo admitted.

Markov's face went from curiosity to shock.

"This isn't a marital disagreement," she quickly added.

"It involves corporate politics and global power. I think my life is in danger."

"From your own husband."

"Yes."

He made a snorting little sound that might have been a halfhearted attempt at a laugh. "At my age! After a lifetime of faithful Communist zeal, one of the world's leading capitalists seeks refuge in the Soviet Union—or what's left of it."

"I'm seeking shelter from a friend," Jo said softly.

"Ah, Jo, if only you had asked me ten years ago. Or even five! We would have set the skies ablaze, the two of us."

She smiled at her old friend. Even eighteen years ago, when they had worked together on Kwajalein, Kirill had pursued her with madly passionate rhetoric. But she had never felt threatened by him. He had an Italian attitude toward women: those who said yes to him were far less interesting than those who did not. Jo knew even then that this was a man who could be her friend without sex, despite all his amorous talk. With most men she could never be so relaxed. Sex was always a factor in every other relationship. No matter what they said, most men saw women first as sexual opportunities and only second as business associates or social friends—if then.

Markov prattled on, trying in his clumsily boyish way to amuse her, thinking that the serious expression on her face was from fear or sadness. Actually Jo was thinking that there were only two men in her life she had ever felt truly happy with. Kirill was one of them, a kindly, gentle, brilliantly clever big brother to her. The other was Keith, the man she had loved, the man she had wanted so desperately to love her.

"You are thinking about him, aren't you?"

Jo stirred in her chair, directing her attention back to the Russian.

"I recognize that look in your eyes," Markov said with a heavy sigh. "You were thinking about Keith."

She looked away without replying.

"I saw him, you know."

"You did?"

'More than a month ago. He called me from Paris and I

flew there to meet him. I was under orders to return him here, but he refused to come with me."

Looking into Markov's eyes, Jo saw how troubled he felt.

"He's changed, hasn't he?" she said.

The Russian actually shuddered. "He was always a remarkable man, but now . . ."

Jo wondered briefly if the office were bugged, then decided she really didn't care. "He told me that he thought the alien had somehow gotten into his mind, while he was frozen in the spacecraft."

With a nod, Markov said, "He eluded a team of special agents. It was as if he could make himself invisible."

"Have you tried to find him?"

"Of course. Our best information is that he went to Africa, to the region where the war is going on."

"One of his children is married to a Peace Enforcer."

"Yes, so we learned," Markov said. "Our own people among the International Peacekeeping Force thought for a day or so that he might have reached a village in Chad called Katai. It was a special project of the Peace Enforcers. A model village."

"But he wasn't there?"

Markov shifted uncomfortably in his chair. "By the time we realized he might have been there . . ."

"He had gone?"

"We don't know," Markov said, shaking his head sadly. "The village was attacked—a senseless, stupid, pointless attack. The Peace Enforcers struck back almost immediately and wiped out the attackers, but it was too late. The entire village was annihilated."

"And Keith?" Jo's voice rose half an octave.

Markov threw his hands up. "We simply don't know. The villagers were slaughtered. High-powered artillery. There was no trace of him in the ruins, but he might have been blown to pieces."

"No," she said, fighting down the trembling inside her. "Not Keith. He got out of it alive."

"The official report says that none of the villagers escaped."

"But Keith did. I know he did. He must have!"

Markov stared at her. Her fists were clenched on the arms of the chair, her whole body rigid. He asked himself silently,

If Keith escaped, then where is he? Why has there been no trace of him for weeks? But he did not voice the question.

To break the tension that had suddenly made the room unbearable, Markov asked instead, "But who would have launched an attack on the village? It was utterly senseless. The village was far removed from the fighting. There was no strategic value to it."

Jo's fists unclenched slowly. She asked, "You said it was a model project of the International Peacekeeping Force?"

"Yes."

"Then whoever ordered the attack wanted to humiliate the IPF."

Markov shook his head again. "How could that be? None of the warring factions in central Africa is stupid enough to attack the IPF."

"What makes you think it was one of the factions in the war?"

"But who else? . . ."

Jo closed her eyes wearily. It all made sense. The monomaniacal sense of a madman. Someone who wanted the war to drag on endlessly. Who wanted to destroy the International Peacekeeping Force. Someone who wanted to kill Keith Stoner.

"Who is it?" Markov asked again.

Jo looked at him and lied, "I don't know." But she knew that she would have to return to her husband. She could not seek the safe refuge that Markov was willing to give her. She had to return to Everett Nillson. If Keith was still alive, she had to prevent her husband from killing him. If Keith had died in that massacred African village, she had to avenge his murder.

CHAPTER 28

Cliff Baker eyed Madigan suspiciously. "Why are you doing this?" he asked.

The lawyer shrugged, trying to make it look nonchalant. "Don't look a gift horse in the mouth."

Baker frowned. "That's what somebody told the Trojans, and look what happened to them."

They were walking down a shadowy underground corridor, featureless walls and floors of concrete that smelled damp and felt clammy. Dim naked bulbs dangling every fifty feet from the pipes that ran overhead were the only illumination, throwing feeble pools of light against the chilling darkness.

"Where are we, anyway? How long have I been here?" Baker demanded.

Madigan said, "That doesn't matter."

The Australian newsman was dressed in a gray one-piece coverall, as featureless and undecorated as death itself. Madigan, usually an impeccable dresser, was clad in a dark blue exercise suit that fit tightly at the cuffs of his wrists and ankles. He wore running shoes.

Baker stopped and grabbed at Madigan's arm. "Hey, I want to know what's going on!"

The lawyer pulled his arm free with a faint smile that was almost a sneer. "You're alive and you're getting out of here. That's enough for you to know."

For the span of a heartbeat they stood facing each other. Baker looked unchanged from the day he had been taken by Vanguard agents in Paris, except that his shoulder wound was completely healed. But his eyes were different: the terror and agony of his interrogation were still in them, together with a smoldering fear and the implacable hatred of a man who had been reduced to a whimpering, pleading, gibbering animal who would say anything, tell anything, betray anyone if they would just stop the pain.

Madigan looked tense. His usual smirk of world weary superiority was gone. His face was drawn tight, eyes locked on Baker's.

"Listen," he said, "I'm taking a huge risk, and I'm doing you the favor of your life. Don't—"

Baker lunged at him, wedged a forearm against his windpipe, and slammed him hard against the concrete wall.

"Don't fuck around with me," he snarled. "I don't care what you're risking. Where are we? Where are we going? Why are you doing this?"

"I'm trying to help you!" Madigan barely could grunt the words past Baker's choke hold on him.

"After they turned me inside out and made me spill my guts?"

"I couldn't do anything about that."

"How long have I been in that cell?"

Madigan's strangled voice rasped, "Six weeks . . . almost seven."

"Where are we?"

"New Jersey . . . old Army base . . . can't breathe!"

Baker took his arm away from the lawyer's throat but kept him pinned against the wall. "Where are we going?"

Madigan coughed, then answered, "I've got a car outside. You can drive it to New York City. Lose yourself there. Then you're on your own."

"You're helping me to escape?"

Nodding, the lawyer said, "Nillson thinks you're frozen. He found out your blood type and tissue samples are compatible with his. He ordered you stored away for organ replacements."

Despite himself, Baker sagged. "Organ . . . Jesus Christ."

"I don't want to be implicated in this," Madigan explained. "I'm helping you to get out. Take my advice and stay out! Forget you ever heard of Everett Nillson and Vanguard Industries. Get out of the country and never do anything to draw his attention to you."

Baker's blue eyes were fiery. "What else is there? There's got to be more to it."

Rubbing his throat, Madigan said, "Under interrogation, you told us about this World Liberation Movement—how it's trying to take power away from the corporations and the industrialized nations and give it to the Third World."

"I spilled my guts, didn't I?"

"You told us everything you knew, which wasn't much. Just that the organization is much better organized than we thought it was, and you do what they tell you."

Baker gave a sardonic little chuckle. "That's all I know. They contact me and tell me what they want me to do."

"Once Nillson was certain that he had screwed everything you knew out of you, he gave the order to have you frozen as soon as you had recovered and your shoulder wound healed."

"And you decided to go against him?" Baker's angry suspicion coated his words with scalding ice.

"I've done a lot for him, over the years," the lawyer said.

"A lot. I even spied on his wife for him. But I've never broken American law. Other nations, yeah, sure. You can buy your way out or just stay out of their country. But now it's different. He's asking me to be a party to kidnapping and murder. On American soil. Under American jurisdiction." He shook his head. "I can't do that."

Baker released his hold on the lawyer. "Seems to me you've already been a partner to kidnapping and torture."

"I'm helping you escape. I'm saving you from being frozen."

"Is that murder?"

"It's moot. Until frozen bodies are revived successfully, most courts will call it murder."

"But the astronaut . . ."

"One case—maybe. There are suspicions that he wasn't an ordinary human being."

Baker frowned, perplexed.

"The scientists think that the astronaut might somehow have been affected by the alien spacecraft's computer or . . . something, they don't know what. But he might be different from other human beings."

"Different how?"

"I don't know!" Madigan snapped. "This is a waste of time. You've got to get out of here before somebody spots that car sitting out there on the highway."

They began moving down the tunnel again, almost at a trot.

"So you're helping me out of the goodness of your heart, are you?" Baker said, almost with his old jauntiness.

"Just remember that I've helped you, if and when the time comes."

"You want a friendly character witness at your trial."

"Damned right."

They could see the end of the tunnel. The buzzing sounds of highway traffic echoed off the concrete walls.

"And I want you to remember," Baker said, "that I can get word to Nillson about who helped me to escape."

Madigan stumbled to a halt.

"We're now partners, my friend," said Baker. "When I need your help, I'll expect to get it."

"You can't . . ."

Baker gripped the lawyer's shoulder and squeezed hard.

"It's an old Chinese custom, mate. If you save a man's life, you are responsible for him forever."

He let go, turned away, and sprinted out to the car that was waiting on the shoulder of the highway, leaving Madigan standing there openmouthed and rubbing his shoulder.

Four days later Cliff Baker was just outside Colombo, Sri Lanka, luxuriating in a private mansion that had once been a maharajah's winter palace. To call it ornate would have been an understatement: each room was gaudier than the last, decorated in gold and ivory, silk draperies of blazing reds and yellows, vivid blues and purples, tables inlaid with silver, goblets dripping with precious jewels, tapestries and cushions and fountains and peacocks strutting unafraid of strangers through the lush gardens that surrounded the domed and minareted palace. A wall of living green guarded the grounds. Baker swam in the pool, ate sumptuously, slept on silk in a maharajah's bed.

Alone. For forty-eight hours he wandered through the palace without seeing another human being. The servants were all robots, exquisitely programmed to make him comfortable and cater to his every physical need, except for sex. But they were totally unable to answer any of his questions.

It was the evening of his second day there. Baker was lounging in a heap of pillows, swathed in loose-fitting pajamas of royal blue threaded with silver. The remains of his dinner had been carried away by robots so identical that he could not tell them apart. A warm night wind wafted the draperies along the open garden doorway, bringing just a hint of salty sea tang with it. Baker held a golden, jewel-encrusted goblet in his hand. A robot stood to one side with a bottle of twenty-four-year-old unblended Scotch whisky in its grip.

"Fill 'er up again, mate!"

The robot swiveled on its trunnions and accurately poured a pony of whisky into Baker's goblet.

"Make it a double."

The robot complied. It was of a different design from the others, different from any robot Baker had seen before. Instead of the usual squat, utilitarian, fireplug shape, this one was a slender cylinder of gleaming stainless steel with a dozen arms folded compactly against its shaft until they were needed for some function. Like a bloody Hindu goddess, Baker thought, with all those arms.

"Make it a triple," he ordered.

The robot's arm did not move. "Three drinks in such a short time interval can lead to intoxication," it said with the sultry singsong voice of an Indian woman.

"That's the whole idea, isn't it? Intoxication? There's nothing else to do in this bloody palace, is there? Not even TV."

"Intoxication is to be avoided," said the robot, almost as if it really cared.

"They had to use a woman's voice, didn't they? Everything under the sun in this fuckin' Taj Mahal except a woman. Where are the dancing girls? What kind of a palace is this, anyway?"

He started to chugalug the beautiful Scotch when an entirely different voice replied, "You are unhappy with the accommodations, Mr. Baker?"

It was a man's voice. Deep basso. Baker sputtered whisky and looked around. A very large Oriental man was standing in the doorway that led out to the garden.

Baker scrambled to his feet. "Who the hell are you?" he demanded, just a bit drunkenly.

The Oriental smiled broadly and walked into the splendid room. He wore a simple khaki jumpsuit and black paratrooper boots.

"I am your host, Mr. Baker. Permit me to introduce myself. You may call me Temujin."

He was big. Well over six feet tall and broad across the shoulders. The jumpsuit strained tightly across his chest and arms. Torso as solid as the trunk of an oak tree. Legs to match. Even his hands looked huge, heavy, powerful. At first Baker thought he was shaved bald, but then he realized that there was no hair at all on his parchment-yellow face, not even eyebrows.

"Temujin," Baker repeated.

"Yes. That is not the name I was born to, but it is the name I have adopted." He extended his arm, beckoning the Australian to come toward him, as he went on, "What's in a name, Mr. Baker? In the tongues of central Asia, Temujin means, literally, Man of Steel. In the languages of the Chinese it means Supreme Man of Earth."

"I've heard the name before," Baker muttered, almost mesmerized by the whisky and the Oriental's imposing presence.

"Indeed you have. It was the birth name of the greatest man of all history, the man you Westerners know as Genghis Khan."

"The barbarian conqueror."

"The Mongol emperor who ruled all men from the China Sea to the Danube River!"

Baker shook his head, trying to clear away the cobwebs. "All right, just who the hell are you, really?"

Temujin laughed heartily. "I am your host. This palace is mine."

"Yours?"

"Yes! I hope you have been comfortable. I regret the lack of human companionship—especially women. I'm afraid that I have been testing you. I find sex to be too disconcerting, too distracting. I wanted to see if you could obey orders and remain here without the pleasant diversions that women offer."

Oh, my God, Baker thought, a king-sized queen. Aloud, he asked, "But why was I told to come here? Why did my contact in New York give me a ticket for Sri Lanka and instructions to find this place?"

"Because I told him to," Temujin said. "This is the headquarters from which I direct the World Liberation Movement."

"*You* direct . . . ?"

Sliding a powerful arm around Baker's shoulders, Temujin said jovially, "Come, let me show you."

He led Baker toward a massive, ornately carved pillar that supported the arch connecting the room with the hallway. It slid away as they approached, revealing an elevator shaft. The elevator door opened automatically, and Temujin gestured Baker inside.

It's like a bloody "Arabian Nights," Baker thought, brought up-to-date by this daffy giant gook. Temujin, he calls himself. A gay egomaniac. Mad as a hatter. No, *two* hatters, considering the blooming size of him.

An hour later, Baker was making drastic revisions in his estimation of Temujin's sanity. The elevator led down to a deep underground chamber studded with display screens and computer consoles. It was a large room, but every square centimeter of space on its walls was covered by green-glowing screens. There were no other lights, nor any need for them. The eerie light from the screens was enough. They hummed like a hive of busy insects and occasionally beeped when new information came up. Baker felt sweat trickling under his chin and along his ribs. The hardworking computers generated enough heat to make the room feel oppressive.

"My situation room," Temujin explained as Baker gaped at the screens lining the walls. "The location and status of every World Liberation Movement unit is tracked here. Some of the units—like that one, up in the right-hand corner—are merely single men, working alone. As you were, when you were in Hawaii, Mr. Baker. Most of the others are teams of people. Some of the teams are quite large."

Baker spent the hour studying the screens, absorbing the information on them, while Temujin kept up a patter of self-congratulatory explanations.

"You've more teams in central Africa than anywhere else," he said at last.

Temujin nodded eagerly. "That's where the action is. There's a war going on there, you know."

"I've heard," Baker said dryly.

"The World Liberation Movement has been able to capture the governments of four of the warring nations. And their armies. What started as a fight over food resources has been turned into a battle for control of an entire continent!"

"All of Africa?"

"Of course!" Temujin boasted. "Slowly but surely our side is winning the war in central Africa. Chad is almost taken, and the campaign for Kenya has begun. After Kenya comes Tanzania, and then the other southern nations will come over to our side."

"South Africa?"

Temujin smiled grimly. "With all their neighbors joining the World Liberation Movement, how long do you think it will take before the blacks of South Africa join us?"

"What about the north?" he heard himself ask. "Algeria, Libya, Egypt, and the rest?"

"In time, Mr. Baker," said Temujin, the greenish glow from the screens casting a weird light on his hairless face. "In time. Our agents are already burrowing into the governments there. Soon enough we may be able to proclaim a

Pan-Arabic union that stretches from Pakistan to Morocco, from the Hindu Kush to Gibraltar, all loyal to the World Liberation Movement.''

"And what then?''

"Asia, Mr. Baker. My own homeland. And once we have the industrial power of China, India, and Japan behind us, Europe and the Americas will fall to us at last.''

For the first time, Baker saw in his mind's eye the slaughter of millions. Men, women, and children. White men. White women. White children. It couldn't be helped. It was as inevitable as the centuries of exploitation that the whites had foisted on the rest of the world.

But he said, "Australia will join the Movement peacefully, willingly. I'll see to that.''

Temujin looked suddenly thoughtful. "That would be a great help to us, Mr. Baker. It would be a significant achievement.''

"Then let me return to Australia and start the Movement there.''

Raising one finger, Temujin said, "Yes. I will. After you have performed one task for me—or rather, for the Movement.''

"What task?''

"The woman you were with in Hawaii, and then in Paris . . .''

"An Linh?''

"Miss Laguerre, yes. She is with the astronaut, Stoner.''

"She's alive?'' Baker felt a thrill of hope race through him.

"Not only alive, but accompanying Stoner. They were nearly killed in a village in Chad, but our people have reliably reported them in a refugee camp near the border between Zaire and Kenya.''

"What are they doing in Africa?''

"You can ask them that when you see them,'' said Temujin. "I want you to find them and bring them to me. It is especially important that Stoner be delivered to our hands. Do you understand that, Mr. Baker? Especially important!''

From the windows of his penthouse apartment, Everett Nillson could see all of Boston spread out before him: the airport and the harbor, the clustered towers of the downtown financial district and the stately row houses of Back Bay, the gleaming golden dome of the state capitol and spire of the Old North Church, where lanterns had once been placed to alert Paul Revere.

A miniature city, Nillson thought, gazing down upon it. Founded by religious bigots, seething with rebellion, steeped for two centuries in greed and petty corruption and racial tensions. Yet still a vital, vigorous city, an exciting place to be. Far better than New York, that dying, sprawling dinosaur where danger lurks on every street. Boston was a livable city.

No, he corrected himself, a *buyable* city. A man of means could control Boston through a few key politicians and civic leaders. Money and flattery, and the skill to use them both to best effect, could deliver a city such as Boston into a clever man's grasp. New York was too big to buy outright, the best you could do was to carve out a fiefdom. Boston you could own entire.

"Excuse me, sir."

He turned from the windows at the soft sound of his servant's voice. She was a lovely thing, not quite nineteen, with limpid doe's eyes and the lithe, tempting figure of an artist's model. Something about her brown eyes and dark hair had reminded him of Jo when he had first seen her. But she had none of his wife's spirit—or intelligence. She was a placid animal, part purring cat, part innocent child.

"What is it?" he snapped.

Her eyes widened. Nillson enjoyed seeing a flash of fear in her.

"Mr. Madigan is here."

"Good. Send him in. No interruptions."

"Yes, sir."

She walked quickly past the long sectional sofa, skirted the sunken area around the fireplace, and opened the door to let Madigan in. She gave Nillson a fleeting, half-worried smile and then closed the door, leaving the two men alone.

"You've changed the decor," Madigan said as he crossed the room toward his boss.

"I have it changed after every visit here," Nillson said. "Before it gets boring."

"Looks great."

Nillson remained standing at the windows, so Madigan stayed on his feet, too. The marble bar in the room's far corner was fully stocked, and both men knew it, but Nillson offered nothing and his lawyer knew better than to ask.

"Well," Nillson snapped, "where is he?"

"Baker's on his way to Africa. He stayed in Colombo exactly sixty-three hours, give or take a couple of minutes, and then took a commercial jet flight to Mombasa."

"And from there?"

"The plane hasn't landed yet!"

Nillson grimaced impatiently. "So the tracker is working right."

"Perfectly. The satellite picks up the signal clear as a bell," Madigan replied with a smile.

"And you're certain that you're tracking Baker and not some decoy."

Tapping his own chest, Madigan said, "That microchip is buried in his thorax. You watched the surgery yourself, didn't you?"

"No, I didn't."

Madigan shrugged and continued, "Anyway, he doesn't know it's in him, and the signal is at a frequency that nobody's going to pick up unless they've got the special kind of receiving equipment we have in the satellite."

"It didn't work with Stoner," said Nillson.

"His was sprayed on his skin. Somehow Stoner turned it off, or more likely the stuff just malfunctioned. But it's working loud and clear on Baker."

Nillson turned away from the lawyer and gazed out the window again. The sun was going down, the concrete ribbons of expressways that sliced through the city were jammed with cars. Ants, Nillson thought. Mindless ants scurrying along on tasks they barely comprehend.

"Apparently the people running this World Liberation Movement think Stoner's still alive," Madigan volunteered.

"And the girl?"

"I don't know. I got a call from her when they were both in Avignon. Since then, not a word. Nothing but that report from our man inside the Peacekeepers, and I still don't think it was very reliable."

Nillson saw Madigan's reflection in the window: serious, carefully dressed, straining to please, as tense as a man juggling vials of nitroglycerin.

"Do you think he's still alive?" Nillson asked at last.

"If he is, we ought to recapture him. He's no use to us dead."

"But he's no use to anyone else dead, either."

"He could help us. . . ."

"He could help the others more."

Madigan fidgeted for a moment, obviously wondering if he dared to say what he wanted to. Finally he made his decision.

"Everett, your wife has given up hope about Stoner. If she's convinced he's dead, then . . ."

Nillson turned to face the lawyer. "Archie, I've given this problem of the astronaut a great deal of thought. I've considered the problem from every possible angle."

Madigan said nothing. He merely stood where he was, almost like a soldier at attention.

"At first," Nillson elaborated, "I thought that our Mr. Stoner was the key to immortality. Worth billions to Vanguard Industries. And to each of us, personally. That would have included you, too, Archie. Immortality!"

"Would have?" Madigan asked.

Ignoring him, Nillson went on, "But then I began to realize that his case was unusual. Unique. Perhaps reviving him from cryonic suspension did *not* mean that ordinary human beings could be frozen and then revived successfully."

He moved carefully across the carpeting and down the three steps to the sunken area before the dark fireplace. "Ahh, but then I realized that if the alien had entered Stoner's mind enough to help him through the freezing, there must be uncountable treasures stored inside his brain! The things he must know! An entire alien civilization! All that technology! The energy shields and fusion power plants must be child's play to such a mind!"

Madigan nodded vigorously. "That's what I think, too. That's why it's so important that we find him and—"

Nillson silenced him with a curt gesture. "Wrong, Archie. It's a trap."

"A trap?"

"Think a moment," Nillson said, almost in a whisper. "Try to follow the line of reasoning. If the alien is inside Stoner's mind, it must be for a reason. Right? Everything has a cause, a reason, doesn't it?"

"I guess so, yes," the lawyer answered slowly, reluctantly.

"Then what is the reason for the alien's being inside

Stoner's mind? Why did the alien come here, to Earth? What is the *reason*, Archie? The *reason*!''

Madigan blinked and stared at Nillson. The man's ice-pale eyes burned with a light he had never seen before.

"The alien came here for a purpose," Nillson insisted. "It picked out this one planet from all the worlds of the universe. It came here *deliberately*."

"But that's not—"

"Don't tell me what the scientists say!" Nillson snapped. "What do they know? The alien came here deliberately. It has invaded Stoner's mind. Deliberately! It is in contact with the rest of its kind. There's no doubt of it."

"In contact?" Madigan's voice was hollow.

"Of course! It's a scout, Archie. It's come here to prepare the way for the invasion. It's turned Stoner into a Judas goat, a traitor to his own species, an agent for the alien invaders!"

Madigan gaped at Vanguard's board chairman. He's gone crazy, he told himself. Great God in heaven, he's gone completely out of his mind.

Nillson leaned against the white brick of the fireplace, tilted his head back until it rested against the wall. "He's dangerous, Archie. This man Stoner is dangerous. He's a Judas goat. He'll betray the whole human race to the aliens."

Madigan staggered a few steps backward.

"If he's still alive, if Baker finds him—kill him!" Nillson commanded.

"But he could be worth—"

"I know what he's worth. This goes beyond profits. It even goes beyond my personal hopes for immortality. He must be killed. Eliminated. There's nothing personal in this, Archie. I'm doing this for the good of the human race. I want him killed."

CHAPTER 29

Calling it a refugee camp was both an exaggeration and an understatement.

It was a clearing in the woods where a dozen huge olive-drab tents had been erected months earlier by the International Red Cross to shelter a medical relief team. Within days the clean, neatly dressed, professional doctors and nurses and technicians were inundated by a flood of miserable, starving, sick and wounded people. They poured into the camp, seeking food and safety from the war that had torn apart their homes and their lives. Mothers carried dead babies in their arms, begging the doctors for help, while other women squatted on ground worn bare by the press of humanity to deliver new babies to a world of starvation and disease. Men carried their aged fathers on their backs for a hundred miles to reach the camp. Children wandered in alone, hungry, crying, skins erupting with festering sores, not knowing where their families were, frightened and confused.

But they found the camp. More and more of them. No matter the flies, the sicknesses, the crowding. The tide rolled in endlessly, overwhelming everything in its path. Now the dead and dying lay side by side in the pitiless sun, jammed together so tightly that the haggard, red-eyed medical workers had learned to step over bodies as normally as they had once learned to walk.

And still they came. The numbers of refugees outran the camp's computer. They poured in, led by rumors of food and shelter and, above all, safety. The food ran out. The water supply, from a respectable stream meandering through the clearing, turned foul from pollution. Helicopters came daily, hovering like impatient birds while the able cleared the landing area of infirm bodies who had collapsed there during the night because there was no other space to lie down.

The worst rat-infested slums of the dirtiest, most crowded

229

cities in the world were luxurious compared to the camp. The inflow of refugees spilled beyond the limits of the clearing. People slept in the trees, among the bushes, and awoke covered with ants or infested with vermin. There were snakes in the bush, too, and some never woke at all.

Disease swept the camp. Dysentery came first, then cholera and a virulent form of whooping cough. But no matter how many died, more came to replace them. The camp swelled like an unlanced boil, fed by the precarious trickle of supplies helicoptered in from a world as distant and alien to the refugees as another star.

"I was born in a camp like this," An Linh said wearily. "How ironic to die here."

"You're not going to die," Stoner told her. "In another few days you'll be strong enough to leave."

If, he added silently, your wound doesn't get infected again. And if we can get enough food to give us the strength to walk out of here.

They had both lost a great deal of weight. An Linh looked frail now, her face gaunt, hollow-cheeked, her eyes sunken behind dark rings. Stoner's beard was full and black, his tall frame rail thin, his clothes hanging loosely on him. He felt tired, always tired, and his mind was numb with the unending misery that stretched out in every direction around him.

An Linh was lying on a cot under the welcome shade of a soaring, spreading acacia tree at the edge of the clearing. Not a square foot of ground was visible, bodies were packed so tightly, some moving feebly, calling weakly for water or help, most of them as still as death under the relentless sun. Not a breath of air moved in the blistering afternoon. Stoner leaned his head back against the bole of the tree and closed his eyes. He heard the incessant hum of flies. And babies crying. Some squalled bitterly, most were too weak to make much noise. But there were always babies crying.

So this is what war is like, he thought. The battles are over quickly, but the misery goes on forever.

The thrumming beat of a helicopter broke the afternoon stillness. An Linh looked up toward the blazing sky.

"I'll go help clear out the landing area," Stoner said, climbing slowly to his feet. "You stay here and rest."

It was an irony of the camp that a beautiful young woman

was safer there than in any civilized place in the world. There had been thefts and even a few rapes when the camp had first been set up. But the refugees were too weak to molest each other now. They had nothing left to steal. Even the meager supplies of food that the helicopters brought were eaten so quickly that only the flies had time to steal any.

Stoner had been helping in any way he could, despite the growing exhaustion brought on by hunger: assisting the medical teams, digging latrines, chopping trees for firewood to cremate the dead. Regardless of religion or custom, all the dead were burned. Every evening there was a huge pyre. No room in the area for burials. And starving people might dig up buried bodies, regardless of the risk of infection.

Will we die here? Stoner asked himself as he lifted dead and dying bodies from the helicopter pad. They were light as birds, and as frail. Nothing but bones and bloated bellies. And flies. Coated with flies. Stoner thought that the flies on some of the bodies weighed more than the body itself.

An Linh thinks it's ironic to die in the kind of camp where she was born. What do *you* think, he asked the other presence in his mind, about crossing all those light-years to find this world and die among starving refugees?

He received no answer. Only a sense of patient, unworried, ceaseless observation; like an automated interplanetary probe gathering data regardless of the conditions it encountered.

The helicopter hung overhead, high enough to avoid swirling up a dust storm, thundering impatiently, jinking back and forth as Stoner and the few other men who still had enough strength moved the bodies away. The sun burned down, but Stoner barely sweated. There wasn't enough in him to generate perspiration.

Finally an area large enough for the big cargo 'copter was cleared away, and the lumbering metal beast, painted glaringly white with a huge red cross on either side, settled slowly down onto the bare ground. Stoner squinted into the dust storm the whirling rotors swirled up, wondering how long he could keep himself from demanding to the camp director that he—or at least An Linh—be evacuated to wherever the helicopters were coming from. Each day the choppers carried off the most desperate cases to a real hospital somewhere in Tanzania, according to the doctor Stoner had talked with. The medics were practicing triage, sending back to civilization only those cases who could recover if they received proper medical care.

An Linh qualified, Stoner thought. Under the pitiless logic of triage, though, the medical staff had decided that she had a fair chance of recovering right here at the camp. She would only be evacuated if she got much worse. And Stoner needed no medical attention at all. His slight leg wound had healed satisfactorily. So the camp rules dictated that they stay, while others were evacuated. But starvation and disease could kill them more quickly than the triage classifications could be changed.

Stoner knew he could talk them into letting An Linh go. And himself, if he wanted to. So far he had not tried to exert his influence over the doctors who made the decisions. So far.

The rumbling, whining roar of the helicopter died away, and its *whoosh*ing rotor blades slowed to a stop. In earlier days, a swarm of refugees would rush to the 'copter's hatch. Sometimes the crew and the medical personnel had to beat them back angrily. But now hardly anyone was strong enough to exert himself. Stoner sensed, though, a thousand listless eyes at his back, staring emptily at the helicopter.

The hatch popped open and a pair of husky, well-fed young men jumped out. Both black, both in olive-drab fatigues. Stoner started helping them to unload crates of food and medicine. A smaller hatch up at the nose of the chopper swung up, and a lightweight ladder plopped down onto the dusty ground. A half-dozen men and women descended, squinting in the sunlight. They were dressed in whites.

Replacements for some of the medical team, Stoner told himself as he took the first wooden crate from one of the blacks in the hatchway and handed it to the next man in the impromptu supply line. Idly he thought that the wood would help as kindling for tonight's pyre.

One of the young women looked familiar to him. No, not really familiar. He knew he had never seen her before, yet there was something about her. . . .

As she walked past him, he saw the nametag clipped to her shirt pocket: Thompson.

"Elly?" he called.

She stopped and turned toward him. She looked puzzled, totally uncomprehending.

Stoner stepped out of the bucket-brigade line to face her. Yes, he could see the traces of the ten-year-old daughter he had known. Her face was fuller now, rounder. There were lines around the eyes and at the corners of her mouth that looked like tension, or fear, or perhaps even grief. And her hair, long and golden curled when she had been little, was a chestnut brown now and clipped almost as short as a man's.

"Elly, it's me." He had to swallow once before he could add, "Your father."

Her mouth dropped open. Her hands flew to her face. "You? You're . . . It can't be!"

Stoner felt incredibly awkward, like a clumsy teenager on his first date. "I guess I could use a shave," he said lamely.

"Daddy? Are you really . . . ?"

"It's me all right."

"But what are you doing here?" Her voice was the same as he had remembered it, a high-pitched squeak when she was surprised or excited.

He smiled sheepishly. "Actually, I was looking for you."

She burst into tears and flung her arms around his neck. For an instant Stoner thought that he would start crying, too. But then he felt his body stiffen, and a wave of cold dispassion flowed through him, like ice crystallizing the water in a test tube that's been suddenly thrust into liquid nitrogen. He felt that other presence in his mind coolly studying this new event, dissecting the relationship between father and daughter as unemotionally as a technician takes apart the components of a machine.

Damn you! Stoner raged silently. Leave me alone! Let me have my daughter to myself.

But within a couple of heartbeats even the surge of protest died away, and Stoner could examine his daughter as if she were a representative of an alien species.

She sensed it and disengaged, stepped back from him. Brushing at her tear-filled eyes, she said in a choked voice, "It's been . . . so long."

"Twenty years," he said. It was like the voice of another creature, an automaton.

"I never thought I'd see you again."

"They brought me back from the dead. I was frozen for eighteen years."

"No one told us you'd been revived."

"I know. I tried to call. . . ."

A short, red-faced man in the same kind of white uniform as Elly's strode up to them and barked, "Thompson! There's work to do!"

Stoner put out his hand and touched his daughter's tear-stained cheek. It took an enormous effort of will to lift his arm.

"I'll talk with you tonight, Elly," he said as gently as he could. "I have work to do, too. I'll see you tonight."

A tumult of emotions raced across her features. Finally she nodded, lips pressed tight, and turned to follow the angry-faced man. Stoner went back to the brigade unloading supplies from the helicopter.

Late that evening, so late that the nightly pyre had burned down to embers glowering redly against the darkness, Stoner finished telling his story to his daughter. He had located her in the main medical tent after the evening meal and brought her to An Linh's cot, leading her by the hand as they picked their way through the bodies packed so thickly on the bare ground. An Linh lay on her cot beneath the big acacia tree. Stoner and his daughter sat on the ground beside her, Stoner leaning his back against the tree's rough solidity, Eleanor squatting cross-legged the way she used to do when she was a child.

Elly listened in silence as the light from the pyre faded. Stoner spoke as unemotionally as a computer, relating the facts of his return to life the way a chalkdust-dry instructor would report on the major events of the Industrial Revolution to a classroom full of freshmen. As the firelight dimmed and shadows darkened his daughter's face, Stoner could no longer see her reaction to his tale. But he felt her stiffen when he mentioned the village where he and An Linh had nearly been killed.

"And you believe," Elly asked, her own voice sounding strangely wooden, dead, "that the village was attacked because of you?"

"I know it sounds crazy, but that's what I think," Stoner replied.

"I agree," said An Linh, sitting up on her cot. "There was no other reason to attack the village. It was not in a battle zone. It had no strategic value, except to challenge the Peace Enforcers."

"Who responded just the way the attackers must have known they would react," Stoner added. "Within a few minutes they obliterated the attacking force."

"Yes, that's the way they work," Elly said, her voice still coldly distant. "Their mission is to prevent aggression by destroying the aggressors. If they are too late to prevent an attack, they will still annihilate the attackers after the fact."

"They did that," Stoner said fervently.

An Linh asked, "But that's only part of their mission, isn't it? The Peace Enforcers seemed to be teaching the villagers how to become self-sufficient."

"The solar power system, yes," Stoner agreed, remembering. "And the new agricultural methods they were learning."

"And birth control," An Linh added. "That's the key to everything the IPF is trying to accomplish, isn't it? You can't raise people's standard of living if they outpopulate their resources. Isn't that right, Eleanor?"

But instead of answering, Stoner's daughter asked him, "What was the name of the village? You haven't told me its name."

The tone of her voice sent a chill of apprehension through Stoner. In the darkness, it was like the creaking of a door that should have been locked. Or the click that might be the cocking of a pistol aimed at your heart.

"Katai," An Linh answered. "The village was called Katai.'

Stoner heard his daughter's breath catch. Then silence. The moments stretched agonizingly. In the darkness he could not see her face. Only the distant glowing ashes of the pyre. Elly seemed to have turned to stone, not moving, not even breathing. Stoner heard a baby crying weakly, off in the distance, and the incessant background hum of insects.

"What's wrong, Elly?" he asked. "Why is the name of the village so important?"

For a few moments more she remained silent. Then she took in a deep breath and answered, "My husband, Wally . . . was killed a few weeks ago . . . flying a helicopter into a village in Chad. . . ."

"Katai," said Stoner.

"Katai," Elly echoed.

Stoner closed his eyes and saw again the helicopter fluttering through the air, the streaking missile lancing toward it, the explosion and the human body hurled out and falling thousands of feet to the ground.

"He was killed because of you," Elly said, her voice suddenly trembling. "Because of you!"

Stoner had no response.

Elly scrambled to her feet in the darkness. She did not raise her voice, but the pain and anger in it were all the sharper because she was not shouting. "Because of you!" she repeated. "You not only robbed me of a father and a mother, you've robbed me of my husband, too! You've taken *everything* away from me!"

She turned and fled into the darkness.

Stoner sat where he was, his back against the tree, unable to move.

"Go after her!" An Linh urged.

He shook his head. "I can't. I never could. . . ."

"Don't leave her alone like this! She needs you. She needs someone to comfort her."

"She hates me."

"No, she doesn't. She may think she does, but she really doesn't."

"I'm responsible for her husband's death."

An Linh swung her legs off the cot and stood up shakily. "She shouldn't be alone."

"She is alone," Stoner muttered. "You're all alone, every one of you."

With a disappointed shake of her head, An Linh started off in the same direction Elly had gone, leaving Stoner sitting there in the darkness.

She has every right to despise me, he told himself. I stepped out of her life and left her without a father when she was just ten years old. She blames her mother's death on me. And now, when I suddenly reappear, it costs the life of her husband.

But something forced him to get to his feet and start out toward the lighted tents where the medical staff lived. I didn't kill her husband. He's a casualty in a war that I've got to stop. I've seen enough of death. Now it's time to find those who are responsible for all this misery and make them stop.

Stepping over the bodies of the sick and the dying, Stoner realized that he had remained in the camp too long. He had

seen all that he had come to see, and then had been overwhelmed by the sense of helplessness that pervaded the
camp. What can one man do? He felt his jaws clenching in a
determined grimace as he approached the medical tent. I'm
going to find out what one man can do. Starting right now.

The Stirling generator that provided electricity for the medical team whined annoyingly as Stoner came up to the tent. A
radio somewhere was playing music that he did not recognize, a thumping, irregular beat overlain by screeching electronic strings. The harsh lights made him squint. The tent
was nearly empty. The surgical table stood bare, unattended.
Beyond it stood rows of metal cabinets, and beyond them a
dozen cots neatly spaced. Four of the Red Cross workers
were sleeping, sprawled exhausted on their cots despite the
noise from the radio. The others were nowhere in sight. Elly
and An Linh sat side by side, arms around each other, on the
farthermost cot.

"What do you want here?"

Stoner turned and saw that it was the little red-faced
martinet who had come in with Elly earlier that day. His
white coveralls were soiled now, no longer fresh and crisp.
The heat and toil had taken the starch out of them. And made
his ill-humored disposition even testier. Stoner saw that his
nametag said DeVreis. Apparently he was the new leader.

"Well, what are you doing here?" he repeated, his voice
rising.

"I want permission to be evacuated in the next flight out,"
Stoner said. "Myself and Ms. Laguerre."

"Impossible! Evac flights are restricted to refugees who
will die unless they are taken to hospital facilities."

"I know that. Neither of us is a refugee."

"Then there's nothing I can do." He spoke English with
an accent that might have been German. Or Dutch.

Stoner looked into his angry eyes. Already the pain and
futility of the camp were reflected in them.

"We must be permitted to leave," he said softly. "I can
do much more good outside this camp than inside it."

"Good?" DeVreis snapped. "What good can you do?"

"Perhaps I can end this war."

"End the . . . What nonsense! Who do you think you
are?"

"That doesn't matter," Stoner said, stepping closer to

him. "What matters is that you've got to give us permission to leave."

"I can't. . . ."

Stoner laid a hand on the little man's shoulder. Gently. Like a father speaking to a son. "I'll carry two refugees with me, if you like. But we've got to leave. You can understand that, can't you?"

DeVreis hesitated. "Yes, I see. But . . ."

"You'll do it, then. You'll give us permission to leave."

The angry scowl left the little man's face. He almost smiled. Stoner felt his body relax as he replied, "Of course. On the next flight."

"Thank you."

"I'll go and make out the necessary papers."

Stoner watched him walk slowly out of the tent, heading for the other lighted tent where the camp's records, such as they were, were kept.

Then he skirted around the surgical table, walked past the rows of cots, and stopped before An Linh and his daughter. Both of them were in tears.

"Elly, I'm sorry about your husband. If there were something I could do to bring him back, I would."

She looked up at him, tears streaking her cheeks, and he remembered that same face streaked with tears on the day he told her and her brother that he was leaving their home, leaving their mother, leaving them. Inside him, Stoner knew that he should be feeling pain, or at least sorrow. But he felt nothing. It was as if he had been anesthetized.

Eleanor finally found her voice. "It seems that you're the only one who can come back from the dead."

He shook his head. "No, Elly. I'm merely the first one."

Her head drooped again. He looked at An Linh, also tearful.

"We're leaving tomorrow, Elly," Stoner said. "An Linh and I. We're going out on the evacuation helicopter."

An Linh gasped. "But how . . . ?"

"I want you to leave, too, Elly. As soon as your tour of duty is finished. Get back to your children in New Zealand. Start your life over again. You're young enough to build a good life for yourself—and for them. I know I'm not much of a father, but that's my advice to you."

Eleanor said nothing, but her head bobbed in what might have been a nod of agreement.

"And call Douglas for me. I couldn't locate him. Tell him that I tried. Tell him . . ." He hesitated, knowing that what he had to say was actually a lie. "Tell him that I love him. I love you both, Elly."

It was as much as he could do. Inwardly, he knew that there was no love in him, no emotion at all. Or if there were, it was frozen as thoroughly as his body had been frozen through all the long years.

Turning to An Linh, he said, "I'll take you as far as the hospital. Then I'll have to leave you and go on."

CHAPTER 30

An Linh refused to leave Stoner.

The helicopter brought them to the International Peace Force hospital near Mwanza, on the shore of Lake Victoria. There on the outskirts of the Tanzanian city, swollen to more than a million by the tide of war, the Peace Enforcers had erected a minimetropolis, prefabricated buildings of plastic and lightweight metals manufactured in the orbital factories a few hundred miles overhead. Crowded, busy, as impersonal as any big-city hospital, staffed by harried doctors and overworked nurses, abuzz with computers filing data and robots whisking along every corridor—still the hospital was infinitely better than the camp.

A brash young intern from Queens examined An Linh's wound and pronounced it healed.

"She's got a slight fever and a mild case of malnutrition," he told Stoner. "It's nothing compared to what we've been getting. A few days' rest, antibiotics, and some real food, and she'll be as good as new."

He was smiling into An Linh's wan but lovely face as she lay on the crisply clean sheets of a real hospital bed, in the long, noisy ward filled with black women who had been

wounded, raped, starved, burned, who had miscarried or
seen their babies killed, who had been too weak to fend off
the diseases that lurked in the very air and turned virulent in
the wake of war. Human nurses and robots answered their
calls, tried to comfort their sobs, ease the pain, quiet the
screaming. An Linh smiled weakly back at the young American and asked, "What about him, Doctor?"

"I'm all right," said Stoner.

But the doctor insisted on examining him, too. Stoner put
up with it and even submitted to the tests that the doctor
ordered. For the remainder of the day he was subjected to
needles, probes, and scanning machines. Stoically he endured it all, thinking, It's just like the space agency's prodding when they took me in for astronaut training.

By that evening the same doctor reappeared in the ward,
stethoscope stuffed in a pocket of his white coveralls, a
knowing grin on his long, horsey face.

"I thought I'd find you here," he said to Stoner as he
strode confidently up toward An Linh's bed. "It's where I'd
be, if I had a choice."

"You're very gallant," she said.

He made a surprising little bow, then turned to Stoner and
said, "I've gotten a bed assigned to you, over in the men's
temporary ward. The only thing wrong with you is malnutrition, but I can't let you out of here until you've gained ten
pounds. Too big a risk of coming down with pneumonia or
diphtheria or any one of the zillion other bugs floating around
the area."

Stoner argued, but only mildly. He stayed at the hospital
for a week, gaining strength each day. And knowledge. He
easily talked the nurses into letting him watch the television
news broadcasts in their lounge. He learned how the war was
going: the alliance of the rebels in Nigeria, Chad, Zaire, and
Uganda had invaded both Kenya and the Sudan, but their
onslaught had been ground to a halt by the Peace Enforcers—
for the time being. Both sides seemed to be taking a breather,
building their forces and waiting for the opportunity to renew
the fighting.

He visited An Linh every afternoon and evening. After the
first two days, they started taking dinner together at the
walking patients' cafeteria.

"I've got to get to this Colonel Bahadur," he told her over dinner. "He's the chief of the Peace Enforcers."

"And where is he?" An Linh asked.

"Not far from here, in a place called Namanga, just over the border in Kenya. It's near Kilimanjaro, from what I hear."

An Linh chewed on her soyburger thoughtfully, then said, "I've always wanted to see Kilimanjaro."

Before Stoner could shake his head, she went on, "I've nowhere else to go, Keith. I've got to stay with you."

A thousand reasons why she shouldn't come with him sprang into his mind. But one look at her trusting, vulnerable face took all the argument out of him. I can't leave her alone, he told himself. And he tried to ignore the feeling that his other self, that observer buried deep inside his brain, wanted to see how their relationship would work out.

"You are an extraordinary man, Dr. Stoner," said Colonel Banda Singh Bahadur.

Stoner nodded an acknowledgment of the compliment. "You are far from an ordinary person yourself, Colonel."

They were walking across a grassy field, past a row of helicopters painted in blotchy jungle-green camouflage, bristling with gun ports and rocket tubes. The morning sun was not yet truly hot, and off in the hazy blue distance the flat, snow-covered summit of Kilimanjaro seemed to hang in mid-air, unsupported, disconnected from the mundane earth below. Stoner could understand why the local tribes worshiped the mountain. It *was* godlike, floating there in the distance, beautiful, unreachable, yet ever-present.

Colonel Bahadur was a Sikh, somewhat of a mountain himself, big in every dimension. His full, curly, iron-gray beard made Stoner's dark growth look almost puny. He towered over Stoner and outweighed him by half again. Yet despite the man's size, Stoner had the impression that Bahadur could move with blinding speed when he wanted to. The colonel wore a white turban and the duty uniform of the International Peacekeeping Force, light blue fatigues decorated only by a pair of silver oak leaves clipped to his lapels, his name stenciled over his left breast, and the Peace Enforcers' shoulder patch: a jagged yellow bolt of lightning on a field of sky blue. Stoner wore similar coveralls, minus decoration.

The colonel's duty, as he saw it, was twofold: to stop the fighting and to build self-sustaining communities in the areas that the war had devastated. His troops were few, but the Peace Enforcers' style of fighting used technology more than manpower. They never initiated hostilities. They never launched an attack. Their task was to discourage others from attacking their neighbors, to stop aggression in its tracks. They were counterpunchers, by design, by doctrine, by training and equipment.

When surveillance satellites saw troops, tanks, artillery, trucks, supplies being massed for an attack, the Peace Enforcers warned the politicians and generals preparing the aggression. If they did not disband their operation, the attackers were met by swarms of drone missiles, either guided remotely by technicians in space stations and aboard high-flying aircraft or running under their own automated guidance systems. The missiles sought out the implements of war—the lumbering tanks and phallic artillery guns, the supply depots and ammunition dumps, the sleekly deadly planes waiting in their revetments—and demolished them. The object of the Peacekeepers was to destroy the implements of war. Soon enough the aggressor's troops learned that it was death to remain near those weapons once the Peacekeepers had spotted them.

The theory was simple enough. But the practice was difficult. Very difficult. Sprawled across a thousand miles of thick tropical forest, mountains, and grasslands, the Central African War was a confused struggle of rebels against central governments, of provinces seceding and guerrillas terrorizing villages. There was no battlefront, no organized confrontation of uniformed armies. The Peace Enforcers reacted where they could, devastated armed concentrations where they could find them. But the Enforcers' numbers were few, and the blood-maddened fighting forces who made war on each other were legion. The carnage went on, mindlessly, it seemed.

"Too many young men," said the colonel to Stoner. "It was a mistake to give these people the means to select the sex of their offspring. They opt for boys over girls, always."

"That hasn't happened in Europe or the Americas," Stoner pointed out. "Or in Asia. Even in your own India . . ."

"We are members of a high civilization! Our religious teachings prevent us from tampering with the natural order of births. Even among a warrior race such as we Sikhs, we know better than to select a huge oversupply of male children."

"But here in Africa . . ."

"They are villagers. Primitives. Still tied to the land, still an agricultural society."

"So they pick boys whenever they have the choice," Stoner said, "and end up with armies of young men who have no jobs and nowhere to go."

"Except to war. Which is why your mission will fail," Colonel Bahadur said. His voice became heavy, deep, as if it came from the bowels of the earth.

"It might fail," Stoner agreed cheerfully.

"No man can bring the leaders of all the various factions together under one roof," the colonel insisted.

Stoner looked up at him. "Then I'll bring them together out in the open, where your satellites can watch us."

Behind his curly beard and mustache, the colonel may have smiled. But he shook his turbaned head. "Not even with such a beautiful woman to help you will you be able to bring them together. We don't even know who half of them are!"

"I'll find them."

They stopped at the helicopter at the end of the row. Unlike the sickly green of the armed choppers, this one was painted all white, with the sky-blue insignia of the International Peacekeeping Force stenciled on its sides. An Linh was already inside the helicopter, dressed in blue fatigues, chatting with the pilot—a golden-haired Norwegian.

"I wish you luck, then," said the colonel, very serious, almost grave.

"Thanks." Stoner put out his hand, and the Sikh's huge paw engulfed it.

Then he clambered into the helicopter and waved a farewell to the head of the Peace Enforcers. The engine whined to life as Colonel Bahadur backed away, and the speedy little helicopter lifted smoothly off the ground.

"He's right, you know," An Linh said over the noise of the engine. "This is a hopeless crusade."

Stoner laughed. "Have you got anything better to do?"

*   *   *

The planet swung around its star in the orbit it had followed for billions of years. Africa's dry season yielded at last to the life-giving rains, and Kilimanjaro took on a new blanket of white that gleamed when the sun shone upon it.

A tall, bearded white man, with a beautiful Asian woman at his side, arrived in Kampala and somehow managed to gain an audience with the chief of state of Uganda. Three weeks later they were seen in Kinshasa, Zaire, and a few days later in Kolwezi, where the rebellious Katangans had made their headquarters. Reports placed them in Chad, in four different locations in Nigeria, on the bank of the White Nile in Sudan, on the shores of Lake Rudolf in Kenya.

It happened that on the very day when the planet was at its closest to its star, men from each of these places flew to a meeting in a dry, wasted gulley carved out of the earth by a river that had disappeared a million years ago. The place was called Olduvai.

It was a strange meeting, witnessed only by a team of paleontologists startled from their digging by the sudden thundering of a dozen helicopters.

The paleontologists, five women, three men, and twenty-eight assistants, watched goggle-eyed as the helicopters descended a respectful distance from their tents. One of the helicopters bore the insignia of the IPF; it had been white, but the hard-driven miles had dirtied its once gleaming finish. The other helicopters all wore battle camouflage, and each carried a different insignia.

One tall, bearded man in sky-blue coveralls ducked out of the white helicopter, then turned to help a slim Asian woman, similarly clad, to alight. No one came out of the other machines, whose rotors kept turning, filling the air with their angry *whoosh*ing roar.

The elderly woman who was in charge of the dig came scrambling up the embankment toward Stoner. The rains had not yet reached Olduvai, and the steep slope was dry and crumbling as she climbed. She was short and squat, and by the time she reached the top she was panting, perspiring, and as angry as a bee-stung mule.

"What's the meaning of this? I've told you media idiots time and again that I—"

But she stopped once she got a good look at Stoner.

"Who the hell are you?" she snapped in a flat Kansan accent.

Stoner lifted both his hands and smiled at her. "I know we're disturbing your work, but this was the only neutral ground that they would all agree on."

The paleontologist looked from Stoner to the ugly green helicopters and back again. The sky was thick with clouds. It would rain soon.

"What's going on?" she asked more gently.

"A peace conference," replied Stoner. Then he added, "If we're lucky."

CHAPTER 31

Stoner watched as the leaders of the various warring factions finally got out of their helicopters. There were eleven of them, and he idly considered the notion that if thirteen was a baker's dozen, then eleven might be a politician's.

He had grave doubts as he watched them step to the ground and look around the dry, wasted gorge of Olduvai. The Katangan was tall and lanky as a basketball player, dressed in camouflage battle fatigues, his face hidden by dark glasses. The president of Zaire was as stubby as a black thumb, strutting imperiously in his splendid uniform of royal blue and scarlet. One of the Nigerians had swathed himself in loose robes; he could be carrying a small arsenal under them, Stoner thought. Another Nigerian wore a Western business suit. A third, the multihued dashiki that was as unique to his tribe as a Scot's tartan is to his clan.

Stoner watched them as they eyed each other, warily, disdainfully, like Hollywood actors portraying Mafia gang leaders gathering for a summit meeting. Nine black men, one of brown skin, one white. None of them trusted any of the others.

They were in this remote place without their usual hordes of sycophants and admirers, without the prying cameras and recorders of the media, without the crowds and honor guards and ceremonies that usually attended meetings of national leaders. No one but a few close advisers and a handful of personal bodyguards for each of the eleven. Stoner had insisted on that, and he saw that each of them had acceded to his demands. He felt a small gleam of hope at that, as fragile as a soap bubble floating in the sunlight—and as beautiful.

How easy it had been to tell Colonel Bahadur that he would bring the warring factions together. Looking back on it, Stoner realized that his glibness had been a façade. He could think of no other way to stop the fighting than to bring together, in one place at one time, the leaders of each faction. He had been confident of his powers of persuasion, and that confidence had not been misplaced. Stoner had talked his way past suspicious soldiers and paranoid security chiefs, past unctuous secretaries and bullying aides, past loyal henchmen and ambitious assistants who harbored treachery in their hearts. But in each case he had finally gotten to the leader. In bustling metropolises, in jungle camps, in redoubts dug into mountainsides, aboard a luxurious yacht cruising on Lake Victoria, he finally saw the man responsible for the fighting in that part of Africa. Sometimes the man was alone, and Stoner spoke with him behind locked doors. Often he was flanked by assistants. More than once, the man sat accompanied by a woman: wife, mistress, power-behind-the-throne.

Each of them agreed to Stoner's suggestion of a peace conference. None of them had any real chance to disagree, Stoner knew, once he got to talk to them face to face.

Now they were assembled beneath a lowering sky on the open plain of Olduvai. Now the real work would begin. But Stoner waited, let them pace around their helicopters, sitting quietly now on the brittle grass like giant metallic grasshoppers, their bulbous canopies catching the fast-disappearing rays of sunlight like an insect's faceted eyes. Stoner stood by the edge of the gorge, arms folded across his chest, watching and waiting. As he watched, Stoner saw the leaders—some proud and vain, some worried and uncertain—slowly, inevitably, approach each other, eye one another, take each other's measure.

He could not hear their conversations from this distance, but he knew what they were saying.

"A strange place to meet."

"Yes. And it looks like rain, too."

"There isn't any shelter around for miles."

"I thought I saw some tents as we flew in. We could commandeer them."

"What ever made us come out to this godforsaken place?"

"That man."

"Yes. Him. He seemed so . . . intense."

"Persuasive."

"What did he tell you to make you come all this way?"

"He was very persuasive."

"What did he tell you?"

"What did he say to *you*?"

"Something laughable."

"Laughable? You came here because he made you laugh?"

"No, of course not."

"He told me that I would be killed by an assassin if the fighting continued another three months."

"He threatened you?"

"It was not a threat. He did not imply that he would send the assassin. He seemed very sad when he told me, as if it were inevitable and there was nothing that anyone could do about it."

"You believed him?"

"Yes."

"He offered you proof?"

"He told me things about myself that no one knew. No one! And things . . . about my aides , my closest comrades. I believed him. Yes, I believed what he told me. That's why I am here. If the fighting does not stop soon, I will be assassinated. I am certain of that."

"He can read minds, then?"

"He can foretell the future."

"You think so?"

"He convinced you to come here, didn't he?"

"Not by frightening me!"

"Then how?"

"Well . . .."

"Come, tell me. You said it was laughable."

"He said that a great statue would be erected in my honor. In Lagos, the capital."

"That must have pleased you."

"But he warned that the statue would be erected only if the

war ended soon. If it continues much longer, I will . . . well, my reputation will begin to dim.''

"You will lose, is that it?''

"He said that I will be blamed for defeats that would be no fault of mine, yes.''

"And your people? The cause that you are fighting to uphold? What of that?''

"Obviously, if a great statue is erected in my honor at the capital—at the *capital,* mind you!—then my people and their cause will have triumphed.''

"Obviously.''

"I believe that he can foresee the future. He has strange powers, this man.''

"He has returned from the dead, you know.''

"Yes. He was frozen in the alien spacecraft for many years.''

"Do you think that is where his powers come from?''

"I have no doubt of it.''

"What else did he tell you? What other predictions did he make?''

"Your province of Katanga will gain its freedom.''

"Truly?''

"Truly.''

For nearly an hour Stoner waited, as unmoving as a patient robot, as the eleven leaders moved cautiously about their helicopter and spoke to one another. He noticed that men who opposed each other did not speak. The Katangan rebel chief did not engage the president of Zaire in conversation. None of the Nigerians spoke to one another. The Kenyan talked with the general from Chad.

Finally he sensed that they were growing impatient, apprehensive. He walked toward them, and the leaders and their aides unconsciously formed a ragged semicircle facing him.

"We are here," Stoner said without preliminaries, "so that we can discuss ways to stop the fighting without the glare and pressure of publicity. No one is making a transcript. This meeting is strictly informal, and no one outside this group need ever know what is said here.''

Turning toward the gorge, where the paleontologists had returned to their work, Stoner said, "I picked this spot not only because it is safe from prying eyes, but because it is one of the earliest known sites of human habitation. The human race had its beginnings here. It is up to each of us to keep faith with those early ancestors of ours, to work on the side of life and civilization, rather than death and destruction."

Stoner knew that there was only one way to make this peace conference actually end the fighting: he had to convince each of these men that he stood to gain more from peace than from war. Why should Zaire give up the resource-rich province of Katanga? How can the central government of Nigeria hold together the tribes that each want to establish their own individual nations? How can Chad feed its starving population unless it has access to the fertile lands to its south?

There were answers to each of these questions, and Stoner patiently coaxed the eleven leaders toward those answers.

It began to rain, and they dashed into the nearest helicopter. No time to argue about protocol or even security; they all ran like schoolboys for the nearest shelter. The helicopter was too small to accommodate all of the aides and guards. Stoner and the eleven leaders squeezed into its interior. The others sprinted through the spattering raindrops to their own helicopters. Radio contact between the choppers was established, so that each leader had access to his assistants. But the eleven of them were sitting pressed together on the plastic bucket seats and bare metal floor of this one helicopter's cabin, seriously discussing ways to achieve peace, while the growing rainstorm raged outside the hatch. Stoner smiled to himself, satisfied with the earnestness of their talk.

A flash of lightning flicked across the darkened afternoon, and an immediate explosion of thunder made more than one of the men wince. The world outside grew darker, turned into a black caldron of fury lanced by sudden blue-white tongues of lightning. Thunder boomed and rain drummed incessantly on the helicopter's metal skin. Ferocious gusts of wind rocked the aircraft. Stoner saw, through the window of the closed hatch, the aircraft's crew tying it down to stakes pounded into the puddled, grassy ground. Still the men talked, argued, hurled accusations and angry denials at one another, waggled fingers, and shook their heads. Yet they kept on talking.

Stoner listened and watched, saying nothing except when an argument would threaten to end rational discussion. Then he would offer a word or two, and the argument would stop. Men would still glare at each other. Hatreds were still strong enough to be felt, like heat radiating from glowing coals. But they got past the shouting and the accusations and forged ahead to find ways to solve the problems that had led to war.

An Linh's with the paleontologists, Stoner said to himself. Her job is to keep them away from here, to convince them that this outlandish political meeting will not interfere with their work, and they in turn should not get anywhere near the politicians. She's probably in one of their tents, having tea and getting ready for a dinner of antelope haunch garnished with the local weeds.

Stoner realized he was hungry. Glancing at his wristwatch, he saw that the darkness outside was not merely from the lashing storm. He pushed through the intently talking men and made his way up to the flight deck. The crew, dried off now after their struggle to tie the helicopter safely down, had already broken out trays of precooked dinners. Stoner used the radio to have each leader's crew bring in a meal. He accepted an extra tray from the helicopter's pilot: frozen steak and whipped potatoes, made in the U.S.A.

The rain slackened and died away completely. After many hours, Stoner crawled down the ladder from the flight deck hatch and stretched his lanky frame in the chilly night air. Tendons popped satisfactorily and cramped muscles relaxed. He saw that the clouds were blowing away, and the stars were in their familiar places, twinkling against the darkness.

Still the politicians talked. Some clambered down from the helicopter and returned to their own machines for brief naps. Others sprawled ingloriously in the helicopter where the conference was taking place. Some stamped out onto the rain-slicked grass in anger, swearing to quit altogether and leave for home. Stoner talked with each one, walking a while under the stars. Each man returned to the helicopter, subdued, willing to make another try. Stoner could hear their voices cutting through the night. Often many of them were speaking at the same time, trying to outshout each other. But as the sky cleared and the stars wheeled around in their eternal cycle, the talking became calmer, more rational, more controlled.

The first hint of dawn was pinking the sky of Olduvai when Stoner decided to go back into the helicopter and see what progress had been made.

The way the men were sitting told him much. All eleven

were back inside the cabin, all of them awake. The four Nigerians were grouped in one corner. The Kenyan and the Ugandan sat beside one another. The tall Katangan had long ago taken off his dark glasses and become the acknowledged chairman of the conference.

He looked up wearily as Stoner ducked through the hatch.

"It is hopeless," he said softly.

"We have tried," said the Ugandan, "but we cannot reach an agreement."

"There are too many differences," agreed the Kenyan. "We'll never be able to settle them."

Stoner stood in the open hatchway, gripping the ribbed metal overhead like an ape clinging to a precarious perch. The brightening sky was behind him. He could see the first rays of dawn reaching into the helicopter's cabin. The eleven men looked haggard, taut with suppressed anger born of frustrated hope and renewed hostility. The cabin reeked of their sweat.

"It's hopeless, you say?" Stoner asked, almost whispering.

No reply. They stared at Stoner like schoolboys caught breaking the rules.

"So you condemn your people to more bloodshed, to more killing." Stoner's voice began to rise. "You're going to leave here and go back to your people and kill still more of them."

"We don't want—"

"You don't want peace badly enough to make the sacrifices necessary to achieve it! You'd rather see your own people blown to pieces, burned alive in their own villages, starved to death. You'd rather kill women and babies than make peace."

The president of Zaire said, "You don't understand how difficult—"

"No, *you* don't understand," Stoner snapped, jabbing an accusing finger at him. "Nor do you, or you, or any of you. If the killing goes on, you will die, too. Don't you realize that? Your own aides will poison you before the year ends." Pointing to the lean, lanky Katangan, "You'll be killed by an assassin in three months." To the Kenyan, "An air raid will kill your wife and children." To the four Nigerians, "None of you will survive the year."

He stopped. Dead silence filled the helicopter's cramped cabin. No one even breathed.

"And worst of all," Stoner went on, his voice lower and calmer, "is that none of your deaths, none of the million deaths that your people will suffer, will matter in the slightest. The problems that you are too stubborn to solve today will remain to plague your survivors."

One of the Nigerians asked in a shaky voice, "Are you saying that if we come to a resolution here, these deaths will not happen?"

"Yes. That's exactly what I'm saying."

"How do you know . . . ?"

"I know. If you don't believe me, leave now and return to your headquarters. You'll learn soon enough that I'm right."

The president of Zaire ran a hand across his dark, stubbled face. He was in shirt-sleeves and suspenders; his gaudy jacket had disappeared many hours earlier. Leaning across toward the Katangan, he asked, "Might it be possible to work out a form of federation, so that Katanga remains within the nation but obtains a measure of independent government?"

"I believe that my people might accept a federation," the Katangan replied.

"And pay taxes to Kinshasa?" demanded the stubby president of Zaire.

"Why should we pay taxes to you?"

"In return for local autonomy."

"How much of a tax?"

Stoner held up both hands. All eyes turned to him. "I want you all to agree to a cease-fire, here and now."

Eleven heads nodded even as they turned to check one another.

"Good," said Stoner. "That is the first step. The most important step. I'll call Colonel Bahadur and ask him to join us here."

The Nigerian in the Western suit called out, "I don't think it is wise to let the Peacekeepers know we are here!"

Stoner smiled at him. "Don't you think they already know? Don't you realize that their satellite cameras tracked your helicopters to this spot?"

"Perhaps so," admitted the Kenyan in his British old-school accent, "but don't you think it's a bit premature to invite him to come here?"

"I will ask him to come as you have come," Stoner replied. "Alone and without saying a word to anyone but his closest aides."

They muttered among themselves but finally agreed that the chief of the Peacekeepers had to be brought into their deliberations sooner or later. Under Stoner's prodding, they opted for sooner. He wormed his way into the helicopter's cramped flight deck and put in a radio call to Bahadur.

CHAPTER 32

"This is astounding," said Colonel Bahadur. "I see it and I hear it, but I still find it difficult to believe."

Stoner said, "It's a chance for peace. The first small step on a long and difficult road."

The sun was setting at Olduvai, beaming reddish-gold light across the barren gorge, glinting in the canopies of the helicopters, throwing long, distorted shadows that reached eerie fingers toward the distant hills. Stoner and the mountainous Sikh stood in front of the Peacekeepers' helicopter, a mammoth machine large enough to house a complete flying headquarters. The eleven African leaders and their staffs had gathered down at the end of the impromptu flight line, where the paleontologists were helping them to put together a dinner of local game and vegetables.

"A cease-fire." Colonel Bahadur shook his turbaned head. "Two days ago I would not have believed it possible."

"It's fragile. And only temporary."

"Yes, I realize that."

"None of them have agreed to give up their arms."

"Of course not."

Stoner went on, "But it gives you a chance to begin the process of making real peace."

"That will require disarming each of the factions," said the colonel, his bearded face grim. "Simultaneously."

"They won't go for that. Not yet."

"Then your cease-fire will break down within a week."

"Not if you can prevent them from being resupplied."

Bahadur's impressive eyebrows rose almost into his turban. "Prevent . . . ?" He broke into a bitter laugh. "My dear man, have you any idea of how many seaports and airports the arms shipments come in to? Do you think my people could blockade all of central Africa?"

"Where do their arms and ammunition come *from*?"

"From?"

"From," Stoner repeated.

The colonel thought a moment, stroking his beard. "I cannot truly say. But I can find out!"

"I think it's important that you do," said Stoner.

"Yes, perhaps you are right." He turned and went back toward his helicopter. Stoner, suddenly alone, jammed his hands into the pockets of his coveralls and, hunching his shoulders against the growing evening chill, headed for the tables that were being set up down at the end of the row of helicopters.

Several of the paleontologists' workers were piling up logs and kindling. A small truck came into view, battered and dust-covered. Stoner saw that it was hauling more firewood. None of the wood was sawed; the paleontologists were picking up windfalls only and resisting the temptation to attack the distant forest with power saws. They respected this desolate land, revered it with almost religious intensity as one of the earliest sites of recognizable human habitation.

Stoner joined the team building the fire. They laid the branches in crosshatched rows several feet high, then filled the ground under it with twigs for kindling. Even before the fire was lit, the exertion began to warm him. He recalled the old Yankee aphorism to the effect that a wood fire warms you twice. The woman who headed the scientific dig climbed laboriously up the slope of the gorge, surveyed their work, and gave a satisfied nod. The chief of her crew, a gaunt, grinning Ethiopian, nodded happily at her approval and lit the kindling with a palm-sized laser lighter.

Within a few minutes the fire was crackling and blazing high into the night air, flinging sparks toward the dark sky. Even as its heat soaked into him, Stoner thought of the pyres lit every night at the refugee camp and knew that this night would be no different: there were still people dying each day from starvation and disease, being killed by bombs and bullets. Men, women, and children.

"They never had fire, you know."

Stoner turned from the leaping, warming flames to see that the chief paleontologist was standing beside him. She was a chunky woman, somewhere in her middle fifties, he guessed. Gray hair. Solid barrel of a body with a man's shoulders and hardly any shape at all. She wore shorts, and Stoner saw that her legs were thick and ungainly. But her hands were long-fingered and graceful; a ballerina's hands on the stubby arms of a longshoreman. The dust of geological ages caked beneath her fingernails. Her eyes gleamed in the firelight.

"The hominids who camped here a few million years didn't have fire," she explained. "Fire came later, much later."

"But they had tools, didn't they?" Stoner asked, looking back at the dancing flames.

"Tools, yes." She dug into the pocket of her shorts. "This is one of them."

He put out his hand, and she placed a small piece of stone in his palm. It looked like a pebble, with one edge chipped and roughened.

"It's a scraper," the woman said. "They used it to clean the hides off the animals they had caught. Small animals, mostly. Rodents, field mice, like that."

Stoner stared at the barely altered pebble in his palm. "How old is it?"

The woman shrugged her heavy shoulders. "Couple of million years, at least. Not more than four million."

"One of our earliest tools." He glanced up at the helicopters standing nearby and thought of the spacecraft he had flown in.

"Thanks for showing it to me," he said, extending his hand back to her.

Instead of taking it back, she folded his fingers around the pebble. "I want you to keep it."

"Me?"

"Ah Linh's told me what you're doing here. How you're trying to stop the fighting. Please take the scraper as a tiny little thank-you from me . . ." She hesitated and smiled shyly. "And from our ancestors."

"But this must be awfully valuable," Stoner said.

"Only to someone who appreciates it."

"Well, thank you, Dr. . . ." He stopped. "I'm afraid I don't know your name."

"No reason why you should," she replied. "I'm just a worker in the field, one of many."

"But you do have a name, don't you?"

The shy smile came back. "It's Delany. Rosemarie Delany. And don't call me Rosie! My friends call me Ro."

"All right." Stoner grinned at her. "Thank you, Ro. I'd like to be considered one of your friends."

"Fine."

"My name is—"

"Keith Stoner. An Linh's spent the past thirty-six hours telling me all about you."

"Really?"

Rosemarie Delany gave him an impish grin. "She certainly did."

They feasted together that night, all eleven of the politicians and their staffs, the paleontologists and their crew, Colonel Bahadur and his half-dozen men, An Linh and Stoner.

I wonder what the original inhabitants of this site would have thought to see us here, Stoner wondered. A motley assortment. So many different tribes, so many different skin colors and backgrounds and loyalties. Yet we can all gather around the fire and share its warmth and protection.

Can we get all the peoples of Earth to gather around one central bonfire and share its warmth and protection? Stoner wondered. How could we accomplish that? How could we begin to try?

An Linh sat next to him on the grass as they ate. Dr. Delany explained the meal to everyone. "We keep goats. Very efficient animals. They eat anything and give us milk and meat."

Stoner felt a slight pang of surprise. The meat was excellent, tender and delicious. His mental impression of goat meat was tough and stringy.

After dinner the politicians went to Colonel Bahadur's helicopter to work out a joint communiqué announcing the cease-fire. They planned to leave in the morning and return to their various headquarters.

Bahadur took Stoner aside. "On the problem of where the arms shipments originate," he said, his voice low, his bearded face etched in firelight, "I am surprised that more than eighty percent of the shipments come from only a half-dozen points: one in Czechoslovakia, two in the United States, one in Singapore, and the final two in Soviet Russia."

"Can you stop the shipments?"

"Not without the cooperation of the local governments."

"Surely the International Peacekeeping Force can exert enough pressure . . ."

Bahadur stopped him with a shake of his head. "It is not so simple. Four of those arms factories are controlled by a single international corporation."

Without asking, Stoner knew which one it was. "Vanguard Industries," he whispered.

"Yes."

"And the Russian government controls the other two."

"That is correct."

Stoner drew in a deep breath. "Then I've got to get the Russians and the people who run Vanguard to agree to stop their arms shipments."

"No one can do that," said Bahadur.

"Maybe. But I can try."

The huge Sikh placed a hand on Stoner's shoulder. "My friend, why even bother?"

"To stop the war."

"Even if you got them to agree to stop their arms shipments, the smaller suppliers would still send weapons and ammunition into central Africa. They would rush in to fill the gap!"

"And you couldn't stop them?"

"There must be hundreds of them," Bahadur said. "Perhaps thousands. The terrorists of the World Liberation Movement have been smuggling weapons in for years. They would merely step up their operations."

Stoner looked deeply into the Sikh's firelit eyes. "Then you'll have to alter *your* operations to stop them."

Bahadur heaved a heavy sigh. "I suppose we could try."

"Yes. We must both try."

"And you? What do you propose to do?"

With a tight smile, Stoner said, "I have an old friend in Moscow. I think it's time for me to visit him. And to renew my acquaintance with the person who runs Vanguard Industries."

"You know him?"

"Her."

"Can you reach these people?"

"I can try. Just as you will try to do what must be done."

Bahadur took his hand from Stoner's shoulder, let his arm drop limply to his side. "You must be insane," he said. "We must both be insane."

Stoner shrugged.

"Yes," said the Sikh. "You are a madman, Keith Stoner. That's the only explanation. A madman. Or a saint."

A man possessed, Stoner thought. That's what he really means. What would he say if he knew that I truly am a man possessed? Stoner felt a faint echo, almost of amusement, inside his mind. Are you a god or a devil? he asked the alien within him. Are you a good witch or a bad witch?

He laughed aloud. "A madman or a saint," he repeated to Bahadur. "Of the two, I think it's easier to be a madman."

"Yes," agreed the colonel. "But if you can get Vanguard Industries and the Russian government to stop shipping arms into Africa, then you will be proclaimed to be a saint. Very definitely."

Stoner laughed again and wished Bahadur good night. He walked back to the helicopter he and An Linh had arrived in. The copilot was sitting on the ground, his back against the 'copter's nose wheel.

"She's off with the scientists, I think." He waved vaguely toward the tents down in the gorge.

Stoner nodded. "Tell the pilot we'll be taking off tomorrow morning."

"He knows. He's already asleep."

"Good. I like a well-rested pilot. And copilot."

The man grinned in the flickering light cast by the dying fire. "Just let me finish my weed, huh?"

Stoner headed down the slope toward the lighted tents. He found An Linh with Delany and the other paleontologists. After an awkward round of farewells, including an impulsive bearlike hug from Delany, he took An Linh back toward their helicopter.

Halfway there she grabbed at his hand and came to a halt.

"Keith . . . there's something I've got to tell you."

The night was cold now. The distant fire had almost burned itself out. The helicopters loomed against the star-bright sky like ancient birds of prey, asleep. The lights down among the scientists' tents were winking out. Darkness and cold were enveloping Stoner. He felt An Linh's hand in his, a small warm candle against the shadows.

"What is it?" he asked.

For several moments she said nothing. Her hand tightened in his, and he almost thought he could feel the blood pulsing in her fingers.

"I love you, Keith." She said it in a rush, as if afraid that someone or something would stop her if she didn't hurry the words out.

He felt his brows knit into a frown. He did not know how to respond.

"Make love to me, Keith. Here in the open, here in this place where people lived millions of years ago."

She pressed close to him, and he automatically wrapped his arms around her tiny childlike frame. The alien presence in his mind allowed him to look at her calmly, rationally, with none of the surging emotions that another man might have felt.

"But what about Cliff Baker?" he asked gently.

"He's dead. I know he is. They killed him—maybe because of me. . . ."

"I don't think so," Stoner said.

"I don't care!" she whispered fiercely. "I want you. Now. I love you!"

"An Linh," he said softly, "I understand how you feel. But I can't make love to you."

She said nothing, merely looked up into his eyes, waiting.

"I wish I could," he said. "I think it would be wonderful. But I can't. I just can't."

"But Keith," she whispered, "I love you!"

"You think you do."

"I do! I love you, Keith. I want to be with you always. I want to bear your children."

"It can't be, An Linh." As gently as he knew how, he said, "It just can't be."

"You don't mean that," she said, anguish in her voice. "I know you can't mean that. I'll wait, it doesn't matter how long. . . ."

He felt a rush of near panic at the thought of physically making love, of stripping and pawing and humping the way animals do, but it was immediately suppressed, frozen, immobilized in the alien's glacial calm.

"An Linh, I can't love anyone. Not the way you want to be loved."

"But I don't understand. . . ."

"Neither do I. Not completely." He hesitated, not knowing how much to tell her. "I don't think that I'm completely human. There's something inside me, something from the alien's starship—maybe it's his mind itself. . . ."

"That's impossible."

"Nothing's impossible," he said fervently.

"Except your loving me."

He had no answer for that.

An Linh pushed away from him, tears glistening in her eyes. Wordlessly she walked back toward the helicopter. Stoner stood in the dark night, feeling cold and alone.

Is that what you want? he asked the alien within him. Am I going to be some kind of freak, completely cut off from all normal human emotions?

There was no reply. None at all.

HIGH ASIA

O day of darkness! What evil spirit moved our minds when for the sake of an earthly kingdom we came to this field of battle ready to kill our own people?

CHAPTER 33

Kirill Markov slouched in the leather sofa, his long legs stretched out across the Persian carpet, his thin white goatee flattened on his chest.

The secretary scowling behind her desk reminded him too much of his late wife. A face like an angry potato, heavy and solid and glaring at him every time she looked up from her word processor. Do you expect me to sit up at attention like a schoolboy waiting to see the headmaster? Markov asked her silently.

He clasped his hands behind his head and wondered what she would do if he started whistling. What tune should I pick? Then he grinned. Why let her turn me sour? Keith is alive. He's alive! And working miracles in Africa.

That was the good news.

The bad news was that Keith's miracle, a ceasefire all across central Africa that actually seemed to be working, was having terrible repercussions here in the Kremlin.

The door next to the secretary's desk swung slightly open, and a thin, ascetic, cadaverous young man slipped through. Bald, hollow-cheeked, he looked to Markov like a zombie from some decadent Western horror video. But he was dressed in a Russian blouse of deep maroon, with billowing sleeves, and heavy dark trousers tucked into glossy boots. Everyone dressed very "Russian" these days, Markov reflected. Everyone wanted to proclaim openly his or her love for the Motherland.

The zombie nodded gravely to Markov. He scrambled to his feet, gave his most charming smile to the secretary—who glared back at him—and went to the door. The zombie slid through the narrow opening like a puff of smoke. Markov thought momentarily of flinging the heavy oak door open wide and striding into the council chamber with his head held high and his shoulders thrown back. Like a soldier. A conquering hero. But instead he edged sideways through the partially open door and tiptoed into the chamber with the meekness born of a lifetime's experience in dealing with high authority.

The council chamber was neither as large nor as grand as Markov had expected, although it was quite impressive. The ceiling was a good five meters high and inlaid with beautifully carved wood. The windows along the wall to his right went from ceiling to floor, although the heavy red drapes were pulled tightly across each of them, so nothing of the outside could be seen. The floor was parqueted and bare, except for runners along the sides by the windows and the gleaming walnut sideboard that held stacks of reports bound in stiff covers, an array of electronic black boxes, and the inevitable ornate silver samovar.

The long conference table was also walnut, polished to a glistening finish. Only nine men sat at it, bunched up at the head. Three portraits hung on the far wall: Marx on the left, Lenin on the right, and the image of the man who sat at the head of the table, Viktor Ulanovsky, general secretary of the Communist party and chairman of the Council of Ministers. In the painting, Ulanovsky was smiling handsomely, his hair was dark and wavy, his eyes shone with dedication.

The man himself was considerably grayer, fatter, sallower than the portrait. And he was not smiling.

Neither were the other eight men grouped around him. They all looked deadly serious. And they all dressed alike. To Markov, it seemed that he was staring at nine imitations of Ulanovsky. They all wore dark, Western-cut business suits, all the ties were Party red, every lapel sported a gold hammer-and-sickle pin, every breast pocket featured a few small Hero of the People medals.

Markov felt suddenly shabby in his gray peasant blouse and tweed jacket.

"Comrade Markov," said Ulanovsky in a surprisingly high-pitched voice, "thank you for joining us."

Markov nodded dumbly, his mind irreverently flicking back to an ancient Marx Brothers film he had seen in his student days. At a decadent Hollywood restaurant a table full of lovely young women call to Groucho, "Won't you join us?" He replies, "Why, are you falling apart?" The rejoinder seemed bitterly appropriate to Markov.

But he kept his lips pressed firmly shut as he walked to the chair being held for him by the zombie.

"Would you like some tea, comrade?" asked the general secretary.

"Thank you, sir," Markov managed to mutter.

"We asked you here, comrade, because you apparently have a personal relationship with this American, Stoner."

Markov nodded as the zombie placed a delicate china cup before him. He saw that the others had cups and even vodka glasses at their places. Ulanovsky, though, had nothing but neatly printed papers before him.

The general secretary leaned forward on his elbows, hands clasped almost as if in prayer, and asked in his strangely piping voice, "Do you realize what problems this man has made for us?"

Before Markov could answer, one of the other ministers snapped, "This American is in league with the so-called International Peacekeeping Force to shut down the Soviet arms industry!"

Markov gaped at him.

"Not shut it down, exactly," Ulanovsky said, more mildly.

"Strangle it!" insisted the minister, a bald, baggy-eyed old man with splotchy skin. "The so-called Peacekeepers actually have had the nerve to demand that we stop all arms shipments to Africa!"

"But isn't the Soviet Union part of the Peacekeeping Force?" Markov asked, puzzled. "Aren't our own men serving with the IPF in Africa?"

"Naturally we have loaned certain units of our own forces to the Peacekeepers," replied Ulanovsky. "To do otherwise would have isolated the Soviet Union and made us appear to be antipeace. Besides"—he allowed a small smile to creep across his face—"how better to keep an eye on the wolves than to join their pack?"

A round of answering smiles went around the table, showing that the ministers agreed fully with their chairman.

"So considering the cease-fire," Markov heard his own voice, so timid that it made him disgusted with himself, "wouldn't it be in the best interests of peace if we . . . uh, suspended arms shipments for a while?"

The room seemed to erupt with angry, sputtering rebuttals.

"Refuse arms to our allies?"

"Turn our backs on comrades who are struggling for national liberation?"

"Allow these thinly disguised imperialists to dictate Soviet policy?"

Ulanovsky raised a hand and they quieted down. All except one of the younger men, bespectacled, dark-haired, his lips curled slightly in a knowing smile that was almost a sneer.

"Think of the economic situation, comrade Markov. Those arms shipments bring hard currency into our treasury. We need hard currency to buy grain to feed our people."

Especially if the Ukraine actually manages to secede from the Soviet Union, Markov realized.

The general secretary said, "Comrade academician, the cease-fire that this American has somehow arranged places us in a delicate quandary. On the one hand, as my comrades have so aptly said, to stop our arms shipments would be a betrayal of our friends in Africa—and an economic hardship we can ill afford."

Murmurs of agreement around the table.

"On the other hand," Ulanovsky continued, "if the other arms exporters suspend their shipments and we do not, the Soviet Union would be held up to public ridicule . . . and possible economic sanctions that could hurt us severely."

"Bah!" snorted the bald one. "This is an *opportunity,* not a crisis. Let the imperialists suspend their arms exports. We can continue to arm our allies, so that when the cease-fire breaks down, our comrades will have an insuperable advantage over the capitalist lackeys!"

"But what if the Peace Enforcers carry out their threat to interdict all shipments leaving the Soviet Union for Africa?"

"They can't possibly. . . ."

"They have threatened an embargo on *all* commerce," Ulanovsky said, his girlish voice rising slightly. "They do not make threats lightly. Even if they are only partially successful, the economic consequences could be disastrous."

"It's the Cuban Missile Crisis all over again," said one of the other ministers. "Only this time, the blockade begins at our own shores."

"And overhead," the young economist added. "They can shut down our major airports if they wish to."

"Then we'll fight them!" roared the bald one.

"Fight who?" Ulanovsky asked mildly. "The International Peacekeeping Force? How does one fight them? They are not a nation. Do we attack their headquarters in Oslo? Do we attack their field stations scattered across central Africa? Every nation in the West and most of the Third World nations in Africa and Asia would rise up against us. The Uzbeks and Kazakhs and Ukrainians would love that, wouldn't they?"

The splotches on the bald man's pate grew redder, and he pulled his chin down into a glowering pout.

Turning back to Markov, the general secretary said mildly, "Comrade, you were asked several months ago to make contact with this American, Stoner, and bring him to the Soviet Union."

"I did make contact with him," Markov said in a choking near whisper.

"But you failed to bring him back."

Instead of going into excuses, Markov cautiously put his trump card on the table. "That is true, comrade secretary. But fortunately, I have reestablished contact with him. He is on his way to the Soviet Union now, at this moment."

Astonishment made Ulanovsky's eyes go round. But just for a fraction of a second. One does not rise to the top of the Soviet government or the Party by allowing oneself to be surprised.

"That is very good, comrade! Very good indeed."

"Better late than never," groused the bald minister.

"Stoner is on a plane from Nairobi, heading for Athens. I plan to meet him there and personally escort him to Moscow."

"Excellent."

"It doesn't do anything for this cease-fire business," said one of the ministers.

"No, but it will be extremely valuable to have this man in our grasp. There may be knowledge locked inside his brain that will make the central African affair look small by comparison."

"Besides," said the young economist, "we can circumvent the Peacekeepers by channeling the arms shipments through the World Liberation Movement. The route is more circuitous. . . ."

"So is the payment," somebody muttered.

The economist's sneering smile widened. "To be sure. But

the results in the field are good. A good percentage of the shipments go through the World Liberation Movement already. We will simply have to put the entire burden on them.''

"Do you think they are reliable enough to handle it all?'' Ulanovsky asked.

"Not really. We will have to place more of our own people in key positions within the WLM to ensure reliability. We may have to take over its leadership entirely.''

Ulanovsky nodded, his mind made up. "Very well. See to it.''

A general murmur of agreement passed around the table.

Turning again to Markov, the general secretary said, "And now, comrade, I believe you have a plane to catch.''

Markov felt the chair being pulled out from behind him by the zombie. He got to his feet and made a smile that he knew was pitifully weak.

"I'm off to Athens,'' he said, "to meet Stoner once again.''

"And this time you will bring him back with you,'' said Ulanovsky.

"Yes, comrade secretary! Of course!''

"Do not fail.'' Ulanovsky said it mildly, almost sweetly. It sent chills up Markov's spine.

With an awkward little bow, Markov backed away from the table, turned, and made his way gratefully toward the door. He cursed himself for being a spineless mouse in the face of power. Yet even as he did, he glowed inwardly: not only was Keith fulfilling the promise he had made, but neither Ulanovsky nor any of the other ministers seemed to know that there would be a third person joining them in Athens—Jo Camerata Nillson.

As he stepped through the doorway, past the zombie holding it open for him, and into the outer office, Markov felt again the disapproving scowl of the secretary glaring at him.

It made him wonder if the ministers actually knew about his message to Jo or not.

"We'll be landing in ten minutes,'' said the pilot's voice over the intercom. It sounded as if he were underwater, but Stoner made out the words with a little effort.

An Linh stirred in her sleep beside him. He looked up from the volume of Vedic hymns that a grateful Colonel

Bahadur had pressed into his hands when they had left Nairobi. After a long night of reading from the lovingly crafted, elaborately printed pages, one verse from the ancient songs stuck in Stoner's memory:

"Harness the plows, fit on the yokes, now that the womb of the earth is ready to sow the seed therein. . . ."

The relationship between sex and agriculture had never impressed him before, but now he saw how miraculous it must have seemed to early men that food crops would grow from tiny seeds, and babies would grow from the seed of their own bodies. To early men. Stoner leaned back in the plane's chair and wondered how early women felt about it. What power they must have had, he realized. And they still have it! No wonder almost every religion pays lip service to male gods but really reveres goddesses.

Even in cultures like those in Africa, where the people were selecting a heavy preponderance of male children over female, this would give women an even greater power within a few years. The fewer the women, the more important they will be to the society's continuation. Stoner nodded to himself: That's a factor that the IPF should exploit. A two-edged sword, certainly, but it could be useful if properly handled.

He smiled to himself. Then, glancing down at An Linh's sleeping face, his smile vanished. How lovely she is, he thought. How fragile and vulnerable she appears. But she has the power of life within her. And the responsibility of choice. She decides who will mate with her. Men compete for her attention, and she decides among them. He sighed out a long, troubled breath. So she decides on me. Of all the men who would fight dragons for her, or lay the world's wealth at her feet, she picks a man who's no longer fully human.

Stoner squeezed his eyes shut and pressed himself deeper into the softly cushioned seat. The twin-engined jet belonged to the International Peacekeeping Force. It was small, but quite comfortable, with generously wide seats that had plenty of leg room between them, even for a man Stoner's height. He and An Linh were the only passengers, which made the flight truly luxurious. But the plane was obsolescent, slow and short-ranged. It had taken nearly twelve hours to reach Athens, with refueling stops in Aden and Cairo.

The plane banked and Stoner looked out the window, surprised to see the sky over Athens clear and clean. He remembered attending a scientific conference in Athens, a lifetime ago, and being shocked at the gray-brown pall of filth that hung over the city. Down in the streets, choked with honking, growling automobiles, he had learned where the pollution dome originated. The noxious fumes were eating away the ancient marble monuments of the Acropolis.

Dr. Richards had told him that cars had gone electric or to clean hydrogen fuels. Stoner could see the result as the plane circled over the ancient rock of the Acropolis. The streets below were just as clogged with traffic as he remembered, but the air was crystalline. And there stood the Parthenon, the most glorious structure in human history, Stoner told himself—and the presence within himself.

Built by the ancient Athenians, nearly destroyed by war, eroded by pollution, the many columns of the Parthenon still stood proud and beautiful, glowing in the morning sun. Stoner saw scaffolding was being erected at one end of the ancient temple. Repairs? Restoration?

Then the plane banked again, and the Acropolis was swept from his sight. He settled back in his seat and listened to the thump of the landing gear being lowered, felt the plane swaying slightly in the gusty wind as the pilot lined up for her final approach to the runway.

An Linh stirred. Her eyes opened.

"Are we there?" she asked, like a little girl.

"Yes, almost," said Stoner.

He had still not made up his mind about her. He knew that the work he had to do with Markov did not involve her. Yet he could not leave her in Athens, alone, penniless, and probably still being hunted by agents of Vanguard Industries. Stoner told himself that he would find Jo, get her to take An Linh under her protection. A tall order, he knew. Jo had wanted to run An Linh out of the corporation. But a life was at stake now, and he was certain that Jo would see things differently once he explained them to her.

For the time being, then, An Linh would have to stay with him. All the way to Moscow. She ought to strike some sparks of interest from Markov, he thought, smiling inwardly. We'll see just how old Kirill really feels once he sees her.

And there he was, standing in front of the hangar as the twin jet rolled to a stop. One hand leaning on his cane,

Markov seemed to be peering intently at the plane, trying to make out Stoner's face in the thick windows. Aged, stooped, his goatee ragged and wispy, his hair white and pitifully thin, still Markov managed to look like an eager schoolboy as he waited for the plane's hatch to open and his old friend to come out and join him.

For a moment Stoner felt the same happy impatience. But then it all dissolved, ebbed away, and the deadened calm enveloped him once again. He thought, with all the passion of a computer readout, that it was unfair of the alien to suppress even welcome emotions. But the thought itself was a mere observation, not even a complaint.

There is important work for me to do, he told himself. I must be free to exert every ounce of strength and will in me to accomplish this task. As he unbuckled his safety belt and got up from his seat, he heard in the dim recesses of his memory his old tae kwan do instructor urging him, "Focus. Focus! Strength and skill mean nothing if they are not focused entirely on the object at hand."

The plane's cabin was so small that he had to bend over to get down the aisle. He ducked through the hatch and clambered down the shaky aluminum ladder to the concrete ramp in front of the hangar. The golden sun of Greece felt good, the morning air was warm without being humid.

And Kirill Markov's eyes lit up when he saw Stoner. Twirling his cane in one hand, he advanced toward Stoner, who half ran to his old friend and clasped him in his arms. The Russian pounded Stoner's back with his free hand, but it felt like the feeble taps of an old man.

"Keith, you look like an Old Testament prophet in that beard: fierce and uncompromising," said Markov.

"I'll shave it off."

"No, no! Keep it! It looks good. Dark and threatening. They'll understand it in Moscow."

Stoner laughed, then saw that Markov's eyes had already shifted to look past him toward An Linh, who was approaching them. Even in the shapeless, oversized blue coveralls of the IPF she looked radiantly beautiful.

"And who is this?"

Turning, Stoner introduced, "This is An Linh Laguerre, my friend and companion. An Linh, permit me to introduce

Professor Kirill Markov, head of the Soviet Academy of Sciences.''

Markov immediately switched to French. *"Enchanté, mademoiselle."*

"Thank you," said An Linh. "I am delighted to make your acquaintance."

"Your beauty outshines the sun," Markov continued in French. "Aphrodite herself would be jealous of you."

"He's a linguist," Stoner said to An Linh, "and a hopeless romantic."

"Who could not be romantic in the face of such loveliness?" Markov retorted. He extended his free arm for An Linh. "Come, you must tell the whole story of your life as we wing our way to Moscow."

"We're going right now?" Stoner asked.

"Yes. That's our plane, there."

"We've just spent twelve hours inside a plane."

Markov's brows knit together. "When did you learn to speak French?"

Stoner made himself shrug.

"You can speak Russian, also?"

"Yes."

Without letting go of An Linh's arm, Markov turned very serious. "Keith, nothing would please me more than to spend a few days in Athens with you and this lovely lady. But we are expected in Moscow immediately."

"I see," Stoner said. "And I promised you I would go, didn't I?"

"Yes, you did."

Stoner cast his eyes toward the horizon. From the spot where he stood, nothing could be seen of the city or its ancient citadel. But the sky was blue, the sun warm, the air clean and fresh.

"Besides," Markov said, "there is a surprise for you waiting aboard the plane."

Stoner looked at his old friend; his aged face was smiling, his eyes sparkled with anticipation.

"A surprise?" he asked.

Markov's smile broadened. He asked An Linh, "I hope this won't be too much of an imposition on you, dear lady. Perhaps after a few days in Moscow, you will permit me to

show you Leningrad. Or we might fly back here to Athens, if
you wish. Or to Paris!"

"You are too kind," she said graciously.

"Yes, it's so. Kindness is one of my many faults. I am
romantic, kind, generous, and sweet. Not like this big oaf of
an American. Take away his good looks and intelligence, and
what have you got? Hardly anything!"

An Linh laughed and Stoner grinned. Markov continued
his bantering chatter as he led them toward the waiting plane
with the red star painted on its raked-back tail.

Another aluminum can, Stoner thought wearily as they
climbed into the plane. But from the brief look he had at its
outside, it was probably a supersonic jet. A swing-wing
design that could make it to Moscow in only a couple of
hours at most.

The interior was even more luxurious than the IPF's jet.
Huge padded chairs covered in leather. They swiveled and
tilted back so far that they could be used as sleeping couches.

Stoner began, "So where's the surprise? . . ."

One of the big swivel chairs turned around, and he saw Jo
sitting in it, dressed in a clinging metallic sheath of gleaming
silver, its miniskirt showing her long legs to good advantage.
The smile on her face froze when she saw An Linh.

"Jo!"

"Hello, Keith." Her dark eyes never left An Linh's.

"What are you doing here?"

"I called her and asked her to join us," Markov explained.

"That's wonderful," Stoner said. He went to the chair
next to Jo's.

Markov showed An Linh to a chair, and as soon as they
were all seated, a uniformed steward brought them a tray of
vodka, fruit juices, ice, and chilled wine. Stoner took juice,
Jo and An Linh both had wine, and Markov knocked back a
pony of vodka.

Stoner could see that the Russian had no idea of the enmity
between the two women. He could feel it, though, like the
heat of molten lava flowing from a volcano.

A voice on the intercom from the flight deck told them to
buckle their seat belts, face their seats forward, and lock
them in place while the plane taxied to the runway and took
off.

"I didn't expect to see you here," Stoner said to Jo.

"I didn't expect you to have her with you," she replied, her voice low with suppressed anger.

Markov sensed the tension, too, as he chattered to An Linh, "You will love Moscow. There's only a few feet of snow on the streets. . . ."

"I love winter sports," she countered, her eyes on the back of Jo's chair.

"And the sun actually peeked through the clouds for a few moments a day or so ago," he continued. "No one has seen a polar bear prowling the streets for weeks now, and the wolf problem is almost under control."

He wanted An Linh to laugh, or at least to smile at him. Instead she merely said, "I'm looking forward to seeing your wonderful city."

"I have a lot to tell you," Stoner said to Jo. "There's a lot that you're not aware of."

"I'll bet," she snapped. Then she turned away from him and stared out her window. Stoner decided not to press her. Not here. Not now. Instead, he marveled at the palpable fury he felt radiating from her. This is more than a business rivalry, he realized. Is she angry because she thinks An Linh was after her husband? Or is she enraged because An Linh is with me?

Both, he thought. All of the above. He had never paid any attention to the competitions between women. Now he wondered how to calm Jo's temper, how to keep it from wrecking the mission he had given himself.

The plane arrowed into the air, and Stoner watched the narrow wings, unpainted aluminum, slide back until they almost touched the fuselage. He pressed his forehead against the cold window glass and saw deeply blue water below. The wine-dark Aegean, he thought. Where Odysseus sailed. The ruins of Troy are off somewhere to the east. The ruins of Knossos and Gizeh and Ephesus are dotted around the shores of these seas. What will be found of our civilization two thousand, five thousand, ten thousand years from now? Maybe we've forestalled nuclear holocaust, but there are other ways to tear a civilization to pieces. The ancients did it by hand, stone by stone, death by death. They didn't need nuclear weapons to destroy Carthage, or Thebes, or even Rome.

He glanced at Jo. Her back was still turned to him. Markov was busily courting An Linh, and Stoner was glad that Jo probably could not understand French. He remembered the legend of Theseus and Ariadne, and the history of Cleopatra and the women of the Roman court. Why must women always scheme and compete against one another? He wondered. Men compete, but that's always for the attention of women, when you come down to it. Conquer an empire or write a sonnet, it's really so that you can get the women you want to notice you and come to your bed. But women compete, too, viciously. For what? They're the ones who decide which men will mate with them. They have the power to decide who will father their children. . . .

And then it struck him. Women compete not merely to get the men whom they desire as mates. They compete for power and security so that their children can be raised in safety. He remembered the Indian woman he had met at the Gare de Lyon, and what she had told him about her duty to her children:

I must protect them as best I can.

That's what it's all about, he realized. It may be buried so deep in their genes that they don't understand it consciously, but that's why women instinctively compete against each other. To get the best mates, the ones with the most wealth, the most power, the most wisdom. Not for themselves. For their children. Even the unborn ones. To protect their children. It's an innate part of their makeup, and a species where the females don't have such an instinct is a species that will die off and become extinct.

The other presence in his mind seemed to ponder that thought for a while, then accept it. Stoner could feel some of the tension in him relax.

Meanwhile, Markov was trying to entertain An Linh, trying to ease the tension in the only way he knew how. "Leningrad is a different city altogether," he was telling her. "A beautiful city, truly beautiful, with splendid buildings and an art museum that you could spend a lifetime in and still not see everything."

"It sounds wonderful." She had swiveled her chair around to face Markov's. "I would love to see it."

Another steward appeared, his hands empty, a slightly sardonic smile on his face.

"I have an announcement to make," he said. In English.

Stoner felt puzzled, almost annoyed. Trouble, he said to himself. This is trouble.

An Linh looked up and felt the blood freeze in her veins. "Cliff!" she gasped.

"Hullo, pet," said Cliff Baker. "I'm afraid it's my sad duty to inform the four of you that this plane will not arrive in Moscow on schedule. In fact, it's not going to arrive in Moscow at all."

CHAPTER 34

Two hours stretched to four, and then to eight. At the high latitudes where they were flying, the sun soon dipped to the horizon and slowly sank out of sight.

When Cliff Baker had announced that their plane had been taken over by the World Liberation Movement, Stoner had thought of the chances of talking to him, persuading him to let them fly to Moscow as originally planned. But Baker was either aware of Stoner's abilities or just naturally cautious. After his cryptic announcement he locked himself in the flight deck with the plane's pilot and copilot.

Stoner turned his chair toward An Linh. She looked stunned.

"He's not dead," Stoner said to her.

"I never thought I'd see him again," she said, her voice hollow with shock.

"Apparently he's escaped from Vanguard. Perhaps the World Liberation Movement freed him."

"Escaped from Vanguard?" Jo asked. "What do you mean?"

Markov demanded, "Who is this man? How can he hijack a Soviet airplane? Where is he taking us?"

For several hours they talked back and forth, Stoner and An Linh taking turns telling their stories to Jo and Markov.

"I had no idea that Everett . . . ." Jo stopped herself, her face suddenly twisted with anguish. Stoner could see she was fighting to hold back tears of frustrated rage.

"Nobody's blaming you for any of this," he said gently.

She shook her head. "My God, I thought I knew what was going on in Vanguard, but I've been nothing but a figurehead! Just a stupid little girl, playing at being the corporation president!"

"You are far from being stupid," Markov said. "This man Nillson must be as devious as a snake."

"He's frightening," An Linh agreed. "Terrifying."

"Nillson isn't our problem at the moment," said Stoner. "We appear to be the unwilling guests of the World Liberation Movement. I wonder where they're taking us?"

"And why?" Markov added.

"That's obvious," Jo replied. "They want you, Keith. The rest of us are extraneous."

"Do you mean expendable?" asked Markov.

Jo shrugged, and the four of them lapsed into silence.

The plane landed once, at an airstrip that seemed empty and abandoned, dust blown, in the kind of dry, brown, barren country that reminded Stoner of Tyuratam, in the Kazakh S.S.R. A pair of fuel trucks rolled up to their plane, and a team of coveralled men quickly, efficiently connected hoses to the fuel tanks in the plane's belly.

"They're not going to let us out here," Stoner said.

Markov, leaning across him to stare out at the refueling operation, muttered, "Kazakhs, or I'll swallow my beard. They're in on this."

"Where are we?" Jo asked.

"Halfway to Tibet," said Markov, "from the looks of things out there."

Within minutes they were airborne again. A dreary silence filled the plane's cabin. The steward who had first served them drinks brought out trays of hot dinners. Stoner saw that the others ate listlessly, picking at the precooked food. It was bland and hardly recognizable, but it felt warm and good to Stoner.

As the sun set and the engines droned on with no sign of their ultimate destination, one by one the others drifted off to sleep. Stoner sat up, though, and stared out at the dark night sky. Far off in the distance he could see the pale flickerings of the Northern Lights, and he remembered those wildly hectic weeks when the alien starship had announced its presence by making the skies dance all across the Earth, night after night after night.

We're heading east, Stoner told himself. To China? I doubt that we can get that far without another refueling. Whoever this World Liberation Movement is, they have things very neatly arranged. An abandoned military airstrip has a refueling team waiting for us. The plane deviates from its scheduled course and there are no problems with ground controllers. We're crossing vast stretches of Soviet airspace and there hasn't been a single interceptor buzzing us.

He thought of the radar operators, air traffic controllers, fuel depot managers, truck drivers, and hundreds of other people who must be part of this hijacking operation. Stoner felt impressed. This World Liberation Movement has organization and discipline. And *money*. You can't pull off an operation like this without lots of bribes, no matter how much confusion and turmoil is racking the Soviet Union. They've had to pay off lots of people, and that takes large amounts of cash.

Leaning back in the leather-covered reclining chair, Stoner realized that the WLM's operations in Africa required huge sums of money as well. Money to purchase arms, money to buy food, money to bribe politicians and customs inspectors. Mao Tse-tung said that power comes out of the barrel of a gun. But you have to have money to buy the gun. It even takes a certain amount of money to steal a gun.

The plane droned on, and when dawn lit the sky at last, Stoner saw vast and rugged ranges of mountains stretching out below. Peaks of rock straining up toward them, pitiless winds blowing the snow from the crags in long streamers of glistening white. Ice choking the ravines between the mountains, glaring in the morning sun, where fog and icy clouds did not hide the rocky landscape.

Jo awoke, stretching and yawning, got up and headed for the toilet at the rear of the plane. She came back a few minutes later and smiled at Stoner.

"I've got a month's supply of clothes in the cargo hold, but I can't get at them."

He gave the glittering, silvery dress an admiring look. "You're fine," he said.

"And what about you," Jo asked, sitting down again. "How are you doing?"

"I'm okay. Curious about where they're taking us."

"Not afraid?"

He made a small shrug. "Not yet."

"I guess as long as we're in the air we're all right. It's when we land that the trouble will start."

"I'll protect you, Jo."

"And Kirill?"

"Yes, of course."

"And her?"

"Her, too," he said.

Jo lapsed into a tight-lipped silence.

"There's nothing between us," he told her. "She's been on the run, trying to get away from your charming husband. I've been sort of a big brother to her."

"She loves you."

He felt himself smile. "How do you know that?"

"It's obvious."

"She thinks she does, yes. She also thought she was in love with this guy Baker, the one who seems to be in charge of this hijacking."

Jo said nothing.

"Are you still angry with her?" Stoner asked.

For a moment she did not reply. Then, "No, I suppose not. But I don't trust her."

It was Stoner's turn for silence. He searched Jo's dark eyes and saw such a turmoil of emotions in them that he could not fathom her intentions.

Markov woke slowly, snuffling and gargling like an old man. He *is* an old man, Stoner reminded himself. His snorts and coughs awoke An Linh, who seemed startled. Her eyes flew open, her hands gripped the armrests of her chair. Then she remembered where she was and, with a deep intake of breath, regained her composure.

The steward came out from the flight deck again, smiling politely. Stoner realized that he was young, probably not much more than twenty. Not very tall, either, but well built; he had the grace of a trained gymnast.

"We will land soon," he announced in studied English. "I will prepare breakfast for you."

"Where?" Jo demanded.

Markov echoed, "Yes, exactly where are we going to land?"

The steward kept the smile on his face. "Truly, I do not know. It is not necessary for me to know."

"You're a Russian," Markov said in his native language. "How can you allow this outrage to take place?"

"I am a Latvian, Academician Markov. Despite nearly a century of being ruled by our Bigger Brothers, we Letts have never accepted the idea that Russians are our natural masters."

The steward went back to the galley. Markov gave an exaggerated shrug of helplessness.

As they ate their cold breakfasts, Stoner could feel the plane being readied for landing. The engines throttled back, the wings slid forward. By the time the steward collected their emptied trays, the plane had noticeably lost altitude. Jagged rocky peaks loomed on both sides now. Stoner and the others saw glittering fields of snow gliding past. The air was bumpy down among the mountains. The plane slewed and jounced badly.

Flaps down. Wheels down. Stoner glanced at his friends. They all had their seat belts tightly fastened. An Linh was gripping the armrests of her chair with white-knuckled intensity. Markov was pasty-faced with fright, staring at the rocks hurtling past, seemingly only a few feet from the windows. Jo seemed more relaxed, her head thrown back against the seat rest, her eyes straight ahead, fixed on the metal bulkhead at the front of the cabin.

There was nothing but snowy ground beneath them, coming up fast. Then the plane leveled off and seemed to coast. Suddenly Stoner saw the dark asphalt of a runway beneath them, and the plane banged down hard, bounced, then settled onto its wheels and rolled along, the engines suddenly roaring mightily with reversed thrust. Without warning they plunged into darkness. The glaring bright snowscape outside the windows disappeared like an electric lamp being snapped off, and they were rushing down a tunnel, the thunder of the engines magnified into a hideous echoing bellow.

An airport built into the side of a mountain, Stoner told himself. I'll bet they have snowplows outside already busy blowing snow back onto the landing strip so no one can see it from the air.

The plane slowed, and a glow of light brightened the windows. By the time they had stopped, Stoner could see a vast cavern lit by strings of lamps high overhead. A team of technicians stood outside, most of them Orientals, dressed in nondescript coveralls. Six carried handguns strapped to their hips.

"Wherever we are," Markov said loudly, trying to cover the quaver in his voice, "we're here."

The door to the flight deck opened, and Cliff Baker ducked through. "Sorry to have put you through such a tedious long flight," he said, grinning slightly. "Welcome to Altai Base."

"What is Altai Base?" Markov demanded.

"Why have you brought us here?" asked Jo. "How long do you intend to keep us?"

Instead of answering, Baker strode down the aisle and went to the hatch. He yanked at the lever control, and the hatch swung open.

"End of the line," he said. "Everybody out."

Stoner unbuckled his seat belt and got to his feet. The others did the same. They shuffled slowly, reluctantly, to the hatch.

An Linh was in the lead. As she came up to the hatch, Baker gave her a crooked grin.

"What's the matter, pet? Not happy to see me?"

"I thought you were dead, Cliff," she said, her voice low and trembling. "I thought they had killed you."

"They almost did." He nodded toward Jo. "Her hubby damned near did kill me. Made me wish I was dead, for a while there. But don't you worry, love. I'm all right now. And I'm going to get back at them. All of them. Starting with her."

CHAPTER 35

The four of them were marched through the big underground hangar by the six armed guards. Baker walked up front with the guards' leader.

He's never been here before, either, Stoner observed. Looking around, he saw that their plane was one of more than a

dozen scattered around the vast cavern. A crew of technicians
was working on one of the planes, off in the distance, a huge
four-engine jumbo jet. Scaffolding ran half its length, and
Stoner could see the flickering blue sparks from a welding
torch scattering like shooting stars. The cavern was so big
that sound seemed to be swallowed up. There were no echoes
of the men working off in the distance. Stoner could hear the
clicking footsteps of the guards' boots on the stone floor and
the softer footfalls of his own soft-soled shoes.

It was cold inside this mammoth cave. He felt no movement of air, which meant that there must be giant doors
sealing off the airstrip from this underground hangar. Still,
the icy chill of the snow-covered mountains seemed to seep
into his bones.

They came to an elevator set into the rock wall, a big open
platform for carrying freight. It bore them down even deeper
into the mountain. Stoner counted four levels before they
came to a stop. The leader of the guards stepped off and
gestured them down the long corridor that lay before them.

"Right this way, ladies and gentlemen," Baker said with
malicious gaiety. They followed him, with the other five
guards trudging silently behind them.

At least it's warmer down here, thought Stoner. The corridor was wide enough for three or four people to walk abreast
and too high for him to reach the ceiling with his outstretched
fingers. Bare pipes ran along the ceiling, with fluorescent
tubes every few feet to provide an eerie bluish light that made
the skin of his hands look sickly gray.

They came to an intersection of corridors and stopped.

The guard leader said in halting English, "Men this
way"—he jabbed a thumb to his left—"women this way."
And he gestured to his right.

"Separate facilities," Baker said. "I'll stick with the ladies
and make sure they're comfortable."

Jo shot a frightened glance at Stoner, but he tried to
reassure her. "I'll see you in a little while," he said.

Baker's sardonic little smile curled his lips. "Don't bank
on it, friend."

Stoner looked into his eyes. "I can see what you've gone
through. Don't let it twist your judgment. You're just as
much a prisoner here as we are."

The crooked smile melted away. His lips tightened. For a

long moment Baker stood immobile, staring back at Stoner. Finally, with a visible effort, he jerked his head away and turned toward An Linh. "Come on, love, I'll show you to your quarters."

Stoner nodded to Jo, and she went with An Linh and Baker. And two of the armed guards.

Stoner and Markov tramped down the other corridor until the guards opened a pair of doors, side by side.

"We will be neighbors," said Markov. "Just like the Siberian salt mines."

Stoner grinned at him. "I hope the food's better."

"I think we will see a lot of rice while we're here. And yak meat."

The guard leader pointed emphatically toward the open doorway. With a shrug and a final look at Stoner, Markov stepped in. Before the leader could swing the door shut, Stoner walked into his own cell.

It was dim inside, with no light except that coming from the corridor. Stoner felt along the wall next to the door and found a switch. He flicked it, and a single small lamp turned on.

Turning, he said to the guard who was closing his door, "Thanks for showing us to our accommodations."

The young man looked shocked that Stoner spoke his language. But before he could say anything the door swung shut. For an instant Stoner heard nothing. Then the lock clicked.

It was a Spartan little room, but far from a jail cell. The bunk looked comfortable enough, though a little short for Stoner's lanky frame. There was a sink and a chest of drawers and a wooden chair. On his left, as he stood by the locked door, was a curtained alcove. Stoner could reach the drape without moving from the spot where he was standing. As he suspected, a toilet. Everything seemed clean. And reasonably warm.

I've seen college dorms worse than this, he reflected.

But how to get out? He tried the door, and it was indeed locked. And quite solid. No one posted outside that he could talk to; or if there was, no way to talk through the heavy door.

Kirill's just next door. Maybe in ten years or so I could chisel through the wall, like Edmond Dantes in *The Count of*

Monte Cristo. He sat on the bunk to think things over. No ideas came to him. No possibilities of escape presented themselves. He was solidly locked into a cell deep underground in the middle of the Altai mountains of high Asia. Moscow lay thousands of miles to the west, Beijing almost an equal distance east.

Stoner leaned back against the stone wall and laughed. Talk about being in the middle of nowhere!

Well, he told himself, if they want something from me, they're going to have to come to me. Then I'll have a chance to do something. Until then, there's nothing I can do except wait.

Then he remembered Baker, and the thought made him sit up straight. The way he looked at Jo. Hatred there. He's been through hell, and he wants to get back at Nillson through Jo.

There's no time to wait, he realized. I've got to protect Jo. But how?

He went back to the door, spread both hands against it, then slid down to his knees. He could feel the metal of the lock against his fingers.

Why this urge to protect the woman? a voice inside his head asked. Instinct, he replied silently. The male instinctively reacts protectively. Built into us. Women bear the children, propagate the species. Men protect women and children. Otherwise the species dies out.

But why this particular woman? Surely the human species will not be endangered if this one is harmed. Do you act on principle or because this one human female is important to you as an individual?

Stoner grimaced, pressing his fingertips against the metal of the lock. She is important to me as an individual. I owe her my life. I can't stand by and allow someone to hurt her, not if I can do anything to prevent it.

The metal of the lock was almost entirely steel, compounds of iron with strong natural magnetic fields. Closing his eyes, Stoner could imagine the whorls and loops of the magnetic field lines, overlapping, intertwining, tiny glimmers of electromagnetic energy emanating from the iron atoms in the steel. He felt sweat trickling down his face, but with his eyes squeezed shut he could picture the magnetic field lines. He could see them. He could feel them.

Concentrating every atom of his being, he focused all his

energy on those magnetic fields. He moved the upraised index finger of his right hand a bare centimeter. It slid across the metal of the lock on a film of perspiration.

The lock clicked.

He slumped to the floor, as soaked and exhausted as a man who has run twenty miles. For long minutes he lay there panting, his only movement the ragged heaving of his chest. His eyesight was blurred, his thoughts a spinning whirl of confusion.

That's why they want you, the voice within him was whispering. They know you better than you know yourself. The tests they put you through at the laboratory. The sessions with Richards. They know that there is knowledge locked within your brain that you yourself are barely aware of. Talents. Abilities. And they intend to get it out of you, so that they can use it for themselves.

An Linh watched Baker carefully as she and Jo were marched down the long corridor. The walls were featureless stone, except for occasional doors set into them. The place looked like a prison to her.

Cliff has changed, she thought. His face looks different, hard. There are no scars showing, but it's almost as if his face had been disfigured. He's ugly now. Brutal and ugly.

They tramped along the corridor in silence, the guard leader up front, Baker striding at An Linh's side, Jo hanging back slightly. Two more guards brought up the rear.

"You're going to love it here, pet," Baker suddenly said. "This is the hub of the bloody universe. They've got everything here: old missile silos, workshops, mess halls, barracks for troops, officers' quarters, cells for prisoners, even a couple of nicely equipped interrogation rooms. They're for your friend with the beard—and for this lady captain of industry we've got with us."

Torture, An Linh knew. He expects to torture Keith. And he's looking forward to torturing Mrs. Nillson.

She kept her voice calm and even. "Cliff, what happened to you? I thought—"

"You don't want to know what happened, love. Don't even ask."

"I thought they had killed you."

"No," he muttered. "That would have been too easy."

The leader of the guards halted their little procession. Two blank doors, side by side. He touched the keypads on their locks, and both doors popped slightly ajar.

Baker swung the nearest wide open and made a mocking little bow. "Special quarters for the president of Vanguard Industries."

Jo stared hard at him, then made a tense smile. "I presume you'll send my luggage?"

"Oh, don't make any presumptions at all, Mrs. Nillson. You're not going to need much in the way of clothes, not with what I've got in store for you."

Jo lifted her chin a notch and stepped into the room. Before Baker could shut the door, she herself grabbed at it and slammed it closed. Baker grinned as the guard tapped one of the buttons and the lock clicked shut.

"And this is your chamber, my dear," said Baker, gesturing to the next door. "Actually, these were officers' quarters when the Chink army used this base."

An Linh asked, "The Chinese army? Then how did you get . . ."

Laughing, Baker told her, "The World Liberation Movement has friends in high places, as well as low."

He pulled the door open and reached inside to turn on the light. An Linh saw a Spartan little cell with a bunk, a chest, a sink. The floor was bare rock. No window.

Her thoughts churning, she turned to Baker. "Cliff, I don't want to be alone. Could you . . . stay with me? For a little while, at least?"

Baker actually licked his lips. He turned to the guard and said loudly, "You go now. I stay with her."

How very English he can be, despite his Australian mistrust of Britain, thought An Linh. How instinctively he lapses into the old theory that if you merely speak English slowly and loudly, a foreigner will understand you.

But the guard eyed An Linh like a man shopping in a whorehouse, then gave Baker a knowing grin. He spoke a single word to his two compatriots, and the three of them headed off down the corridor.

Baker ushered An Linh into the cell, then closed the door. She turned and immediately slid her arms around his neck. He held her tightly and kissed her fiercely. An Linh opened her mouth and let his tongue probe into her.

After several moments, Baker whispered huskily, "What's the matter, pet, didn't the space man treat you right?"

"He never even touched me," she replied. "He isn't interested in such things."

"Really?"

"Even if he were, I would save myself for you, Cliff."

He gave out a low chuckle. In days long gone, An Linh would have interpreted his laugh as pleasure at her words. Now she was not sure. There was an edge of sarcasm to it, an undertone of bitterness. He could be telling her that he didn't believe a word she was saying.

But he moved her swiftly to the bunk and unzipped her coveralls. An Linh responded to him eagerly, knowing that every moment he spent with her was a moment he would not be tormenting Keith.

Stoner took a deep breath and hauled himself slowly to his feet. Cautiously, he pushed his cell door open a crack. No one in the corridor. He stepped outside, then closed the door again, gently.

He looked down at the buttons on the lock of Markov's door. After an instant's hesitation, he tapped out a four-digit code. The lock snapped open.

Smiling inwardly, Stoner thought, It's much easier doing it that way than using mental energy to move the magnetic fields. That must be why human beings developed speech and tools instead of mental telepathy and telekinesis: speech and tools take far less energy. Faith really can move mountains, but it's a helluva lot easier to use bulldozers.

He swung the door open and found Markov sitting on the edge of his bunk, eyes wide with apprehension, both hands gripping the bunk's thin mattress, his body shrinking away from the door.

"It's all right, Kirill," he said softly, stepping into Markov's cell. "It's only me."

"Keith! How did you get out of your own cell?"

"I picked the lock," he answered half-truthfully. "Come on, let's find the others."

Markov stayed on the bunk. "Do you think that's wise? Won't it make them angry to have us wandering around the corridors?"

Stoner looked at his old friend sadly. Already Kirill is

thinking like a prisoner: Don't break the rules, don't call attention to yourself, don't do anything to make them angry at you.

"Kir," he said, "they didn't ask us to come here. Why should we stay if we don't have to?"

Markov got to his feet slowly, shakily. "How can we escape? We're a million kilometers from anywhere."

With a laugh, Stoner said, "Maybe we can commandeer one of their planes. You can fly a jumbo jet, can't you?"

Markov smiled back weakly. "Oh, yes, certainly. And I can crash one even more easily."

"Great. Come on, Kirill. Let's find Jo and An Linh."

They walked along the corridor side by side. No one else in sight. Stoner told himself, There aren't all that many people here. The World Liberation Movement may have taken over this base, but they certainly haven't staffed it very fully.

They came to the intersection, and Stoner turned down the corridor to the left.

"You're sure that this is the right way?" Markov asked.

"Certain."

After passing several unmarked doors, Markov wondered, "How will we know which one—"

"That one," Stoner said, pointing to the next door on their right. "Jo's in that one."

"How do you know? . . ."

"Trust me."

Stoner looked at the digital lock for a moment, then tapped out four numbers. The door sprung slightly open.

Jo was standing between the bunk and the sink, her face set determinedly, her back rigid, arms at her sides, hands balled into fists, her jaw stubbornly clenched. Then she realized who had opened the door, and the tension sagged out of her.

"Keith!"

"Don't get your hopes up," he said as he and Markov entered the little room. "We're just visiting."

"But I thought they had locked you . . . I mean, I tried that door. . . ."

"I have a way with locks, it turns out."

She dropped down onto the bunk. Markov sat next to her, looking worried.

"Baker is vicious," Jo said. "He's looking forward to hurting you. And me."

"He won't get that chance," replied Stoner.

Markov shook his head. "Do you think you are just going to walk out of here, leading the rest of us like the Pied Piper?"

Stoner grinned. "Leading the children *out* of the mountain instead of into it? Yes, that would be a new twist on the old story, wouldn't it?"

"You laugh," Markov marveled. "Doesn't this frighten you? Have you no fear in you?"

No fear, Stoner thought. No anger. No love or hate or joy. They've all been buried in ice. All submerged, frozen in an ocean as deep and cold as interstellar space.

Aloud, he answered, "Fear has two components to it, Kirill. There's the intellectual awareness of something that might harm you. And there's the emotional, glandular reaction to that perception. I'm fully aware of the danger we're in. But it won't do us any good to let our glands dominate our brains, will it?"

Markov stared at him. "Cool as ice. You must have little glaciers running through your veins in place of blood."

How close you are to the truth, my old friend, Stoner replied silently.

The door slammed open suddenly, and Baker stood there, mouth agape.

"How in the hell . . . ?"

An Linh appeared behind him, her eyes wide, too.

"Don't look so surprised," Stoner said as pleasantly as if the man had just dropped by for a cocktail. "You brought me here to learn about things I can do. Well, it turns out that I'm pretty good at handling locks."

Baker's eyes narrowed to suspicious slits. "You're in a jovial mood, are you?"

"Come on in, don't stand out in the hall," Stoner invited. "Join the party."

Baker took An Linh by the arm, and they both entered the little room. Now it felt crowded, and Stoner could feel the heat of their bodies, make out their different scents.

"You must think you're pretty clever," Baker said.

Stoner shrugged. "And you must think that I've got some tremendous secrets locked up in my brain, and if you can get me to tell what they are, your World Liberation Movement will be able to topple all the governments and take over control of the whole Earth.''

"Something like that.''

"Fine,'' said Stoner, "I'll tell you everything I know. Happily. It won't help you much, but I'll hide nothing from you.''

"Really?''

"Providing you let my friends go.''

Baker smiled crookedly. "So that's it. Let them go, and you'll sing sweetly for us.''

"That's it.''

"And if we don't?''

"I won't sing at all,'' answered Stoner.

"Then we'll have to persuade you, won't we?''

"Do you think you can?''

Baker turned his gaze toward Jo, still sitting on the bunk. "Oh, I think maybe *she* can. Properly encouraged, of course.''

Stoner looked deep into Baker's eyes and saw the cynicism, the anger and hurt that went far back into his childhood. Very early in his life, Cliff Baker had learned that he could not trust people, especially people who held authority over him. As a youngster he had feared his father and known that his mother would never protect him against her husband. The university instructor who had recruited him for the World Liberation Movement had played on that distrust, Stoner knew. He could envision the moment. The instructor, as youthful and cynical as Baker himself, turning the student's angry bitterness at his parents into an angry bitterness against Them: the invisible, ubiquitous, all-powerful Them; the enemy, the university administration and big corporations and national governments and banks and politicians and corporate executives and anyone and everyone who held more power, flaunted more wealth, stood one step higher in society than he did himself.

Stoner smiled back at him sadly. "Cliff, I know who you want to hurt, and it's none of us.''

"You'll do for starters,'' Baker snapped.

"No, Cliff. You don't want to hurt us. You don't want to hurt anyone but yourself.''

"You think so?'' Baker said uncertainly.

Stoner noticed the rhythm of his breathing had increased

ever so slightly. Baker's mouth seemed suddenly dry. He swallowed hard. Picturing the living heart pumping beneath Baker's ribs, Stoner watched it skip a beat.

"I know it's true," he said. "You want to die. I can see it in your mind. And you will die, unless you turn away from the violence you're planning."

Unconsciously rubbing a hand across his shirt, Baker growled, "Stop trying to hypnotize me. It won't work."

Stoner went on, "Cliff, you want to know what's stored up in my head. I don't know the full extent of it myself. All I can tell you is that whatever's there seems to come to the surface of my consciousness when I need it. It's as if the alien is inside my skull, like another person, and when I need his help he gives it to me."

Baker said nothing.

"So don't push me to the point where I need to show you your own inner self. That would kill you, Cliff. You'd kill yourself, willingly."

CHAPTER 36

The crowded cell fell silent. In the distance, Stoner could hear footsteps clicking on the stone floor. They drew nearer. All heads turned toward the open door.

"Guards coming," An Linh whispered.

"They will find us here," said Markov, a hint of fear in his voice.

Baker said nothing. His eyes still locked on Stoner's, but a relieved little smile crept across his lips.

Jo got to her feet to stand beside Stoner. She did not touch him, nor he her, but he knew that she felt somehow safer by being close to him. Mammalian instinct, he thought. The warmth of the body gives comfort. How we hate to be alone and in the cold.

Stoner tried to estimate the number of men approaching

from the sounds of their footfalls. At least six, he thought.
No more than eight.

Suddenly the footsteps stopped, and the doorway was filled
with the huge bulk of a tall, broad-shouldered, thick-set
Oriental wearing outlandish battle fatigues of green jungle
camouflage, glistening black paratrooper boots, and a wide
black leather belt. A heavy gold medallion hung around his
neck. His head was completely hairless, his face as beefy and
large as the rest of him.

Wordlessly, he looked over the five people inside the cell.
Behind him, a squad of six guards in tan coveralls stood at
grim-faced attention. Each of them carried a submachine
gun.

The Oriental broke into a huge grin. "I couldn't believe
my eyes," he said in a deep, reverberating voice. "I watched
you on the closed-circuit television, Dr. Stoner. How on
earth did you open the lock on your door? From the inside, at
that! Fantastic!"

Stoner felt a wave of astonishment wash over him. Obviously this man was the leader here. But to Stoner he seemed
more like a clown than a threat.

"Mr. Baker, please introduce me to your friends," he
commanded.

"This is Temujin," said Baker with just a tinge of sarcasm, "the supreme chief of the World Liberation Movement."

Stoner found himself thinking, No, not the supreme chief.
He can't be.

"I am very impressed with your talents, Dr. Stoner," said
Temujin, still smiling cordially. "Perhaps we can discuss
them over dinner."

Like the host of a summer weekend at a country villa,
Temujin led the five of them down the corridor.

"I am afraid that the food here isn't all that it should be,
but I will endeavor to see that you at least don't go hungry."

They reached a metal door set into the rock wall. Temujin
touched his medallion and the door slid open, revealing an
elevator cab big enough to hold a dozen people. He gestured
them into the elevator, then followed himself. The guards
remained outside. They rode up; Stoner estimated two levels,
but it was impossible to tell inside the closed elevator car.
The door opened onto a large chamber, empty except for a
long dining table set for six. And three gleaming robots

standing off to one side like a trio of cylindrical metal sculptures, their multiple arms neatly folded to their sides.

Doors were set into the far wall, and bare tubes of fluorescent lights ran across the ceiling.

"Please, be seated. Dr. Stoner, Dr. Markov, next to me, if you please." Temujin strode to the head of the table and took the chair there.

Slightly more than an hour later they were picking at a dessert of melon and yogurt, flown in every week from Afghanistan, according to Temujin. Through most of the dinner he had talked discursively about his choice of name for himself, his humble origins, how he had founded the World Liberation Movement, its growth, its accomplishments, its goals.

"Being a Korean," he was saying, "my first object was to reunite the two halves of my country, cruelly separated at the whim of the two so-called superpowers. My father fought for national unity; he was a captain in the North Korean Army. Killed in action in 1950. I was merely a baby then, but I vowed to carry on his work."

Stoner ate slowly, sipped at the warming tea that the robots kept bringing. They never allowed a cup to go dry, and they never missed a cup when they poured.

"By the time I reached my manhood," Temujin rambled on, "it became apparent to me that the problem of reuniting Korea was actually a small part of a much larger problem, a global problem. That was when the World Liberation Movement was born."

"And eventually absorbed the PLO, the IRA, the Red Guards, and most of the other liberation movements," Baker added from the far end of the table.

Temujin favored him with a small nod. "Yes. By the time I was thirty, we were consolidating the world's freedom fighters into a unified entity—with the help, I should mention, of the Soviet Union."

Markov's white brows climbed toward his scalp.

"But the leaders in the Kremlin began to fear us," Temujin went on, scowling slightly in Markov's direction. "They did not want to allow liberation of *their* colonial possessions! They turned against us."

Stoner suppressed a smile as he watched Markov's face across the table from him.

"You have overlooked one tiny detail," Markov said. "Scientists from the Soviet Union and the United States learned how to make a defense against nuclear weapons."

"Yes, they learned it from the alien starship." Temujin gave Stoner a sour glance.

Markov went on, "This defense, this ability to protect ourselves from nuclear terror, changed the entire world political situation."

"Not the entire situation," Temujin shot back. "It changed the power struggle between your two nations. It encouraged you to combine against the poor and nonwhite peoples of the world. It *intensified* the struggle between the rich and the poor!"

This Temujin behaves like a pompous fool, thought Stoner. But then I guess Hitler gave long, rambling speeches after dinner, too.

"Even so," Temujin continued, "we continued to receive some help from the Soviet Union. And from elsewhere. China has been most cooperative. And the various leaders of Islam have been generally favorable toward us, despite their internal differences."

"Yet the Islamic Republic of Iran was overthrown and a secular government installed in its place," Markov pointed out.

"With the help of the Soviet Union," Temujin said. Then, nodding his gleaming bald head toward Jo, "And with even more generous help from Vanguard Industries, I might add."

With a slight nod of her own, Jo said, "We also managed to stop your terrorist movement in Latin America."

"Temporarily, Mrs. Nillson. Only temporarily. There is no way that we can be permanently stopped. The will of the people always prevails, in the long run. And we prefer to call ourselves revolutionaries, not terrorists."

"But the people want prosperity," said Jo. "They want jobs and money in their pockets, not terrorism and hunger. Above all they want peace."

"They will have jobs, and money, and peace—once we have wrested away the wealth from your rich nations and your fat corporations that hold down the nonwhite peoples of the world."

"Those corporations," Jo shot back, "are spreading more wealth among the people than you'll ever be able to do. All you can do is tear things down, destroy and kill. We can build. We can create. We generate wealth and we spread it all around the world."

Temujin laughed. "Yes, of course. I know your philosophy. But you move too slowly. Too much of the wealth stays in your pretty white hands, not enough gets to the people who generated it with the sweat of their black and brown and yellow brows."

"Your way just spreads misery and death," Jo insisted.

"We shall see, Mrs. Nillson. History shall be our judge."

"What do you plan?" Stoner asked.

Temujin spread his powerful arms wide. "What do we not plan?" He laughed. "Members of our Movement are at work on every continent, in every nation—yes, Mrs. Nillson, even inside every multinational corporation."

"Doing what?" prompted Stoner.

"Not far from here, in the missile silos where the Soviet government has replaced their nuclear warheads with warheads containing genetically altered viruses that will produce diseases for which there is no cure—my men are infiltrating the missile crews, preparing to seize the silos and aim those missiles at Moscow and Paris and New York."

Markov gasped.

"In Hanoi"—he shifted his gaze to An Linh—"secret adherents to the World Liberation Movement have penetrated the highest levels of government and will soon arrange a border incident that will allow Vietnam to invade south China."

"But the Chinese are helping you!" An Linh blurted.

Temujin's answer was a booming laugh. "And so are many others who will be brought under our control!"

Stoner shook his head. This man is a windbag with delusions of grandeur. He can't be in control of all these efforts; he hasn't the capacity. He may *think* he's running the show, but somebody is controlling him.

"And in the meantime," Stoner said aloud, "you fomented the war in central Africa."

"Fomented?" Temujin looked insulted. "We fomented nothing, Dr. Stoner. Could the World Liberation Movement, or any human organization, *foment* the spread of the Sahara Desert into the farming lands of the south Sahara regions? Could we *foment* mass starvation?"

"Perhaps not," Stoner admitted. "But what did you do to help feed the starving?"

"We struck at the inequalities that caused the starvation!"

"You let them starve while you started a war that's spread all across the middle of the continent."

"Yes! Exactly! And what did your Europeans and Americans and Japanese do? They created this so-called International Peacekeeping Force to fight against us!"

Jo, sitting at Stoner's right, said, "The people of Chad and Nigeria and other African nations asked for help. . . ."

"Not so! The *governments* of those nations asked for help. Not the people. The people are with us."

"I don't believe that," said Stoner.

"They are!" Temujin insisted. "And we were winning the war, until you came along with your cease-fire agreement."

Stoner said calmly, "The people in the villages, the people you claim to be liberating, want an end to the killing. The Peacekeepers can help them to learn how to deal with the encroachments of the desert, how to take their energy needs from the sun instead of deforesting their countryside, how to grow food and balance their population growth. They can teach the arts of peace—once the fighting stops."

"What you mean is that they can teach the Africans how to become slaves of the Europeans once again," Temujin rumbled.

"No. That time is long gone. You're living in the past."

Scowling darkly, Temujin said, "Your cease-fire will not last, Dr. Stoner. I will not allow it to last."

"You want more blood on your hands?"

"Yes. If killing is necessary to free the captive peoples of the world, then let there be blood! Let there be rivers of blood! Oceans of blood!"

Stoner heard himself say, "Then let the blood be yours."

Temujin stared at him. "What do you . . ."

Stoner looked deep into the big man's eyes, so deeply that he could sense the intricate lacework of microscopic blood vessels within them.

A tear welled in the corner of Temujin's left eye and rolled down his broad cheek. A tear of blood.

The others gasped.

Temujin flinched back in his chair, looking wildly from one astonished face to another. He grabbed his napkin and rubbed at his cheek, then stared at the bloody smear on the cloth.

"Do you truly want rivers of blood?" Stoner asked, his voice as cold and hard as a stiletto of ice.

A flow of blood cascaded from both of Temujin's eyes. He gave out a strangled cry and reached for the medallion on his chest.

Stoner said nothing, yet Temujin's hands froze in midair. He squeezed his eyes shut, but they streamed blood nevertheless.

"I can't see!" he screamed. "I'm blind!"

Baker jumped to his feet, knocking his chair over backward. Stoner froze him with a glance. An Linh sat in horrified silence next to him. Markov's face looked ashen, and Jo gripped Stoner's shoulder as if she would fall to the floor if she didn't have his support.

"Yes, you are blind," said Stoner to the mammoth Oriental. "You have been blind for many years."

Still the blood flowed from Temujin's eyes. It streaked down his jungle camouflage fatigues, over his gold medallion, dark stains spattering, growing, puddling against the mottled greens.

"You tell us that you direct the World Liberation Movement," Stoner said to him, "yet you know that you are little more than a tool for others. Your weapons, your technology, your money all come from outside sources. You have told us that the governments of Russia and China have been helpful to you. Who else has helped you? Where does the bulk of your resources come from?"

"I can't see!" Temujin shrieked. "I can't see!"

"Your eyes will heal," Stoner said coldly. "In time you will be able to see again. If you tell me where your resources come from."

"I'll tell you . . . I'll tell you. . . ."

"Good. The bleeding will stop in a few moments. Keep your eyes closed. And speak."

"Most of our weapons and technology . . . most of our money . . . is contributed by sources in the West. Europe and America."

"They come from one single source, don't they?" Stoner prodded.

"No. From many. Arms from Czechoslovakia. Computer systems from Japan. Aircraft from the United States."

"And the money? The money to bribe air traffic controllers in the Soviet Union? The money to keep officials in the Kremlin and the Pentagon and the Forbidden City feeding you information and assistance? The money to feed and clothe your troops? Where does that come from?"

"Zurich," Temujin gasped. He pressed his hands to his face. "London. New York. Sydney."

"Who provides these resources? Do they come from one single entity or from many?"

"Many! The hard-liners in Moscow and Beijing—and Washington. The government officials who do not agree with their leaders' policies of peaceful coexistence. Revolutionary groups everywhere. Muslims, Filipinos, Irish, Argentines—they exist in every part of the world."

"But they're not poor, downtrodden peasants, are they?" Stoner demanded. "The poor and the weak couldn't give you any help, except for their expendable bodies. The people who supply your resources are important people, high officials in governments and global corporations, aren't they?"

"Yes. . . ." The bleeding seemed to have stopped, but Temujin still pressed the heels of his hands against his eyes. Blood caked his cheeks, his clothes.

"And there's one corporation in particular that's been especially generous, isn't there? One corporation that either owns or controls the factories in Czechoslovakia and Japan and the United States. Right?"

"Yes." Temujin's voice was a weak, pleading sob.

"Which corporation is that?" Stoner asked.

"He doesn't have to answer," Jo said. Stoner turned toward her, as did the others around the table.

"I know which corporation it is," she said. "It's Vanguard Industries."

CHAPTER 37

"It's Everett," Jo said. "I didn't realize how mad he really is until this moment."

Markov leaned across the table toward her. "Your husband? *He* is the mastermind behind these terrorist movements? But why? Why would he . . . ?"

"He must be insane," An Linh said.

Baker, still standing between the table and his knocked-over chair, seemed to stir and breathe again like a statue coming to life.

"Nillson can't be the man behind the World Liberation Movement! He tortured me to get information about . . ."

Jo gave him a pitying glance. "Don't you think he's capable of torturing you to see how loyal a member of the Movement you are? Or just for the sadistic pleasure of it?"

His face went white. An Linh reached up and took Baker's hand in her own.

"Everett could do it," Jo said. "He's crazy enough to use the World Liberation Movement as a counterforce to the Peacekeepers. He'd do anything to keep Vanguard Industries on top. It's a game to him. A power game."

"I don't understand," said Stoner.

"The Peacekeepers are the first step toward a world government," Jo said. "An *effective* world government with the power to disarm the individual nations and enforce international law."

"And impose taxes," added Markov.

Nodding, Jo agreed, "Taxes, yes, and all sorts of other laws and regulations. Everett is dead set against that. So are most of the other corporate powers around the world."

"They want to run the world their way," said Markov.

"They're already running the world," Jo said. "And I've been one of them. They're not going to give up their power to anyone—not willingly."

Stoner asked, "How do we get to Nillson?"

"We must first consider," said Markov, gesturing at the stone walls around them, "how we can get out of this place."

Temujin still sat in his chair, hands pressed to his eyes, face and clothes streaked with drying blood. He was crying, chest heaving with deep, racking sobs.

"He's finished," Stoner said. "He'll never have the strength to recover, even if his sight comes back."

"*If* his sight . . ." Jo's question petered out into silence.

Grim-faced, Stoner said, "He'll spend the rest of his life in a monastery. He'll make a good monk, doing penance for the lives he's taken."

The others stared at him.

Rising to his feet, Stoner said, "Come on, it's time we left. Cliff, you can stay here with him or come with us. Which will it be?"

Baker shuddered visibly. He swallowed hard, then answered in a choked voice, "I'll . . . I'll come with you."

"Good," said Stoner. "Come on."

Within a few hours they were back in the air, aboard the same Russian swing-wing jet they had come in, flying at supersonic speed toward Moscow. Markov was up on the flight deck, using the radio to call his superiors in the Kremlin. After only a few minutes in the air, Stoner saw a pair of Soviet fighter planes streaking toward them.

Jo saw them, too. "My God, what are they going to do?"

"Relax," said Stoner calmly. "They're our escort."

And the fighters took up stations on either wingtip of their jet. Stoner saw one of the pilots in his bubble canopy wave at them with a gloved hand.

"We're safe now," he told Jo. "We'll get to Moscow all right."

He swiveled his chair to face An Linh and Baker, sitting behind him.

"How long were you working for the World Liberation Movement, Cliff?" he asked.

The Australian looked uncomfortable. "Since college, really."

"I thought so."

He nodded warily. "You haven't ended the WLM, you

know. Even if Temujin is a total loss, you haven't ended the Movement.''

"You think not?"

"It'll just split up again into a lot of separate movements, the way it was before. You may have broken up our central organization, but the Movement will go on."

"I don't want to end it," said Stoner. "All I want is to see the Movement turn to a peaceful pursuit of its goals. The fighting's got to stop, Cliff. The killing's got to end."

Baker snorted. "And I suppose the rich nations and the big corporations are going to share their wealth out of the goodness of their hearts, like Father Christmas bringing presents to good little boys and girls."

An Linh put a hand on his knee. "Cliff, don't lose your temper."

He ignored her. "I suppose you"—he jabbed a finger toward Jo—"will sell all your jewels and give the proceeds to the poor, huh?"

"What good would that do?" Jo countered.

Before Baker could reply, Stoner said, "Cliff, there are two ways to help the poor. One is by redistributing the world's wealth. The other is to generate more wealth, to make a bigger pie so that there can be more slices available for the poor."

"Don't give me that eyewash!" Baker snapped. "I've been hearing that since school days."

"It will work, Cliff. You can create enormous new riches. . . ."

"And *she'll* get fatter while the poor keep on starving!"

"Not if you work together to see that the wealth reaches those who need it most."

"Work together? Who? Me and her?"

"Why not?"

"I don't trust her, that's why."

Jo gave him a derisive sneer. "What makes you think I trust you?"

"Well, that's one thing we agree on. The rich and the poor can't trust each other," Baker said. "They're cut from different cloth."

"Really?" Stoner asked.

"I was poor," Jo told him. "I was born in Chelsea,

Massachusetts. My father was a shoemaker. I went to MIT on a scholarship. I've worked hard all my life.''

"And I was born on a sheep ranch in New South Wales and got a scholarship to university to study journalism. I've worked hard, too, but I'm never going to have the money you have. Not unless I can take it from you, and you won't give it up without a fight, will you?''

Stoner asked. "Cliff, do you want to help the poor, or are you just jealous of the rich?''

The Australian opened his mouth to reply, but no words came out.

"Use the calculator function on your wristwatch to do a little long division," Stoner said. "Divide all the budgets of the multinational corporations and the industrialized nations of the world by the number of people alive today." He looked over at An Linh and asked, "What's the world's population today?''

"More than seven billion," she guessed.

"I know what you're driving at," Baker said. "You're going to claim that there isn't enough money in the world to make everybody rich.''

"Almost," said Stoner. "The thing is, it won't do any good to make everybody equally poor. We've got to find ways of creating new wealth, ways that will allow the poor people to make themselves rich.''

"It'll never happen.''

"Of course it can happen!" Stoner insisted. Tapping his temple, "Do you think that the energy shield and fusion power are the only things the aliens have to offer? There's an entire universe of riches out there in space. Wealth beyond your dreams.''

"And you expect me to believe that Vanguard Industries is going to let the poor peoples of the world share in that wealth?''

"No. I expect you to work to *make* Vanguard and the other corporations and rich nations share that wealth. I expect you to work with the poor nations to help them learn how to tap that new wealth. And I expect myself to work alongside you, to see that it gets done.''

Baker fell silent. Stoner could see a lifetime's worth of bitterness and cynicism struggling with the new hope that he could dimly visualize.

"You've tried it your way," Stoner urged gently. "All your life, terrorists have been killing people, revolutionaries have been fighting wars, all in the name of the poor. And what have they accomplished?"

Baker's eyes shifted. He seemed uncertain, wavering. Stoner knew he could convince the man of anything—for a while. What he needed to do was to have Baker convince himself, permanently.

"Killing leads to more killing, Cliff, and damned little else. When you take from the rich to give to the poor, you build hatred and violence; you guarantee that the rich are going to fight back."

"But they'll never give up what they have voluntarily," Baker argued back heatedly. "D'you think *she's* going to sell what she has and give it to the poor? The hell she will!"

Stoner smiled grimly. "Let's ask her." He swiveled his chair back toward Jo. "What about it, Jo?"

"What about what?" Jo snapped. "I could give away everything I own and it wouldn't make a dent the size of a pimple on the world's poverty."

"See?" Baker said.

"Wait a minute," said Stoner. "Jo, would you be willing to give a certain percentage of Vanguard's profits to an international fund for helping poor nations to develop their economies?"

She said, "We've tried that before. The World Bank—"

"Suppose all the multinational corporations were taxed equally," Stoner suggested, "and the fund was administered by a nonpolitical organization."

"Would the corporations be represented on the administrating board?" she asked.

Stoner turned toward Baker again. "Would that make sense to you?"

"Not a whole hell of a lot," he grumbled.

"A tax," Stoner explained, "that is paid by every multinational corporation. No hiding behind national borders or getting favorable tax deals from a friendly national government. No tax shelters anywhere on Earth."

"What about space?" An Linh asked. "Couldn't a corporation move its operations into orbit to escape the tax?"

Stoner grinned at her. "Then we'll have to extend the

reach of the tax law to space—as far as the Moon, I guess. That should do it.''

"Maybe," Baker admitted.

"Would you sit on the governing board of such an organization, Cliff, to help see that the money raised by this international tax is spent to help the poor nations develop their economies and feed their people?''

He waved his hands in the air. "This is all theoretical! Nothing but hot air!''

"It's something to aim for," Stoner insisted. "A way to accomplish the goals you claim you want to reach, without bloodshed.''

"I would sit on that governing board," Jo said firmly.

"Sure you would," Baker snapped.

She leaned toward him. "Then why won't you? Scared?''

"Of what?''

"Of trying to solve the problems that have given you a goal in your life. Of trying to build something new and good, instead of tearing down what you don't like and leaving nothing but rubble.''

"You'd have a chance to make something of yourself, Cliff," An Linh said.

Stoner added, "It's always tougher to create than to destroy. But you've got to try, Cliff. You, and all the others who've spent their lives in destruction. You've got to turn your energies to creating a new society.''

Baker looked at each of them in turn: An Linh, Jo, and finally Stoner. His face was a strange mixture of emotions: hope and uncertainty, fear and longing.

"You all think you're pretty smart, don't you? This is nothing but talk! What good will it do?''

"For you personally, Cliff," said Stoner, "it will be a way of changing your life. You're rushing toward death now. Work for life! Try to build instead of destroy, because it's your own life that's either growing or withering away. Choose life over death.''

"By becoming an international bureaucrat." Baker snorted derisively.

"You could help to change the world," An Linh said.

"I'll work for such a system," Stoner repeated, "if you will.''

"And I will, too," Jo said.

"You?"

She grinned at Baker. "You don't think I'm going to let you radicals set up an international tax system by yourselves, do you? I don't trust you enough to let you do that."

A small grin played across his face. "I see. Well, if you're going to meet with your fellow plutocrats to set up an international tax system, I sure don't trust *you* enough to let you do it by yourselves."

"You're in, then?" Stoner asked.

Baker eyed him for a moment, his old cynical smile returning. "This is a lot of hot air, y'know. But—for what it's worth—yeah, I'm in."

"Good!" An Linh clapped her hands together.

Stoner got up from his chair. "I'll get Markov. We shouldn't let the Socialist nations get away from paying their fair share."

Hours later, as the plane flew on through the darkening evening, Jo leaned across the aisle separating their two seats and asked Stoner:

"Did you mean what you said to him?" She cocked her head slightly toward Baker, sitting behind them, talking with An Linh.

"Yes, of course. Didn't you?"

"Do you think we could really do it? Do you have any idea of how much resistance . . ."

"Are you willing to try?" Stoner asked.

She thought for a moment, then nodded. "Yes. Sure. Why not? If it can be made to work."

"Can you bring Vanguard into the scheme?"

"Everett will never agree."

"Can you take the corporation away from him?"

She shook her head. "No way. As long as he's alive, he's got the power and I'm just a figurehead."

"As long as he's alive."

Jo stared at Stoner.

"Where is he now, do you know?"

"I can find out," she said, getting up swiftly from her seat as if anxious to get away from Stoner.

He watched her go forward to the door of the flight deck. It opened, and he could see Markov standing, hunched over, between the two pilots. Jo squeezed into the compartment and closed the door behind her.

Stoner leaned back in his chair and thought over the situation. Can we really turn the World Liberation Movement away from violence? Can we bring the multinational corporations into a global tax system that will provide the funds to attack the problems of world poverty and hunger?

We? he asked himself. Who are we? The president of a corporation. An undercover agent for terrorists. A Russian academician. An orphaned victim of war. A scientist—and an alien intelligence living inside his brain, like an interstellar parasite.

Parasite? He sensed a waspish reaction, an almost angry denial of the term. Symbiote, thought Stoner. Maybe that's a better name for our relationship. The mind of an alien who's been dead for millennia, combined with the living body of a man of Earth. By combining, by working together in symbiosis, each is more than he could be by himself.

So now you intend to change the world. No, Stoner corrected himself, *we* intend to change the world. Why? What difference does it make? In all the vast starry universe, does this one little planet with its scurrying, chattering, monkey-descended people make any difference at all? Are we so important? Do we matter in the cosmic scheme of things?

Stoner shook his head. He had no way of knowing. Not yet.

Is there an answer? Did the starship pick out Earth deliberately, from all the myriad worlds it must have encountered? Is this alien in my mind for a specific purpose? Does he have a special reason for being here?

He thought back to one of his first nights after reawakening, when he had still been at the research lab in Hawaii. The night he had briefly escaped from his room and gone out onto the beach. How he had waited for a message, a communication, some sign or signal from the alien who was inhabiting his mind. There had been no sign, no communication. There was still no message to tell him why he had been picked to carry this symbiotic presence from the stars.

There's got to be a reason! Stoner told himself. All this can't just be happening because of a blind throw of the dice. There is *order* in the universe, no matter what the quantum theory claims.

But he could see no reason. No message reached him. The plane simply droned on through the deepening night, on its way to Moscow.

The voices behind him had long since stopped their murmuring. Stoner turned slightly in his chair and saw that Baker and An Linh were both asleep, holding hands across the aisle between their chairs. Like two children, he thought. Hansel and Gretel, lost in a wilderness they barely understand.

She's content to be with him again. An Linh knows she can't have me, so she'll settle for Cliff. I hope they can be happy together. I hope she can help him to choose life over death.

The door up at the front of the cabin opened, and he saw Jo coming out, with Markov behind her. She came toward him and took her seat next to his. Markov sat heavily in the seat in front of Stoner's, with a weary sigh, and swiveled it around to face him.

"I've located Everett," Jo said. Her face looked grave, fearful.

Stoner said, "He's gone up to the orbiting complex where the starship is, hasn't he?"

"How did you know?"

"And he left a message for me," Stoner added.

Jo threw a startled glance at Markov. Then she looked back at Stoner, her eyes filled with fear. "Everett's message is that if you want to find him, he'll be up there in orbit, demolishing the alien's spacecraft."

Stoner nodded. "That's what I thought he'd do."

"He's gone totally crazy," Jo said. "He's really dangerous now, murderously dangerous."

Looking to Markov, Stoner asked, "Do you think your government might give me another ride into space, Kirill?"

"You want to go back to the alien ship?"

"Yes."

Jo reached out toward him. "Keith, don't you understand what Everett's up to? He *wants* you to come after him!"

"I know."

"He's planning to kill you!"

"No," Stoner corrected. "He's planning to kill the star traveler, by destroying his ship."

"What do you mean? . . ."

"I've got to stop him from destroying the spacecraft, Jo."

"At the risk of your own life?" Markov growled.

"Whatever the risk. The future of the human race is tied up with that starship. If Nillson destroys it, he destroys humanity's future, too."

THE STARSHIP

Human evolution is nothing else but the natural continuation . . . of the perennial and cumulative process of "psychogenetic" arrangement of matter which we call life. . . . Life, if fully understood, is not a freak of the universe— nor man a freak in life. On the contrary, life physically culminates in man, just as energy physically culminates in life.

CHAPTER 38

It hung in the black emptiness like a shining golden globe.

Stoner blinked as he stared out the space shuttle window. He had expected to see the small oblong shape of the alien starship surrounded by other spacecraft, like a queen bee attended by glittering metallic workers.

Instead there was a huge, smooth expanse of gleaming gold, like a gigantic polished gemstone. It shimmered subtly, and Stoner realized that it was a screen of energy that now encased the alien ship and all the human structures that had been built around it.

"It's an energy screen," Jo said.

She was sitting beside him in the shuttle's passenger cabin, dressed in the functional coveralls everyone wore in zero gravity. Hers were coral red, and they accented her figure rather than hid it. Jo's hair was neatly pulled back and tied in a little ponytail that floated weightlessly off the nape of her neck.

Stoner could not take his eyes off the gleaming ovate immensity of it. He felt the shoulder straps of his seat restraint harness cutting into him as he pressed his forehead on the cold plastic of the window.

"It must be miles wide," he said to Jo.

"Four thousand meters from end to end," she said. "Same dimension top to bottom. Almost three miles."

"More like two and a half miles." Stoner did the math in his mind. "Two point four eight something."

"But who's counting?" she joked weakly.

Markov, hovering weightlessly over their chair backs, chimed in, "I'm surprised that you don't have the metric system ingrained in your very souls. It is such a logical system, so scientific."

"We have both systems in our minds, Kirill," answered Jo. "Metric and English."

311

"Such confusion." The Russian wagged his head. It made him float slightly sideways, and he pressed his hand against the cabin's curving bulkhead to steady himself.

The Russian looked younger in zero gravity. The lines in his face and the pouches beneath his eyes had smoothed out.

Markov, An Linh, and Baker had all started to get sick when the Russian shuttle had coasted into zero gravity. Stoner could see their faces go white, sense the dizziness and nausea each of them was experiencing. He said a few soothing words as he reached into their minds and eased the disorientation that plagued them. What usually took new space travelers hours to achieve, they accomplished in minutes—an inner equilibrium. They found that they enjoyed zero gee and marveled that they had acquired their "space legs" as quickly as any veteran astronaut.

Stoner laughed inwardly at Markov's disdain of the English system of measure. Kirill's worried about the confusion of having two mathematical systems in your head. How about having two minds inside you? Two different persons in one body? He suddenly thought of his childhood Sunday school classes. God must find it even more confusing, with three persons inside.

But his eyes never left the curving wall of the energy screen, growing bigger by the moment as their shuttle approached. The huge bulk of the Earth slid into view, ponderous and incredibly bright, with deep, swirling blues and streaming swirls of dazzling white clouds. The energy screen glowed against it, big enough to blot out the subcontinent of India as it glided past.

The Indian Ocean was a wide swath of purest lapis-lazuli blue, decked with a procession of pearl-gray domed thunderclouds which cast long shadows ahead of them. Stoner saw the coast of Australia coming up, then suddenly squeezed his eyes shut against the unexpected brilliance of the island continent's interior.

"What's that?" he asked, opening his eyes again to see a vast glittering swath too bright to look at directly.

Jo leaned against him to peer out the tiny window.

"Oh," she said. "The Outback Project."

"Outback Project?"

"The Aussies are converting their desert into solarvoltaic cells. Automated machines scoop up the sand at one end and leave solar cells on the ground on the other. They've been going on for years now; must have done several thousand square miles."

"A solar-energy farm," Stoner marveled. "Converting sunlight into electricity."

"It's not very efficient," Jo sniffed. "But trust the Aussies to think *big*. Australia's an electricity exporter now. Vanguard's been negotiating with them to run a power link all the way to Japan."

Stoner squinted at the glittering strips of solar cells reflecting sunlight at him like the facets of a continent-wide jewel. Then the golden-hued energy screen slid across his view, so close now that it blotted out Australia and New Zealand both as it swept by in its Earth-circling orbit.

Elly's on her way back there, Stoner thought. That tiny speck of an island is home to her now. Her children are there. She'll find a new husband, he told himself. She's a good woman, warm and intelligent and caring. Maybe someday she'll get over the hurt I've caused her. Maybe someday I can visit her in her own home.

He looked across the curving bulk of the Pacific Ocean toward the coast of California, coming into view. Douglas, he thought. Douglas.

Once they had landed in Moscow, Stoner had put through a call to Los Angeles. With Jo's help, he'd tracked down the Douglas Stoner who was his son.

Douglas was a man now, with the beginnings of pouches under his eyes and a tight, suspicious downturn at the corners of his lips. He wore a light gray jacket over a silk pullover shirt. His hair was ash blond from the sun, as was the drooping mustache that had surprised Stoner. In the background, Stoner saw a marina filled with sailboats.

Douglas stared out of the phone's picture screen with narrowed eyes, warily, as if he were facing a trap of some kind. "You're my father?" His voice was dark with suspicion.

"Underneath this beard, yes, it's me." Stoner had tried to sound light-hearted. It was a mistake.

"I don't have a father. My father's dead."

"I'm back, Doug. I've been trying to reach you to tell you—"

The thirty-three-year-old stranger reached out and snapped

off the connection. The phone screen before Stoner went suddenly blank gray.

He heard Jo's sharp intake of breath behind him, saw Markov's sad shake of head. Wordlessly, Stoner touched the button on the phone's keyboard that redialed the same number. For the span of a heartbeat he wondered what he could say to the son whom he had not seen in twenty years.

The phone screen lit up with the words "CALL REFUSED." They glowed blackly against the gray background.

Stoner hit the off button and got up from the phone. Neither Jo nor Markov said a word. He stood and waited for some feeling to hit him: anger, pain, remorse, something, anything. But there was no emotion at all. It was as if some stranger had refused to tell him the time of day.

"Well," he said to his two friends. "At least he knows I'm alive."

And he walked out of the room, leaving Jo and Markov staring at his retreating back.

Markov tugged worriedly at his thinning beard. "He frightens me."

Nodding, Jo admitted, "Me, too."

"He's not human."

"He was when he first awoke. In Hawaii . . . in Italy, Keith was more human, more alive than he'd ever been."

"But now . . ."

"Now he's like a machine, almost."

The Russian sighed deeply. "Not a trace of emotion in him. Not love or fear or anger. Nothing. As cold as an iceberg."

"What he did to that Oriental, Temujin . . ." Jo shuddered.

"He's not human," Markov repeated.

"He was always driven," said Jo.

"But not like this. He had emotions before. Passions. He could get drunk. He could get angry. Now—now he's like a man possessed."

She stared at the empty doorway that Stoner had left behind him. "Do you think it's really a good idea to let him go up to the alien spacecraft?"

"What do you mean?"

"I don't know," Jo said, feeling the tension within her turning to actual fear. "I just think . . . maybe if he gets in contact with that spacecraft again, with the alien and all . . .''

Markov stared at her silently.

"Maybe we ought to keep him away from it," Jo suggested.

The Russian slowly shook his head. "I don't think we could keep him away, even if we tried. I don't think there is any way we could possibly stop him from doing whatever he wants to do."

As Stoner stared at the approaching wall of energy, with the Earth reduced to a beautiful backdrop rather than a world of living, suffering people, he felt as if all the things that had happened to him since awakening had really happened to someone else. It was like watching a video biography of some stranger's life. The Earth was merely a distant place, a locale, a stage, and those strange people who inhabited it were odd characters in someone else's struggle.

Here was home. Here, in the clean, empty silence of space.

For an instant Stoner thought he might get up from his seat, go to the airlock, and step out into the void. How simple it would be. How clean and neat. I did it once, he told himself. And he felt the chill of death seeping into him. He shuddered, not from the cold, but from the conflict. Part of him *wanted* oblivion, an end to struggling. Part of him looked forward to returning to the cold and emptiness.

Not yet, a voice within him whispered. We have not come all this way to give it up now.

We. The voice spoke of we. The alien and I. Linked together irretrievably.

"The screen holds in air and heat, and it shields against meteoric dust, even good-sized meteors." It was Jo's voice, far in the distance. She was talking to Markov and the others.

He stared at the approaching wall of shimmering energy, and his eyes saw the sarcophagus riding against the glorious sky of the homeworld up at the top of the tower that rose into orbital space. His funeral cortege carried his body with reverence and placed it lovingly on the bier inside the sarcophagus. None of his crèche mates was there, of course. Born on the same day, they had each terminated their lives on the same day, according to the ancient custom. But he was starting a new custom, something unheard-of in all the ages of their civilization. Sending his dead body, preserved by the cold of infinity itself, off among the stars. Some called it foolishness. A few spoke of sinful pride. But he was beyond their words now. His body would ride the starways, perfectly preserved, waiting to be discovered by creatures who could understand, creatures who could care, creatures who could look to the stars and finally *know*.

The space shuttle thumped against an airlock, and Stoner was jarred out of his reverie.

"The airlock projects out beyond the screen," Jo was saying. "It was easier than trying to open the screen every time we wanted to dock a shuttle."

Wordlessly, Stoner unlatched his harness and rose to his feet. Stretching an arm upward, he balanced himself a few inches off the floor and eased out into the cabin's central aisle. Jo and the others were ahead of him. The shuttle was otherwise empty, except for the flight crew up in the cockpit.

The hatch swung open and a pair of technicians ducked their heads inside. One wore white coveralls with the stylized Vanguard monogram on his shoulder. The other, a chunky young woman, was in khaki coveralls that bore a hammer-and-sickle insignia.

An Linh, Baker, and Markov all wore Russian-issue coveralls, plain khaki with no shoulder patches or nametags. Stoner still wore the faded blues he had acquired from the Peacekeepers, partly because Markov could find no coveralls long enough to fit him. Jo's outfit of coral was the only touch of vivid color among the five of them.

She took an electronic stylus from the white-clad technician and signed his hand-sized display screen. The tech came aboard the shuttle as the Russian woman led them away and into the orbital complex.

Stoner saw that they were in a transparent tunnel that led toward the center of the complex. From inside, the energy screen looked a dull, flat gray. Other transparent tunnels led from different parts of the screen toward the center, with cross tunnels connecting them here and there. It reminded Stoner of a drawing he had studied in a biology class, ages ago, showing blood vessels threading through the human body.

And we're the corpuscles, he thought as they floated through the tunnel.

"These were built before the energy screen went up," Jo said, like a tour guide. "They're airtight, so they give us some redundancy if the screen should blow out."

"Blow out?" Markov's voice squeaked.

"Not to worry, Kir," said Jo, laughing. "This whole complex is built to man-rated specifications. All the safety precautions we can think of. Like the airlock coming up: these tunnels are divided into airtight segments, so if something happens in one area, the rest of the tunnel can be sealed off and kept safe."

Markov gave her an unconvinced look.

The Russian woman halted them in front of the airlock hatch.

"From this point onward there will be gravity," she said in British-accented English. "It will be very slight at first, but as we approach the center of the complex it will increase to the full value of gravity on Earth's surface."

"Gravity?" Baker asked. "How?"

"It's fairly new," Jo replied. "We've been experimenting with it for a few months now. Same principle as the energy screen, really, but here we apply the energy to create a gravity field."

Stoner watched Baker's face as the new information swirled in his mind. The Australian's mouth grinned, but his eyes were calculating. He's trying to figure out how an artificial gravity field could be used as a weapon, Stoner saw. He's picturing a city being uprooted and flung off into space.

And these are the people you're trying to save, he told himself. Savages whose first thought is always how to kill their enemies, how to increase their own power.

Why? he wondered. And looking deeper into Baker's cold eyes he saw the anger that drove the man, and the fear that lay beneath it. Strike first, Baker's fears commanded him. Hurt them before they can hurt you.

Stoner turned his eyes away from the Aussie. They went through the airlock, and within a few moments he could feel the gentle, insistent tug of gravity. An Linh's hair, which had been floating wildly in all directions like a mini-Afro, began to settle down. Jo's ponytail bobbed against her neck. Markov's face began to sag again and look its age.

Looking forward, Stoner strained for a glimpse of the alien spacecraft. But the area where all the main tunnels converged was a jumbled mass of metal-walled structures. Like the holy places in the Middle East, Stoner thought. They cover over them with churches or mosques or temples. The more important the site, the bigger the structure they've built over it.

Still, he felt a tingle of anticipation as they made their way down the tunnel. From floating they went to the long-striding, half-loping walk that astronauts use in the meager gravity of the Moon. But that quickly gave way to the more solid tread of full Earthly gravity. Stoner soon heard the heavy, purposeful clicking of half a dozen pairs of booted feet against the plastic tiles of the tunnel's floor.

More airlock hatches, and then they were inside a laboratory building, striding along a corridor that was flanked by labs and offices. Through the computer center they walked, then more labs and a wide, dimly lit storage area where arcane pieces of equipment were neatly shelved.

Another section where white-smocked men and women bent over display screens and light tables, and then a final airlock.

They stepped out onto a wide metal catwalk. It ran in a circle all around a hollow area brilliantly lit by so many arc lamps that there were no shadows whatsoever.

The nucleus of the atom, Stoner thought. The DNA in the heart of the cell.

At the center of the brilliantly lit hollow was the alien starship, just as Stoner had remembered it. A smooth metal oblong with gently rounded edges, twenty-five meters long, six deep. Light tan, almost the color of the coveralls that Markov and Baker and An Linh wore.

"So that is a starship," said Markov, awe in his voice.

"Not awfully big," Baker said.

"But think of how far it's come," said An Linh.

An extension of the catwalk led to a platform alongside the spacecraft. Without asking, Stoner walked to it. The others followed. They crowded shoulder against shoulder on the metal platform and peered inside the ship. Its entire top half was dimly transparent.

"He's gone!" Stoner said.

The bier was empty. The body of the alien that had once rested upon it was missing. The artifacts that had surrounded the bier were also gone, and one whole bulkhead of the compartment had been removed to reveal a mass of stacked crystals, like diamond necklaces hanging by one end, that glittered in the light of the arc lamps.

Two human technicians stood inside the spacecraft now, clad in white coveralls. One held a hand-sized display screen which she peered at intently, checking off items on a list with an electronic stylus. The other bore a heavy backpack of metal cylinders. He bent down on one knee and slid a transparent visor down over his eyes. Then he started cutting the floor plates of the spacecraft compartment with a laser torch.

"The alien's been taken away," Stoner repeated.

Jo nodded. "They removed him years ago, so they could examine the body."

"But . . ."

"The body has been cremated, Dr. Stoner," said a new voice. "Burned to an ash. At my order."

They all turned to see Everett Nillson, lean and pale as death, standing at the railing of the catwalk, grinning at them. Behind him stood a quartet of uniformed guards, each carrying snub-nosed submachine guns.

CHAPTER 39

In the shadowless light of the arc lamps, Nillson's pale, bony face looked almost like a death mask. The guards behind him stood impassively, hard and grim, their submachine guns held firmly in their hands and pointed at the five people standing at the edge of the alien starship.

"The body has been cremated," Nillson repeated, "and the ashes have been fired off in a rocket that will plunge into the Sun. You'll never find a trace of your alien, Stoner."

For an instant Stoner stood rigid, staring into Nillson's nearly colorless eyes. Then, in his mind, he heard a voice telling him, He does not understand. The physical body means little. I am with you, crèche-mate from another world.

I am part of you now, my brother. Eternally. My body has served its purpose. Its loss is hardly a loss at all.

Still standing at the railing of the circular catwalk, Nillson gloated, "Now we are dismantling the spacecraft itself."

Stoner glanced down at the technician slicing the floor of the spacecraft's compartment with the laser cutting tool. Both he and his female supervisor kept their eyes on their work and made it clear that they were ignoring the byplay going on alongside them.

"I'm having it cut apart into small pieces. Then the pieces will also be propelled into the Sun."

"You cannot do this!" Markov protested. "This starship belongs to the entire human race, all of mankind. It's not yours to dispose of."

Nillson laughed. "Possession is nine-tenths of the law. By the time your government learns about this, it'll be too late to do anything about it."

Stoner studied the tall, lank, cadaverous man who loomed before them. The man who was Jo's husband. Nillson's eyes were dilated, his face covered with a fine sheen of perspiration. His knobby, long-fingered hands were gripping the railing of the catwalk tightly, as if he were afraid of swaying or even falling down if he let go. He was dressed in an elegant suit of deep blue, but its high mandarin collar was hanging open and the suit seemed baggy, overlarge.

He's lost weight since that suit was tailored for him, Stoner judged. And he's high on something.

"In another few hours," Nillson was saying, his voice rising shrilly as he spoke, "there won't be a trace of the alien or his starship left. Or you, either, Stoner. You're going on a one-way trip to the Sun also. Going out in a blaze of glory." He giggled.

Jo said, "Ev, you can't . . ."

"Who says I can't?" His tone turned truculent; his face hardened. "I can do whatever I damned well please, wife of mine. The only question is, what do I do with *you*?"

Baker pushed past An Linh and stood in front of her protectively. "You're insane, you bloody bastard. Stark staring bonkers!"

"Ah, Mr. Baker." Nillson made a vague gesture with one hand, seemed almost to lose his balance, then clasped his hand onto the railing again. "What should I do with you? A loyal member of the World Liberation Movement. You didn't know that I run the WLM, did you? That *I'm* the mastermind behind you!'' He lifted his head and laughed, his eyes squeezing shut, the noise coming from his throat sounding more like the yowling of a feral animal than human laughter.

Baker took a step into the short gridwork bridge that connected the platform girdling the starship with the catwalk where Nillson stood. The four guards immediately turned their gun muzzles to focus on him.

''You don't see how funny it all is, do you, Baker? So grim! So angry!'' Nillson wiped at one eye. ''How loyal you were under torture. Taking such punishment to resist telling me what I already knew. Can't you see the humor in that? The irony of it all?''

''I'd like to get my hands on you. . . .'' But Baker stood rooted where he was, immobilized by the threatening guns of the guards.

Nillson seemed totally unconcerned. ''For years now I've been bankrolling that fat Korean and letting him think he directed the World Liberation Movement. Just as I let you think you were actually running Vanguard Industries, Jo.''

She flinched as if he had slapped her.

Nillson went on, ''But it was I who brought the different terrorist groups together. I did it! Me! I could control them better if they all worked under one leader. I made Temujin my puppet, and he never even realized it.''

''But why?'' Jo asked.

''Why not? There was power to be had, and a man should never pass up the chance to gain power.'' Nillson ran the back of his hand across his forehead as he said, ''I inherited a multinational corporation at a time when the world was tottering. I had the vision, the courage, to buy out the terrorists and bring them under my control. I let you, Jo, go after the alien starship. It was a gamble, but it paid off handsomely. It made Vanguard the biggest, richest corporation in the world. But it brought some unacceptable risks. So today I'm getting rid of those risks. Eliminating them.''

Jo turned toward Stoner, who stood unmoving, watching, listening.

''The only question in my mind,'' Nillson said, ''is what to do with the rest of you.''

''If you think . . .'' Jo started.

But he paid her no attention. "Baker, how would you like to be the new head of the World Liberation Movement?"

"You're crazy!" Baker snapped.

Nillson fixed a cold stare on him. "Say that once more and you'll go back to that interrogation table."

Markov raised his voice. "I am a representative of the government of the Soviet Union. You cannot—"

"You are a dead man!" Nillson snarled. "You had a heart attack on the flight that brought you here and died before disembarking. I've already got a writer working on the news release."

Markov's face went white. He stumbled backward half a step, and Stoner took his arm.

"Jo, my beloved wife—I think you're going to fly off into the Sun with your lover. You've always wanted to be with him. I'm going to grant you your fondest wish."

He turned his glittering eyes to An Linh. "And you, pretty girl. You've been a great disappointment to me. I wanted you to accept the fetus I had frozen and carry my son to term. Now I don't think I need you for that anymore."

Stoner finally spoke. "Do you think you'd live long enough to see a son born?"

All eyes turned to him.

"You won't last nine months," Stoner said, his voice low and hard.

Nillson gripped the catwalk railing even harder, struggling to control the fury that shook his body.

Stoner said, "Having yourself frozen won't work for you because you don't know if you can be revived successfully when and if the cure for your cancer is discovered. My case is suspect, and all the other trials failed miserably."

"How can you . . ."

"It started in your gonads, didn't it? And it's eating away inside your guts. The pain gets worse each day, and the only end to it will be death."

Jo's voice was hollow with shock. "Cancer? Terminal cancer?"

"They discovered it just about the time I was revived, didn't they?" he asked Nillson. Without waiting for an answer, Stoner went on, "So you blame me for it, in your subconscious. And it's running wild, accelerating. No way to stop it."

Baker stared at Stoner, then swung his gaze to Nillson. "There's no cure? You didn't discover a cure?"

Nillson's mouth opened, but no words came out. Only a ragged, groaning sound. Spittle flecked the corners of his lips.

"There never was a cure," Stoner said. "That was nothing but your own propaganda."

"But I thought . . ."

Turning back to Nillson, Stoner said, "That's why you don't really care anymore what a mess you make of the world. It's all a game to you now, a toy that you're going to break so that nobody else can use it."

Jo objected, "But we did freeze fertilized ova, more than a year ago. He wanted a son. He still wants one."

Stoner shook his head. "Maybe he did then. But now he wants immortality." Turning back to Nillson, "That's it, isn't it? You want to live forever."

"The alien," Nillson said, his voice dropping nearly to a whisper. "What did he tell you? What was his message?"

Stoner said nothing.

"I'll let you live! I'll let them all live. Just tell me what the alien's message was. It was about immortality, wasn't it?"

"There is no message," said Stoner.

"Don't lie to me!" Nillson snapped, his voice stronger, angrier.

"No message."

"That's impossible! Out of all the worlds in the universe he came *here*. He was looking for us, searching for us. For a reason! There has to be a reason for the alien coming to us."

Stoner said calmly, "It was random chance, nothing more."

"It couldn't be random chance! There's a purpose behind his coming here. I know there is!"

"No purpose," insisted Stoner. "None at all."

"I don't believe you!"

"The alien has no message for you or anyone. And there's no hope of immortality for you."

"You're lying!"

"And you're a dead man."

"I'll kill you! I'll kill them all!"

Stoner looked deeply into those watery, pallid eyes and saw madness behind them. "I know," he said, his voice almost sorrowful. "You'll bring down the whole Earth, plunge them all into war and starvation and death. If you can't live, no one will. Just like Hitler. Just like a spoiled neurotic little boy who breaks his toys in spite. If you can't live, no one's going to live."

"Starting with you!" Nillson screamed. "Kill him! Shoot him down! Shoot them all!"

The guards raised their guns again, then hesitated.

Stoner said to Nillson, "The only person who's going to die here is you."

Slowly, like sleepwalkers, the four guards turned their guns toward Nillson himself. Blank-faced, they cocked the weapons and pointed their blunt muzzles at the lean, tottering chairman of the board.

Jo gripped Stoner's arm. "Keith, what are you doing?"

"Putting him out of his pain. It's what he really wants."

But Nillson had turned to face the guards, his back pressed to the catwalk railing. "No," he screeched, his voice high and pleading. "Not me! Not me!"

"Keith, please," Jo begged. "You can't murder him in cold blood!"

"It's a mercy killing," he said, his voice flat and calm. Within himself he felt no emotion whatever. Like a scientist terminating an experimental animal. Like a surgeon excising a cancerous tumor.

Nillson collapsed to his knees in front of the quartet of guns. "Please, *please!* I don't want to die."

A new voice boomed out of nowhere. *"Let him go, Stoner! Let him go or none of you will get out of there alive."*

Stoner looked up at the loudspeakers spotted above the catwalk.

"You've come out into the open, finally," he said.

Archie Madigan's voice replied, "You forced my hand, Stoner."

Nillson lay huddled in a blubbering heap on the catwalk. Jo, Markov, An Linh, and Baker were staring wide-eyed at the loudspeakers. The two technicians inside the spacecraft had stopped their work and were standing, stiff with shock, watching the drama being played out in front of them.

"Show yourself," Stoner said to Madigan.

The lawyer chuckled. "Ah, now, that wouldn't be the

wisest thing for me to do, would it? You've a sort of hypnotic way about you, I've found.''

"Archie!" Jo shouted into the empty air. "Help us! Send somebody if you can't come yourself."

"Well now, before there's any helping done, we've got to come to some terms," said the lawyer.

"Terms? I don't understand."

Stoner said to Jo, "Archie's the one who's been behind all of this. Your husband thought he was controlling the World Liberation Movement, but Archie has actually been controlling your husband."

Loud enough for the microphones by the speakers to pick up his voice, Stoner went on, "You've been the power behind the throne for years now, haven't you, Madigan?"

"Indeed I have," the lawyer replied. "Old Everett thought he was running the show, but he was jumping through *my* hoops without even knowing it."

"You've been controlling Vanguard and the WLM both," Stoner said.

" 'Controlling' is a bit strong," said Madigan. "I'd say I've been influencing my dear boss to a considerable extent." The voice hesitated, then asked, "Does he really have cancer?"

Stoner nodded. "Terminal."

"So that's why he was so interested in you, at the outset."

"You didn't know?"

"It's the one secret he managed to keep from me."

"But once he began to suspect that my revival was a fluke, he lost his last chance to beat the game," said Stoner.

Madigan's sigh, amplified by the loudspeakers, sounded like a high wind rustling through a forest. "You've forced me to come out into the open, Stoner. I didn't want to do that."

"But now it's done."

"I haven't made any plans for this. I thought Ev would finish you off, and I could go on pulling his strings."

Stoner glanced back at Nillson, whimpering on the catwalk floor, and the four guards standing uncertainly over him, looking back and forth at one another and up at the loudspeakers.

"To what purpose?" Stoner asked. "Why have you been helping Nillson to promote terrorism around the world?"

"Ah, if you'd been born in Belfast in the year of our Lord 1970, you wouldn't have to ask such a question."

"That's a good excuse," Stoner countered. "But it's not the real reason."

"Little matter. It's reason enough. The only question now is how to kill the five of you with as little mess as possible."

CHAPTER 40

"There will be no killing, Madigan," said Stoner, "unless you want to die."

The voice from the loudspeakers chuckled. "Not me! I'm in good health, and I'm enjoying the power of running the world's largest corporation—and the World Liberation Movement. I'm even planning to infiltrate the Peace Enforcers. That should complete the job. I'll be emperor of the world, and nobody will know it!"

Turning to Jo, Stoner said softly, urgently, "Get Kirill and these two back to the shuttle. Disconnect from the airlock and go onto the shuttle's own life support system. Take the two technicians with you."

"What are you going to do?"

"Keep Madigan busy until you're safe. You've got ten minutes, maximum. Get going!"

"But—"

"Go!"

Jo took charge of Markov, An Linh, and Baker with a single glance over her shoulder. The two technicians clambered up from the interior of the spacecraft and followed them as she strode across the little bridge and up to the catwalk, where her husband lay crumpled on the gridwork flooring.

"Pick him up and take him to his quarters," she commanded the four guards.

They stirred as if waking from a dream. They looked at Jo, glanced at one another.

"He's obviously had a breakdown," she snapped. "If you want to keep working for Vanguard, you'll do what I tell you. Otherwise you'll be in the unemployment line back Earthside tomorrow morning."

They shouldered their guns and picked Nillson up from the catwalk floor.

"Take him to his quarters, call the chief medical officer, and stand guard over him," Jo said.

They marched off, hauling Nillson, who seemed barely conscious.

"Now just a minute here," Madigan's voice boomed from the loudspeakers. "You're not going anywhere, Jo. Neither you nor your friends."

Jo raised her face toward the speakers, her eyes blazing fury. "You're the power behind the throne, Archie? Well, the throne just collapsed! I'm the president of this company, and the people around here will do what I tell them!"

"No, they won't," Madigan insisted.

"We'll see about that!"

"I'm warning you, Jo. If you don't stay exactly where you are—"

"Fuck you, Archie," she snapped. To Markov and the others she said, "Follow me."

Through this Stoner remained standing by the side of the spacecraft, eyes closed. He pictured the loudspeakers with his mind, the electrical wiring that led from them through the maze of passageways and workshops that made up this orbiting complex. He saw where Madigan sat, at a control center crammed with desklike consoles and display screens. His mind's eye went past that and sought out the electrical power generator, the compact metal sphere at the heart of the fusion reactor, where a plasma hotter than the core of the Sun transmuted matter into energy. From there he directed his mind along the pulsing web of electrical circuits to the life support system that sustained the complex's air and heat.

He opened his eyes. Jo was herding her charges along the catwalk. She stopped at the door that opened onto the passageway they had come through. As if she felt his gaze, she turned to look at him.

"Hurry," he called to her. "Your lives depend on it."

Jo seemed to understand him. She gave a single curt nod,

then pulled the door open and gestured Markov and the others through it.

"I'm warning you, Jo," bellowed Madigan's voice.

Stoner could see him mentally, hunched intently in his chair at the control center, staring angrily into the display screens that showed every corner of the orbital complex. Madigan had cleared the control center of all other personnel. He sat there alone, trusting no one, playing God.

There's no way to simply shut off the air to his compartment alone, Stoner saw. No way to choke him off without killing everyone else.

Deep within him, Stoner knew that it would be a tragedy to kill the thousands of men and women working innocently throughout this complex. It would be even worse to kill Jo and Kirill and An Linh. But those feelings were smothered over by a glacial deadening of all emotion as the details of the situation came into clear focus for him.

Madigan. The master puppeteer. Pulling Nillson's strings and, through the hands of that half-insane dying man, torturing half the world.

Madigan. Born in bloody Belfast. Raised in violence. Stoner touched the lawyer's mind and looked into the past. Murders in the street. Bombs in department stores. Buses burning in the night. Father shot dead by British soldiers. Mother blown to pieces by a car bomb. A cold wind sliced through Stoner as he saw that the car bomb had been planted there by the teenaged Madigan himself. He had murdered his own mother. By mistake. A mistake he could never atone for.

Escaping to the south. Cutting his ties with the terrorists. Emigrating to America. To Boston. To a scholarship and a law degree and the gradual realization that the real power in the world was held by the enemy, the huge corporations that controlled national governments. And what better way to bring them down, what better way to steal their power, than to join the largest corporation of them all and work and scheme and smile and kiss your way to the top of it?

Madigan. The nexus of power. The key to it all: the war in Africa, the secret alliance between Vanguard and the World Liberation Movement, perhaps even the convulsions racking the Soviet Union.

One man. Stoner hesitated. Can one man truly be the

difference between war and peace? Can one man prevent a whole world from moving forward to find the solutions to its problems?

Yes, he decided. This man could. This one man barred the way to humankind's future. There were others, of course. But this one man was the obstacle to be cleared away. Now. Unless he could move Madigan out of the way, no progress could be made toward real peace.

Madigan had to die.

But how many had to die with him?

As he stood there by the side of the alien's starship, its jeweled inner workings glowing and glittering with otherwordly power, Stoner saw Madigan frantically snapping out commands, punching buttons on the control consoles in front of him, trying to force the men and machines of this orbital complex to stop Jo and the others from reaching safety.

With a gentle pressure, Stoner shorted out the communications console that Madigan was using. Its display screen went blank, and the lawyer's face twisted in anger. But he simply slid his chair to the next console and began tapping the keyboard in front of it. There were dozens of screens flanking him, row upon row, on either side of where he sat. Madigan could see every room, every passageway, every laboratory and storage bay and workspace in the complex. Stoner knew that he could short them all out, one by one. But it would take time. Too much time. Madigan would have all the airlocks sealed and guarded by then.

Perhaps a diversion will help, Stoner thought. He concentrated his attention.

The shimmering grayish wall of the energy screen vanished. In the blink of an eye it disappeared, and Stoner could look up from the edge of the alien spacecraft and see the stars staring back at him, solemn and steady as the eyes of God against the infinite blackness of space.

Klaxons hooted and emergency hatches slammed shut throughout the complex. People dropped their work and ran for safety. Stoner realized that the area where he stood was domed over by an airtight bulkhead of clear plastic. Yet his ears popped as the air pressure dropped slightly. He felt the chill of the dark void sapping at him.

Madigan stared at the screens, his face going from fury to fear.

"Let them go, Archie," he said flatly to the microphones above him. "Let them go and I'll let you live."

"You'll let *me* live?"

Stoner nodded, knowing that Madigan could see him in at least two of the display screens.

"You can't kill me without killing yourself, Stoner," the lawyer shouted.

"Are you certain of that, Archie? Are you sure that you're safe as long as you're not in face-to-face contact with me?"

Madigan said nothing.

"My powers are growing. Perhaps being next to the space-craft is giving me an extra boost. Cremating the alien's body didn't harm me, Archie. I can see you."

"You're bluffing!"

"And you're sweating, there in the control room. Your nice toast-colored shirt jacket is getting stained with perspiration. Your bladder's giving you trouble, too, isn't it?"

Madigan jerked away from the console as if it had turned red hot and jumped to his feet.

"Come down here and meet me, Archie. Come down here now, before I have to turn off the air and kill everybody in the complex."

"You'd be killing yourself, too!"

"Would I? I'm not really certain about that."

"You're not human!"

Stoner nodded patiently. "That's right, Archie. I'm not. Come down here and meet the ambassador from the aliens, Archie. Come down *now.*"

Madigan stood uncertainly, staring at the banks of display screens lining the control center. Stoner strained every atom of his strength, trying to control the lawyer's mind from a distance of more than a mile. He felt perspiration dampening his face, trickling along his ribs beneath the faded blue fabric of his coveralls.

No use. Madigan's will was strong, his ego powerful. He was not a twisted, terrified mental cripple as Nillson had been, drugged half out of his mind against the pain of an incurable cancer. Nor a pompous popinjay of small intellect and overwhelming self-esteem, as Temujin had been. For all his murderous hatred of the world, Madigan was healthy in mind. Raised in a world where violence was normal and murder was commonplace, his desire for power and his willingness to use any means at all to achieve it were perfectly understandable to Stoner. The lawyer had even rationalized his mother's death: it was *Them*, the ubiquitous hated enemy, who had murdered his mother. The bomb had been meant for Them. If it hadn't been for Them, he would never have touched the bomb, never have handled it, never have put it in that car. *They* killed my mother, Madigan had told himself every day of his life until he almost really believed it. Not me. Them.

Stoner could not control him. Not at this distance. Not with all the bulkheads and electrical circuits between them. He could see the lawyer, dimly, in his mind. Instead of coming to him, Madigan was reaching into a locker on the other side of the control center, pulling some sort of clothing over the shirt jacket and slacks that he wore. Something white and smooth and . . .

A space suit! Stoner felt a tremor of shock inside him. Madigan sealed the front of the suit and then reached into the locker where it had been hanging and pulled out a clear plastic fishbowl helmet. He put it over his head and sealed it to the collar ring of the suit. Stoner saw that the suit included a slim backpack for life support.

"I'm protected now," Madigan said, needlessly. His laughter echoed from the loudspeakers. "Go ahead and turn off the air, Stoner. You can kill everybody in the complex—except me."

Stoner said nothing. He shifted his inward focus to the four fleeing people. He saw Markov, An Linh, and Baker standing in front of an airlock. Armed security guards were there, preventing them from going any farther. But he did not see Jo. Where was she?

"I've got a deal to offer you, Stoner," Madigan's voice said.

He looked up at the loudspeakers. "What kind of a deal?"

"I'll let Jo and the others live—under my hospitality, of course, in a suitably remote location. Maybe an island in the Pacific. Or a space station. Vanguard owns several."

Stoner shut his eyes again and pictured Madigan in his space suit. The lawyer was smiling. He held the upper hand.

"In exchange for what?" Stoner asked.

"For the knowledge that the alien has put in your mind," Madigan replied, licking his lips.

"Knowledge?"

Madigan's head bobbed up and down eagerly inside the fishbowl helmet. "Yes! Knowledge is power, you know. I want it. All of it. Every scrap of knowledge the alien has given you."

Stoner blinked. "I don't think you understand . . ."

The lawyer's face was becoming indistinct. Stoner's mental image of him was blurring, fading.

"Oh, yes, I do," Madigan insisted. "I want to pick your brain clean, Stoner. I want to know everything that you know."

The words boomed in Stoner's ears. He felt tired, achingly weary. Maintaining mental contact with Madigan was straining him. He could barely keep the image focused in his mind.

"Nillson taught me one important thing," Madigan said. His amplified voice seemed to have weight, power. It pressed against Stoner's ears, made his head throb. "Old Everett taught me that if you can't have something for yourself, the next best thing is to deny it to your competitors."

Why am I so weak? Stoner wondered. What's happening to me?

"So either you agree to share your knowledge with me, or I make certain that you'll never share it with anybody." Madigan chuckled, and the sound echoed painfully.

Stoner shook his head slowly. "The knowledge you want isn't mine to share. It belongs to . . . the other one. . . ."

Madigan's voice roared from the loudspeakers, "You've got to tell me, Stoner! Agree to it now, before it's too late."

"Too late? . . ." Stoner could no longer see Madigan's image. His mind was drifting, drifting aimlessly. "Too late for what?"

"You're dying, Stoner," said the voice from the loudspeakers. "I've been pumping the chamber you're in full of carbon monoxide gas. You'll be asleep soon. And you'll never wake up."

"Asleep." Stoner thought about that for a moment. It would be good to sleep. He wondered what his alien brother would do if he went to sleep, but the alien's voice inside his mind had gone silent.

"Just tell me you'll cooperate," Madigan urged. "Before

you die, agree to cooperate with me. Don't let his knowledge die with you!"

It took an enormous effort of will for Stoner to answer slurringly, "Better that no one gains the knowledge than you gain it, Madigan."

"Stoner, I'll let you live if you tell me!"

"No."

"You've *got* to!"

"No."

"You'll die, and all that knowledge will die with you!"

Stoner closed his eyes. It would be good to sleep. Deep within him, the alien stirred. Is this the way the experiment ends? Have I come all this way merely to be snuffed out by the fears and angers of these advanced apes?

I can move, Stoner said silently. I can walk out of this chamber. He looked out across the bridge to the catwalk and the airtight door that led to safety. It seemed a million miles away.

His foot weighed several hundred tons. But he moved it. He actually lifted it from the metal flooring and forced it to take a step forward. Then the other foot. He reached out for the railing and leaned heavily on it. Sweat was streaming from every pore of his body, soaking his coveralls, blurring his vision. His hand slipped on the metal railing, and he fell heavily. He lay on the metal gridwork, thinking, Just like Nillson. I'm huddled here just like he was. At least I'm not whimpering.

A bolt of energy shot through his consciousness. With a sudden clarity he saw the control center again in his mind, saw Madigan in his space suit, his face white with shock and pain, saw Jo standing at the doorway, a slim steel-gray pistol bucking in her hand as she emptied its clip. Each time the gun fired, a fresh black hole appeared in Madigan's gleaming white space suit and the lawyer twitched and jerked backward like a puppet in the hands of a mad, spastic master.

Then everything went black.

CHAPTER 41

Slowly, reluctantly, Keith Stoner awoke. He opened his eyes and saw a ceiling of gray metal above him. He was lying on his back in a softly comfortable bed. The sheets felt like silk against his bare skin. They were perfumed, subtly, and his nose wrinkled at the cloying sweetness.

Turning his head slightly, he saw Jo sitting on the edge of the oversized bed, watching him intently. She was still in her coral coveralls, her hair slightly disheveled, her mouth an anxious taut line. But when she saw that his eyes had opened, her face relaxed into a relieved smile.

He began to sit up, but Jo touched a hand to his naked shoulder.

"It's all right," she murmured. "You can rest."

Stoner let his head sink back into the pillow. He took a deep, testing breath, then said, "I'm okay. I feel fine."

It was true. He felt perfectly normal. No pain or dizziness, only a slight headache that was rapidly fading away. He felt strong and good.

"Everything's taken care of," Jo assured him, her voice almost cooing like a mother gentling an infant. "There's no need for you to do a thing except rest."

Stoner luxuriated in the plush extravagance of the huge bed. It was warm, exactly body temperature. Sensors in the silken sheets, he decided. Not a waterbed, but almost as good. He realized that soft music was purring from speakers hidden somewhere above his head.

"We're still in the orbital complex." It was more than a guess.

"Yes," Jo replied, a touch of tenseness returning to her face.

Looking around, Stoner saw that the bedroom was an attempt to bring Earthly creature comforts to the starkly functional compartment of a space habitat. Splendid antique

334

furniture crammed the narrow room; a trio of wildly tortured Van Gogh paintings hung against the metal curving ribs of the walls. There were no windows, but a holographic projection of Earth spread across the low ceiling.

"This was Ev's quarters," Jo admitted. "He liked to flaunt his luxuries."

Stoner nodded, then remembered. "Madigan."

Jo's lips pressed together even tighter. Her dark eyes flared with barely controlled anger. And guilt.

"He was killing you," she said.

"So you killed him."

"There wasn't anything else I could do. There wasn't time for anything else."

"And your husband?"

"He's in sick bay. I'm having him sent back to Earth, where they can care for him better."

"Kirill?" he asked. "An Linh, Baker?"

"They're all fine. On their way Earthward. But they want to see you as soon as they can, and thank you."

"Thank me?"

"For stopping Everett and exposing Madigan. For saving the world."

Stoner felt an echo of ironic laughter in his mind. "I haven't saved the world."

"They think you have."

He looked at her. "What do you think?"

Some of the tension eased out of her face. She smiled tightly at him. "You've come back to me. That's all that's important. The world can take care of itself."

Stoner studied her. Jo had been a beautiful, headstrong girl when he had known her eighteen years earlier. Now she had matured, grown in knowledge and strength. Now she possessed the classic womanly beauty of an earth goddess. For long moments neither of them spoke a word. Only the softly muted music kept the room from total silence.

"What is that?" he asked.

"What?"

"The music."

"Oh! It feeds through the headboard speakers automatically. I'll turn it off. . . ."

He grasped her wrist. "No. I like it. Tell me what it is."

Jo leaned across his reclining form and touched a button on

the keypad set into the bed's headboard. Turning, Stoner looked at the computer screen display: *Maurice Ravel, Piano Concerto for the Left Hand; Robert Casadesus, piano, with The Philadelphia Orchestra, Eugene Ormandy, conductor. Recorded 1955.*

Stoner closed his eyes and let the music reach into him. He felt a questioning probe from his alien brother, feather light yet puzzled, filled with wonder. Ravel was a Frenchman who wrote this concerto for a pianist who had lost his right arm in World War I. The pianist was an Austrian, an enemy of France during the war. Inside him, Stoner's alien brother glowed with new understanding. Creation can rise above destruction. Human beings have the capacity to overcome evil.

"Keith?"

He snapped his eyes open and saw that Jo looked worried, almost frightened.

"I thought you had passed out again," she said, her voice trembling slightly.

"No," he said, reaching out to take her hand in his. He hesitated a moment, then decided he had to tell her. "Jo— you remember what we talked about that night at your villa in Naples? The alien inside my head?"

She nodded somberly.

"He really is there, Jo. Permanently. He's within me. It didn't matter that Ev destroyed his body. His mind, his memories, his soul—he's part of me now."

"In Naples," she said, so low that he could barely hear her, "you were alive, and human. But . . . later, in that mountain base, with Temujin, and then in Moscow, and now here . . ."

She was fighting for self-control, Stoner saw. He said nothing.

"You were so distant, Keith. So cold and controlled. Like a machine. Like you had turned into an alien creature yourself. You frighten me, Keith! The things you're able to do, the powers you have—they're not human!"

"And yet you're here, with me," he replied softly. "Not because I'm controlling you, but because you want to be."

"I love you, Keith," she said, tears brimming over and spilling down her cheeks. "I've loved you all my life."

"But you're afraid of me."

"I don't know who you are! Or what you are."

He smiled at her. "I'm human, Jo. Maybe more human than I've ever been."

"But the alien? . . ."

"He's there, inside my head. He's become part of me." His grin widened. "You'll just have to accept the two of us, I guess. It's a package deal: can't have one without the other."

She wiped at her eyes with the backs of her hands, like a little girl.

"It's been like a new life for me, Jo. I've seen the world for the first time, really, since you revived me. In a way, I was an alien, too. Now—with the help of my brother—I've become a full human being."

Jo looked troubled, almost fearful.

"It's true," he insisted. "I understand things now that I never even thought about in my earlier life."

"What kinds of things?"

He took in a deep breath, puffed it out. "This will sound corny, Jo, but I've learned that I really am my brother's keeper. Each of us is. We're interdependent. One human being living alone in the wilderness isn't a noble savage, he's a dead naked ape."

"But what does that mean to me? Or to you?" she asked.

"We've got to work together. Each of us. All of us."

"The way you were talking about to Baker? Setting up a new economic system?"

"That's part of it," Stoner said, pushing himself up into a sitting position, feeling the intensity of the need to convince her. "We're at a pivotal point in human history. . . ."

"And you think a few people like you and me can change the course that the whole human race takes?" Jo sounded utterly unconvinced.

"Yes!" he snapped. "The forces of history are massive, like a glacier moving down a mountainside. But they can be changed, shaped, directed by human effort, if that effort is applied intelligently at the pivotal points."

"I wish I could believe that, Keith."

"You've already seen it happening! Nillson concentrated the world's major terrorist groups into one worldwide organization. . . ."

"Because Archie Madigan manipulated him into it."

"More than that, Jo. It was the right time for the terrorists to combine forces. The movement of history pushed them in that direction."

"The movement of history?"

"Yes. And once they were concentrated it was easy to shatter their organization."

"So now a thousand little terrorist groups will spring up again out of the ruins."

"Not if they can't get arms," Stoner said. "Not if they can't raise money. Not if the multinational corporations and the national governments and the Peacekeepers can work together to alleviate the *causes* of terrorism."

Jo gave him a skeptical frown. "Keith, it's a wonderful dream, but . . ."

"But we can make the dream come true."

"How can you believe that?" she demanded. "The world is disintegrating. It's falling down around our ears! So you stopped the war in Africa. For how long? Nations are breaking apart, the whole social order is unraveling."

"Look deeper, Jo," he urged. "Look behind the politics, find the underlying human emotions. Okay, national boundaries are changing. So what? What looks like fragmentation to you is actually homogenization at the economic and social levels."

"Homogeni . . . What do you mean?"

Grinning, Stoner replied, "Farmers in Chad want to be as rich as farmers in Kansas. Uzbeks and Ulstermen want to be free of distant governments that make bad decisions for them. Every group of people in the world is trying to achieve what Western society already has: economic plenty and individual freedom."

"Blue jeans and a sports car," Jo muttered.

Stoner ignored her sarcasm. "At the economic, the industrial, the social level, they all want to be rich and free. *That's* what's causing all the turmoil around the world. Instead of fighting it, instead of trying to hold on to the status quo, we've got to help the peoples of the world to get rich, and free. Instead of clinging to yesterday, we've got to help build tomorrow."

"Christ, you sound like a politician."

"God forbid!"

"Well, you do," Jo said. But she was smiling.

"Listen, Jo. People want to make life better for themselves. But even more, they want to make life better for their children. That's a basic human urge, to make life better for your kids. We've got to help them to win that struggle, Jo—without tearing down all the gains we've already made over the centuries."

"You don't really think you can. . . ."

"*We* can do it," he insisted. "You and me, Jo. And Kirill and Baker and a few billion others. Working together. Yes, we can do it."

"You're serious about this. You're really going to try to save the world."

He gestured up at the hologram of Earth on the ceiling. The planet seemed to float above them, a brilliantly beautiful sphere of blue, decked with streams of white clouds.

"It's a world worth saving, Jo. We've got to try. Otherwise everything will disintegrate. It'll all fall apart under the pressure of runaway population growth."

Jo sighed deeply. "But for every one of us there's an Everett, or a Madigan. Or worse."

"It won't be easy," he admitted.

"It seems so hopeless."

"No. It's not. Never hopeless. As long as we live, as long as we can dream, we can hope. And work. We can heal their wounds, Jo. We can help them build a better world."

Jo leaned her head against his bare shoulder. "So now you're going out to save the world. I'll lose you all over again."

"Lose me?" He felt surprised, puzzled. "I thought you were going to work alongside me in this."

Looking up at him, she said, "Keith, if there's one thing I've learned about you, it's that I can be right beside you and you'll still be a million miles away."

She seemed to hold her breath, waiting. For what? Stoner wondered. There was fear in her eyes. What could she be afraid of? What is she searching for?

In the sudden silence between them, the music flowed over Stoner, reached into him, drove along his nerves, lifted him with its exhilarating relentless power. He felt his alien brother's confusion at the swirling turmoil building within him and laughed inwardly as he realized that he was feeling emotions, true emotions, pleasure and sorrow, joy at being alive, bitter regret at all the lost days, all the things he had been unable to do, all the pain he had seen or caused or failed to ease. His alien brother relaxed and began to sample complexities that he had never understood before.

Like ice breaking on a river that had been locked in winter, like snow packed deep on a meadow melting under the springtime sun, Stoner felt all the pent-up emotions within him suddenly released, thawed, freed from the iron control that had held them so rigidly. At last he and his alien brother were one, trusting each other, true brothers now, unafraid.

He gripped Jo tightly, held her closer than he had ever been able to before, felt the warmth of her body against his own.

"Jo . . . Jo . . ." His voice broke. His vision blurred as tears filled his eyes. "I love you, Jo. I really do. I know what it means now, I know what it is to love, and I love you, my dearest, dearest woman. I'll love you forever."

The fear and doubt in her eyes were washed away by fresh tears, and she clung to Stoner gladly, wildly happy at last.

They made love slowly, languidly, exploring each other's bodies gently and patiently, unheeding of time, alone in their own secret universe where nothing else existed except the two of them and the rising heat of passion that grew fiercer and hotter until they felt like twin novas exploding into the star-filled night.

At last they lay side by side, their bodies covered only by a fine sheen of perspiration, the only light in the bedroom coming from the glorious shining sphere of the Earth revolving slowly in the overhead hologram.

Jo grinned at him knowingly. "You really are human, after all."

"I told you, didn't I?"

"Maybe just a little bit superhuman."

He turned and traced a finger along her lovely cheek, her neck, her shoulder. She sighed and turned toward him. He kissed her lightly.

"Keith," she whispered, her face growing somber. "I have a confession to make."

"Is it something serious?"

"Very."

"Then let it wait until later."

"No, I've got to tell you now," she insisted.

He propped himself up on one elbow. "Okay. What is it?"

"Those frozen embryos . . ."

"The ova that Nillson had fertilized?"

"They weren't fertilized with Everett's sperm," Jo said.

Stoner looked down at her for a moment, then realized what she was trying to tell him. "My sperm? You took sperm from me?"

Jo nodded gravely. "While you were frozen."

He lay there for a moment, head resting on his fist. Jo seemed perfectly calm, glad she had told him the truth and totally unrepentant.

Stoner broke into a low chuckle. "I should have guessed." He flopped down onto his pillow and laughed. "Of course! That's exactly what you'd do."

"I wouldn't bear his child," Jo said. "I wouldn't allow anyone else to bear his child."

"But you'd have mine."

"I *want* yours!"

"I'm glad you do." He tried to be serious, failed, laughed again.

"I don't see what's so funny about it," Jo complained.

"It's the difference between men and women," he said. "Men see sex as a goal. Getting laid is what they want, and that's it. Women see sex as a *means* to some other goal: usually it's having children."

"That's not true."

"Isn't it?"

"No."

"Then why did you take the risk of crossing Nillson to substitute my sperm for his?"

"Because I wanted to," Jo said with great finality, as though dismissing the subject.

Stoner tried a slightly different tack. "Look at An Linh. When you thought she was trying to invade your territory, you were determined to get rid of her."

"That's natural enough."

"Of course it is. And although she was willing to use sex as a means of attracting Nillson's attention, she really was in love with Baker."

"I don't understand what she sees in him."

"The same thing you see in me, Jo," he answered. "A father for the children she's going to create."

Jo frowned but said nothing.

"When she thought Baker was dead, she turned her sights on me. Nothing calculated about it. Nothing devious or Machiavellian. She was just seeking a father for the babies inside her, the same way the female of any species seeks out a mate."

Jo's frown deepened. "Is that what the alien's taught you? That human women are nothing more than baby machines?"

His grin returned.

"If that's what you think," Jo said, "then you men are nothing more than brainless sperm carriers."

He moved over toward her. "Oh, you're a lot more than a baby machine, Jo. Human beings are much more complex than that. But making babies is fundamental. It's more important than anything else we do."

She smiled up at him and twined her arms around his neck. "I thought you just wanted to get laid."

"Of course I do. That's all men want, didn't you know that?"

"Like nightingales singing or bullfrogs croaking," Jo said, teasing him. "That's what you told me, remember?"

"That's right. Everything men do, from graffiti on cave walls to exploring new worlds in space—it's all done to attract women."

"Okay, so you've got my attention."

He laughed and took her in his arms once more.

Later, as they lay in each other's arms, flesh against warm flesh in the shadows of the darkened bedroom, Jo teased, "I'll keep the frozen eggs as a backup."

"Do you think we'll need them?"

"Hardly."

He gazed up at the blue-and-white globe in the hologram projection. "It's a good world, Jo. Well worth saving."

But she reached toward the headboard and turned a dial. The picture shifted. The Earth slid away to reveal a field of stars glittering in the infinite expanse of the universe.

"I wonder which star he came from," Jo whispered in the darkness.

"You can't see it in this view," Stoner said.

She turned her head sharply. "You mean you know?"

"Yes. Of course."

"Is it close to us? . . . I mean . . ."

He laughed. "It's more than ten thousand light-years away."

Jo looked back at the stars, pinpoints of light against the blackness.

"To think he came all that way. All that time."

Stoner felt himself smiling inwardly. Distance means nothing. Time means nothing. The universe is vast, but it can be spanned by intelligence.

"And he just stumbled blindly here," Jo murmured. "Just happened to find Earth, out of all the billions of worlds. . . ."

"Not blindly," Stoner said. It was such a low whisper that she almost missed it.

"What did you say?"

"It wasn't blind chance that brought the starship to Earth."

Even in the darkness he could sense the thrill of excitement that raced through her. "But you said . . . I mean, when Ev asked you if the alien had brought a message, you told him. . ."

He smiled gently at her. "Do you think I'd trust a madman with the message from the stars?"

"You mean there *is* a message?"

"Of course."

"What is it?" Jo's voice was high with anticipation.

Stoner saw the world that his brother had left behind, the beauty and harmony of it.

"It's a very simple message, Jo. So simple that someone like Nillson or Madigan would never have believed it."

"Tell me!"

He smiled and kissed her and said, "The message is this: We are not alone. There are other intelligences among the stars, but they are very far apart, spread very thinly. The universe welcomes us, Jo. We can spread through a million star systems, if we want to. If we don't destroy ourselves here on Earth."

"The universe welcomes us," she whispered back.

He nodded. "How would you like to find the world where my brother came from?"

He could barely make out the features of her face, but he heard her breath catch.

"Could we?" Jo gasped. "I mean, do you think . . . ?"

"I know the way there, Jo. We've got a lifetime of work

to accomplish here on Earth first, but we've also got several lifetimes after that, ahead of us."

"I wanted to be an astronaut when I was a kid," Jo said.

Smiling, Stoner replied, "You will be. We'll sail out to the stars together, Jo. The universe welcomes us."

She was trembling with joy.

"When?" she asked. "How soon can we . . ."

Stoner took in a deep breath, then let it out slowly. "There's so much to do here on Earth first, Jo. It won't be easy, and it won't be quick."

"But someday? . . ."

"Yes," he said. "Someday we'll seek out my brother's homeworld and meet his people."

"Someday," she whispered, like a promise to herself.

Stoner nodded. "We'll do it together, Jo. But for now—I think I can use a little nap."

And for the first time since his reawakening, he closed his eyes in sleep.